BEAUTIFUL
Journey

Kenna White

Bella
BOOKS

2008

Bella Books, Inc.
P.O. Box 10543
Tallahassee, FL 32302

Printed in the United States of America on acid-free paper
First Edition

Editor: Cindy Cresap
Cover designer: Linda Callaghan

ISBN-10: 1-59493-128-3
ISBN-13: 978-1-59493-128-4

In loving memory of my Annie

Dedication

This book is dedicated to my mother.

At the tender age of nineteen and against her father's wishes, she climbed into a single-engine Piper cub J-2 trainer, rolled across a grassy Missouri field and into the summer sky as she began her training to become a ferry pilot. As did many young women in the pre-war days of 1941, she accepted the challenge offered by her country and was ready to answer the call if she was needed.

Acknowledgements

I would like to acknowledge all the women who served so bravely and without fanfare, delivering aircraft into the teeth of battle. Without their sacrifices and dedication to duty, the victories out fighting men achieved in the air and on the ground would have come at much higher a cost. Unlike the male combat pilots during World War II, the women ferry pilots had to pay for their own uniforms, meals and housing. They served without equal pay, health insurance, transportation, paid vacations, or even the common respect their rank was due. These women deserve our gratitude and respect for doing a job so many doubted they could do. They not only completed their assignments but did it without complaint.

About the Author

Kenna White was born in a small town in Southwest Missouri, but has lived from the Colorado Rocky Mountains to New England. Once again back in the Ozarks where bare feet, faded jeans and lazy streams fill her life, she enjoys her writing, traveling, substitute teaching, making dollhouse miniatures and life's simpler pleasures with her partner of ten years.

Chapter 1

Kit checked her fuel gauge then rubbed a gloved hand over the condensation on the side window of the single-engine Hawker Hurricane, the workhorse of the RAF fighter command.

"Five minutes more, sweetheart," she said through clenched teeth. "Just five minutes more. Don't give up on me now."

Kit considered climbing to two thousand feet, giving her more time to find an emergency landing spot if the battle-scarred plane lost power before she reached Alderbrook airfield, but she doubted the Hurricane could climb above five hundred feet without dropping damaged parts and the loose rudder all over the English countryside. The stick was heavy, pulling against her grip. It took both hands and all her strength to hold the nose up and keep the airplane from heading into a steep dive.

"Come on, you pretty thing, you. Show them what you're made of. Stay with me."

She braced her feet and squeezed the stick between her knees for support. The jarring and bouncing rattled her cheeks and shook her body until it ached. As she roared over the S-curve of a river and the gray stone bridge marking the edge of the township, the engine belched smoke and coughed several times. The fumes rolled through the cockpit and teared Kit's eyes. The burned out shell of a house in the clearing below, the most beautiful clearing Kit had ever seen, brought a relieved smile to her face. It was just two more miles to the aerodrome.

"Oh, you lovely airfield," she said as she began cranking the undercarriage into place. The wheels were sluggish and slow at first, but she could feel them lowering. Kit roared over the airfield, dipping her wings and waiting for the steel cables holding the barrage balloons to be lowered. As soon as the airstrip was clear, she eased the stick forward, throttled back and dropped in for a perfect landing. A last plume of smoke belched out the side of the engine as she rolled to a stop. Though harrowing for some pilots, returning another combat-damaged aircraft for repairs was just another day at the office for Flight Lieutenant Katherine "Kit" Anderson.

"Thank you, sweetheart," she said, kissing the dashboard. Kit treated every airplane she flew like a lover, giving it her full devotion and respect for those moments they were together, and expecting the same in return. She slid the canopy open and climbed out as several members of the ground crew raced across the field toward her.

"Nice landing, Lieutenant Anderson," one of the men called as he examined the bullet-riddled tail section.

"Thanks, Willie. She handled like a dream." Kit unbuckled her parachute harness, leaving it hanging over one shoulder. She grinned confidently in spite of the hair-raising flight. It was a standard joke that any landing you could walk away from was a good one. Kit knew the British mechanics would love to hear a woman pilot, especially an American woman pilot, complain about a rough go, as they called it. Her fingers could be frozen to the controls and her legs cramped into a ball, but they would never hear a word about it from her or any of the women in her squadron.

"Not bad, considering you're a Yank." Willie wiggled the damaged rudder, and it came off in his hands. A group of men lined up along each wing and began pushing the plane toward the hangar for repairs.

Willie Thorn was a feisty little man with a cocky curl to his lip and more hair over his beady eyes than on his head. He wore a dirty cap with the bill turned slightly to the side as if he couldn't find the front. Before the war he had been a welder and mechanic for the London underground. In his eagerness to help the RAF and do his part in the war, he accepted the job as mechanic at Alderbrook. He was good at his job and rapidly advanced to foreman, but when he realized he would have to answer to women officers as well as men, he made it clear he wasn't happy about it.

"Have Officers Loveland and Peacock landed yet?" Kit asked, pulling her goggles to the top of the her head and unzipping her leather flight jacket.

"Not yet," Willie replied, dragging the broken rudder panel. "They probably got lost. Most of your girls couldn't find the ground without a map."

"I hope you don't get lost on your way to the hangar, Willie," Kit said as she started for the commander's office. "It's that big building with the open door. You can't miss it."

When Kit arrived fifteen months ago from the United States she, like most women in the British Air Transport Auxiliary, or ATA, was received with much less than an enthusiastic welcome. But it didn't take long for her skill and experience to earn her the rank of Flight Lieutenant. Britain was at war, a war for its very survival. German Luftwaffe had been bombing British airfields, industrial centers and major cities in nearly nonstop attacks for months. The assaults were brutal. Every British pilot and aircraft had to be used as efficiently as possible to combat wave after wave of German bombers. When British high command decided women, though not allowed to fly combat missions, could be used to ferry airplanes and cargo from factories to airfields and repair centers, women with pilot experience jumped at the chance. Kit heard about the British need for women pilots and left her small but profitable flying service based in Kansas City to join up. Flying VIPs and special delivery cargo across the Midwest couldn't compare with the exhilaration of flying military aircraft. Where else could she fly a Spitfire, a Mustang and a Lancaster bomber all in the same day? It was her flying skills that brought her to England. It was her tenacity and experience that kept her there. Not only did she fly ferry service missions, but she was also an instructor. This was Kit's domain, and she walked it with confidence.

The women of the Air Transport Auxiliary shared the airfield with the RAF's number twelve group fighter command. A mechanic's unit, or MAC, also shared the field and runways. Damaged airplanes that couldn't be repaired at forward airfields were brought to one of the MAC units. Bringing a damaged fighter or bomber back to a MAC unit was one of the more harrowing jobs for the ferry pilots. Sometimes the blood from wounded combat pilots still stained the cockpit. Flying test flights for the repaired aircraft was another of the women's duties.

"Don't get too comfortable, Lieutenant," Willie called as she walked away. "We've got a Spitfire that needs to go back north straight away."

"Where to?" she said over her shoulder. She loved the way the British said Lieutenant, making it sound like lefttenant.

"Ringway."

"Okay. I'll check with Commander Griggs." Kit hung her flight bag over one shoulder and her parachute over the other as she crossed the field. Her shoulders squared and the green scarf around her neck flagging behind her, she was the picture of self-assured determination. That's what the women in her squadron saw and that's what they got. There was no doubt Kit could do her job and expected the same from each and every pilot who wore the ATA emblem on her sleeve. Kit had a pair of wings on her collar and wore them proudly.

Alderbrook was an unassuming air base but a vital one in the scheme of things. Even though it had only grass-covered runways, unlike the smooth pavement at larger airfields, it had a nearly constant buzz of incoming and outgoing aircraft from the RAF and the ATA. The buildings were scattered along the edge of the two runways. The three-story fighter squadron command building was at the center. The top floor had a balcony where the officers could watch the takeoffs and landings. There were three hangars, all of them constantly full of damaged aircraft awaiting repair. Mechanics by the dozens swarmed over the Spitfires, Hurricanes and other aircraft in an attempt to keep them ready for the next day's missions. Several single-story buildings dotted the perimeter of the field, including a dining hall, living quarters for the male pilots, motor pool and supply depot.

The ATA command office was a wood building divided into two sections. The front two-thirds of the building was an open room lined by mismatched wood chairs and two uncomfortable benches. Two crates pushed together and covered with a canvas tarp were the closest thing to a table. A coal-fed stove with its monstrous chimney pipe served dual purposes. It attempted to take the chilly dampness out of the air, usually with only marginal success, and it also supported a copper kettle. With its broken porcelain handle and dented lid, the kettle steadfastly held the sustenance that carried England through even the grizzliest task, namely tea, strong, reheated, nearly undrinkable and foul smelling. The teakettle was never allowed to fall empty. As if by some magical hand or wandering gnome, the kettle always seemed to have water in it and enough bits of tea leaves to make a toxin savored by the faithful. This gathering room, or ready room as the pilots called it, was where the ferry pilots congregated while waiting their next assignment. The women's toilet was a small, hastily constructed and drafty shed behind the ATA building. It wasn't much, but at least it was off-limits to the men.

The back third of the ATA building was Commander Mary Griggs's office. All business having anything to do with the auxiliary's ferry service, from ferry pilot training to passenger and cargo transfers, fell across her desk. And because she put a great deal of trust in Kit's ability, much of that trickled down to her as well. Kit's office was little more than a second-hand desk in the corner of the ready room. But she didn't want more. More office would mean more paperwork, and she would much rather be flying than writing.

"I heard the Hurricane gave you a bit of bother bringing it down," Commander Griggs said, following Kit into the ATA office. Mary Griggs was a demure woman in her forties with a neatly pressed military uniform and her hair in a tight bun at the back of her head. Her skirt hung past her knees, and she wore black military heels. There was a stoic and deliberate set to her jaw and a placid reserve in her eyes. Many thought her lack of emotion was ambivalence to the war and her duties. She had quickly risen to the post as Wing Commander in the ATA, giving orders to both women and men under her command with crisp efficiency. Before the war, she had been a pilot for British Airways, flying cargo across Great Britain and onto the continent. On her first day as Wing Commander, she heard the rumors circulating around the airfield that she wasn't qualified and had only acquired the post by sleeping with someone from the Admiral's office. Instead of facing the accusations head on, she stepped into a flight suit, pulled on a flight cap and goggles and climbed into a Hawker Hurricane. She took off and buzzed the airfield in a daring inverted pass, saluting the men on the ground as they watched with their mouths open. When she landed, she stepped out of the flight suit, took off the goggles and cap and returned to her desk. It was two days before anyone dared enter her office.

"It wasn't too bad," Kit said, dropping her parachute and flight bag in the corner of the ready room. "I got her down. That's all that matters."

"Come in my office, Lieutenant," Griggs said, leading the way through the door. "We've got a new girl coming in today. Second Officer Andrea Paisley. Not much experience, but I'm told she's a quick study. Take her under your wing, Lieutenant. We can use the extra pilot." She took her seat behind the desk, her posture military rigid.

"How old is she?"

"Does that matter?" Griggs looked over the report on the new pilot.

Kit looked at her expectantly.

"She's twenty," Griggs finally said.

"What is her rating? Class Two, Class Three?" Kit asked hopefully, already planning how the extra help could ease the flight load in moving the fighters and medium bombers.

"Class One."

"One? I don't need another pilot to fly light trainers. I need help with the bombers. We've got Class Ones coming out our ears. Class Twos, Threes and Fours are what we need, Commander. How am I supposed to train another amateur if I don't have help delivering the big bombers?" Kit scowled down at Commander Griggs. "We've only got two other pilots on this airfield who can fly Class Three planes. Two," she repeated, holding up two fingers. "You've got to get me someone in here to fly the heavy bombers, or we'll have them stacked on top of one another. Unless of course you want to use the combat pilots to ferry aircraft back and forth. I've got three bombers out there now, and they won't deliver themselves."

Commander Griggs didn't argue with her. Instead she folded her hands across her paperwork and stared up at Kit.

"Lieutenant Anderson, when you return from delivering the Spitfire to Ringway, I'd appreciate your using a few minutes to map out directions to the tree where we might harvest the Class Three pilots. I'm sure the Commodore will be most interested in having that location. What with the war and all, I'm sure they have overlooked that bit of information. I will let Commodore

Gower know Flight Lieutenant Anderson from the United States will be providing an endless supply of highly trained and experienced pilots for the Air Transport Auxiliary straight away. It will be a great relief to the Admiralty to know all our worries are over." She gave Kit a cold, hard stare.

Kit knew she had been reprimanded in the most polite manner Commander Griggs could use. Any further remarks by Kit ran the risk of bringing on a much harsher tirade, something she knew good and well was within Griggs's ability to deliver. Kit straightened her posture and snapped a salute.

"Yes, ma'am. I'm sorry, Commander Griggs."

"I believe that's Loveland and Peacock coming in now," Griggs said, turning her attention out the window as the faint sounds of engines grew in the distance. "Have you talked with Officer Loveland about her landings?"

"Yes, ma'am. I think she is getting better."

Commander Griggs rolled her eyes up to Kit's.

"I'll mention it to her again, Commander. Is there anything else, ma'am?"

"Second Officer Brown has been given a leave of absence."

"Helen Brown? Why? She has three flights scheduled for tomorrow."

"She had an accident yesterday during a landing in Dublin."

"Is she all right?"

"Broken arm and collar bone. The doctor said she would be out at least two months, maybe three. Nasty break."

"I'm sorry to hear that. But there goes one of my Class Threes."

"Is anyone ready to be promoted?" Griggs asked.

"Not yet. Close, but no one I'm ready to sign off on."

"We need pilots with good skills, Lieutenant, but don't hold them back on technicalities," Griggs said, cocking an eyebrow as if to say good pilots were sufficient when great ones couldn't be found.

"Yes, ma'am. I'll remember that."

"By the way," Griggs said, changing the subject. "While you're in Ringway, could you see if they could spare a bit of tea? Even a small tin would be lovely."

"Tea. Anything else?" Kit wasn't surprised at Commander Griggs's request. Ringway airfield was outside Manchester, a large city with lots of shops and hopefully lots of places to buy what Alderbrook shops didn't have. Ringway was also a larger aerodrome where the supply depot could sometimes provide a few procurements when backs were turned.

"Sugar perhaps. A tin of milk, even powdered milk, would be nice."

"Yes, ma'am. Tea, sugar and milk."

"Carry on." She nodded then went back to her paperwork. "One more thing, Lieutenant. I noticed you haven't responded to the letter regarding your re-enlistment yet." She opened a folder and sifted through a stack of papers. "Can I expect your signature before the end of the week?"

"I've got three months."

"Your experience is very valuable, Lieutenant. You've been trained and given a great deal of responsibility. It would be a shame to waste that training."

"You never know. I might just want to go home to civilian life. The food is better. The pay is better. The planes don't have bullet holes in them, not to mention the Luftwaffe can't reach Kansas City."

"The United States will be in this war eventually. I don't see how they can avoid it. We'll need all the ferry pilots we can get to keep up with the added missions. Are you planning on flying for the American women's ferry service? Is that why you haven't signed the renewal? They can't possibly need pilots as badly as we do." There was a pleading in Commander Griggs's voice even her stoic British façade couldn't hide.

"I have no idea what I'm going to do, Commander. For now all I plan on doing is finishing my eighteen months." Kit opened the office door and stood ready to be excused.

9

"We'll talk about it later," Griggs said as if realizing it wasn't the right time for this discussion.

Kit collected her gear and went out to the runway to wait for the two biplanes to land. They were trainers being brought to Alderbrook to help convert wide-eyed young men into experienced flying aces. Kit watched as the first aircraft crossed the row of trees at the end of the field and settled onto the runway, touching down softly and rolling to the end of the grassy airstrip. The second aircraft followed, clearing the treetops by only a few feet. Kit sucked air through her teeth at how close the wheels were to the branches.

"I bet that's you, Lovie," she said, shaking her head and smiling. "No one gets that close to the trees but you."

The airplane floated down, the engine throttling back as the landing gear touched down. But the wheels didn't stay down. The airplane bounced across the field, hopping up and nearly taking flight twice before settling onto the runway and rolling to a stop. Kit shook her head and heaved a sigh. "Yep, that's my Lovie."

The two pilots waved at Kit as she crossed the field to greet them.

"Nice landing, Red," Kit said to the first pilot as she climbed out of the cockpit.

"Nothing to this flying thing. I may have to get a license." Red laughed loudly, removing her leather flight cap and shaking out her long red hair. Even the flight dust of the open cockpit couldn't hide her mass of freckles.

"How about me?" Lovie said, sliding down the wing and removing her cap. She waved at Kit and came to give her a hug.

"Nose up, wheels down," Kit said, ruffling her hair. "And no bouncing the landing, Lovie."

Darlene Loveland, or Lovie, as her friends called her, was Canadian. She was twenty-three, vibrant, enthusiastic and had a perpetual smile on her face. She had arrived a year ago as an innocent, naïve pilot. She was now an experienced veteran, having flown her fair share of nail-biting missions. Lovie had bouncy blonde hair and a peaches and cream complexion usually dotted with rouge and red lipstick. There was nothing deep or complicated about Lovie. She was just as her nickname implied. She loved everyone and everything. Kit worried she might be a little too naïve for her own good.

"Did I bounce?" Lovie asked, smiling demurely.

"Yes, you bounced," Red said in her thick Aussie accent. "I could hear the thud all the way over there." She gave Kit a hug as well.

Mildred "Red" Peacock was a saucy Australian with a hot temper, flaming red hair and more balls than many of the men in the RAF. Red took nothing from anyone. She had been a crop duster with her father back in Queensland since she was fifteen. At twenty-six, she was experienced and could fly any of the RAF's single-engine aircraft. She could take off in less than half the distance any other pilot required and could stretch her fuel better than even the most seasoned veteran. What Red couldn't do was keep from saying whatever was on her mind. She had been promoted and demoted more times than Commander Griggs could count, seesawing back and forth between Second Officer and First Officer. Her stripes were usually attached with safety pins to make them easier to change.

"Officer Loveland," Willie said as he and the ground crew swarmed toward the airplanes, ready to push them to the edge of the field. "What was that? Surely you can't call that a landing."

"The landing gear was a bit soft," Lovie said. "You better take a look at it."

"A bit soft? If you land like that, it'll be broken, not soft."

"Are you on your way in or out?" Red asked Kit.

"Out." She pointed to the Spitfire waiting for her at the edge of the field.

"A Spit?" Lovie asked, her eyes wide with envy. "How did you rate a Spit? We've been flying these old trainers all week."

"Lieutenant Anderson rated a Spit because she can land without smashing the undercarriage," Willie said.

"Where to, Kit?" Red asked.

"Ringway."

"Do you think you'll be back by this evening?" Lovie asked. "I thought we'd finish our game of cribbage."

"I'll try, but I don't know if they have anything for me to bring back," Kit said, pulling her flight cap over her head and tucking her hair under the earflaps.

"Did you hear? We've got a new girl coming in," Red said, unbuckling her parachute harness.

"Yes, I heard. Andrea Paisley. Class One."

"One?" Lovie asked. "Has she ever flown before?"

"Probably not," Red scoffed. "I bet she doesn't know a Spitfire from a spittoon."

"If she arrives before I get back, please don't scare her off," Kit said, patting Red's cheek. "We need all the help we can get."

"I promise I won't let Lovie teach her how to land."

"You'd better deliver that Spitfire to Ringway before the bloody thing rots on the runway," Willie said smugly.

"Yeah, I better."

"Fly safe," Lovie said, giving her a goodbye hug.

"I will." Kit slipped into her parachute and buckled the crotch strap.

"Kit," Lovie whispered, touching her arm and leaning in to her. "If you happen to see any face cream, would you be a dream and pick me up some? I can't find it anywhere in Alderbrook. The shops have been out for ages."

"Okay," Kit winked at her.

"And soap flakes."

"I had that on my list too. I'll see what I can find. How about you, Red? Anything you need?"

"A good bottle of Scotch," Red said instantly.

Kit laughed.

"I'm not fussy. I'd take any bottle. It doesn't have to be good," Red added.

"I could use a bit of that myself," Kit said then headed toward the waiting airplane.

"A new pair of goggles would be nice, but those are harder to find than the crown jewels," Red called, looking at her scratched pair.

"New goggles? What are those?" Lovie laughed.

"Don't forget to sign in," Kit called over her shoulder. "You both forgot your log entries yesterday."

"That was on purpose," Red teased then waved goodbye.

Kit climbed into the cockpit and waited for the crewmen to help with her seat harness. She tossed a wave then slid the bubble canopy closed and headed down the runway, the engine roaring loudly as she eased back on the yoke and soared into the midday skies. She tipped her wings to Red's and Lovie's waves then banked to the north. In a little over an hour she would be circling Ringway airfield, waiting for the barrage balloons to be lowered so she could land.

Kit swooped in and touched down on the tarmac, the smooth landing surface a welcome change from the grassy runway at Alderbrook. Ringway was a large airfield with rows of Spitfires, Hurricanes and American P-51 Mustangs poised for takeoff if the signal to scramble was sounded. She taxied to the end of the runway and rolled to a stop where a group of mechanics awaited her arrival. They swarmed over the Spitfire like locusts, ready to add a radio, armaments and other instruments before its first mission. Kit checked in at the command office. Occasionally she delivered an airplane but was on her own to get back to Alderbrook if no other aircraft was in need of her services. She was relieved to learn she would have a twin-engine transport to fly back later that afternoon.

"You have time for a spot of tea and a bite to eat, Lieutenant," the flight commander informed her. "The crew is loading the plane."

"What am I taking back?"

"Scrap parts to the MAC unit and empty petrol cans."

"Oh, swell," she said, not pleased with the potentially lethal cargo. She knew an emergency landing with the flumes from even empty gas cans could be a bomb just waiting for a spark to ignite a huge fireball.

"Don't worry, Lieutenant. You won't have to bring them back once they're full." He chuckled.

"I need strong coffee," she groaned and went in search of lunch.

Chapter 2

It was after three when the Ringway ground crew had the aircraft full of empty fuel cans and scrap parts for Kit's return to Alderbrook. She revved the engines, turned the big transport onto the runway and lumbered into the afternoon skies. She flew at 600 feet, low enough so she could keep the window open and the cockpit clear of the fumes. She circled the field at Alderbrook and set the big plane down as softly as her years of experience would allow. She rolled to a stop and wasted no time in climbing out.

"Thank you, baby," she said, kissing the side of the fuselage.

"You sure took a lot of runway to land that thing," Willie said, striding out to meet her.

"She's full of empty gas cans. I gave her all the room she wanted."

"Commander Griggs said there's someone waiting for you in the ready room. It's the new girl, Second Officer Paisley," he said, grinning like a school boy. "I caught a glimpse of her."

"I'm sure you did," Kit muttered under her breath as she headed in that direction. When she stepped inside the ready room, a young woman stood and snapped a salute.

"Officer Paisley reporting for duty," she said with nervous enthusiasm, her eyes frozen on the wall straight ahead. She held her salute until Kit returned it.

"Hello, Paisley. I'm Flight Lieutenant Anderson," she said, hanging her jacket on a peg and unzipping her flight boots. "Have a seat." She pointed to one of the chairs. The young woman perched on the front edge of the seat as if waiting for a starting gun to signal the beginning of a race.

"Thank you, Lieutenant." She looked up at Kit expectantly.

Kit had seen this look before. Andrea Paisley had the unmistakable eagerness of a rookie pilot, ready for her turn to show off her flying talents. There was a fresh innocence in her face, one that told Kit she had no idea how hard things would become for her once she began shuttling airplanes in a war zone.

"Where are you from?" Kit lowered herself into a chair with a groan, her body tired and sore from the missions.

"Haftrist, north of Manchester."

"There's a base near Haftrist. Why didn't you request to be stationed there?"

"My brother asked me not to. He's an engine mechanic there and thought it might be awkward having us both on the same airfield."

"Why awkward?"

"He isn't very keen on me joining the ferry service. He thought I should do something more . . ." Andrea shrugged as if she didn't know how to finish.

"Refined?"

"That and less dangerous. I think he was a bit jealous that he didn't qualify for the RAF. He's blind in one eye from a motorcar accident."

"So good old brother wanted his baby sister to cook for the

women volunteers or answer telephones at headquarters."

"Something like that."

"Did you fly before you joined the ferry service?"

"Yes. My cousin was a pilot. He flew bombers until he was injured. Then he became an instructor. He taught me to fly on his days off. It was just little planes, but it was exhilarating. I don't think I've ever felt anything quite like that before." Andrea's eyes gleamed as she relived her early days in training. "I knew I wanted to be a pilot. I just knew it. Was it like that for you, Lieutenant?" she asked eagerly. "Was it wonderful for you that first time you roared across the sky on a wing and a prayer?"

"Yes, it was wonderful." Kit smiled reflectively.

"I can hardly wait to fly my first mission. Where do you think I'll go? Scotland? Ireland? Northern England?" Andrea asked, her excitement revving her engines.

"Paisley," Kit said, trying to interrupt delicately. "Before you get yourself all worked up—"

"Oh, I know, Lieutenant. I have to wait my turn. I know I'll be flying short trips at first. But that's all right. I just hope it isn't too long before I'm flying those long missions with you."

"Relax, Paisley. Andrea, isn't it?"

"My friends call me Babs," she said cheerfully, then thought better of it. "But yes, Lieutenant, it's Andrea."

"How did they get Babs out of Andrea?" Kit asked, stretching her legs to work out the cramps.

"My middle name is Barbara, after my mother."

"Why didn't your friends call you Andy?"

"They did for a while, but my mother didn't like it. She put a stop to it when I was ten."

"Why? Andy is kind of cute."

"She said it was too boyish." Andrea shrugged. "I don't really like Babs either."

"So, Andrea, how many hours do you have?"

"Twenty in Hawkers," she said proudly.

"Hawker Hurricanes?" Kit asked, hoping this fresh recruit

had some experience she could use flying the agile fighter.

"No. Furies."

"Hawker Furies?" Kit practically choked on her own words. Hawker Furies were single-engine biplanes popular in the 1920's and much less sophisticated than the fighters used by the RAF.

"Yes, Lieutenant. I soloed after just three days."

"Have you flown a Hurricane or a Spitfire?"

"No."

"How about a P-Fifty-one Mustang?" Kit scowled.

Andrea shook her head, reading the disappointment on Kit's face.

Kit went to the window to keep Andrea from seeing her frustration. Griggs was right. The newest pilot to join Kit's squadron had flown little more than basic light aircraft dating back to pre-war standards and had been hurried through her training without being given the skills to fly most of the aircraft she would be expected to deliver.

"Is something wrong, Lieutenant?" she asked.

"Tomorrow morning. Be here by seven. If I can shake a Hurricane loose, we're going to take a little ride." Kit looked back at her. "I need you flying every plane in your class by the end of the month, Officer Paisley. Every time there's a free plane or a test flight to be taken, you'll be in it. I want you to know every type of single-engine fighter on this base. If there's a Mustang sitting in the hangar getting repairs, you be in it getting accustomed to the controls. Ask the mechanics questions and take notes. You can't learn this stuff sitting in the ready room. Be out there on the field. The other ferry pilots will help you. Officer Loveland and Officer Peacock both fly Class Twos. If there's a spare seat in one of their flights, be in it."

"Yes, ma'am." There was a moment of silence as Andrea lowered her eyes. "I'm sorry, Lieutenant," she said solemnly. "But I'll work very hard. I promise I will."

"It isn't your fault. It just takes time. You'll do fine."

The door to the ready room burst open and Lovie stepped in,

Red following close behind.

"There you are," Red declared. They were both in their dress uniforms with their hats set carefully atop their neatly curled hair.

"Officer Andrea Paisley, these are two of your fellow pilots. Officer Peacock." Red stepped forward and shook her hand. "And Officer Loveland," Kit added. Lovie shook Andrea's hand as well and smiled broadly.

"Welcome to Alderbrook, Andrea," Lovie said.

"Thank you, Officer Loveland."

"I'm Lovie and this is Red. What do we call you? Everyone has a nickname. What's yours?"

"Just Andrea, I guess," she said, smiling over at Kit. "Yes, Andrea is fine."

"So, Andrea, how do you like our little corner of England?" Lovie asked. "We've got all the comforts of home. Rainy weather, bad food, leaky roofs."

"Shortages, drafty rooms," Red added.

"Terrible communication and transportation," Lovie said.

"But we do have a great Flight Lieutenant," Red said in Kit's direction. "She'll send you to hell and back and never think twice about it."

"Lieutenant Anderson is one of the best pilots and best officers in the ferry service. Where else can you find someone who will complain about your flying and order you up in rainy weather all in the same breath?" Lovie said, adding to the teasing.

"I heard she was an excellent pilot, even if she was a . . ." Andrea looked over at Kit and stopped herself.

"A Yank?" Kit supplied with a smile.

"Yes, ma'am."

"She's still getting back at England for the tea tax," Red said.

"Tea tax?" Andrea asked innocently.

"The Revolutionary War. You know, the Boston Tea Party, tossing the tea in the harbor."

"Oh," she said hesitantly, clearly not understanding the reference.

"Didn't you read about the colonists' revolution in history class?" Lovie asked.

"I don't remember. I wasn't very good at history. I liked geography but not history. I could never remember all those dates. Too many wars and too many kings." Andrea smiled shyly.

"That's okay. Right now geography will be more important to you than history," Kit said.

"We're going to Brindy's. Would you like to come with us?" Red said, wrapping her arm around Andrea's shoulder. "I think you'll fit right in."

"What is Brindy's?" Andrea asked carefully.

"It's a pub. Small, dark, smelly, smoky and the only place within walking distance where you can get a glass of anything stronger than tea."

"The sandwiches aren't bad," Lovie added. "I had some chips there the other day, and they weren't bad. The fish was a bit rank, but the chips were all right."

"Brindy's is in the basement of the hotel on Queen's Way Court," Kit explained, reading the doubt on Andrea's face. "It was just a bomb shelter, but Mrs. Brindy started selling sandwiches and coffee during the air raids, sometimes even ale when she could get it. When people started staying after the all-clear was sounded, she decided to keep it open. She put in a few tables and a dart board and called it a pub."

"You're coming, aren't you, Kit?" Lovie asked.

"Not tonight. The only plans I have for this evening are to take a bath and to wash my hair. If I'm not too tired I may wash out some laundry." Kit collected her gear, ready to head home. "By the way," she said, opening her tote sack and rummaging in the bottom. "I nearly forgot." She pulled out a jar of face cream and tossed it to Lovie.

"Oh, Kit. You are a dear." She opened the jar and examined the treasure. "It's wonderful. Thank you. How much do I owe you?"

20

"Maybe an extra mission sometime. I'll let you know." She dug out a can labeled Bearing Grease and tossed it to her as well.

"What do I need with bearing grease?" Lovie asked as she opened the lid. "Soap flakes," she said gleefully, peeking inside. "Oh, Kit, thank you."

"Wow, where did you find those?" Red asked, admiring the treasure trove.

"Never mind where they came from. Just remember to thank the officer's laundry at Ringway in your prayers. And here, Red." Kit pulled a paper sack from her tote and handed it to Red. "Treat these like gold. It was the last pair on the shelf."

"Goggles," Red exclaimed, opening the sack. "I won't ask where you got these, but you should be promoted to Wing Commander for this."

"If certain people knew I took them, I'd be bounced back to window washer."

"Are you the supply officer too, Lieutenant Anderson?" Andrea asked.

"No." Kit laughed.

"Come on, Kit. Come with us," Lovie said.

"Yeah, Kit," Red added.

"Don't let me get in the way of your night out, Lieutenant," Andrea said.

"No, thanks. You three have fun. Just remember we have missions to fly tomorrow morning." Kit headed out the door. Lovie, Red and Andrea followed. They watched as Kit crossed the yard and stepped onto the road.

"Don't blame us if you have a boring evening," Red called.

"Maybe she has plans," Andrea said loud enough for Kit to hear. "Maybe she has a date or something."

"Kit?" Red teased. "Our Kit? A date? I doubt it." She laughed it off.

Kit waved and disappeared around the corner of the building. She knew as soon as she was out of earshot Red or Lovie would explain to Andrea that Lieutenant Anderson didn't date. She flew airplanes. Period. That was her reputation and she was fine with it. Her squadron didn't need to know anything about her private life.

Although Kit's second floor room in her landlord's house was small and drafty, she was looking forward to a quiet evening alone. She followed the lane that skirted the airfield then wound through the village. She turned at the corner marked by only a clump of thorny raspberry bushes. All over Britain, the streets signs had been removed with the hopes of confusing any possible German invasion troops. It was a quarter mile to the brick house, then a flight of steep steps up to the front door. It wasn't a large house, but it was the only one with a room for rent within walking distance of the airfield. Kit paid a shilling a week for the room with use of the bathroom and kitchen when the family wasn't using them. She was allowed three baths a week using no more than five inches of water per bath, an amount dictated by the British Ministry in an attempt to conserve water, something her landlord followed to the letter. Dinner was available for a small additional charge if she gave Mrs. Ettlanger notice the night before. Kit seldom knew where she would be by dinner time the night before, so she rarely ate with the family. She had to wash her own sheets and towels and was not allowed overnight guests in her room. The idea her tiny room was large enough for an overnight guest was almost laughable. Kit had a cot with a lumpy mattress, a wooden chair, a two-drawer dresser better described as a night stand, a lamp with a single twenty-five watt bulb and a coat rack. That was all. She did have a window that overlooked the garden. The stairs creaked with every footstep, and the wind whistled through the cracks in the window casing, but Kit had learned to accept it since it was all that was available.

The Ettlangers were nice enough people. They had two boys, aged nine and twelve. Mr. Ettlanger was a school teacher. Mrs. Ettlanger was a housewife, mother and busybody. She was also director of the neighborhood clothing center, recycling out-grown and donated items to families in need. Ration coupons restricted the clothes available for purchase, so a "make do and mend" policy was quickly adopted. Government-imposed conservation of available fabric limited garments to a few basic styles, most of them drab and out of date. Trousers had no cuffs or pockets. Dresses were limited in length and the number of pleats. Collars were restricted, as were ruffles, darts and hems. The only items that remained constant were military uniforms made from a poor grade of scratchy wool. As for civilian clothes, Kit owned one pair of trousers, one skirt, a blouse, a sweater and a pair of brown shoes. Everything else in her closet was provided by the ATA. She had traded away most of her civilian clothes for the few luxuries she enjoyed: a radio, an American coffee pot and a down comforter. Winters in Britain were cold, damp and depressing. She could do her job even in the worst conditions if she could at least keep warm at night. The comforter had cost her a pair of leather boots, two pair of socks and a wool coat, but it was worth it. The blankets issued by the ATA were the same rough wool that the British soldiers carried, and they were good for little more than additional padding under the thin military mattresses. Kit had rented the room shortly after she came to Alderbrook, and she treasured the location, if not the amenities. Like most British families asked to help out, the Ettlangers tried not to show displeasure at having to open their home to strangers.

"Hello, love," Mrs. Ettlanger said, opening the front door and holding it for Kit. She had a thick Cockney accent Kit occasionally still had trouble understanding. "How was your day?"

"Fine. How was yours, Mrs. Ettlanger?" Kit set her gear on the bottom step of the staircase and flexed her weary fingers. Mrs. Ettlanger seemed overly friendly, but Kit assumed she and Mr. Ettlanger had found their once a month private time in the bedroom, something that usually put a smile on both their faces. When Kit heard the headboard on the other side of the wall creaking, she knew Mrs. Ettlanger would be offering fresh biscuits instead of porridge for breakfast for no reason other than she thought they'd be nice for a change.

"Would you like a nice cuppa, dearie?" Mrs. Ettlanger asked, wiping her hands on her apron nervously.

"No, thank you," Kit said, her eyes drifting down the hall to a cardboard box and a pair of satchels that looked suspiciously like hers. They were filled and waiting as if someone was going on a trip. Mrs. Ettlanger noticed where Kit's eyes had fallen, and she instantly took her by the arm and led her into the living room.

"Lieutenant Anderson, I'd like you be meet my older sister and her family," she said, smiling apprehensively at her husband who was also in the living room. A man, a woman and three children immediately stood and formed a row, tallest to shortest, giving Kit a polite smile and greeting. "This is Frances and her husband James. And this is James Junior—Jimmy. He's fifteen," she said, pointing to the lanky teenager. "And this is Paul. He'll be eleven in June. And this is Gracie. She'll be six next Friday."

"How do you do, Lieutenant Anderson?" Frances said.

"Hello," Kit said, suspecting something. There wasn't a confident expression in the group.

"They're from London," Mrs. Ettlanger added as if that should explain everything.

"Glad to meet you. How do you like living in London? Bet it's busier than out here in the country."

"We got bombed," Gracie blurted out but was quickly hushed by everyone in the room.

"I'm sorry to hear that. I hope no one was injured," Kit said sympathetically.

"Their house was in the east end of London. Fortunately, they were in an air raid shelter. Lord knows what would have happened if they had been in the kitchen or upstairs in bed," Mrs. Ettlanger said.

"We even lost our ration books," Frances added, a sorrowful look on her face.

"I'm glad you weren't hurt. It must be very hard to have your home damaged like that. How long will it take to repair it?"

"There isn't anything to repair," her husband said resolutely. "Wiped it right off the street, that bomb did. Our whole block is gone. A pile of bricks and sticks, that's all that's left. Took out my shop as well."

"Gee, I'm so sorry."

"We tried living in the shelter for a few days, but it was too crowded. More families coming in every day. So cramped the kids barely had room to stand," Frances said.

Kit immediately knew why she was getting the royal reception and why her bags were packed and waiting in the hall. Frances and her family had moved in with the Ettlangers, and the tiny room under the eave that Kit had called home was now their home. She was about to be hand-shaked right out the door and into the street.

"Oh, I see," Kit said, looking around the room. "Those bags in the hall are your way of telling me my room has been given away, right?"

"I'm sorry, Lieutenant," Mr. Ettlanger said, finally reading the scowl on his wife's face to offer some help with the explanation. "You see, Frances and James have no other place to go. His family in Nottingham is too far away, and their mother isn't able to have the children. She gets too upset by all the noise."

"You know how it is, love," Mrs. Ettlanger said sympathetically.

"Yes, I know how it is. Do you mind if I go check the room? I don't want to forget anything." Kit knew there was no use in arguing. Blood was thicker than uniform.

"We've already packed the lot. It's all there." Mrs. Ettlanger followed Kit back into the hall as she looked in the box. "I put your coffee pot in the bottom and I wrapped your sweater around the radio to protect it."

Kit trusted the Ettlangers, but she checked her suitcases anyway. Mrs. Ettlanger watched, her hands nervously fiddling with the hem of her apron.

"You can keep the shampoo," Kit said when she noticed it

25

wasn't in her toiletry bag.

"Oh, thank you, love."

"But I would like my comforter," Kit said, almost sorry she had to ask for it. "It was on the bed."

"Yes, the comforter." Mrs. Ettlanger opened the cabinet under the stairs and pulled out the rolled up comforter tied with one of Kit's belts. "I'm sorry. I forgot the comforter." She gave an apologetic giggle.

"Thank you." Kit stuffed it in the box.

"I know you just paid for two weeks in advance, but would it be all right if we return the rest of it next week?" Mrs. Ettlanger asked apprehensively. "We had a rather large grocery bill, what with the extra mouths to feed."

"Sure, no problem." Kit nodded, knowing they probably didn't have it to give her. She had left a stack of pennies on the dresser, and she knew they probably weren't in her satchels either. "Tell you what," she said, closing her cases. "You can keep the two shillings if I can get some help getting my things over to the airfield."

"Sure, we'd be glad to help you, Lieutenant," James said at once, motioning to his sons. "Let me get my coat." He hurried toward the stairs but stopped halfway up and looked back at Kit. "Thank you for understanding, Lieutenant."

Kit nodded and smiled up at him knowing, as a husband and father, he must feel helpless to take care of his family. Any independence he once enjoyed was now gone, snuffed out by one German bomb.

"Do you really fly airplanes, Lieutenant Anderson?" Gracie asked, squatting next to Kit and helping her examine the contents of the box.

"Yes, I do."

"Is it fun?"

"Yes, it's lots of fun," Kit said, smiling at the little girl's innocence. "I get to touch the clouds and fly with the birds."

"Wow. I wish I could fly airplanes."

"Maybe you will some day," Kit said, smoothing the little girl's hair.

Gracie skipped down the hall into the kitchen, waving her hand through the air like it was an airplane floating on the breeze.

"I'm sorry about all this, love," Mrs. Ettlanger said, pulling a napkin from her apron pocket and dabbing at her nose.

"I understand." Kit gave her a hug. "Thanks for everything."

"Ready, Lieutenant?" James said, picking up one of the satchels while his sons carried the rest. Mr. Ettlanger followed along carrying Kit's parachute over his shoulder and puffing on his pipe.

Kit led the way back to the airfield. With a little luck, she hoped to talk Commander Griggs into allowing her to spend the night in the ready room. James thanked her repeatedly for understanding and being congenial about giving up her room. Mr. Ettlanger also thanked her, but Kit suspected he would rather have her rent and a single person in the spare room rather than the five extra mouths to feed. As for Kit, she had no idea where she was going to live. The small village was bulging at the seams from all the extra employees working at the airfield. For tonight, Kit would sleep in a chair, and her bath would be a splash of cold water from the sink. Tomorrow she would fly her missions, instruct the fledgling pilots and hope to find time to look for another place to call home.

Chapter 3

"You're here bright and early," Red said, stepping into the ready room.

"So are you," Kit said through a yawn.

"It was my turn to get the stove going, but I see you already did that."

"I spent the night here," Kit said, rummaging in her satchel for a clean flight suit.

"You spent the night here? Why?" Lovie asked, following Red inside.

"I have to find a new place to live. I got the royal boot last night. Mrs. E's sister's house got bombed. She and her brood came in, and I am out."

"You're kidding. Bombed?" Lovie asked. "Anyone hurt?"

"No, but I think they lost everything they owned. The kids looked like they had been wearing the same clothes for a week."

"That isn't your fault. You were there first," Red said. Kit just stared at her. "Okay, I know. Family comes first. Why didn't you come over to the rooming house last night? You could have slept on the floor or something."

"No, thanks. I already checked with your landlady and with every other landlord in town. There isn't a room to be had anywhere. Andrea got the last bed at the community housing. I put my name on the list, but there are five names ahead of me for a room at the hotel."

"How about the officer's quarters?" Lovie asked.

"No women," Kit reminded her.

"I heard they had some rooms at the church near Didcot," Red said.

"Only for widows or those displaced by the bombing. I don't qualify," Kit said, peeling out of her dirty flight suit and stepping into a clean one.

"Get married then drop hubby out at three thousand feet," Red teased.

"Very funny."

"I remember seeing something in the field commander's office on the message board," Lovie said, wrinkling her forehead as she thought. "Something about a small cottage or a shed for rent. I don't remember exactly."

"A shed?" Kit laughed. "That would make my day. I go from second-floor bedroom to a tool shed in the woods."

"It didn't say tool shed, I'm sure. Shall I go see where it is?"

"Sure. I guess it can't hurt to look."

"Maybe you could stay here for a while, or at least until there's a room available at the hotel," Red said. "You could fix it up. Put something over the windows for a little privacy."

"Commander Griggs said one night. That's it. She didn't really want to let me do that, but I think she took pity on me. She told me to use today to find something because I have to be out by sunset. Airfield rules. By the way, how did Andrea do last night? Did she get along all right?"

"Oh sure. She was fine. A little quiet at first."

"Shy, probably."

"And young," Red added, looking out the window. "She doesn't quite get it, you know."

"The war?" Kit asked.

"Not that. But she thinks all she has to do is run out there and hop in a plane. She thinks her training is enough to make her a flying ace."

"She's just eager."

"Well, I'm not ready to have her be my navigator."

"I seem to remember a certain Class One pilot from Australia who forgot to buckle her seat belt on her first mission and nearly—" Kit began.

"All right," Red interrupted, hunching her shoulders at the memory.

"Give Paisley some time. She'll be okay."

"Here it is," Lovie said, waving a slip of paper as she rushed in the door. She handed it to Kit then looked over her shoulder as she read it.

"For Let. Furnished cottage. Clean. Digby Lane Southwest. It doesn't say how much and there's no telephone number," Kit said, checking the back of the paper. "That isn't much information."

"Cottage sounds good," Lovie said.

"Where is Digby Lane Southwest?" Kit asked.

"I have no idea," Red said.

"Good morning, ladies," Commander Griggs said as she entered the room.

"Good morning, ma'am," Kit said. The three saluted. Griggs returned the salute.

"Commander, do you know where Digby Lane Southwest is?" Lovie asked.

"Yes. Digby Lane runs through the middle of town then winds along the river."

"There's a place for let on Digby Lane Southwest, but it doesn't say where. No house number," Kit said, handing Griggs the paper to read.

"If I'm not mistaken, about a half mile past the church is a bridge that crosses the river on the left. I believe that is Digby Lane Southwest," she said, studying the listing. "It's more of a private road than anything else. There is probably just one house at the end of the dirt lane, so there is no need for a house number." Griggs handed the paper back to Kit.

"Would you mind if I go see if it's still available?" Kit asked hopefully. It would be unlike Commander Griggs to agree to anything trivial if there was work to be done, but knowing Kit needed a place to live might be enough to convince her to allow it just this once. Griggs straightened her posture and narrowed her eyes as she considered it.

"All right, Lieutenant. Go check and see about the cottage. Peacock and Loveland, I'll have assignments for you shortly. Carry on, ladies," she said, heading for her office. She stopped and looked back. "By the way, Lieutenant, did you have something for me? A package from Ringway?"

"Oh, yes, Commander." Kit pulled a paper sack from her tote bag and handed it to Griggs. "I almost forgot. With Commander Philips's compliments, ma'am."

Griggs clutched the parcel to her chest but didn't open it. She seemed to know what it was even without looking. Kit knew she would covet it like water in a desert.

"I'm sorry, but the other supplies weren't available. I did try though, ma'am."

"Thank you, Lieutenant. Carry on," she said, disappearing into her office and closing the door.

"What was in the package?" Lovie whispered.

Kit held her hand up as if she was sipping tea, her pinkie finger curled in the air.

"No wonder she allowed you to go see about the room," Red said.

"It may be the only place to rent in the whole town, so I hope it's still available and isn't too expensive," Kit said, changing into

31

her uniform trousers and jacket. She set her cap on her head, checked her looks in a pocket mirror then headed out the door.

Kit hitched a ride on a delivery truck as far as the bridge then walked up the lane that drifted back and forth through the woods. As she came around a bend, she noticed a narrow path that led through the woods to a small cottage with a red tiled roof. It was tucked between the trees, and she might not have noticed it if not for the white painted walls. Vines climbed up over the door and down the other side in a green tangled arch. There was a window on either side of the door and a stove pipe sticking out through the roof. At least it had heat, she thought. The windows were covered on the inside by newspaper and the door was padlocked. She pushed her way through the scrubs and vines as she circled the cottage, hoping to find a window with a view inside.

"You there," a man's voice called from the path. "What are you doing there?" He was a thin man in his seventies wearing black trousers and a matching vest over a white shirt. He walked bent forward at the waist as if his back hurt him. He studied Kit menacingly. "You are on private property. I should have to call the constable if you don't leave at once."

"I'm here to see the owner," Kit said, taking the paper from her pocket and holding it up to the man as she walked toward him. "I'm Lieutenant Anderson from the airfield. I understand you have a room for rent."

"To let," he corrected as if he didn't approve of her American expression. "Yes, well. Perhaps we do. You'll have to talk with the lady of the house about that." He turned and started up the path, giving Kit a small wave to follow.

"Who is the lady of the house?"

"Lady Lillian Marble."

"Lady Marble?" Kit asked, surprised that a member of British nobility would be offering a room to rent. She followed the man's slow but deliberate pace up the path and back onto the lane. As soon as they rounded the bend Kit gasped as she caught sight of a stately English Tudor house. The three-story estate with its massive gables, stone chimneys and shuttered windows looked like something right out of a storybook. The grounds were covered with trees and gardens seemingly untouched by the tragedies of war. Massive trees flanked the entryway and the edges of the driveway. Kit had flown over such estates many times, but the view from the air was nothing like the impressive view gained from walking up the path and having such a home present itself in all its grandeur. Somehow just the looks of the place made Kit think of marble floors and silver teapots. The man headed for the single door off the side portico. He wiped his feet on a mat then turned to Kit, pointing to the bench outside the door.

"Please wait here, miss. I'll see if her Ladyship has time to see you," he said then went inside and closed the door.

After several minutes, the door reopened and he motioned her inside.

"Lady Marble will see you in the garden, miss," he said then led the way through the kitchen, dining room and down a long hall to the back of the house and a pair of French doors. Kit's head was on a swivel as she followed him through the house, noticing the highly polished furniture and antiques. The walls were covered with tapestries, paintings and gilded décor. Mahogany paneling, detailed woodwork, ornate chandeliers and bouquets of flowers brightened every room. Even the blackout curtains the defense department ordered every home to install were covered by more dramatic tapestry drapes to retain the dignity of the room.

Kit stopped at a portrait of a man in a naval dress uniform, his chest covered with medals. His bushy moustache was as white as snow, and his eyes looked as cold as steel. The brass plaque at the bottom of the frame read Lord Edmond Ambrose Marble.

"This way, miss," the man said, noticing that she stopped.

"He looks like, what is it you Brits call it? A brick?" Kit said, studying the portrait.

The man looked up at the painting and frowned.

"Sir Edmond was far more." He stood a bit straighter as he

said it. "I dare say he'd show these Jerries a bit of bother." He opened the French doors to a terraced patio and garden. "What was your name again, miss?"

"Lieutenant Anderson, Kit Anderson. Kit is short for Katherine, but no one calls me that."

"Lieutenant Katherine Anderson to see you, madam. She is here about the cottage," he announced clearly.

Kit looked around but didn't see anyone. There was a table and several rattan chairs, but no one was occupying any of them. Kit had expected a matronly looking woman with a big bosom and heavy shoes to be sipping tea with a linen napkin across her lap. But there was no one around. Kit was beginning to wonder if the man, presumably the butler, was so old or nearsighted he didn't realize Lady Marble wasn't there.

"Nigel, would you make us some tea?" a woman's voice said from somewhere in the midst of the flowerbed.

"Right away, madam," he replied as if he could see her. "Would you care to have a seat, miss?" he said in Kit's direction, motioning toward the table and chairs before going inside.

Kit eased into a chair as she searched for the person behind the voice.

"Do you like to garden, Lieutenant Anderson?" the woman asked, still out of sight.

"Um, yes. When I have time," Kit answered, squinting into the flowers where a clump of dried out blooms were waving as if they had been disturbed.

"I don't know what I'd do if I didn't have my garden. It is such comfort during trying times, don't you think?"

Kit was making judgments based on the voice she could hear and the face she could not. Lady Marble sounded friendly enough. There was softness in her words, but a definite British aristocracy in the crispness of her diction.

"I'm sorry, Lieutenant Anderson. I have to finish this graft or I'll lose the entire shoot. You don't mind, do you?"

"No, I don't mind. I'm sorry if I disturbed you."

"I understand you have come about the notice, is that correct?" she asked, the clump of flowers shaking violently.

"Yes." Kit leaned back and forth, looking for the woman in the flower bed. "I'm a ferry pilot with the Air Transport Auxiliary, and I need a place to live that's close to the airfield."

"Where have you been living?"

"A private home in town."

"Why aren't you still there, if you don't mind my asking? Did you have a problem with the family?"

"No. The Ettlangers were very nice. The kids were great. But Mrs. Ettlanger's sister and her family lost their home in an air raid in London. They didn't have any place to go, so the Ettlangers took them in, and they needed every inch of space they could find."

"So you were pinched out?"

"Yes, you'd say that. But they couldn't very well leave a family with three children to live on the street, could they?"

"What kind of person are you, Lieutenant Anderson?"

"What kind?" Kit wasn't sure what the woman wanted to know. She was gainfully employed and was good for the rent. What else could Lady Marble possibly need to know?

"Yes, tell me about yourself, Lieutenant."

"I'm a pilot and I have logged over four thousand hours. I'm thirty-four and I'm American. What else did you want to know?"

"Is that your résumé, Lieutenant Anderson? An American thirty-four-year-old pilot?" the woman asked with a sarcastic chuckle.

Kit frowned at her insinuation. She thought it was a respectable résumé. She had worked very hard to earn her pilot's license in a world where men dominated the skies and the workforce.

"I attended the University of Nebraska and have a master's degree in mathematics," she added defensively.

"Good. What else?"

A master's degree in a difficult subject like mathematics should have been accomplishment enough, Kit thought. She wasn't sure what Lady Marble wanted to hear. But whatever it was, she had the feeling her chances of renting the cottage were rapidly slipping through her fingers. This British formality of an interview with a suitable résumé seemed to be all Lady Marble would need to find some excuse not to rent to her.

"I like Glenn Miller music, chocolate cake, coffee with cream and sugar, and I sleep naked," Kit blurted out then wadded up the rent notice and stuffed it back in her pocket, expecting this woman to thank her for stopping by, and say she was sorry that the rental was no longer available.

"All the time?" Lady Marble asked calmly.

"All the time what?"

"Do you sleep naked all the time or just in the summer?"

"All the time unless it's snowing."

"I do too. I much prefer to feel the soft sheets against my body than the harsh flannel nightgown." Lady Lillian Marble stuck her head up from behind the flowers. She had silver gray hair that fluffed out under the brim of her straw gardening hat, and a pleasant, though restrained, smile. She wore wire-framed glasses that were hanging perilously close to the end of her nose, and a pair of pearl earrings that looked like anything but gardening wear. "There is nothing like a thick feather bed and a cool breeze through the open window."

"So long as it isn't a damp breeze," Kit said.

Lady Marble laughed discreetly.

"That's all we have here in England," she said. "It does take a bit of getting used to."

"How long?" Kit joked, surprised at the woman's lighter side.

"If there's one thing you should learn about the British people, it's that we are a patient lot. We have been waiting for centuries for the weather to improve."

At that exact moment a bank of clouds rolled across the sky and blocked out the sun. Lady Marble and Kit both looked skyward at the coincidence then back at one another and laughed.

"So, you are in rather desperate need of a place to live. Is that what brings you here, Lieutenant Anderson?"

"Yes." Kit pulled the crumbled paper out of her pocket and smoothed it on the table as Lady Marble climbed to her feet and brushed the dirt from the knees of her tan coveralls. "And you may call me Kit. Everyone else does."

Lady Marble gracefully ascended the three steps to the patio with a scowl on her face.

"I have no intention of calling you Kit," she said firmly.

Kit's eyes widened at her remark. She hadn't meant to be disrespectful. To the contrary, she was trying to be friendly.

"I have no intention of diminishing the importance of your rank or your accomplishments, Lieutenant Anderson. And neither should you. I know how hard women have to work to acquire equal acknowledgement during this terrible time. Are you proud of your rank?"

"Yes. Of course, I am," Kit stammered. "I just thought—"

"Lieutenant Anderson," Lady Marble interrupted, "I consider it an honor to address you by your name and rank. You need do little more than accept the compliment with a slight nod of the head." She folded her hands over her stomach and stared down at Kit.

Kit gazed up at her, reading the wisdom in this woman's pale blue eyes. She had never heard anyone explain something so succinctly and directly that made her feel so good about herself. She gave a slight nod to her.

"Now, when did you plan on taking up residence, Lieutenant?"

"You mean I can rent your cottage?"

"Of course. Isn't that why you came? I planned on it the moment you came through the door. I judge people on their carriage. The way a person walks tells a great deal about them. And you, Lieutenant, have told me volumes." She circled the table, dropped her straw hat on the bench and took a seat. Even though she was wearing baggy men's coveralls several sizes too large, she sat delicately, her knees pressed firmly together and her posture straight as a string. She folded her hands in her lap and looked over at Kit. "Nigel will give you a key. He keeps track of those things. You may move in at your leisure, Lieutenant."

Kit dug in her pocket and pulled out a handful of coins. She fished around, reading each one, trying to count out two shillings for her deposit. She had no idea how much the rent would be, but she hoped this would be enough to at least get her moved in.

"Here," she said, handing the coins to Lady Marble, smiling for having made the correct change.

"What is this for?" She stared down at the coins in her hand as if they were something foreign.

"Two shillings for a deposit. That is two shillings, isn't it? Is that enough?" Kit mentally recounted the coins.

"Deposit?" she scoffed. "Why would I want two shillings deposit?"

"Most landlords ask for a deposit. It's for breakage, damage, wear and tear."

"Do you plan on breaking things, Lieutenant Anderson?"

"Well, no. But it's customary to make a deposit when you rent an apartment."

"I try to do as little of the customary as possible." Lady Marble placed the coins back in Kit's hand. "I do not require two shillings for breakage."

"Are you sure?"

"Quite sure." She turned to the door. "Nigel," she said in a quiet but commanding voice. "Lieutenant Anderson will be renting the small cottage. Has it been cleaned?"

"Yes, madam. Miriam prepared it," Nigel said, stepping out onto the patio with a tray in his hands. He placed the tray on the table and checked the teapot. "Would you like me to pour?"

"No, thank you, Nigel. We can manage. Will you get Lieutenant Anderson a key to the cottage?"

"Excuse me, madam." Nigel leaned over her shoulder, a worried look on his face.

"It isn't a large cottage, Lieutenant, but the roof is tight," she continued. Nigel cleared his throat and waited for her to notice him. "What is it, Nigel?"

"Madam, may I remind you about Miss Emily?"

"Yes, Nigel. I know what you are trying so delicately to tell me. My granddaughter won't be pleased that I'm renting the cottage. We discussed this before. I am well aware of what I am doing. After all, I am lady of the house, am I not?" she said sternly, turning her gaze to meet his.

"Yes, madam. I just thought . . ." he said then thought better of it.

"The key, Nigel," she said in a perfunctory tone.

"Yes, madam." He went inside and returned a minute later with a skeleton key. He placed it on the table then excused himself, giving Kit a last look of concern.

"Will your granddaughter be upset if I move into your cottage?" Kit asked, watching Nigel close the doors.

"My granddaughter is young and she will get over it," Lady Marble said, pouring a cup of tea. "How do you take your tea, Lieutenant?"

"It sounds like she will be disappointed if a stranger moves in."

"Disappointments are the obstacles placed before us that build character."

"Too many disappointments can crush the spirit," Kit said quietly.

"Don't underestimate the human spirit, Lieutenant." Lady Marble continued to pour tea. "It is more resilient than a rubber band, but unlike a rubber band, it grows stronger with age. Now, do you take milk and sugar?"

"Yes, but if you don't have it, that's fine," Kit replied, knowing many people couldn't get milk or sugar because of the rationing and shortages.

Lady Marble poured a bit of milk in the cup and dropped in

a cube of sugar.

"One lump or two?" she said without hesitation.

Kit wanted to say two, the way she normally drank tea to hide the taste, but she didn't want to sound greedy if Lady Marble was using the last of her sugar stores for this event.

"One is fine. Thank you."

Lady Marble looked over at her and studied her eyes.

"Two, Lieutenant?"

Kit smiled shyly.

"Yes, please. Two."

Lady Marble dropped in a second lump and placed the tiny spoon on the saucer then handed it to Kit. She then made a cup for herself, dropping in two lumps as well. She removed a linen napkin covering a small plate of cookies. Kit thought they looked like her grandmother's Christmas sugar cookies. There was a tiny dollop of jam nestled into the top of each one. Lady Marble picked up the plate and offered a cookie to Kit.

"Miriam's shortbread cookies are heavenly. Would you care to try one, Lieutenant?"

"Thank you," Kit said, resurrecting her best manners.

Take the one nearest you, Katherine. Not the big one on the other side. Two fingers, pinkie up.

Kit's mother's words echoed in her brain like nails on a blackboard. So did the thump her mother would apply to the top of her head when she forgot her table manners.

Don't eat like a field hand, Katherine. No man wants a wife who gobbles. Dainty is better.

She plucked one of the cookies from the plate and waited for Lady Marble to retrieve one for herself. Together they bit into their sweet tidbits, the buttery richness making them moan softly.

"Oh, wow. These are so good. I haven't had cookies like this since I was a kid." Kit popped the rest of it in her mouth and closed her eyes as she enjoyed it, sighing deeply.

"Please, have another," Lady Marble said, holding up the plate again. "I'm so glad you like them."

Kit hadn't had anything to eat since last night, and although she knew she shouldn't, she couldn't help herself. She took another cookie and ate it in two bites. She washed it down with the tea, finding it surprisingly pleasant, unlike the repulsive substitute for tea in the teakettle in the ready room.

"This is very good tea. I'm surprised since I don't usually like it." Kit finished her cup and set it on the table.

"Would you like some more?" she asked, lifting the teapot.

"Thank you, but no. That was just enough. Those cookies were excellent. Miriam is quite a baker. You are lucky to have her." Kit glanced toward the door, hoping to see who Miriam might be so she could thank her personally.

"I'm glad you enjoyed them. Miriam has been baking pastries and lovely surprises for me for years." Lady Marble sipped her tea slowly, her eyes lowered. "Those are the last of her shortbreads. Miriam's neighborhood was bombed last Tuesday. It was a lovely section of Oxford. She was on her way to the air raid shelter and was struck by a tiny piece of shrapnel. It was no larger than a fountain pen." She sipped again, a noticeable shake to her hands as she held her cup and saucer, but her voice never cracked. "Miriam died just after midnight." Lady Marble took a long breath as if resigning herself to the fact then raised her eyes and forced a small smile. "Yes, her shortbreads are lovely, aren't they?"

Chapter 4

"Lieutenant Anderson?" a woman asked as she stepped into the ready room.

"Over there," one of the pilots said, pointing at Kit.

"Lieutenant Anderson," the woman said, striding up to her decisively. She had crisp British diction and a determined set to her jaw. She wore a camel-colored wool coat and matching leather gloves. The woman was somewhere in her late twenties. She had auburn hair and brown eyes. Her creamy complexion was accented by a small amount of lipstick drawn across pleasingly full lips. Her hair was shoulder length and held back on one side by an enameled clip. There was a strong sense of confidence in her walk and her posture.

"Yes," Kit said, reading a weather bulletin.

"Lieutenant Anderson," she repeated. She seemed a bit. "I'm Emily Mills."

"Uh, huh." Kit was only marginally listening. The threat of

rain and sleet seemed more important for delivering the row of aircraft on the runway than this woman's nagging persistence.

"Are you hard of hearing, Lieutenant? Or are you just rude?"

Kit assumed this woman was used to getting her way. Whatever she wanted, Kit would put her in her place then return to work. She slowly rolled her eyes up to the woman's arrogance but was instantly taken back at her striking beauty, so much so Kit nearly tripped over the leg of her desk.

"Can I help you, Miss . . ." Kit stammered.

"Mills, Emily Mills."

"Can I help you, Miss Mills?"

"I believe it is *may* I help you, and yes, you may."

"Let me guess. You want a ride in an airplane. Or better yet, you want a private flight to Edinburgh or Manchester because you don't like the train service."

"I do not require a ride in an airplane." Emily cocked an eyebrow at her.

"We don't do personal deliveries either, miss," Kit added. It was a standard request from the locals to "drop off" packages to northern towns since the postal service was notoriously slow and unpredictable. The higher the official or the richer the resident, the larger the request for ATA deliveries.

"You seem to enjoy jumping to conclusions, Lieutenant," Emily said, scowling at her.

"Okay, I'm sorry. If you don't want a ride or something delivered, what may I do for you?" Kit pinned the weather report on the bulletin board.

"I'll tell you what you may do for me, Lieutenant Anderson. You may collect your possessions and find another place to live, before dinner, if possible." She said it as if the mere suggestion of it made it a simple and doable task.

Kit tossed a look at her, not sure if she should laugh or dismiss the remark as absurd.

"I have no idea what you are talking about, but if this has anything to do with me renting Lady Marble's cottage, I have already paid two weeks in advance. You're too late, honey. You'll have to look somewhere else for a room. You could put your name on the waiting list at the hotel."

"I do not require a room. You, on the other hand, do. You simply must be out of the cottage by sunset." Emily made a slight nod at the end of her statement as if to leave no doubt about her instructions.

"Lieutenant Anderson, we need to get those planes up before the weather changes. They're only giving us five hours before the ceiling drops," Commander Griggs said, striding into the ready room. "Get your girls up, Lieutenant."

"Yes, Commander," Kit said then looked back at Emily. "I don't know who you are, Miss Mills, but let me assure you I do not plan on moving out of the cottage and looking for someplace else. First of all, there *is* no other place to rent within twenty-five miles of the airfield unless you are a man, a widow or have a house full of kids. I don't have time to run all over the English countryside anyway. I have a job to do."

"Is everything all right in here?" Griggs asked.

"Everything is fine," Kit reassured her.

"Everything is not fine. Perhaps I didn't make myself clear, Lieutenant. The cottage was rented to you by mistake, and you are required to move out today."

"Lady Marble owns the cottage, doesn't she?" Kit asked. "It is on her property."

"Well, yes."

"And you are not Lady Marble," Kit continued.

"No, of course not, but I am here on her behalf."

"If Lady Marble wants me out of the cottage, she can contact me directly. Now if you'll excuse me, I have some airplanes to deliver. We are at war, Miss Mills. Surely you heard about it somewhere, perhaps over tea."

Emily gave Kit a last cold stare then turned and stormed out the door.

"Who was that?" Red asked, looking out the window as Emily

rounded the corner of the building and disappeared.

"That was Miss Emily Mills, a day late in getting to the little white cottage I rented yesterday. She thinks she can bully me out of it because she is some snooty Brit with fancy diction. But I have news for her. I am *not* moving. She can try that act on someone else, but not me. I rented from Lady Marble, and she is the only one who can kick me out," Kit said, spreading the map across the desk. "Come on, ladies. Let's get a look at where you're going today." The women crowded around the desk and studied the routes, headings and landmarks for their flights. Red and Lovie were assigned to deliver a pair of Spitfires. They were to pick up a cargo transport and deliver it to another field then wait for a pair of obsolete trainers to be brought back to Alderbrook. The triangular flights were the most efficient use of fuel and pilots. The other women were assigned flights according to their class ratings, leaving Kit to fly the larger bombers, most of them needed as fast as they could be built or repaired and delivered.

"Officer Paisley, you are going with me," Kit said, waving Andrea up to the map. "Study this and make some notes. We're going to Lossiemouth."

"Scotland?" Andrea asked. "That's on the North Sea, isn't it?"

"Actually, it's Spey Bay at the mouth to Moray Firth," Kit said, pointing to the bay that sliced into northern Scotland. "Find Burghead Point then go due east. Get your flight suit on. We'll leave in ten minutes."

Kit gave last-minute instructions to the pilots then watched as they rolled down the runway and into the partially clouded sky. Then it was their turn. Kit sat in the left pilot's seat but gave Andrea the job of doing the pre-flight check, taxiing into position and starting the throttle up to takeoff speed. When she felt the tail wheel lift off the grass, Kit took the yoke and pulled back, easing the big bomber skyward.

"Undercarriage up," she said, flipping the switch and listening to the mechanical churn as the wheels folded under the fuselage.

"At what altitude do you throttle back, Lieutenant?" Andrea asked, watching Kit bank away from the airfield and head north.

"I don't. We are flying at five hundred feet. I want all the power I can get at low altitudes. If an engine cuts out at five thousand feet, I have time to adjust. At five hundred, I don't."

"Why five hundred? It's mostly open spaces once we get past Leeds."

"They haven't put the squadron insignia on the wings yet. I don't want to be mistaken for a German bomber. At higher altitudes some spotters can't tell the difference."

"It sort of makes the parachute worthless then," Andrea said after a minute of thought.

Kit smiled over at her.

"Makes the seat more comfortable to sit on," Kit said.

Andrea gave a nervous smile and nodded.

"Relax, Paisley. I haven't lost a new girl in weeks." Kit rocked the wings, teasing Andrea into a gasp.

"Do you have to do that, Lieutenant?" she asked, looking as if her stomach was about to come up.

"Are you going to ride the entire flight with your hand choking that seat belt strap?"

"Oh, I didn't notice I was doing that," Andrea said, easing her fingers off the webbing.

"Is this your first flight in a bomber, Paisley?"

"Yes. Big, aren't they?"

"That's why the boys call them heavies. But the Lancaster is bigger."

"How long did it take you to learn to fly the heavies, Lieutenant?"

"I flew commercial airplanes in the United States before I came over here. It sort of came naturally to switch to military aircraft."

"That sounds exciting. Crisscrossing the United States from New York to San Francisco. Flying big commercial planes."

"It wasn't like that. I flew for a small company. Our service is limited to Kansas City, Chicago, St. Louis and sometimes Wichita."

"Where is Wichita?"

"Kansas. Right smack dab in the middle of the U.S. The sunflower state. Land of wheat fields and dust storms. Dorothy and the Wizard of Oz." Kit grinned reflectively.

"Dorothy who?"

"The Wizard of Oz. You know, Toto and the Tin Man." Kit looked over at Andrea. "Didn't you see the movie *The Wizard of Oz* with Judy Garland? It came out a couple years ago about the girl from Kansas who was sucked up by a tornado and lands in Oz then can't get home."

"I'm sorry, I didn't see that one. Was it any good?"

"Yeah, it was. It was one of those movies with a deep moral."

"What moral was that?"

"Dorothy thought she wanted to leave home and find happiness someplace else, only to discover happiness was right under nose, right in her own backyard."

"So she wanted to go back to Kansas?"

"Sure, everyone wants to go home, don't they?"

"I suppose so, unless they are happy where they are."

"Why don't you take the stick? We're leveled off. Watch the airspeed and altitude. Don't drop below five hundred feet." Kit relinquished the controls to Andrea's nervous hands. "Are you watching for an emergency landing spot?"

"I haven't noticed any place big enough." Andrea scanned the fields below as they roared above the treetops.

"What happens if the engines quit?"

"I guess I'd have to find a place."

"Don't wait until that happens to be picking out a place to set down. Always have one in mind. Keep your eyes moving and scanning for someplace. And remember, at this altitude, you could ease down onto a field and clip off a wing but still walk away. We're not asking you to go down with the ship. You are more important than the aircraft. We'd like to have it back to repair, but don't be a hero, Andrea. There's always another plane to be delivered tomorrow."

"Have you ever had to crash land?"

"No, not crash land. I've had to make a few emergency landings, but that isn't the same as crash landing. If you plan ahead and keep your eyes open, you won't have to crash land a plane. These planes are tough old birds. Don't be afraid to set one down if you have to."

"Yes, ma'am."

"Of course, we'd prefer you deliver the aircraft to the intended destination," Kit said. "Makes life much easier if we don't have to do the same mission twice."

"Yes, ma'am."

Kit and Andrea took turns at the controls, Kit pointing out features and tricks of flying heavy bombers at low altitudes. Once they reached Burghead Point, Kit eased the heading due east for a straight-in approach to Lossiemouth airfield. As usual, they had to do a fly by so ground spotters could identify the airplane and signal for the barrage balloons to be lowered. Once they were lined up for a landing, Kit throttled back and set down on the runway. By the time she had cut one engine and began her roll to the end of the taxiway, a jeep full of ground crew was roaring across the field toward them, ready to receive the airplane into service and finish the preparation for its first mission. Kit and Andrea checked in at the field office and received their orders for returning a single-engine light bomber to Alderbrook. With the weather closing in, they took a thermos of hot tea and a paper sack of sandwiches with them rather than waste precious time on the ground, time they would need to get back before the cloud cover kept them from finding landmarks for the homeward leg of the trip. Kit rolled down the runway and lifted off, skipping through the checklist as they reached takeoff speed. She opened the throttle and roared south, her eyes watching the growing cloud bank. Andrea was in the second seat behind Kit, familiarizing herself with the instrument panel and controls. It was another airplane she had never seen before and her wide eyes told Kit she was trying her best to soak up all she could.

"Try out the stick," Kit yelled over the roar of the engine. "It'll seem a bit loose to you, so watch the altitude. The nose gets heavy if you don't keep a firm hand." Kit could tell when Andrea took the controls. "That's it. Don't over control it."

Kit let Andrea test her skills navigating as they raced for Alderbrook ahead of the weather front.

"Watch your altitude," Kit said, resisting the urge to grab the controls when Andrea's attention to landmarks allowed the airplane to dip to three hundred feet.

"Oops," Andrea said and eased them back up to a safe altitude.

"These planes respond pretty fast. Some don't. You've got to keep an eye on the altimeter."

"Sorry, Lieutenant."

"You can throttle back. Cut your airspeed to one-twenty."

"I thought we wanted to get back before the rain closed in," Andrea said as she eased back on the throttle.

"I did, but did you notice the fuel gauge?" Kit asked calmly. "This speed is a more efficient use of fuel."

"Oh my. Lieutenant, what happened? Did I use all that?"

"No. It wasn't you. They sent us off with just a partially full tank."

"We'll have enough to make it back, won't we?" Andrea asked nervously.

"I hope so. Better let me take it. I want to straighten us out." Kit took the controls and made a slight course correction, using her experience at flying this route to help reduce fuel consumption.

Kit showed Andrea the little clues that they were approaching Alderbrook. After Kit lined up with the row of trees on one side and the barn on the other, she allowed Andrea to land the airplane, calling out last-second corrections. Once they were over the runway, Kit sat quietly while Andrea set the wheels on the grass. It was a good landing, one Kit hoped Andrea would keep in her arsenal of skills.

They no sooner climbed out and checked in at the office than the heavens opened up and it began to pour, covering the field with puddles and muddy ruts. Kit and Andrea were the last pilots to return for the day. Red and Lovie had already returned and left again on a short delivery to Luton just forty miles away. With no aircraft to be returned, they would have to hitch a ride on a military truck or wait for one of the buses that occasionally ran through Alderbrook on the London to Oxford route.

Kit reviewed the missions her squadron flew that day and talked over concerns with her pilots before calling it a day. She stopped in at Brindy's for a bite to eat then headed for Digby Lane and the white cottage. She had moved her few possessions into the cottage the night before and had slept in the bed but had time to do little else. Tonight she would settle in and get used to her new home. She was halfway home before she remembered the conversation with Emily Mills from that morning. Whatever the woman's problem was, Kit wasn't going to let it bother her. She was too tired to dwell on an overbearing woman with a surly disposition. By the time Kit unlocked the door and dropped her coat and bag on the chair, her body was near collapse. With only a small fireplace and a two-burner wood stove for heat, the cottage was cold and damp. She started a fire in the fireplace, coaxing a flame from the green branches in the wood box outside the door. She reminded herself she would need to collect firewood if she planned on keeping warm for more than just a few days. She stood by the fire, warming herself as she studied her new residence.

The narrow room had two distinct regions. The kitchen end had a sink, the stove and a small though modern refrigerator. Two shelves were suspended over the sink, one for dishes and one for canned goods. A white lace curtain covered the shelves as if to disguise their unpainted crudeness. There was one sauce pan with a warped lid, a teakettle, a cast iron skillet, a stack of mismatched dishes and several pieces of silverware standing in a glass. A shoebox on top of the refrigerator held the odd kitchen utensils that seemed to have found their way to the cottage. Kit wasn't sure what some of them were, but the scissor-type clamp made a good lid lifter, and a long-handled pokey thing worked well stirring the coals in the fireplace. The sitting area had a wooden table strategically placed in front of one window with the leaf folded down to conserve space. There were two wooden chairs with worn green paint on the seats. An antique blanket chest with a warm polished patina was the largest piece of furniture in the room. It held extra linens and provided storage. The room wasn't large enough to hold a sofa, but there was a comfortable upholstered wingback chair and a floor lamp. A short bookcase next to the chair was filled with old magazines, tattered copies of leather-bound novels and a large unabridged Oxford dictionary. Kit hadn't noticed what was in the limited library since she seldom had the energy at the end of a long day to read. It was all she could do to wash and flop into bed. A random collection of art and sculpture hung from the walls, many of them childishly simple or damaged.

In the far corner of the sitting area, near the fireplace, was a free standing bathtub. It was short but deep. The plumbing for it had been run up through the floor, something Kit assumed meant it was an afterthought. The bathroom was off the kitchen and housed only a small sink and a toilet, the tank and chain variety. The bedroom was a small room extending out the back of the cottage and had a single bed and narrow wardrobe. Surprisingly, the bed was comfortable and the rugs on the floor were warm underfoot. The sheets were worn but smelled fresh and inviting. It was a small cottage and very British, but it offered many of the conveniences she craved since leaving Kansas City.

Kit considered unpacking and settling in, but she eyed the bathtub instead. The strict orders to conserve water and the fuel to heat it were the furthest things from her mind. She hadn't had a long hot bath in weeks. At the Ettlangers she often had to settle for quick dips in lukewarm water, long enough to get clean, but they did little to warm the soul. Tonight she wanted a bath, one that did more than wash away the dirt and grime of her open cockpit flights. She wanted to soak away the tired, achy loneliness of being so far from home. It hadn't bothered her in months, that emptiness of being half a world from anything she called familiar. Tonight she needed to block it out. She needed to ignore the reasons she left her world behind and came to this Godforsaken war.

She filled the tub, stepped out of her clothes and into the bathtub, sinking down until her chin was barely above the water. It was the first time in days she had been completely warm. She closed her eyes, smiling as she enjoyed the warmth and the peaceful solitude. The fireplace crackled and the candle she had lit flickered softly, a serenity so compelling she could almost forget where she was. Kit had nearly fallen asleep in the tub when a loud knock on the door jolted her awake.

"I know you are in there. Open this door at once," a stern voice called, pounding again.

"Go away. I'm busy," Kit said sleepily, too comfortable to allow the angry voice to interrupt her tranquility. She snuggled down in the warm water and closed her eyes again.

"Lieutenant Anderson," the voice demanded. "Unlock this door immediately."

Something in the way the woman on the other side of the door spoke instantly told Kit who it was. The woman who had ordered her to move out was again trying to disrupt her world. And Kit knew why. Emily Mills wanted her to move out and abandon the cottage so she could have it. But it didn't work this morning, and it wasn't going to work now.

"Go away, Miss Mills. I told you I am not moving out. Go find your own place to live. This is mine and I'm not giving it up." There was a silence Kit suspected meant the irritating woman had left her to her bath. After a moment there was a rattle at the door and the sound of a key in the lock. Suddenly the door burst open and Emily Mills stepped in, an angry scowl on her face.

"Hey, what are you doing?" Kit shrieked, trying to grab her towel, but it was out of reach. "How dare you barge in like that?" Kit searched for something she could use to cover herself, but there was nothing within reach. She was naked, and there was nothing she could do about it. She folded her arms over her chest and clamped her knees shut.

"Lieutenant Anderson, I gave you instructions to vacate this cottage before sunset, which happened to be two hours ago. But you have chosen to ignore me. Unless you pack your bags this instant and remove yourself from this property, I will be forced to call the constable and have you arrested. Do I make myself clear?"

"Miss Mills, I am taking a bath. Would you mind closing the door?" Kit asked as goose bumps covered her skin. "Preferably with you on the outside."

Emily frowned at her but closed the door.

"I will wait," she said, lowering herself into a chair then folding her hands across her lap. As dignified as she tried to appear, Emily's eyes raced down Kit's naked body, pausing at each delicate detail. It only lasted a few seconds, but it was unmistakable.

Kit slid as far under the water as she could, hoping to hide her breasts from this woman's view.

"I don't think you understood me this morning, Miss Mills. I have rented this cottage and I am staying. Until Lady Marble tells me in person she has changed her mind and refunds my rent, I am not leaving. Now, you can get out, or I will be the one calling the constable and telling him you are trespassing."

Emily gave a disgruntled gasp and opened her purse. She counted out four shillings and slapped them onto the table.

"There is your rent."

"I really am getting tired of you harassing me, Miss Mills. I may not be British, but I know my rights. I do not have to move out unless the landlord tells me to. And you are not my landlord."

"I most certainly am," Emily said harshly. "I am Lady Marble's granddaughter. And you are trespassing on private property."

"You are the granddaughter?" Kit asked with a snicker. "I thought you were a child."

"I am not a child. I am twenty-eight and this cottage belongs to me. My grandmother rented it to you without my permission."

"I thought it was on her property," Kit said, a bit confused by Emily's statements.

There was another knock at the door and a rattle of the doorknob.

"Hello," Lady Marble's voice called. "Is anyone in there?"

Emily opened the door and greeted her grandmother with a frown. Lady Marble stepped in before she noticed Kit was in the tub.

"Oh my, Lieutenant Anderson. Are we interrupting?" she asked, diverting her eyes, seemingly more embarrassed than Kit.

"I *was* taking a bath when your granddaughter decided to let herself in." Kit scowled at Emily, hoping Lady Marble would intervene and convince her to leave.

"Emily, I told you Lieutenant Anderson has my permission to rent the cottage."

"Lieutenant Anderson is an American," Emily said, making it sound as repulsive as possible. "She can find a place to live in town. I am sure there is something suitable for her elsewhere."

"Because she *is* an American and a pilot for the ferry service, Lieutenant Anderson deserves a place to live. We owe her and the other pilots like her a great deal." Lady Marble tried tact to make her point, but Emily seemed undeterred.

"You told me this was my cottage and I could do with it as I saw fit. I do not want it rented out and certainly not to an American."

"Emily, dear, we all must do our share. The cottage has been empty for years, and there is no reason it can't go to good use."

Emily opened her mouth to argue, but Lady Marble held up her hand as if to stop her.

"Emily, please don't countermand me. Lieutenant Anderson is renting the cottage as long as she is flying for the ATA." Lady Marble's tone was decisive without being demanding. "You no longer use it. While you are in Alderbrook, you will stay in the big house with me."

Emily shot a fiery stare at Kit.

"Now, let's leave the lieutenant to finish her bath in peace." Lady Marble motioned Emily out the door then followed. She looked back, keeping her eyes discreetly on the floor. "I'm sorry we interrupted your evening."

"Good night," Kit said, the draft from the door again chilling her exposed skin. She could feel her nipples hardening and a shiver racing up her body.

"Good night, dear," she said then closed the door. Kit could hear their voices fade into the night as they walked away.

"Am I going to have to deal with you and your attitude every day, Emily Mills?" Kit groaned then slipped under the water and blew a long trail of bubbles.

Chapter 5

Kit locked the door to the cottage and started up the path to the lane. If she hurried, she had just enough time to make it to the airfield before the first flights were scheduled. It wasn't like her to be late. Usually she was up and dressed before her alarm clock rang. But the surprise intrusion by Emily Mills left her so angry and befuddled she spent most of the night tossing and turning. Why she allowed the obtrusive woman to destroy a night's sleep was a complete mystery. She had faced irritating people and emotionally sensitive situations before and never lost a night's sleep over it. But this woman had her gnashing her teeth at the mere thought of it. Granted, Emily wasn't hard to look at, and the delicate scent of her perfume that lingered in her wake made a definite impression on Kit's psyche.

"Lieutenant Anderson," Nigel called, hurrying up the path to her.

"Good morning, Nigel."

"Would you have a moment, miss?" he said, nearly breathless.

"Actually, I'm late. I have a meeting in six minutes," she said, checking her watch. "No, four minutes."

"Lady Marble asked me to invite you to breakfast. She would like to talk with you, miss."

"I'm sorry, but I can't. Tell her thank you but not this morning," Kit said, quickening her pace up the lane. Nigel followed, trying unsuccessfully to keep up.

"It wouldn't take but a few moments, miss," he persisted.

"I'll come by this evening. I should be back by six."

"I'll tell her. She'll be expecting you."

Kit hoped the invitation wasn't to inform her she had changed her mind about renting the cottage. She didn't have time to go house hunting again.

"Gather around, ladies. Let's get the assignments sorted out," Kit announced, stepping into the ready room where the pilots were waiting.

The day was a full one, several of the pilots flying three and four missions. Lovie drew the short straw and had to deliver an open cockpit biplane to Ireland, a cold and windy flight in an older, slower aircraft. But it was her turn and she did it without complaint. Red delivered an American P-51 Mustang fighter to an airfield near London, a mission considered a plum assignment. Any assignment that sent a pilot near London and its shopping district brought jealous sighs and teasing from the group. Kit had three missions, all of them returning damaged bombers to the factory near Manchester and bringing back repaired ones. Andrea went along for the ride and helped navigate, something Kit explained she couldn't practice enough. On the last flight, Kit allowed her to take off, navigate and land with little help or instruction. She was impressed with Andrea's confidence and talent at picking up the traits of the aircraft. She seemed to have the ability to watch and learn faster than Kit expected.

The airfield hummed with incoming and outgoing flights. The mechanics and ground crews worked nonstop to keep the aircraft repaired and ready. Two scramble orders sent the fighters off to intercept German bombers. A rumor spread across the base that one of the Spitfires had been shot down, but confirmation was slow in coming. Finally, word was received. Officer Philip Norton, twenty-two and the son of a London shopkeeper, was shot down over the English Channel. He was the first pilot lost from Alderbrook's squadron in a week and a particularly tragic loss since his wife was eight months pregnant with their first child. The atmosphere around the airfield was somber as the last fighters returned home, their outline silhouetted against the fading evening skies.

"You may dismiss your girls, Lieutenant. It's too dark to send anyone else up," Griggs said as Kit entered the office after her last flight of the day. "And there's a gentleman to see you," she added, nodding toward the back door. "He said he would wait in the car out there."

"Who is it?" Kit said, looking out the window at the long black car. She couldn't see who was inside.

"I have no idea, but he was adamant about waiting for you. Said it was most important." Griggs raised her eyebrows to affect a sinister scowl. "What have you done, Anderson? Flown too low over someone's house and broken the glassware?"

"Not that I know of, but you never know who you're going to upset these days." Kit draped her jacket over her shoulder and headed out the back door. The driver's door of the car immediately opened and Nigel climbed out.

"Lieutenant Anderson," he said politely. "May I offer you a ride?" He opened the back door of the car and stood waiting for her to get in.

"I don't need a ride home, Nigel. I can walk."

"Yes, miss. But Lady Marble is most anxious to visit with you, and she instructed me to pick you up. I would be remiss in my duties if I allowed you to walk." He nodded toward the open door. When she hesitated, he raised an eyebrow stiffly. "You wouldn't want the petrol ration to be wasted, now would you, Lieutenant?"

"Okay. You can stop trying so hard to make me feel guilty, Nigel. I'll take the ride." She tossed her jacket on the seat then climbed in.

"Thank you, miss," he said, closing her door then settling into the driver's seat. He started the car and carefully pulled out onto the road. It seemed to take all Nigel's strength to hold himself up enough to see over the huge steering wheel as he crept along the road. Kit sat back and enjoyed the ride. It was easier than staring out the front knowing she could walk faster.

The interior of the car was covered in rich burgundy upholstery and burled wood paneling. She knew it was none of her business, but she couldn't help peeking in the small cabinet fitted into the back of the front seat.

"Would you care for a drink, Lieutenant?" Nigel asked, glancing at her in the rearview mirror. "I believe you'll find a flask of Scotch in the bar. I'm sorry there is no ice."

"No, thank you." She quickly shut the compartment door. The idea of a stiff drink did sound appealing though. She noticed a small glass vase attached to the window frame. A single yellow rosebud stood in a dab of water, filling the back seat with a heavenly scent. Kit leaned over and took a deep sniff. "Is this one of Lady Marble's roses?"

"Yes, miss. The Queen's Crown. Lovely, isn't it?"

"Yes, it's very delicate." She took another whiff.

"The roses will be most impressive this year. That is one of the last roses from the greenhouse."

"Thank you for the rose, Nigel."

"You're welcome, Lieutenant."

Nigel crossed the bridge and wound along the lane, coming to a stop in front of the house. Before Kit could find the door handle he was out and holding the door for her. After she climbed out, he led the way up the steps and opened the front door.

"This way," he said, his footsteps clattering across the shiny marble floors and down the dark wood-lined hall. He pushed back a pair of heavy paneled pocket doors and motioned Kit inside. "I'll let her Ladyship know you are here. Please make yourself at home, Lieutenant." He waited for Kit to go inside then closed the doors behind her.

"So this is how they live," Kit said under her breath, scanning the stately, though unassuming, opulence. Everything was large, from the pair of leather sofas flanking a tiled fireplace to the mahogany desk polished to a mirror shine. A stained glass desk lamp and two leather-bound volumes Kit assumed were great tomes to history and culture were the only items on the desk. Bookshelves stretched along one wall from the floor to the high ceiling and were filled with thousands of leather-bound books, many of which looked antique to Kit's unskilled eye. A huge bouquet of flowers was placed on the table between the sofas, making it impossible to see over if seated on either of the sofas. A heavily carved table stood in front of the pair of tall windows. It held a silver tray with two cut glass decanters and four matching glasses. There was also a crystal bowl of ice with a pair of silver tongs hanging on the side. Kit was tired and she was thirsty. Her long day of flights was catching up with her, and the sight of ice, something she didn't see very often, was more than she wanted to ignore. She was dying for a cool drink of water. And Nigel did say to make herself at home. She placed several ice cubes in one of the glasses and sniffed the contents of the decanters, hoping the clear one was water. It had no smell. She poured three fingers worth into the glass and took a big gulp. Her eyes instantly widened as she choked it down.

"Wow, that is definitely not water," she gasped, coughing and choking.

"No, that is vodka," Emily said from the open door.

"I found that out." Kit covered her mouth as she finished coughing and cleared her throat.

"What are you doing in here?" Emily asked critically, frowning her disapproval.

"I have no idea. Nigel picked me up at the airfield and brought me here. I'm just the nasty American here to steal the family vodka," she said sarcastically, taking another sip.

"Emily, dear," Lady Marble said, coming up behind her. "Don't be rude. Lieutenant Anderson is my guest. Go on in the library and quit acting like someone stole your doll." She escorted Emily inside and closed the doors. "Oh, I see you found some refreshment, Lieutenant. Good for you."

"I'm sorry, ma'am. I thought I was pouring water. It's vodka."

"Why would I keep water in a decanter?" Lady Marble asked, coming to the tray and refilling Kit's glass. "Would you like something, Emily?"

"No, thank you." Emily stood just inside the closed doors, seemingly uneasy with Kit's visit.

"Well, I do." She poured herself some vodka then smiled up at Kit, clinking their glasses together. "Long live the King," she said in salute.

"God bless America," Kit said, taking another sip.

"Emily, dear, come in and sit down. Don't stand over there while we have company. Be sociable."

"I don't understand why I have to be here," Emily said, crossing her arms.

"Lieutenant Anderson, please have a seat," Lady Marble said, motioning her toward one of the sofas as she circled the desk and lowered herself into the large leather desk chair. "I won't waste any more of your time. I'm sure you had a very difficult and exhausting day. I'll get right to the point." She took another sip from her glass. "Do sit down, Emily, dear," she scowled, motioning to the sofas. Emily begrudgingly took a seat across from Kit. Kit tried not to show it, but it was hard not to snicker at Lady Marble's disciplinary tone at her granddaughter.

"Nigel said you needed to talk with me. Is there something I can do for you, Lady Marble?" Kit asked.

"Yes. First of all, you may call me Lillian. When I'm out in public, I'm Lady Marble out of respect for my late husband and his family. But here at Bellhurst, in my home, I am Lillian. I find Lady Marble a rather cold and remote greeting."

"Is that why I'm here? To call you Lillian?"

"No." Lillian took a sip then set her glass on the desk and folded her hands.

"This is ridiculous," Emily declared, standing up and storming to the door.

"Emily," Lillian said.

"I do *not* need Lieutenant Anderson's help. I am quite capable of finding my own position." Emily thrust the door open and disappeared down the hall.

"Emily, come back this instant," Lillian demanded. She and Kit watched, but Emily didn't return. Instead, Nigel appeared in the doorway.

"Is there something else, madam?" he asked.

"No. Thank you, Nigel." Lillian's forehead wrinkled with anger.

"Does this have anything to do with me?" Kit asked.

"I am sorry for my granddaughter's behavior, Lieutenant. And I want to apologize for barging in on your bath last night as well."

"That's okay. I survived."

"It was unspeakably rude. Please excuse Emily. She just arrived three days ago. She'll need a few days to settle in."

"Is that what this is all about? Is Emily settling into the cottage after all?"

"Absolutely not. My granddaughter will be staying with me here in the house. The cottage is yours as long as you require housing. Emily never actually lived in it. When she was a child she used it as a playhouse. As she got older she used it for more of a retreat, a place to find solitude on her visits to Bellhurst. Sometimes I think it was just a place for her to hide. She hasn't used it since she went off to school."

"She's a university student?" Kit asked, noticing a photograph of Emily on the bookshelf behind Lillian's chair.

"No. Not a student. Emily is a teacher. Or at least she was. The school was destroyed in a bombing raid. They have tried unsuccessfully to rebuild it, but materials just aren't available."

"What did she teach?"

"Literature and grammar."

"I could have guessed that," Kit muttered sarcastically.

"I understand she is very good at it," Lillian said proudly, opening the desk drawer and pulling out an official looking paper. "Emily applied for work here in Alderbrook. She was in hopes she could transfer to one of the schools near here, but there are no positions available. In fact, she hasn't been able to find employment anywhere within miles. Many of the schools have either been closed or damaged in the air raids. Many families have sent their children to northern England or to the United States until the war is over. Those students who are left are being taught in overcrowded schools with far more teachers than classrooms. It appears the only jobs available for women of her age in Alderbrook are with the Air Transport Auxiliary."

"Is she a pilot?" Kit asked.

"No. That's the trouble. My granddaughter is an intelligent, sensitive woman, but she has little in the way of practical skills. Since Parliament has decided all unmarried young women are to work in some capacity, I was in hopes she could live here with me and find adequate employment in Alderbrook, but in order to do that she will have to find work at the airfield."

"Does this have anything to do with the restrictions on hiring at the airfield?" Kit asked, sipping her drink.

"Regrettably, yes. Emily was told she had to have at least two references to even be considered. And both must be from airfield officers."

"What is she applying for?" Kit came to the desk and looked at the paper.

"I don't believe she knows. Surely there is something available for her ability and education. My granddaughter earned very high marks in school and is very well read."

Kit smiled to herself. The jobs available on the airfield were as far from literature teachers as you could get.

"Emily is furious with me for asking you, Lieutenant, as you could tell. But there just isn't anything else for her in Alderbrook. I was counting on her being here with me. I worry about her and was so in hopes something—anything—would be available to her. Is it terrible of me to ask if you know of something suitable?" She looked up at Kit with the eyes of a concerned grandmother rather than the stiff expression of British nobility.

"Teacher, no. There are no schools on the airfield. About all we teach is pilot training." Kit read over the paper carefully. "There are other jobs that become available occasionally. Cooks, mechanics, anything that helps keep the planes ready and the pilots flying them. We aren't a large airfield like Manchester or Whitechurch. We don't have lots of offices." Kit squinted at the name scribbled on one of the lines at the bottom of the page. "I see Commander Frost signed as a reference."

"Yes, Charles is an old friend of the family. He isn't with the ATA however."

"And you'd like the other signature to be an officer with the Air Transport Auxiliary, right?" Kit knew at last why she had been asked to come to the house.

"Yes, Lieutenant Anderson. It would be a great favor to me if you would agree to be Emily's other reference. It would mean she could remain here in Alderbrook with me. This has absolutely nothing to do with your renting the cottage. I want you to know that. I will understand if you prefer not to sign. My granddaughter has been less than hospitable to you," Lillian said, smiling slightly. "I could understand your not wanting to help someone who burst in on you while you are taking a bath."

Kit chuckled to herself, but Lillian was right. The idea she should forget Emily's behavior and outright hatred for her seemed a bitter pill to swallow. Kit had done nothing to bring on Emily's disgust for her other than rent a cottage and be an American pilot. Ordinarily, she would wad up the paper, toss it in the fireplace and walk out, leaving Emily to her own devices. She could find a job or not. It didn't matter to Kit. But Lillian had a look on her face that told Kit she loved her granddaughter very much and felt helpless to protect her. Like so many people throughout England, adjustments and concessions had to be made. Kit was no different. This was war. It seemed like a small enough request that she sign her name on the bottom of the paper if it would bring a measure of relief to a woman she had grown to admire. Kit dug in her pocket and pulled out a pen. She signed the paper and handed it back to Lillian.

"For you, I'd be happy to sign. Thank you for asking me."

"Thank you, Lieutenant Anderson," she said, standing up to shake Kit's hand. "This means a great deal to me. And I will instruct Nigel to put water in one of the decanters. I hope you will join me on occasion." Lillian walked Kit to the door.

"I'd like that. Good night. And tell Emily good night for me." Kit had no idea why she said that. Emily's British tea-sipping arrogance and her stick-up-the-ass posture grated on Kit like a piece of sandpaper. But for Lady Marble, she would accept her, at least for now. As Kit walked down the drive toward the cottage, she had an eerie feeling on the back of her neck, the one that told her someone was watching her. She discreetly tossed a glance over her shoulder and caught sight of a face in the upstairs corner window. The face quickly disappeared behind the curtain, but Kit was certain it was Emily staring down at her.

"Yes, Miss Mills. The Yankee signed your application. I hope it doesn't give you a rash." Kit slipped her hands in her pockets and continued down the drive, whistling happily.

Chapter 6

It was four o'clock and tea time. The women in the ready room were huddled around the stove waiting for the teakettle to begin whistling. Kit had just returned from Luton, swapping a fighter for a light bomber to correct a mistake in the deliveries. She and her squadron had flown fifteen missions and were all cold and tired. Late winter temperatures were giving way to early spring, but there was still a chill in the air that pinked their cheeks and numbed their fingers even in closed cockpit aircraft.

"Tea, Lieutenant Anderson?" one of the girls asked as Kit walked through on her way to Commander Griggs's office.

"No, thanks. When you find some coffee, call me."

"You're in England. When are you going to understand afternoon tea?"

"Oh, I understand it. I just don't like it." She laughed and opened the door.

"Don't like what?" Griggs asked, looking up from her desk.

"Tea."

"I can't believe you Yanks. Always in a hurry. Never taking time for a civilized cup of tea in the afternoon." Griggs already had her afternoon cup of tea on her desk, the delicate bone china cup and saucer a testament to her determination to carry on the tradition.

"I don't mind the afternoon custom of tea and crumpets. I just prefer coffee and crumpets." Kit placed a stack of papers on Griggs's desk. "By the way, what the heck is a crumpet anyway? I haven't had one since I got to England."

"Yes, you have. I saw you eating one in the dining hall just yesterday."

"No, I didn't. I had an English muffin."

"That was a crumpet, Lieutenant Anderson. You Yanks may call it an English muffin, but here it's a crumpet."

"Learn something new every day." Kit chuckled lightly.

"Speaking of learning something new, how is Officer Paisley doing? Is she passing muster?"

"She's doing okay. She's a little nervous, but that's to be expected. She hasn't balked at anything I've thrown at her so far. I'd like to get her qualified on Hurricanes this week. I don't think she'll have any trouble."

"How about Loveland and Peacock? Are they ready to move up? You could use a bit of help with the bombers."

"I don't know if they're quite ready yet," Kit said, furrowing her brow apprehensively. "Lovie still has a little trouble with her landings, and Red flies a little too loose for the big bombers just yet."

"It's your call. By the way, I understand you signed as a reference on an employment application." She took a paper from the stack. "Emily Mills."

"Yes, I know her grandmother, Lady Marble."

"Isn't that the woman who rented you the room?"

"Her cottage, yes."

"What do you know about this Emily Mills?" Griggs asked,

scanning over the application.

"Not much. She was a teacher, but the school was bombed. Lady Marble thinks she is intelligent and sensitive. As least that is her opinion."

"And what is your opinion?"

Kit raised her eyebrows. "I don't know that I have one."

"Well, I have to sign this and send it on to Captain Bower or reject it. Give me some guidance, Lieutenant." Griggs stared at her pensively. "We get too many of these applications to accept them all."

"Why does it fall to me to make the decision?" Kit asked.

"Because you signed it, that's why."

"I didn't know my signature carried such weight." Kit thought a moment. "Okay. Sign it, I guess. I think she's harmless."

Griggs signed the paper and placed it in her out basket. "See? That wasn't so difficult."

"I hope it doesn't come back to nip me in the rear."

"Do you have some problem with this woman I should know about?"

"No, not really," Kit said hesitantly. "I just hope she has some of her grandmother's common sense."

"If she doesn't, she won't last long. She'll be booted out before the sun can set on her backside."

"Anything else, Commander?"

"No, I think that's it for today. You can dismiss your squadron when you're ready. By the way, some of your girls are getting a bit slack with their paperwork. Log entries should be completed daily." She tossed Kit a little scowl that meant as a flight leader, it was her job to rectify.

"I'll take care of it, Commander." She saluted and closed the office door behind her. "Ladies," she announced, repeating Commander Griggs's scowl for all her pilots to see.

"Don't say it," Red said, closing her eyes and holding up a hand. "Log entries, right?"

"If you already know it, why is Griggs chewing my ass about

it? Finish them." Kit made eye contact with each girl, punctuating her point.

Lovie set her cup down and rushed over to Kit, throwing her arms around her dramatically.

"Oh, Lieutenant Anderson, I'm so, so sorry for neglecting my log entries. I feel just horrible about it. I promise I will never, ever forget to complete my duties again." Lovie buried her face in Kit's shoulder, pretending to sob mournfully. "Please forgive me, Lieutenant, ma'am." She peeked up at Kit.

Before Kit could reply, two other pilots rushed her, wailing and crying at their failures and pleading for absolution.

"All right, all right." Kit was unable to hide her amusement. "I will forgive you this once. But . . ."

"Oh, thank you, Lieutenant Anderson. Thank you," Lovie said, throwing herself at Kit's feet and kissing her boots. "I promise I won't let you down. You'll see. We'll be little angels. We promise. Don't we, girls?" she said, winking at the others.

"Yes, we promise," the group said, fawning over Kit, making as big a joke out of it as possible.

"I'm going home. You can stay here and plan your next lie." Kit collected her things and pulled a poncho over her head as protection from the mist that had begun to fall. "Tomorrow, ladies. Early and eager."

"Lieutenant?" Lovie said angelically from her kneeling position on the floor.

"What?" Kit said from the open door.

"Cribbage tonight?"

"Sure. Come by about seven. Just don't bring the marked deck this time."

"I don't need a marked deck to beat you," Lovie teased, climbing to her feet. "Tell her, Red."

"Keep me out of this," Red said, dipping a stale doughnut in her tea.

"You better come too," Kit said. "I'll need a witness to my victory. See you later."

Kit walked home, the mist growing to a full shower as she crossed the river bridge and started up the lane to the cottage. In spite of the poncho, she was drenched by the time she opened the door. She stomped and shook, shivering from the cold. She lit the fireplace and coaxed it to a full blaze. By the time she had finished her dinner and washed the few dishes, Lovie and Red were knocking at her door.

"Oh, Kit. This is *so* cute," Lovie said, hugging Kit then rushing past her to see inside. "Red, look. She has a fireplace."

"Wow, Kit, old girl. You really found a goodie here," Red said, following Lovie in the door. "Look at that, a bathtub in the main room."

"I think it was added recently. There isn't room for it in the bathroom," Kit said.

"It's wonderful. We only have a tiny tub. I have to sit with my knees up under my nose," Red said. "That's if you can get in the bathroom at all. Four girls and one bathroom is a constant struggle."

"Our bathtub isn't that bad," Lovie argued, taking off her coat and warming herself by the fireplace. "You're just too tall."

"I am not too tall." Red stood gazing into Kit's bathtub longingly. "Now this tub is nice and deep."

"It doesn't matter. The silly water ration means five inches is all you can use regardless of how deep the tub is," Lovie said.

"And I bet you stick to that five inches, don't you, Kit?" Red winked at her.

Kit went to put a kettle of water on the stove. She knew Lovie and Red would want tea.

"What is this I hear about you and that woman?" Lovie asked, rubbing her arms by the fire.

"Yeah. How about that?" Red stared at Kit suspiciously.

"What woman?" Kit asked.

"I heard you signed the application for an Emily Mills so she could work for the ATA. Isn't she the woman who was causing the scene in the ready room the other day?" Lovie asked. "Why would you be a reference for her? Do you know her from some-place?"

"It's no big thing." Kit dropped a few pinches of tea in the kettle.

"She isn't going to be a ferry pilot, is she?" Red asked.

"No. She's a school teacher. They'll probably find something clerical for her to do."

"What did she teach?"

"Literature," Kit said.

"Literature?" Lovie pronounced it like the British do. "Well, la de da." She flipped her hand and batted her eyelashes. "She can teach Shakespeare to the mechanics. *King Lear* during the day. *Romeo and Juliet* at night."

Red laughed at the idea.

"I doubt she'll be teaching anybody anything," Kit said. "She's a tea bag."

"Tea bag?" Red asked.

"Yeah, you know," Lovie said. "One of those stiff British women who never smile."

"Like Commander Griggs?" Red laughed.

"Mary Griggs isn't a tea bag," Kit said. "She's a great pilot."

"So Emily Mills is a tea bag?" Red asked.

"From what I have seen, I think so."

The teakettle began to whistle. Kit poured two cups and brought them to the table.

"Oh, boy. I could sure use a hot cup of tea. I'm cold through to the bone," Lovie said, holding her hands around her cup to warm them. "I hate to tell you, Kit, but you aren't supposed to make tea like that. You boil the water then pour it over the tea in a teapot. Never, ever boil the tea in the kettle." She grinned at her. "But I forgive you."

"No wonder your tea is always nasty," Red said, wrinkling her nose as she sniffed her cup.

"Do you want to make it next time? Help yourself," Kit replied.

"I'll make it," Lovie said. "I love to make tea. I feel so British when I make tea."

"You're Canadian, Lovie," Red said over her shoulder as she settled into the big chair.

"I know. But sometimes I think I was born British. I just have this feeling I was born to be queen," she said regally. "I want to live in a big house with servants that say 'yes, ma'am,' 'no, ma'am,' 'whatever you would like, ma'am,' 'dinner is served, ma'am.' I think I could get used to that." Lovie grinned demurely. "You can be my personal pilot."

"And fly you where?" Kit asked, bringing her cup of coffee to the table.

"I don't know. Someplace with really good tea." Lovie giggled.

"Where's the cribbage board, Queeny?"

"Right here," Lovie said, pulling it from her purse. "And I have decided to be nice to you. We will start over. I will wipe out the score altogether," she said proudly. "I can beat you anyway. I don't need a head start."

"She's only doing that because she lost the score pad," Red said with a chuckle as she read through the titles on the bookshelves.

"Sit down and shuffle the cards," Kit said, taking her seat. "This is my lucky night. I feel it." She rubbed her hands together eagerly.

Lovie set up the cribbage board and shuffled the deck of battered cards. Kit was just a beginner, but no one else would play with Lovie, knowing she could trounce even the most experienced player. Kit didn't offer much competition, but the fun of the game was the point. And she suspected Lovie allowed her to win occasionally just to keep her playing. Red watched for a few minutes, but she didn't understand the strategy and soon lost interest. She found a mystery to her liking on the bookshelf and settled in to sip her tea and lose herself in fiction.

"What was that?" Red asked, looking at the door.

"What?" Kit mumbled, her undivided attention on the game, trying desperately not to get skunked the first hand.

"Didn't you hear that?" Red put the book down and went to the door. "I heard something outside," she whispered. "Footsteps or something." She snatched the door open, but no one was there.

"Who is it?" Kit asked, playing a card then looking up.

"No one, I guess." Red stuck her head out and looked into the night. "I would have sworn I heard something."

"If it's Hitler, tell him to buzz off," Lovie said, playing a run of three.

"Shh," Red whispered, holding her finger to her mouth. She listened intently. "Sounds like someone is coming up the path."

Kit came to the door to listen.

"Where?"

"Over there." Red pointed, but the sound had faded and there was only silence. They both strained to see into the darkness, their ears trained on whatever sound was out there. Suddenly, Emily popped out from behind a tree, her umbrella making a ghastly figure in the darkness.

"What are you doing out there?" Kit shrieked, her heart pounding wildly at being surprised like that.

"I was cutting across the woods. I saw your light was on. Don't you know there is a blackout order? You could be fined for showing a light from the window," she said harshly. "You'd think a pilot would know about that. I could see it from the house."

"I forgot." Kit quickly closed the black curtains across the window, chastising herself for forgetting.

"It's raining outside," Red said, frowning at Emily. "You couldn't see anything above two hundred feet."

"Rules are rules." Emily stared righteously at the women. "Didn't they instruct you about the laws governing such things?"

"Actually, no. They don't tell us Yanks stuff like that," Kit shot back. "They know we can't read or write, so they figure what's

73

the use? They want us to spend our time learning two and two is four, or is it five? I never can remember which."

"Good one, Lieutenant." Red snickered, giving Kit a slap on the back.

"I don't think sarcasm is necessary," Emily said, glaring at her.

"What's going on out here?" Lovie asked, sticking her head out the door and broadcasting one of her let's-all-be-happy smiles.

"Nothing. Miss Mills was just being her usual informative self," Kit said, glaring right back at Emily.

"Oh, so this is Emily Mills?" Lovie said, stepping outside and offering her hand to Emily. "I'm Darlene Loveland, but you simply have to call me Lovie. Everyone else does." She shook Emily's hand as if they were long lost friends. "This is Mildred Peacock, but call her Red. Come inside out of the rain. We're playing cribbage and drinking Kit's terrible tea." She pushed Kit and Red aside, wrapped an arm around Emily and pulled her through the door. Emily may not have wanted to come inside, but she didn't stand a chance against Lovie's bubbling enthusiasm. "Would you like some tea, Miss Mills?" Lovie led her to a chair and pulled it out for her. "Sure, you would. You're soaked to the skin."

"No, thank you," she said, but Lovie didn't seem to hear it. She rushed off to get her a cup.

"It's perfectly horrible, but you know what they say, any tea is better than no tea."

Kit and Red were left standing in the doorway, watching Lovie's animated performance.

"This is the tea bag, right?" Red whispered into Kit's ear. Kit nodded.

"Sit down, Emily," Lovie said, setting a cup in front of her. "It's okay if I call you Emily, isn't it? I hear you may be working at the airfield with us." Lovie was hardly giving Emily a chance to respond. She sat down across from her and hitched her chair in closer. "Emily, tell me, what's it like to be nobility?" Lovie leaned in and gave Emily her undivided attention. Emily had just taken a sip of tea and choked slightly at the question.

"Well . . ." she started.

"Have you met the King and Queen?" Lovie asked eagerly. "Have you been to Buckingham Palace? Do they have satin sheets on the beds?"

"As a matter of fact, yes. I have been to the Palace," Emily said then took another careful sip of tea.

"Really?" Lovie's eyes were huge. "Did you spend the night? Did you meet Princess Elizabeth?"

"No. I understand the royal family was in Windsor. And it was just an hour tour. We didn't spend the night." Emily sipped again, a tiny curl appearing at the corner of her mouth.

Kit and Red laughed as Lovie's face melted with disappointment.

"I'm sorry, Officer Loveland. I didn't mean to tease you like that. My grandmother is Lady Marble. I'm just her granddaughter. I have no title. She was married to my grandfather, Lord Edmond Ambrose Marble. Her title is through marriage."

"Call me Lovie. And I thought you'd be Lady Mills."

"No. My mother would inherit the title if she chose to use it since she is daughter to Lord and Lady Marble."

"Then you would inherit it from her?" Red asked.

"Yes, I suppose so," Emily replied nonchalantly, swirling the tea in her cup.

"Has your grandmother ever spent the night at Buckingham Palace?" Lovie asked, determined to find some shred of pomp and circumstance.

"No, I doubt it."

Lovie heaved a sigh and slumped in her chair, a withered look on her face.

"My grandfather met the King though," Emily said, seeming to realize Lovie's disappointment. "He was a naval officer during the first war. King George the Fifth used my grandfather's ship on several occasions when he needed to cross the channel."

"Really?" Lovie brightened.

"Yes. And he told me the King liked big cigars and drank dark ale," Emily added as if divulging a secret. "And he ate his dessert first."

"Me, too." Lovie grinned over at Kit and Red. "I told you I was born to be royalty. Will you two sit down? You look like bank guards."

Red turned the big chair around and sat down. Kit perched on the blanket chest. She had trouble not staring at Emily, and Emily seemed to know it.

"If you are going to work for the ATA ,what exactly is it you plan on doing at the airfield?" Red asked, sitting on the edge of the seat.

"I'm not sure." Emily's eyes drifted over to Kit's. "I have an interview tomorrow."

"I understand you are a literature teacher," Lovie said, still eager for anything Emily wanted to say.

"Yes."

"Wow, literature. I bet you've read lots and lots of books," Red said.

"A few."

"Like what?" Lovie asked, hanging on Emily's every word.

"Lots of things. Shakespeare, Oscar Wilde, Tolstoy."

"Anything fun?" Red asked.

"Fun?"

"Yeah, you know. Fun," she said with a wink and a grin.

"Oh, you mean suggestive or bawdy." Emily pulled a half-smile.

"Yeah, really raunchy books," Red said. "The kind you see in plain brown wrappers at the back of the bookstore."

"Actually, you don't have to go to the back of the bookstore for that kind of thing. Some of the great works of literature are full of very provocative passages."

"Like what?" Kit asked, surprised Lady Marble's granddaughter, the very essence of British reserve and propriety, would discuss such things.

"Chaucer's *Canterbury Tales*, for one. It's full of immorality and depravity."

"Gee, I wish I had paid more attention in class," Red declared. "Do you have an extra copy I could borrow?"

"There should be one there in the bookshelf," Emily pointed to the stack by the chair. "Of course, if you don't care for four-teenth-century literature you could always read *Flames of Desire*," she added, a teasing little twinkle in her eye. "It's in there too."

"Now that sounds more my speed," Red said, searching the stacks.

"Don't take that one. Kit might want to read it first." Lovie giggled.

"Is that the kind of literature you read, Lieutenant?" Emily asked, giving her a sideways glance.

"Not hardly. They seldom live up to the real thing." Kit's gaze captured Emily's and held it.

"What kind of books *do* you read?" Emily asked, still locked in Kit's stare.

"I like adventure stories."

"True accounts of real people struggling to overcome the desperate challenges in their everyday lives?"

"Something like that."

"I didn't know you read stuff like that," Lovie said.

"I figured you for the fantasy novels," Emily said. "Or maybe the escape stories."

"I don't have anything to escape from. I'm perfectly happy right where I am," Kit said.

"I assume you are referring to renting this cottage from my grandmother."

"Not necessarily. But, yes, I guess I am."

The air in the room became brittle as Emily and Kit exchanged stares. Lovie cleared her throat as if to defuse any explosion between the two.

"Would you like to play a hand or two of cribbage, Emily?"

Lovie asked, "We just started, and it wouldn't be any trouble to deal you in."

"No, thank you. I have to go." Emily stood up, her eyes still on Kit. "I appreciate the tea, Lieutenant. It was very different."

"She boils the tea," Lovie said in a hushed tone then snickered.

"I didn't know I would be serving tea to royalty," Kit said, standing up and opening the door for Emily. "Next time I'll try to do better," she added sarcastically.

"On the bottom shelf of the bookcase there is a book by Alicia McCloud titled *Pondered Moments*. May I suggest you read chapter six, Lieutenant? It's all about humility and understanding," Emily said as she stood in the doorway. "Nice to meet you, Lovie and Red. I'll look forward to seeing you again. And thank you for the hospitality, Lieutenant." Her sarcasm matched Kit's perfectly. She reached over and tucked the black curtains together in the middle. "Good night."

"Good night," Lovie and Red said in unison, standing next to Kit in the doorway. They watched as Emily disappeared up the path, her umbrella bobbing into the night.

Lovie grabbed Kit by the arm and squeezed.

"Kit, Emily is not a tea bag," she said, scowling at her. "She is very nice."

Kit scowled. "You have *got* to be kidding."

"Lovie's right, Kit." Red nodded in agreement. "She seems very nice to me."

Kit walked away from the door, laughing out loud.

Chapter 7

Even before Kit entered the ready room two days later she could hear raucous laughter from the women inside.

"Can you believe it?" Viv exclaimed, barely able to control herself.

"I wish I had been there to see the commander's face when he read it," another woman added, wiping the tears that rolled down her face as she tried to bring her laughter under control.

"What's so funny?" Kit asked, coming to the stove to warm her face and hands. She had just returned from her mission in an open cockpit biplane, and she was cold.

"We've found a new way to end the war," Viv said, swallowing a giggle. "We've got a new secret weapon." Everyone again erupted in laughter.

"Tell me." Kit smiled eagerly. "I could use a good laugh."

"I'm serious," Viv said, trying to hold a straight face. "The Germans have the Luftwaffe. We have the Mills." She snickered again.

"The Mills?" Kit asked.

"Yes. The ultimate weapon to end the war within the week. Of course, we're going to lose unless we can convince the Germans to take her."

"Hey, maybe we should drop her behind German lines and let her go to work for them," one of the girls said.

"What are you talking about?" Kit asked, suspecting this had something to do with Emily Mills.

"Good idea, Janie," Viv said. "They'll have their bombers going in every which direction. They'll probably bomb their own factories." Everyone had another big belly laugh.

"Okay," Kit said. "What are you talking about? What's going on here?"

"Lieutenant, didn't you hear? That new girl, Emily Mills, was working in the command office as a typist, and she made a few corrections she shouldn't have." Viv stifled another snicker.

"What kind of corrections?"

"I'm not sure the exact wording, but she was supposed to type a memo from Flight Commander Hollingsworth, but I guess it had some grammar omissions and misspelled words."

"She fixed them," Janie added, unable to keep from helping with the explanation. "Every single one of them."

"So?" Kit didn't see the problem with Emily using her education to correct the Commander's mistakes unless he didn't like being shown up for his lack of language skills.

"They were supposed to be there. It was coded. When she fixed the memo, she gave word for an entire squadron to bomb some island in the North Sea." The girls laughed again, bumping one another playfully.

"An entire squadron?" Kit's eyes grew large. "My God. Was anyone hurt?"

"No. At the last minute the weather grounded the squadron in Scotland. Before it cleared, someone checked to make sure the bombing run was still on," Viv said.

"That's when the roof really fell in. You should have seen the commotion. Commander Griggs looked like she was going to bust a gut," Janie said. "She's been over in the flight command office all afternoon."

"But no one really bombed anything, right?" Kit asked carefully.

"Thanks to a storm off the Atlantic, no. We heard if it hadn't rained, our boys would have wiped out a fish cannery." Janie giggled.

The door to the ready room burst open and Commander Griggs flew in, a scowl on her face and purpose to her stride.

"My office, Lieutenant Anderson," she said, storming through. Kit followed her into the office and closed the door.

"Yes, Commander?" Kit stood at her desk. By the look on her face she suspected this too had something to do Emily and her over-eager corrections.

"Your Emily Mills," she began with restrained anger. "Do you have any idea what she could have done today?"

"I heard there was a problem with a certain memo," Kit said, standing at attention.

"*Problem* is the understatement of the century," Griggs said, her jaw rippling. "Your Miss Mills sent a squadron to bomb one of the Orkney Islands."

"But it didn't actually happen, did it?"

"No, but your Miss Mills could have killed hundreds of innocent people."

"First of all, Commander, she isn't my Miss Mills. I didn't hire her."

"That's beside the point. You signed as her reference and I approved it. Do you have any idea how this will look on our records?"

"Commander Griggs, you and I didn't do anything. And I would guess Miss Mills was only doing what she thought was right. I sincerely doubt she meant to bomb anyone. You have to remember she is a teacher. I'm sure she was just doing what came naturally. It's not as if she sent bombers to intentionally bomb Buckingham Palace. She isn't a spy, Commander. What did she do, fix a dangling participle?" Kit asked as a little snicker crept out. She could just imagine Emily shaking her head at the Commander's terrible spelling and giving his memo a teacher's critical red pencil editing.

"This is very serious, Lieutenant. Do you know that if she had changed frequent to frequently she would have sent two squadrons?" Griggs stared harshly at Kit, but Kit couldn't help it. She burst out laughing.

"You've got to watch out for those adverbs. They'll get you in trouble every time." She covered her mouth with her hand, but it was no use. She was a goner.

"Lieutenant," Griggs snapped.

"I'm sorry, Commander." Kit brought her laughter under control and straightened her posture. "But you'll have to admit it's kind of funny. And since no one was hurt, I think we can at least have a small chuckle over it. I assume Miss Mills is no longer typing memos."

"Miss Mills is lucky she wasn't arrested. And yes, she is no longer typing."

"Is she out of the ATA?"

"No." Griggs heaved a sigh. "We are going to give her another chance. She will be assigned to a less sensitive position."

"Like what?"

"Miss Mills will be working in the officers' dining room."

"Cooking?" Kit asked skeptically.

"The general consensus was that she could do little harm in the kitchen. There are no bombers stationed there." Griggs folded her hands on her desk and looked up at Kit. "Do you have any reason to doubt this assumption?"

Kit shrugged. "I have no idea, Commander. You'd think serving potatoes and beans would be pretty safe."

"That's all, Lieutenant." Griggs went back to work. "You may return to your duties."

"Yes, Commander." Kit was out the office door and had closed it before she shook her head and chuckled.

"What happened?" Janie asked. "Are they going to fire Emily?"

Before Kit could answer, the door opened and Emily walked in, her face pale and drawn. The women watched in silence as she crossed the room and knocked on Commander Griggs's office door.

"Hello, Miss Mills," Kit said, realizing Emily felt everyone's eyes on her.

"Good afternoon, Lieutenant," she said in a restrained voice.

"Come in, Miss Mills," Griggs said, opening her door.

Kit watched as Emily stepped into the office, their gaze once again meeting as Griggs closed the door. Emily looked humiliated and vulnerable, something Kit hadn't seen in her eyes before. As much as she would have loved to see that look a week ago when Emily was harassing her over renting the cottage, Kit felt a surprising empathy for her. Kit had absolutely no idea why, but for some shockingly unknown reason, she wished she had offered Emily a hug and a word of encouragement over the incident.

"Don't let her map your next trip, Lieutenant," Janie joked.

"No kidding." Viv giggled. "You'll end up in Italy."

"Okay, ladies," Kit said. "Let's break this up. Don't you all have something you could be doing?"

Kit gave a last look at Commander Griggs's door then made the assignments for the afternoon. As much as Kit wondered how things went for Emily in Commander Griggs's office, she had her own work to do.

It was after seven and Kit was nearly home when Nigel came hurrying down the path, waving his arm to get her attention.

"Lieutenant Anderson," he said. "Please wait."

"What is it, Nigel? Is everything all right?"

"Lady Marble," he began, gulping to catch his breath.

"Is Lady Marble all right?" Kit asked, grabbing his arm.

He nodded as he continued to breathe heavily, unable to

speak yet.

"Take it easy, Nigel," she said, wrapping an arm around him. "You shouldn't be running like that."

"Lady Marble asked me to invite you to the house for tea and a sandwich. I have been watching for you."

"Thank her very much, but that isn't necessary."

"She is very adamant, miss," Nigel added, still trying to recover. "She said to tell you she doesn't require your signature on anything. She just wanted to thank you for your assistance."

Kit thought a moment. She had no real reason to say no to Lady Marble's invitation. A nice cup of something warm and a bite to eat sounded good. And Lady Marble was a pleasant conversationalist, so why not?

"Okay," Kit said, unlocking the cottage door. "Tell her I'll be there in ten minutes."

"Very good, Lieutenant." Nigel turned and walked back up the path to the house, this time at a slower pace.

Kit washed her face and combed her hair before walking up the hill to the house. As soon as she knocked on the side door, Nigel opened it and frowned at her.

"Lieutenant Anderson, we were expecting you at the front door." He stepped back. "Come in. Madam is waiting for you. Follow me, please." Nigel led the way to the living room. Unlike the paneled and polished details of the library, the formal room was dressed with elaborate tapestries and plush furniture. Portraits adorned the walls and antiques dotted the tables. A grand piano stood open, its gleaming black finish polished to a mirror shine. Lillian was sitting in a large wingback chair, reading.

"Hello, Lieutenant. I'm so glad you could join me." She set her book on the table and reached up to Kit to shake her hand. "I didn't feel like dining alone tonight. We are just having a light dinner, but it's always nice to have someone join you, don't you think?"

"Isn't Emily joining you?"

"She telephoned and said she would be late this evening.

Something about training for her job. I was going to ask you how her first day went. I'm so anxious to hear how she did today. I know it is silly of me to be so nervous, but this kind of work is so foreign for Emily. Even when she was a little girl she would sneak off to read rather than run and play like the other children. She would read dozens and dozens of books during summer holiday."

"I understand she had a very busy day." Kit decided it wasn't her place to break the news that Emily's first day as typist was also her last.

"I can't wait for her to tell me all about it."

Nigel brought them dinner and they ate casually, enjoying fresh potato soup and nibbling finger sandwiches as they visited. The fire in the large fireplace warmed the room and lit it with a soft glow, one Kit found homey and soothing after a long day at the airfield. For a moment she remembered a winter back in Kansas City when she too entertained a guest, a guest with long raven hair and skin so soft she wanted to nuzzle herself against it and never leave. Kit hadn't thought of her in months. Like many of the things in her past, she had locked them away where they could no longer hurt her.

"Emily," Lillian called when she heard the front door open and footsteps in the hall. The footsteps hesitated then came closer.

"Hello, Grandmother," she said. "How was your day?" She came to give her a kiss.

"I had a lovely day, dear. And yours?" Lillian patted the chair next to her for Emily to sit down. "Are you enjoying your work?"

"Yes, it's very interesting." She seemed to choose her words carefully then glanced up at Kit. "Hello, Lieutenant."

"Good evening, Emily." Kit wondered if Emily planned on admitting what really happened at the airfield.

"I invited Lieutenant Anderson for a late tea. Do sit down and join us, dear. Tell me all about your first day with the Air Transport Auxiliary. Was it exciting?"

85

"Oh, yes. It was definitely exciting," Emily said. She went to the table and poured herself a cup of tea. On her way back to her chair, her eyes met Kit's as if pleading with her not to embarrass her in front of her grandmother.

"Does Emily work for you, Lieutenant?"

"No."

"Of course only pilots would work for you. How silly of me," Lillian said, laughing at the suggestion.

Nigel came to the doorway and waited for Lillian to finish speaking.

"There is a telephone call for you, madam. A Mrs. Baldwin. She insists it is very important, concerning repairs to the community center."

"Oh, yes. I'll be right there, Nigel," Lillian said, setting her cup on the table. "I really should take this call. I am on the committee to fund the reclamation. Please excuse me, girls." She hurried out of the living room, across the hall and into the library, closing the door behind her.

"Thank you, Lieutenant," Emily said after Lillian was out of sight.

"For what? And please call me Kit. We aren't at the airfield."

"Thank you for not telling my grandmother what really happened today. I appreciate your restraint."

"I'm not going to tell her, Emily. That is your job. If you want her to know, tell her. If not, don't."

"Absolutely not," Emily said without hesitation.

"She may surprise you. She may be very understanding and supportive."

Emily shook her head adamantly. "It was humiliating enough. I don't need my grandmother's disappointment."

"You may not be able to keep it from her." Kit went to stand by the fire.

"So you are going to tell her after all?"

"Not me. I told you, that is your business. But it isn't exactly a secret. Every one of my pilots seemed to know about it. I assume the news will race across the airfield and into town as well. It will probably just be a matter of time before someone tells her. Don't you think it should come from you?"

"How do I tell my grandmother I have disgraced her? How do I explain I almost caused a terrible catastrophe that could have cost hundreds of lives, and it was out of pure stupidity?" Emily lowered her stare. "I heard the laughing and I saw the faces today. I know I'm the joke of Alderbrook. Like everyone else, I'm sure you've been waiting for a chance to have your say about it. Here's your opportunity. Go ahead." Emily sat stiffly, her eyes down and submissive, looking like a medieval peasant awaiting her trip to the guillotine.

"I don't want to say anything." Kit sipped from her cup.

"Oh, come on, don't hold back. I'm sure you have some little jab you'd like to offer—some tidbit of sarcasm at my expense. While my grandmother is out of the room, go ahead and get it over with."

"Emily, I mean it. I don't have anything to say. What happened was not just your fault. The command office has to share responsibility as well. You may have actually typed the memo and made the assumptions about what your job was, but they should have given you better instruction. They should have told you to type exactly as it was given to you. And if the memo was that important, they should have proofread it before giving it to the currier. I have a feeling they know that. Changing your job was the mildest punishment they could have issued."

"I can't help but think what would have happened if the weather hadn't grounded those bombers. I don't think I could have lived with myself if even one person had been injured because of my stupidity." She slowly looked up, tears streaming down her cheeks and her chin quivering.

"But it didn't happen. No one was hurt. You'll get over it. Someday, you'll be able to smile about it. And I know a great way to start."

"How?" she asked, discreetly wiping the tears from her face.

Kit nodded toward the library where Lillian had gone. Emily looked in that direction then back at Kit.

"Tell Grandmother? Absolutely not." Emily gasped, shaking her head. "I couldn't. It would humiliate her too much."

"It's up to you. She's your grandmother. I just know if it was my grandmother, I'd want the bad news to come from me, not a stranger who might not get the story straight to begin with. I can imagine how embarrassed she would be standing at the butcher counter and having someone bring it up, blindsiding her with the story how her granddaughter tried to have one of the Orkney Islands bombed."

"I did *not* try to bomb one of the Orkney Islands," Emily argued. "That isn't what happened at all."

Kit raised her eyebrows and stared at Emily as if to point out how easily the truth could be misconstrued.

"Lieutenant, please. I'll handle this in my own way," Emily said, wiping the tears from her cheeks as she regained her composure. "Your help is not required in this matter." As soon as Emily said it, she seemed sorry for the remark. She looked away then back at Kit regretfully. "I'm sorry."

The library door opened and Lillian rushed back into the living room.

"I have wonderful news," she said, clapping her hands together and grinning widely.

"What is it, Grandmother?"

"Charlie Dooley and Michael Bostwick have donated the lumber and their labor to repair the roof over the community center. The job should be finished within a week." Lillian glowed with the news as if it was second only to winning the war.

"That's wonderful," Emily said happily. She seemed relieved the topic of conversation was no longer her fiasco at the airfield.

"The women's guild may now continue with their plans for a social event."

"What kind of social event?" Kit asked.

"A dance," she said enthusiastically. "Heaven knows the young men and women could use an evening of gaiety. I hope you'll plan on attending, Lieutenant."

"If I'm in town, sure," Kit said but knew she probably wouldn't go. She didn't like spending an evening telling men she didn't want to dance with them.

"Emily, dear, I hope it's all right. I told Mrs. Baldwin you would be available to help with the refreshments."

"That's fine," Emily said.

"Will you need my help too?" Kit asked.

"Oh, no. You and your pilots will be our guests, dear. If you'll excuse me, girls, I really do need to make a telephone call or two. We have so many things to plan." She went to the doorway and looked back. "Please forgive me."

"Thank you for dinner and tea," Kit said, holding up her cup.

"Thank you for sharing it with me and for such encouraging words about Emily's new position."

Kit nodded, her eyes falling on Emily.

"Good night, ladies," Lillian said then disappeared into the library.

"She gets so excited when she's on a project," Emily said, smiling as the library door again closed.

"It seems to give her a goal and a purpose." Kit set her cup on the tray. "If you'll excuse me, I think I'll turn in myself."

"I didn't mean to scare you off, Lieutenant."

"You didn't." Kit crossed the room and stood in the doorway. She looked back at Emily, her eyes doing an involuntary scan down her body and back up again. She didn't mean to be so obvious about it. The slight hesitation at Emily's curves and bumps was just habit, a habit she hadn't used in over a year. She also didn't mean to cause the blush that raced over Emily's face.

"Good night, Lieutenant," Emily said, seemingly well aware of where Kit's eyes had been.

"Good night." Kit left through the front door, her strides long as she crossed the yard and found the path to the cottage.

Kit was confused. In spite of the sharp edge to their conversation, she had seen something in Emily's eyes, something that surprised her. She wasn't sure what it meant. But whatever it was made Kit tingle. That much she was sure of. This crusty Brit hated her. That much Kit did know. And all the while Kit was undressing her with her eyes. How stupid could she get?

Chapter 8

"Ladies," Commander Griggs announced from the door-way to her office. "The clouds will be breaking up from the east within the hour. Get yourselves organized. We've got aircraft to deliver."

"It's pouring rain," Red said under her breath, glancing out the window of the ready room.

Griggs crossed the room to Kit's desk and handed her the list.

"Weather command just telephoned. This squall line will move off toward the channel and leave us six to ten hours of clear skies. That P-Fifty-one needs to go first."

"Okay," Kit said, slipping her paperwork into a folder and looking over the list. "Why are we taking the trainers back to Manchester?" she asked as Griggs was about to walk away. "We just brought them down last week."

Griggs tossed her a gaze that meant don't ask, just do it.

"Gather around, ladies," Kit said, moving to the map. "Viv, I promised you the next Mustang, so the one on the runway is yours." She handed her the assignment sheet. "Lovie, the Hurricane to Prescott. Check with flight operations. You may be delivering some engine parts as well."

"Right." Lovie nodded.

"Red, you, Patty and Dee, Spitfires to Lyfirth."

They nodded.

"Watch for runway damage. I heard they got bombed last week and may not have it all filled in yet. Come in from the west and set down quick. You'll be bringing something back. But I'm not sure what." She checked the list then handed out the assignment sheets and any information she thought would help the pilots have a safe mission. As soon as the clouds began to pull away, the skies over Alderbrook were filled with ferry pilots on their way to combat bases. Kit stood outside the ready room with her binoculars trained on each airplane as it roared down the runway. Andrea stood next to Kit, watching and waiting for her first solo mission. No sooner had all the aircraft disappeared and the air above the field returned to calm than the scream of the siren split the silence.

"Scramble, scramble!" a man shouted from the observation deck of the command office. "Bombers from the northeast at eight thousand. Zero four zero." The airfield instantly was abuzz with men racing toward their fighters and ground crews helping to get them skyward as the sirens wailed.

"Lieutenant, what do we do?" Andrea asked, looking to Kit for guidance.

"Come on." Kit rushed into the office. Like every scramble order, the entire airfield was in frantic mode, everyone running and preparing to get the airplanes up as fast as possible to meet the threat.

"Get into your flight suit," Kit ordered as she grabbed her gear.

"Lieutenant, we've got two DHC's waiting canopy repair,"

Griggs said, bursting into the ready room.

"We'll get them up." Kit pulled on her heavy leather flight jacket. "Find gloves and anything else warm you can put on, Paisley."

Andrea stepped into her flight suit and pulled on a sweater and jacket.

"Come on. You're going to get your first taste of this war," Kit said, waving Andrea to follow her across the field.

"What are we going to do?"

"We're going to get those De Havilland Chipmunks up," Kit said, pointing to a pair of single-engine trainers that looked like small RAF fighters. Their sliding canopies had been removed.

"But they aren't repaired yet. Where are we taking them?"

"We aren't taking them anywhere. But we aren't leaving them on the ground as targets either." Kit tossed her parachute into the seat. "Put that parachute on, Paisley. Check your fuel."

"Half," Andrea said, standing on the wing and looking at the gauges.

"Good. Climb in and follow me. Stay on my left. Watch for hand signals. Conserve your fuel. No steep turns or climbs. The tail wheel will come up at forty-five knots, but don't try to lift off until you reach sixty."

"Where are we going? What is our heading?"

"We're heading the hell out of the way." Kit climbed in and hit the switch, spinning the propeller into action. The engine belched black smoke and coughed but didn't start. Andrea started her engine, the rumble shaking the cowling, but the propeller spun and caught. Kit adjusted the choke and hit the switch again. "Come on, baby." This time the engine started. She signaled for Andrea to follow her as she rolled into position for takeoff. Kit pulled the flaps on her flight cap down over her ears and set her goggles into place. She eased the throttle to full and released the brakes. As the airplane began to roll across the grass, she looked over at Andrea and gave her a thumb's up for takeoff. Kit was sure Andrea's stomach was doing flip flops and her mouth must be as dry as the Sahara Desert. There wasn't time to ease her into her first solo flight. This was war, and experience would not come easy. And if she couldn't cut it, Kit needed to know that now, in an expendable training aircraft rather than in an indispensable Spitfire or Hurricane fighter. This was Paisley's chance to show what she was made of and how cold her nerves were.

Andrea followed Kit across the field, pulling up and shadowing her turns until they were heading due west. The cold wind whistled through the cockpit, stinging their faces. Kit kept them at a few hundred feet where the temperature wasn't as cold as at higher altitudes. For over an hour, they flew racetrack patterns, using landmarks to keep their course constant. Andrea showed surprising abilities to stay with Kit, remaining twenty feet off her left wing tip as if she were glued there. On a pass near the corner of the airfield, Kit rocked her wings and looked for a signal from the ground. The red flare meant it wasn't yet safe to land. Kit signaled Andrea they would be making another pattern and asked how much fuel she had. Andrea signaled she still had a quarter of a tank, enough for two, maybe three circuits over the countryside. Kit gave her a nod and headed them away from the airfield. She also kept an eagle eye out for German aircraft. They shouldn't be flying where Andrea and Kit were, but there was always the chance a lost Luftwaffe pilot might see two RAF airplanes and want to claim a quick kill, another reason to keep their altitudes low and harder to detect. Kit noticed her own fuel tank was wobbling dangerously close to empty. She throttled back, easing the strain on the engine and hoping to stretch her flying time. She kept an eye out for a suitable emergency landing spot.

"Give us one more time around, pretty lady," Kit said to the airplane, adjusting the throttle and the flaps. She wanted to pull up, giving herself an extra margin of safety in case the engine conked out, but she could see Andrea's nearly frozen cheeks. Any higher altitude and they ran the risk of hypothermia or frostbite. Kit kept them low and slow, cruising just above the treetops. At the end of the circuit, Kit once again tipped her wings and watched for a signal from the ground crew. After an agonizingly long hesitation, a green flare exploded over the runway. Kit immediately signaled Andrea to land and waited for her to set down. Her own fuel gauge now showed an empty tank. Just as Kit banked over the hangar, lining up for her landing run, her engine gave out a cloud of smoke and fell silent. The only noise was the wind whistling through the open cockpit. She grabbed the stick with both hands and stomped on the rudder pedals, forcing the nose up as she finished her slow arc over the end of the field.

"Find the wind, sweetheart," she gasped, gritting her teeth. She leveled her wings just a few feet before the wheels touched down heavily, jolting her in her seat. The trainer rolled to a stop in the middle of the runway, bringing a truck roaring across the field toward her.

"Is it empty, Lieutenant?" the driver shouted.

Kit nodded and jumped out. She waved at Andrea, who was taxiing back to the hangar where the airplane had been waiting repairs. Two men hooked a tow cable to the tail wheel of Kit's airplane and pulled it off the runway. Andrea climbed out and hurried to catch up with Kit as she headed for the ATA office.

"That was fun, Lieutenant," she said, the fresh sense of exhilaration glistening in her eyes. She found Kit's stride and joined her in lock step.

"You did okay, Paisley," Kit said. "Watch the turns on take-off."

"Yes, ma'am." Andrea was barely able to contain her excitement over her first assignment, even if it was just flying in circles. She didn't seem to realize she was cold and wind-chapped. It was clear Andrea had been bitten with the bug. She was now officially an ATA ferry pilot, and nothing else seemed to matter.

Kit wanted to tell her not to get too excited about her missions, but she refrained. She didn't want to spoil the moment for Andrea. There would be time for sobering reality soon enough. For two hours, all Andrea could talk about were the scramble orders and their harrowing flight. Kit tried to finish some paperwork, but Andrea was like a wind-up toy chattering away about flight patterns, emergency takeoffs and what it would be like to face a German fighter at 500 hundred feet. When several of the women returned from their missions, Andrea found new ears to hear her stories. Kit used the diversion to escape. Just as she stepped out of the ready room on her way to the hangar, a chilly mist once again darkened the afternoon skies. She rolled the collar of her flight jacket against her cheeks and trotted across the field knowing full well there would be no test flights or pilot checks this afternoon. Lovie and Red were waiting for her, their checklists and assignment releases in hand.

"Did you order this lousy weather, Kit?" Red asked, standing just inside the hangar door, watching the drizzle.

"No. I ordered sunny and seventy. Someone in weather and logistics can't read." She shook her head and tried to push some shape back into her limp hair.

"We've missed more missions because of bad weather than we've made this week," Lovie said, hanging her flight case over her shoulder and pulling out a cigarette. She lit it and flipped the match into a puddle. "I want sun!" she yelled skyward. "I hate this."

"I know, Lovie, sweetie," Red said, wrapping an arm around her. "You are starved for affection. You and your aircraft become one with each other. You need to feel the stick between your knees and the pull of the rudder under your seat."

"You bet I do. I love to fly. And so do you. I did not join this flying circus to just polish my wings. I want to go someplace. Do something." Lovie threw her head back disgustedly. "I feel like I'm trapped. And don't tell me you don't feel just the same, both of you." She pointed a finger at them menacingly.

"Relax, Lovie. You'll get your chance. By the weekend we should have enough clearing so we can get caught up. You'll have more missions than you can handle." Kit steered Lovie's hand up to her own mouth and pulled a drag on her cigarette then coughed. "God, no wonder I decided to quit that smelly habit."

"Did you hear what they are telling women in the tobacco shops?" Lovie asked, taking a drag then blowing a smoke ring.

"What's that?"

"The government made an announcement asking women not to smoke."

"Just women?" Red asked.

"Yep, just us sweet, dainty creatures." She batted her eyes.

"Why just women?" Kit asked.

"They said there is a national shortage of cigarettes and tobacco, and it should be reserved for, and I quote, 'His Majesty's Fighting Men.'" She took a drag then spit a bit of tobacco from the tip of her tongue. "Yes, ladies, we now have been officially instructed to allow the men fighting and dying for jolly old England to have our cigarettes. It was *suggested* to the shop owners not to sell cigarettes to women."

"They can't do that," Red said with a frown. "I'm a member of the ATA and a citizen of Australia. I'm putting my life on the line just as much as any bloody Jack. I ought to be able to buy cigarettes if I want to."

"Well, let me know if you find any shop in Alderbrook to sell them to you. I'll buy a dozen packs," Lovie said. "Last month it was tea. This month it's cigarettes. What are they going to ration next? Toilet paper?"

"I wouldn't be at all surprised," Kit quipped. "I need a cup of coffee. You want to join me in the mess hall? At least it's dry in there."

"Yeah, I could use something hot to drink," Lovie said, taking a drag then offering the cigarette to Red, who finished it off and stomped it out.

"Come on. I'll buy," Kit said and started for the dining hall. They ran through the rain, ducking behind the command office and through the alley that ran behind the row of buildings. Just as Kit was about to round the back of the mess hall, the back door opened and a huge pot of dirty water came flying through the air. It caught Kit full in the face, drenching her from head to toe, and nearly knocking her down. Red and Lovie jumped out of the way, gasping in horror. Within a moment, their shock changed to restrained giggles as Kit stood stunned, the nasty water dripping down her front.

"Oh, Kit," Lovie said, unsure what to do to help. "Are you okay?"

"Goddamn it." Kit blinked hard. She spit and shook, wiping her hands across her face. "Who the hell did that?" Kit, Lovie and Red looked to the back door only to see Emily's terrified face. She was frozen in place, her hands gripping the pot as evidence she was the culprit. She didn't say a word. She couldn't. Her mouth was open, but she was clearly unable to form a single syllable.

"It's her." Red laughed. "The memo fixer."

"You have got to be kidding me," Kit said, looking at Emily then down at her soaked clothing. "I can't believe this. There are two hundred people on this airfield. Why did it have to be me?"

"Lieutenant Anderson," Emily stammered, rushing down the steps. "I didn't think anyone was coming round the back. They said throw the water out, so I did."

"Don't you have a sink or something to pour it in?" Kit shook one leg then the other. She pulled at the legs of the flight suit, trying to coax them from their grip on her skin. She could feel the water puddling in her shoes.

"It's in use at the moment. I truly am sorry."

"What is that smell?" Kit sniffed her wet hand. "What was in the pot?"

"Burnt food. I've been scrubbing it for hours." Emily seemed sorry to admit it.

"Burnt what? Whale blubber? It reeks." The fetid stench was rapidly becoming overwhelming.

"Wow, Kit. You have some serious body odor, honey," Lovie said, waving at her nose. "You smell like rotten garbage."

"It was cabbage and some kind of meat, tongue or something," Emily said.

"How did it get burnt so badly?" Red asked, wrinkling her

nose at the smell. "The cooks must not have been paying any attention."

"I'm afraid that was my doing. I was supposed to bring it to a boil then lower it so the meat would simmer, but . . ." Emily started then lowered her eyes.

"But you forgot to turn it down?" Kit said.

"There was so much going on in the kitchen. I had other duties, and the cooks kept giving me jobs. It was only my first day, and I just couldn't keep up. I am so sorry for drenching your clothes. If you'll give them to me, I'll have them cleaned and returned to you in the morning." She unzipped Kit's jacket and began peeling it off her shoulders.

"Never mind, Miss Mills. I'm not surrendering my flight jacket to anyone. I'll clean it."

"Please, Lieutenant. It is my duty to have them cleaned."

"No, thank you," Kit said stubbornly, pushing her hands away. "I'll take care of them myself. You've done enough."

"Miss Mills," Commander Griggs's voice boomed from the doorway. "What have you done now?"

"Emily is issuing free showers, Commander," Red said with a chuckle.

"I'm not talking about this," Griggs snapped. "I'm talking about the wasted food. I understand you allowed a substantial amount of food to be lost due to inattention. Is that true?" Griggs crossed her arms and glowered down at Emily. "Three pots full."

"Three?" Kit asked, glancing over at Emily. "My God, woman. What happened? Did you forget all three?"

"The officers' dining room will be serving cheese sandwiches for dinner tonight."

"Can't they salvage some of the meat for the sandwiches?" Lovie asked.

Griggs turned to the counter just inside the door and stabbed a lump of burned meat that resembled a large charcoal briquette.

"This is what is left, Officer Loveland. Help yourself," Griggs said, holding it up by the knife. "This was to be served to Admiral Gordan and his staff for dinner this evening. He is here from central command to discuss efficiency in personnel placement."

"I'm sorry, Commander Griggs," Emily said. "I know I should have been paying more attention, but as I told Lieutenant Anderson, it was my first day and things got out of hand so quickly. The gravy needing stirring, and the salt and pepper shakers needed filling, and the silverware was in a dreadful state, not to mention the potatoes needed peeling. There were buckets of them."

"It seems you have problems adapting on your first day of any job," Griggs said, the wrinkles on her forehead growing deeper.

The light rain had changed to a steady downpour, but Kit couldn't be much wetter. On top of that, the smell of the burned cabbage was beginning to turn her stomach.

"I am going home to change. If you need me, send someone. Otherwise, I'll see you tomorrow," Kit said, her shoes squishing out disgusting sounds as she walked away.

"Maybe you could boil your clothes in a big pan of water and have a nice soup," Lovie said, unable to hold back her laughter any longer.

Kit glared back at her.

"I truly am sorry, Lieutenant," Emily said, rushing after her. "You have to believe me, it was unintentional."

"If I thought it wasn't, I would have registered a complaint. As I see it, you're just an accident roaming around the airfield looking for places to land."

"I am not," Emily said stiffly. "I am quite capable of doing my job."

Kit narrowed her stare at Emily.

"Well, I am," Emily added indignantly.

"Do me a favor, Miss Mills," Kit said. "Don't do your job anywhere near my pilots, my airplanes or me." She peeled a strip of burned cabbage from the sleeve of her jacket and flicked it across the yard then turned and strode away, gagging from the stench.

Chapter 9

"You smell much better today," Red said, sniffing Kit's jacket. "I did like the cabbage cologne though."

"Do you know how long it took to get the smell of burned cabbage out of my clothes?" Kit poured herself a cup of whatever was in the kettle. It didn't matter what it was. She was cold and damp from her walk to the airfield.

Lovie came bursting through the door, holding a piece of cardboard over her head as an umbrella.

"Where is your umbrella, honey?" Kit asked.

"I wish I knew. The last time I saw it was Monday and I was on my way to flight headquarters."

"Then maybe you should go back to flight headquarters and get it," Red said, helping her out of her rain-soaked coat.

"I did. No one has seen it. I bought it at Harrods in London and paid a pretty penny for it. No wonder no one wants to admit they saw it." She shook out her coat then hung it on a chair near the stove to dry.

"So, Kit," Red said, raising her eyebrows suspiciously. "Where do you think she'll be today?"

"Where will who be today?"

"Emily Mills, of course."

"What makes you think she's being moved?"

"You know they won't leave her in the kitchen, especially in the officers' dining room. I bet Commander Frost about bit the stem off his pipe when he heard what she did to his big dinner for the Admiral."

"She's right," Lovie said. "He isn't known for his forgiveness. He demoted his aide for accidentally spitting on his shoe. I like Emily and I feel sorry for her. I'm sure she was completely and thoroughly embarrassed over what happened."

"Lieutenant Anderson," Griggs bellowed through her closed office door.

"Yes, Commander," Kit said, opening the door with a smile. "Good morning."

"You'd think so, wouldn't you?" she said without looking up from a folder of papers. "Can Miss Mills drive?"

"Emily Mills? I have no idea. Why?"

"Find out." Griggs tossed the folder aside then opened another one.

"May I ask what this is all about?"

"I received orders from headquarters. Miss Mills's position in the officers' dining room has been suspended. I have been given two days to find something suitable for her here in Alderbrook, or she will be sent to Manchester. They are in need of file clerks."

"Two days?"

"Yes, Lieutenant. Two days, and I must say I won't be surprised if she fails to meet the requirements for any of the available jobs here in Alderbrook."

"And the only job available requires a driver's license?"

"The motor pool needs drivers. I realize I am taking a terrible chance putting her behind the wheel of a truck full of fresh pilots, but we need drivers."

"And there isn't anything else available?" Kit asked skeptically, tugging at her ear. She couldn't help thinking Emily's abilities would be put to better use at a desk rather than in a garage full of greasy trucks and cars.

"Not unless she can repair a De Havilland engine or fly a heavy bomber. If she can't or doesn't want to join the motor pool, you'll be delivering her to Manchester on your next run."

"How about answering telephones in flight operations?"

"I have my orders, Lieutenant. And now you have yours. Find out if Miss Mills is capable of working in the motor pool, or have her ready for transfer to Manchester on Friday. That's all, Lieutenant." She went back to work, dismissing Kit.

"That'll teach me to sign as a reference," Kit muttered as she went through the office door and pulled it shut behind her. She was tempted to call Bellhurst and ask Nigel or Lady Marble if Emily knew how to drive, but thought better of it. If Emily hadn't yet told her grandmother about her difficulties with the memo translation or the burnt food, Kit didn't want to be the one to enlighten her. Lillian was a doting grandmother, and it was up to Emily to confess her problems.

Just before nine o'clock Kit saw Emily peddling her bicycle across the infield.

"Miss Mills," Kit called, intercepting her before she could enter the dining hall.

"Yes?" Emily was busy straightening her clothes and finger-combing her hair. Then she tossed her hair, and it sent a wild shiver down Kit's back. Emily had no idea what she had done. She had no idea the soft settling of her curls had stopped Kit's heart in mid-beat, completely captivating her in the moment.

"Can you toss your hair?" Kit asked, staring straight at her, unaware of her slip of the tongue.

"What did you say?"

"Drive, can you drive?" Kit said, realizing her mistake.

"Drive what?"

"I have no idea. A car, a truck. If you can drive one, you can drive them all."

"Why do you want to know? Has someone misplaced a vehicle and you want to blame it on me?"

"Commander Griggs wants to know if you can drive. She asked me to find out. So can you?"

"Yes, I know how to drive. Nigel taught me on grandmother's car when I was eighteen." Emily checked her watch. "I'm going to be late for work. If you'll excuse me, I need to check in with Mrs. Kelly."

"Um, you might not really need to do that." Kit stumbled over her words. She didn't want to be the one to tell Emily she was about to be dismissed from another job.

"Of course I do. I pride myself in always being on time." Emily opened the back door to the kitchen then glanced back at Kit. "And once again, I am sorry about the mess yesterday. I honestly didn't mean to drown your clothes like that. I hope you will forgive me."

"It's done. No problem." Kit turned around to show off the cleaned jacket. "It all came out."

"I'm relieved to hear that. Good day, Lieutenant." She stepped inside and closed the door.

Kit knew she would be back. She sat down on the back step and waited. Sure enough, it didn't take long. Slowly the door re-opened and Emily stepped out. It was obvious Mrs. Kelly had wasted no time in discharging her.

"What are you doing still here?" Emily's face had lost its color.

"I need to talk with you."

"You knew about this, didn't you? Did you plan on gloating?"

"Sit down, Miss Mills," Kit said, patting the step next to her. "And no, I didn't plan on gloating."

"What do we need to talk about?" Emily sat down next to Kit, leaving a space between them.

"Driving." Kit looked over at her. "The motor pool needs

drivers. Are you interested?"

"I know how to drive, Lieutenant. But that doesn't mean I want to be a professional driver. I haven't driven a car in years. I rely on the bus or the train."

"But you know how, right?"

"Yes, I told you I do."

"And you want to stay here in Alderbrook and work for the ATA, correct?"

Emily suddenly glared suspiciously at Kit.

"Does my continued work for the ATA have anything to do with the motor pool's need for drivers?"

Kit thought about trying to soften the news, but she saw no reason to extend Emily's curiosity. She nodded succinctly.

"There are no other positions available to me?" Emily asked carefully.

"Not at Alderbrook."

"Where then?"

"Manchester," Kit said.

Emily heaved a disappointed sigh.

"It's motor pool or nothing, right?" Emily said. "That's what you have been sent to tell me."

"I'm afraid so. You'll be transporting pilots to the factories to pick up aircraft as well as moving parts and personnel."

"I assume you know why I want to stay here, why I don't want to work in London or Manchester?"

"To be near your grandmother."

"Did you know she had a heart attack last year?"

"I didn't know that. Is she all right?"

"Yes. It was small, thank goodness. But I worry about her." Emily lowered her eyes as if considering how much to divulge. "Lieutenant, I am Lady Marble's granddaughter, her only grandchild. My mother and my grandmother have very little to do with one another. I could request and probably be granted a waiver from the ministry of labor excusing me from the employment required of most women. But I don't want it. I don't want to get out of my responsibility. There is work to be done, and I want to do my part."

"So you'll accept the motor pool assignment?"

"I don't see that I have much of a choice."

"You can tell Lillian you were needed as a driver instead of a cook."

Emily smiled discreetly at the ground then raised her eyes to meet Kit's.

"The other evening when you were having dinner with her, she already knew about my disaster with the memo. Nigel said someone telephoned that afternoon with the news. She just chose not to mention it. She told me I could allow my mistakes to conquer me or I could conquer them."

"Very sound advice."

"So now I have something else to conquer." Emily gazed across the field.

"Maybe it's true what they say. Third time's a charm."

"I hope so."

"It's stopped raining, so I have aircraft to deliver." Kit climbed to her feet. "Commander Griggs has your orders if you want to come with me," she said, offering Emily a hand up.

"I almost hate to enter that building again," Emily said, walking her bicycle next to Kit.

"Don't let my girls bother you. If someone says anything, tell me and I'll take care of it."

"I don't need your help with everything, Lieutenant, but thank you."

When they entered the ready room, the pilots were climbing into their flight suits.

"That's right, ladies. Button them up. We've got missions to fly and no time to waste," Kit said, stepping to the map. Griggs had just placed a list of deliveries on her desk and was on her way back into her office when she saw Emily.

"Miss Mills, I have your new orders. Follow me." Griggs led her into her office.

"Lovie and Red, bicycles to Ringway." Kit's eyes were on

Emily as she followed Griggs through the door.

"Don't you mean Spitfires, Lieutenant?" Red said with a curious smile.

"Yes, Spits," Kit corrected quickly, bringing her attention back to the pilots. "Viv, you're flying test flights for the MAC unit today. I heard they have six or seven Spits ready to go. Be sure you get a look at the repair sheets before you take them up. Paisley, you have a short flight to Luton." Kit looked up at her, knowing this was Andrea's first solo mission. "I'm sending you over in a trainer. You're picking up an RAF pilot, an Officer Powell. He's fresh out of training and is being assigned here."

The women collected their assignment sheets and checked the map before heading to the runway.

"Thank you, Lieutenant," Andrea said, snapping a salute. Her grin was so wide Kit thought her face might crack.

"Check your headings on the map. Watch out for crosswinds as you line up for your landing. Luton is known for gusty winds." Kit returned her salute.

"Yes, ma'am." Andrea studied the map again then rushed out onto the field, so eager for her first flight she could hardly keep her feet on the ground. Kit watched from the window as she climbed into the airplane and waited her turn for ground crew assistance.

"Paisley taking her first solo?" Griggs asked, coming to stand next to Kit and watch the departing flights. Kit nodded and raised her binoculars to her eyes.

"She's eager as hell."

"Weren't we all?" Griggs said then went back into her office. "Mills is on her way to the motor pool. Let me know if she crashes into something."

"Fortunately, I have a Lancaster to deliver. I won't be here."

"I know you think this is funny, Anderson. But I don't. If she has any problems at all in the motor pool, if I hear she even has a puncture in a tire, she'll be relieved of duty." Griggs gave a stern look then closed her office door.

Chapter 10

"Lieutenant Anderson," Commander Griggs said, waving her into her office.

Kit had just returned from a delivery. Her cheeks still stung from the cold.

"Yes, Commander," Kit said, coming in and closing the door.

"Did you hear Officer Paisley had a bit of trouble?"

"Andrea? No, I just got back. What kind of trouble? Is she all right?"

"It seems your newest chick lost a few feathers today."

"What happened to her?"

"You sent her to Luton to pick up that new pilot, an Officer John Powell." Griggs frowned.

"And?"

"The RAF can have him. I wouldn't allow him to fly for me."

"What happened, Commander? Did she have trouble with the plane?"

"Not the plane. It handled splendidly. I can't say the same for Officer Powell."

"What did he do?"

"Don't misunderstand me, Lieutenant. He didn't actually *do* anything. But from what I heard around the field, he certainly made an obnoxious horse's ass of himself. He was spouting all sorts of unpleasantries."

"Such as?"

"Such as how dare we send a woman to pick him up, and the only thing Officer Paisley was good for was flying a mattress."

"You're kidding." Kit chuckled, unzipping her jacket. But Griggs just stared coldly. "You mean he actually said that?"

"Officer Peacock overheard him. It seems it didn't stop once they arrived. Powell continued to harass and berate her for some time."

"What did Andrea do?"

"I don't know what she said to him, but I know she was upset. She should have come to me to register a formal complaint straight away."

"Are you going to say anything to Powell? Surely you plan on a reprimand."

"Not unless Paisley registers a complaint."

"Can't Red, I mean Officer Peacock do that?"

"I'm afraid it has to come from Paisley."

"Which way did she go?" Kit asked, turning for the office door.

"I'm not sure." Griggs followed her into the ready room.

"There you are," Red said, bursting into the room, her face flushed with anger. "Kit, you can't believe what that new RAF idiot said to Andrea."

"I just heard."

"You've got to do something. She's in tears. That stupid little pipsqueak needs his clock cleaned. Come on. I'll show you where he is." Red started for the door.

"Officer Peacock, you are not to do any clock cleaning,"

Griggs said loudly. "Do I make myself clear?"

Red's hot temper was well known around the airfield. It wasn't uncommon for her to take a swing at someone if he crossed the line, regardless of rank.

"I'll take care of it, Red," Kit said, pulling her back inside. "You stay out of it."

"You may need some help. He's small, but he might be wiry."

"Red, I'm not doing anything to Powell. I'm more concerned with Andrea. Did you see where she went?"

"She was crying so hard I doubt she could see where she was going, but I think she was headed for Brindy's. She was probably going to drown her sorrows in a pint of ale. I'd like to drown Powell's big mouth," she said angrily.

"Stay here and stay out of it. You and your red-headed hot temper won't help. That's an order," Kit said, wagging a finger at Red. "Just stay here and cool off."

"Tell her I am prepared to register a formal complaint with Powell's commander if she wants me to," Griggs said as Kit started out the door.

"I'd like to register something on that bastard," Red muttered, kicking a chair.

It was nearly dark as Kit crossed the airfield and made her way to Brindy's. The narrow staircase at the back of the building opened into a musty cellar full of smoke and the smell of fish. The evening crowd had not yet filled the long, narrow room, but a few die-hard customers leaned against the bar, sipping glasses of ale and exchanging stories about the bombing a few weeks ago. Kit squinted into the dim light and scanned the room. Andrea Paisley was the only woman in the pub. She was sitting at the corner table, an untouched glass of beer on the table in front of her. She stared at the floor, fumbling a handkerchief between her fingers and dabbing at her nose.

"Hello there," Kit said, gazing down at her.

"Hello." Andrea didn't look up.

"Do you mind if I sit down?"

"No, I don't mind. I assume you heard." She sniffled.

"Yes." Kit hitched in her chair. "Are you okay?"

"Oh, yes. I'm fine," she said, stiffening slightly. "But I become a blubbering baby at the drop of a hat." She dabbed at her eyes.

"From what I heard, you have good reason."

"I'm sorry, Lieutenant."

"Sorry for what?"

"For any embarrassment I might have caused you."

Andrea sniffled again then blew her nose.

"You caused? Why would you have caused me any embarrassment?"

"I am under your command. I am a member of your squadron, and I certainly didn't act accordingly. Members of His Majesty's service should conduct themselves with more dignity. I allowed myself to wallow in self-doubt and inadequacy rather than stand up for myself," Andrea said then lowered her eyes again.

Kit smiled to herself. This eager young woman was trying so hard to do her job and impress her superiors, she couldn't allow herself any room for mistakes or frailty.

"What exactly did you say to Powell?"

"Nothing," Andrea insisted. "I didn't say anything, honestly, I didn't, Lieutenant."

"So you just allowed him to have his say without interrupting?"

"Oh, yes, ma'am." Andrea nodded.

"That's good." Kit leaned back in her chair. "But tell me, what would you like to have said to him? Just curious, of course."

"I beg your pardon."

"I'm sure there is something you wanted to say to him when he said all you were good for is flying a mattress."

"Well . . ." Andrea started then hesitated, a blush racing over her face.

"It's okay. Tell me what your first instinct was."

"My first instinct was to slap his face," Andrea said.

"And then?"

111

"I wanted to tell him he had no right to say such things to me. I am an officer with the ATA, and he should show me the same respect he would show any other officer, man or woman. I was doing my job, and if he had an issue with my ability to fly the mission, I would be glad to listen, but his personal attack was completely unwarranted." Andrea's confidence seemed to be returning.

"And?" Kit encouraged.

"As for him, I sincerely doubt his experience was enough to justify his opinion of my flying. After all, he hadn't flown a single mission. He only had twenty hours in a trainer. How dare he think he knows more than I do? I took the same training and passed with exceptional marks." She was growing more confident by the moment. "And his uniform was a mess and his breath was disgusting. He wasn't even good looking."

"But you didn't say that?"

"No, ma'am. I didn't. I would never . . ."

Kit just stared at her without expression.

"I should have said something, shouldn't I?" Andrea's energized and self-assured expression began to melt as she studied Kit's face. "Instead of running away in tears like a frightened child, I should have stood up for myself, shouldn't I?"

"You allowed Officer Powell a victory he didn't deserve. Not only did he serve you an injustice, but you have set a precedent, Officer Paisley. You gave him the idea that what he said was acceptable."

"But it wasn't."

"He thinks it was. You told him so. By not standing up for yourself and explaining his rude behavior just like you explained it to me, he thinks it's all right and he will undoubtedly remember that."

"I'll get over it," she said with a resolute sigh.

"Are you ready to apologize to the next girl he says that to?"

Kit suspected Andrea hadn't thought of that. She was trying so hard to do the right thing in Kit's eyes, but it was clear she hadn't considered the consequences.

"You think I should have said something, stood up for us ATA girls?"

"I would have. All but the slap. Now Red would love to slap the guy silly for you. She's been known to stand up for herself from time to time."

"What should I do? Should I go back and talk to him?"

"I think the perfect moment for your reply is gone. But now you know what to say. And unfortunately, I'm afraid you probably will have to deal with those kind of narrow-minded people again. But you knew that when you joined the ATA. You knew it wouldn't be easy."

"Yes. I heard some of the terrible things people say about women taking jobs from our fighting men. But it isn't true, is it, Lieutenant?"

"No. It isn't. Everyone has a job to do. Next time you overhear someone say the girls in the ferry service are taking jobs from men, you tell them if they want your job you'll be glad to trade. They can fly the planes and you can lean on the bar and hoist a few. This isn't easy for anyone, Andrea. And we women have enemies on several fronts. Don't let the critics get to you. You're a good pilot, and the ATA is lucky to have you. Just keep flying safe and don't take any nonsense from anyone. Most of those poor idiots don't have the brains to read a flight manual, let alone fly a plane. If it wasn't for us, who would deliver the planes?"

"So if it ever happens again, you won't be upset with me if I tell the guy to bug off?"

"I'd be honored." Kit smiled at her.

"Thank you, Lieutenant." Andrea snapped a salute. "I can hardly wait."

"Just don't get carried away."

"Lieutenant, may I ask you something? Did you have any trouble when you first started flying missions? With men and all?"

"Yes, I did."

"What did you do?"

Kit smiled at the floor and thought a moment. It seemed like ages ago, but in reality it was only ten months since she had her first confrontation with a prejudiced mechanic.

"When I first got to England I spent a month at an airfield in Hutmouth. It was a tiny little field with a couple of buildings and only six airplanes, one Spitfire, two Hurricanes and three old bi-wing trainers. I could run faster than they could go on takeoff." Kit was fiddling with the napkin under Andrea's glass of beer.

"Here, Lieutenant. You can have it. I don't drink beer anyway." Andrea pushed the glass over in front of Kit.

"Are you sure?"

"Absolutely."

Kit took a sip then leaned back in her chair.

"I was supposed to take one of the Hurricanes up for a test flight. It had some bullet holes in the wing and the side of the engine. The pilot, a Captain Langmire, said it landed okay but was acting sluggish. The mechanics worked all night to fix the damage so I could test it before Langmire was scheduled to take it to Prescott to join a mission over the channel. The head mechanic, a Scotsman named Royce, was waiting for me when I arrived just after seven in the morning. He had the plane all fueled and sitting at the end of the runway, ready for the quick test flight. I climbed in and started it up. He waved me down the runway, so I took off. As soon as I got up I realized what he had done. He had removed the undercarriage crank. I couldn't get the wheels up. I was supposed to perform some rolls and dives. Have you ever tried to roll a Hurricane with the wheels down?"

Andrea shook her head.

"Don't. It's hard to keep the nose up. But that wasn't all he did. He changed the pitch of the stick. It was tilted back further than it was supposed to be. It was okay when I took off, but once I got in the air it was a different story. With the wheels down and making more drag, I had to hold the stick against me through the entire roll and loop. It was like sitting down on the bar of a boy's bicycle."

Andrea's eyes widened.

"What did you do?"

"I did the test and landed the plane. As I was rolling to the end of the runway I could see his face, grinning like an idiot. He asked how the flight went. He wanted to know if I liked the way the plane handled, then he laughed at me. When I climbed out of the plane I was so sore I could barely walk. My crotch was sore for days."

"Didn't you say something to him?"

"No," Kit said then smiled. "But I heard Royce came down with a terrible rash. Something about all the tools in his toolbox covered with some sort of itching powder. They said he had a rash in lots of unfortunate places."

"Oh, that's wicked." Andrea frowned then grinned devilishly. "I like that."

"I have no idea how it happened. Just one of those things, I guess." Kit winked at her.

"May I remember that bit of advice too, Lieutenant?"

"Be my guest." Kit chuckled then finished the glass of beer.

"If you'll excuse me, I need to return to the airfield and complete my log entries." Andrea stood up and saluted. "Thank you, Lieutenant, for your understanding."

"Anytime, Paisley." Kit watched as Andrea strode out of the pub, her shoulders back and her head up. Her confidence was back, something Kit knew she would need to fly her missions and return safely.

Chapter 11

Kit headed up the path for the big house. It was her first day off in weeks, and she planned on spending it taking a quiet walk across the meadow or perhaps napping away her afternoon. What she hadn't planned on doing was repairs to the plumbing in the cottage, but when she awoke to a growing puddle on the kitchen floor, she knew her plans had changed.

"Lieutenant Anderson?" Nigel exclaimed, answering her knock on the side door.

"Good morning, Nigel."

"Good morning, miss. Do come in. May I help you with something?"

"Thanks, but I just need to borrow a wrench. Do you have one?"

"Are you having problems that require repair?"

"Nothing major. Just a leak under the kitchen sink."

"Oh, dear."

"Lieutenant," Lillian said, coming into the kitchen. "I thought I heard your voice. I'm so glad you stopped by. Would you join me for tea, or perhaps a cup of coffee?"

"Lieutenant Anderson requires a wrench, madam," Nigel said. "It seems the cottage plumbing has acquired a leak."

"Oh, dear," she said with a worried look.

Kit loved the way the British handled adversity. There was no panic, just reserved confusion and stoic apprehension.

"Nigel, who are we calling for plumbing repairs?" Lillian asked, looking as if she had no idea what to do herself.

"I believe Jonathan Roland is still in practice." He said it as if he were recommending a physician for surgery.

"I can fix it," Kit said. "The water line has just come loose from the faucet. A few turns of the collar should take care of it."

"Lieutenant, I'm so sorry for the inconvenience. I thought the cottage was ready for inhabitants. Mr. Roland is a quite knowledgeable plumber, I am sure," Lillian said. "Nigel, call Mr. Roland and make an appointment at once."

"I can fix it," Kit insisted, touching Lillian's arm. "I've done it before. My apartment in K.C. had plumbing leaks all the time. The landlord wouldn't fix them, so I started doing it myself."

"Nonsense, Lieutenant. I wouldn't dream of having you make such a repair. Such things aren't your responsibility."

"I don't mind, really I don't. I wouldn't have even mentioned it, but I couldn't find any tools in the cottage. A wrench or a pair of pliers is all I need. Do you have any tools?"

Nigel had already picked up the telephone, but Kit stopped him.

"I can save you a big plumbing bill and do it in five minutes. And by the time Mr. Roland gets here, the water will be running out the front door," Kit said.

"I can't ask you to be a common plumber, Lieutenant," Lillian said.

"Believe me, it's no problem." Kit smiled reassuringly.

Lillian hesitated.

117

"She may be right, madam," Nigel said. "In matters of plumbing, timing is of the utmost importance."

"I have no idea if we have pliers, or what was the other thing you mentioned?"

"A wrench, pipe wrench, if you have it."

"Perhaps the carriage house, madam," Nigel said.

"Where is the carriage house?" Kit said.

"I believe you Americans call it a garage," Lillian said. "Follow the driveway around the back. It's beyond the greenhouse. But are you sure you don't want Mr. Roland to handle it? It might be a very unpleasant job."

"Don't worry," Kit reassured her. "It'll take longer to find the wrench than fix the leak."

Kit followed the driveway to the carriage house. She pushed back the big door, its squeaky rollers making it impossible to sneak inside. The black car Nigel had used to pick her up at the airfield was parked inside. A canvas tarp covered the windshield and hood, partially protecting the car from the bird droppings. A barn swallow dove at her head then flew out the door and into the fresh air. Kit coughed and sneezed, the stale air thick with dust and dank odor. The sunlight streamed in a pair of windows illuminating a shelf filled with odd paint cans, flower pots, dust-covered shoe boxes and a wooden crate of hand tools. Kit pulled the crate from the shelf and dug through the rusty tools for something she could use to repair the sink.

"Ah ha." Kit fished out a pair of red-handled pliers and replaced the crate on the shelf. As she turned to leave she caught her toe on a greasy drop cloth. She reached out to catch herself from falling and accidentally pulled the cloth back, exposing a handlebar. "What's this? A bicycle?" She peeked under the cloth. "Wow. You are no bicycle." She carefully lifted the cover to reveal a motorcycle. It was chocolate brown with yellow trim. The spoke wheels were dirty but intact. The large seat was also covered with a layer of dust, but the leather upholstery was still in good condition. The fender skirts and gas tank had yellow pin-striping, and there was an Indian head decal on either side of the tank. "I wonder who rides this." Kit squeezed the hand brake. After a last look, she covered it up and went to fix the leak.

Just as Kit had predicted, it took only a few turns of the pliers, and the nagging dribble stopped. She tightened the other side and the ones in the bathroom while she was at it. She returned the pliers to the wooden crate and went to the side door to report the job was finished.

"All done," she said, brushing the dirt from her hands.

"Do come in. Lady Marble will want to pay you for your services." Nigel stepped back and motioned her inside.

"I don't want anything. Just tell her the leak is fixed and I put the pliers back in the carriage house. And in case you want to know, you don't have a wrench." She smiled at him. "Thanks."

"Lieutenant," Lillian called, hurrying into the kitchen. "Do we need to call Mr. Roland?"

"No. The leak is stopped. I tightened the fittings on all the faucets just in case."

"I'm impressed. I want to pay you the going rate for plumbing repairs. What would you consider an equitable rate?"

"Honestly, I don't want any money. I was glad to fix it."

"That isn't fair. I would have had to pay Mr. Roland. I insist on paying you for doing the same work."

"Nope, I won't take it." Kit turned for the door.

"Are you sure?"

"Positive. If you have a leak, give me a call. I can't fix everything, but I've learned to be pretty handy."

"You're very thoughtful."

"Tell me, Lillian, out in the carriage house you've got a motorcycle. I didn't mean to snoop, but I tripped over the tarp covering it and saw the handlebars. May I ask who rides it?" Kit didn't mean to be nosy, but her curiosity had been piqued.

"What motorcycle?" Lillian asked, wrinkling her forehead.

"The brown Indian," Kit said, but Lillian still didn't seem to know what she was talking about.

"Sir Edmond's toy, madam," Nigel said quietly.

"Oh, yes." She laughed. "No one rides that. I don't even think it runs. My late husband bought that from a man in town who was having a bit of financial trouble. He wouldn't take charity, so the next best thing was to buy something from him. Edmond had this wild idea he would learn to ride it. He planned on using it on his hunting trips." Lillian shrugged and sighed. "I had forgotten it was there."

"Would you mind if I tried it out?" Kit asked, worried she was interfering with a family keepsake.

"Try out the motorcycle?" She chuckled. "As I said, I doubt it runs. And they are very dangerous vehicles, Lieutenant."

"I understand. I didn't mean to meddle."

"Oh, no. You aren't meddling, Lieutenant. I don't mind at all. But I didn't know you knew how to ride a motorcycle."

"It's a lot like riding a bicycle only less work."

"You are welcome to try, but it probably just needs to be sent to the scrap metal center for recycling."

"Don't do that. If you'll let me tinker with it, I might get it running enough so I can use it to get to the airfield."

"Help yourself," Lillian replied, offering Kit a warm smile. "Just promise you'll be careful."

"Yes, ma'am. I will."

Kit hurried back to the carriage house to look over the motorcycle and see what she had to work with. To her surprise, the tires still had air. The gas tank was empty, but that didn't surprise her. She checked the oil and the hoses. Everything looked good. The brakes seemed to work, as did the clutch and shifter. All she needed was gasoline. Without a ration card it was going to be hard to get her hands on even a small amount. She considered siphoning out a pint or two from the car but refrained, knowing how hard it was to get. She was sure Nigel had planned every trip and every mile from what he had in the tank. Kit knew the only place she could find gasoline was at the airfield. The officer in charge of the supply depot was known for coveting the gasoline stores like they were gold. Getting him to cough up enough to test the motorcycle would be a challenge, but one she had every intention of accepting. Rumors circulated around the airfield of an admiral's wife who traded a look under her skirt for a tank of gasoline. Kit wondered how much gas she could get for a quick peek down her shirt.

Kit dressed in her uniform and walked to the airfield, being careful to steer clear of the ATA office. She didn't want to be snagged and coaxed into delivering an airplane on what remained of her day off. She circled the supply depot and waited until the truck loading cots was finished and pulled away.

"Sergeant Deebs," she said, smiling broadly. "How are you today?"

The man in the office looked up from his desk, the short stub of his cigar wedged in the corner of the mouth.

"I told you girls before, Lieutenant, whatever it is you want, you must have a requisition. This isn't a bloody shop for your convenience."

Kit placed a glass jar she had found in the carriage house on his desk.

"What's that for?" he asked, scowling up at it.

"I need some petrol. It's top secret," she said, looking over her shoulder then leaning in. "I can't tell you why, but trust me. This is big."

He took the cigar out of his mouth and held it over the jar.

"Top secret or not, you need a requisition." He tapped the cigar, allowing the ashes to fall on the lid. He stuffed the cigar back in his mouth and went back to his work.

"I thought we were all working on the same side here. One canning jar of gasoline won't jeopardize the military's war effort, I'm sure. One lousy liter," she added, holding up a finger.

He pulled a blank requisition form from his desk drawer and placed it on the jar without looking up.

"You should be very proud of yourself," she said, snatching up the jar, leaving the form to float to the floor. "Because of your stubborn commitment to duty, you have prevented a pilot from having transportation to the airfield."

"Let me guess, Lieutenant," he said, continuing to scribble at his paperwork. "You found a car in someone's barn and want RAF petrol so you can spend a day shopping and sipping tea in London, right?"

"I did *not* find a car in someone's barn. How dare you accuse me of such a thing?" Kit frowned at him. "Is that what you do with RAF petrol? Or do you just drive to a pub for an evening of ale and darts?" She was trying her best to act indignant.

"I have work to do," he said, moving the cigar to the other side of his mouth. "Don't you?"

Kit tried secrecy and guilt. Neither worked, and she realized it was fruitless to try further. She would have to think of something else. She stepped outside, squinting at the sunlight. She didn't notice a truck roaring toward her. The driver honked and leaned out the open-sided cab, shaking a fist at her.

"Watch where you're going, Lieutenant," the woman shouted, swerving sharply.

"Sorry." Kit jumped back then suddenly snapped a look up the road where the truck had gone. The only other place on the airfield to have gasoline was the motor pool, or at least they had access to it. Perhaps someone could be persuaded into allowing a squirt or two to fall into her jar. She walked up the narrow alley to where the cars and trucks were parked. A woman in a dress uniform was signing out a car, presumably to transport an officer to a meeting. Several other women drivers were milling around, waiting for their assignments.

"Kit," Lovie said from the loading dock. "What are you doing here? I thought you had the day off."

"I do."

"Hey," Red yelled, coming out the door. "There's our fearless leader." She jumped down from the platform, her parachute pack slung over her shoulder.

"What are you two doing here?" Kit asked.

"We hitched a ride back from Luton on a delivery truck," Red said.

"And you'll never guess who our driver was," Lovie said with a coy smile.

"Who?"

"Oh, come on, Lieutenant." Red chuckled. "Surely you can figure that out."

"Emily Mills?" Kit asked cautiously.

Red and Lovie nodded in unison.

"So she did all right?" Kit asked. She remembered what Griggs said about even the smallest problem being enough to send her off to Manchester.

"She drives like my grandmother," Lovie whispered.

"Slow?" Kit asked.

"S-L-O-W, sloooooowwww. Painfully slow," Red said then rolled her eyes. "We could have gotten home faster by walking."

"It wasn't *that* bad," Lovie said. "She was just being cautious."

"Uh, huh," Red grumbled.

"But she did okay, didn't she?" Kit said.

"Yeah," Red finally said. "She did okay."

"What are you doing with the jar?" Lovie asked.

"I need some gasoline," Kit said. "Just a little, but the jerk at the supply depot is tighter than a rusty bolt. He won't cough up even a drop."

"Hey, I saw a petrol can in the back of the truck. I remember thinking Emily was driving so slow she might need it just to get back," Red said.

"Do you think it had any gas in it?"

"I can check." Red took the jar then climbed the steps to the loading platform. She looked both ways then disappeared into the back of truck. When she reappeared she was tightening the lid on the jar. She hopped down and handed the jar to Kit, smiling coyly. She handed Kit a blue rag to cover the jar.

"Thanks." Kit wrapped the rag around the jar to disguise its contents.

Kit, Lovie and Red were all standing in front of the truck Emily had backed up to the loading dock. Lovie was the first to notice the front bumper of the truck was slowly moving toward them and stepped aside.

"Hey," she said, watching it roll a few feet farther, slowly picking up speed. "Watch out, you two."

"What?" Red looked back at Lovie.

"The truck," she gasped in horror.

"Look out, Kit!" Red pushed back on the front fender as she jumped aside. But Kit was trapped between the bumper and a fence. The only place for her to go was down the alley.

"Run, Kit!" Lovie yelled as the truck continued to gain speed down the alley. The truck's wheels were caught in the deep ruts left from days of rain. It was rolling down the narrow alley like a train on a track. The alley was lined on one side by a tall board fence and on the other by rows of oil drums and storage bins. Kit searched for an opening where she could duck out of the way, but there was none. As the slope down the alley steepened, the truck's speed increased, lumbering steadily toward Kit.

"Don't look back, Kit. Just run!" Red shouted, dropping her parachute and running along behind the truck.

"Lieutenant Anderson!" Emily screamed from the dock. "Someone stop the truck."

"We're trying," Lovie yelled.

Kit stumbled over the rut and nearly fell but regained her balance. She looked over her shoulder, hoping the truck was slowing, but no such luck.

"Keep going," Red said breathlessly.

"Catch it, Red," Lovie shouted, frantically trying to keep up.

"I can't catch it," Red said.

"Run faster, Lieutenant," Emily called.

Just as Kit saw an opening in the fence at the end of the alley, she stumbled over a rock and fell face-first into a puddle, sliding several feet along the mud. Lovie and Emily screamed as she went down.

"Stay down. Keep your head down," Red said wildly.

The truck rolled over Kit, the oil pan passing mere inches above her head as it continued down the alley. Red pulled Kit to her feet, brushing off the clumps of mud that coated her face.

"Are you all right?" Red said. All Kit could do was cough and spit mud.

"Is she okay?" Lovie said as she rushed up to them.

"Please don't let her be injured," Emily said as she caught up with them.

Kit gagged and coughed up a mouth full of muddy water as if it came from her toes. Red slapped her back, trying to clear the last of the mud and yuck. Just as Kit looked up, able to take a full clean breath, they heard a thud from the end of the alley. The truck had come to a stop against a concrete barrier.

"Are you all right?" Lovie asked, grabbing on to Kit's arm. She looked her up and down as if expecting major injuries.

"I'm just peachy," Kit grumbled, looking over at Emily.

"But nothing is broken?" Emily asked nervously.

"Broken? Naw," Kit said sarcastically. "There's nothing broken. I was chased down the alley by a runaway truck that someone forgot to set the brake on, but there's nothing broken. I was run over by said truck, missing my head by only inches and was forced to eat mud, but nothing's broken. And oh, yes, once again my clothes are covered with disgusting, nasty water, but no, nothing's broken." Kit spit another bit of mud.

"You make it sound like it's my fault," Emily said defensively.

Kit grabbed Emily's wrist and headed for the truck, pulling her along behind.

"What are you doing?" Emily tried to pull away, but Kit kept a firm grip on her arm.

"Come with me, Miss Mills. And please, feel free to take notes," Kit said angrily. She pointed into the cab of the truck. "See that? That is the brake. It stops the vehicle from rolling. You pull it. That's all it takes. You just pull it."

"I thought I did pull it," Emily replied, looking in as well.

"Does that brake lever look like it is set to you?" Kit said.

"Well, no. But I was certain I set it."

"Show me." Kit stepped back so Emily could climb in the cab. Once in the driver's seat, Emily gave the lever a tug. But it fell back when she released it. She tried again, and once again it failed to remain in the locked position.

"It's defective," Emily said, trying it several more times.

Kit heaved a frustrated groan and climbed into the cab, waving Emily over. She settled into the driver's seat and looked over at Emily. With a slow, methodical motion Kit pulled up the brake lever and slid it to the side, locking it into place. She removed her hand and placed it on the steering wheel. The brake lever remained locked.

"Oh," Emily said weakly, melting back in the seat with an embarrassed smile. "I'm sorry." Kit didn't reply as she climbed out. "I said I'm sorry, Lieutenant," Emily repeated, sliding out of the truck. "I honestly thought I set the brake. It was just an accident."

Kit looked back at her, perching a hand on her hip.

"Miss Mills, if you are absolutely set on killing me, please find a pistol and do it quickly. I am confident even you can handle that. You just point the gun in the general direction of your target and pull the trigger. If you'd like, I can stand real still. I doubt even you could miss."

"That is a terrible thing to say. Just because I have had a few mishaps, you make it sound like I'm an evil person."

"You are," Kit said starting back up the alley. "And it is my own fault. What did I expect? I signed as your reference, and now it's coming back to haunt me. I said you were safe. Safe? Huh! You are about as safe as an unexploded bomb. Go home, Miss Mills. Lock yourself in your room, and pray you don't hurt anyone else this week."

Kit stared down at the broken jar that once contained her precious gasoline. She reached down and retrieved the lid then placed it in Emily's hand. "This is for you, Miss Mills. You have found a way to make things even worse." Emily opened her mouth to say something, but Kit held up her hand. "This jar contained gasoline. Not a lot, but it was important to me. Now it's gone. Congratulations." Emily again tried to say something, but Kit stopped her. "I am going home. Please don't touch *anything* until I am completely off the base." Kit strode away, again sloshing in her shoes.

"It really was an accident," Emily said apologetically.

Chapter 12

Kit stepped out her front door the next morning and was about to lock it when she noticed a basket on her porch. It held something wrapped in newspaper and a small note tucked in the side. She pulled out the note and read it.

Lieutenant Anderson, Please accept this small gift as an apology for my careless mistake yesterday. I truly am sorry for any damage, inconvenience or embarrassment I may have caused. If you will leave your uniform in the basket I will be most happy to have it cleaned and returned to you right away. Respectfully, Emily Mills.

"What's this? A grenade with a missing pin?" Kit said sarcastically. She folded back the newspaper and revealed two glass jars filled with an amber liquid. She carefully removed the lid and took a sniff. "Gasoline? Well, what do you know? Miss Tea Bag did something right." She reread the note then set the jars of gasoline inside and locked the door. She wished she had time to try out the motorcycle that very minute, but it was nearly eight o'clock and she was going to be late for a meeting with Commander Griggs as it was.

It was a slow day. With only six airplanes to deliver and two to test, the pilots completed their assignments by two o'clock.

"Might as well let your squadron leave early, Lieutenant," Griggs said, passing Kit outside the ready room.

It wasn't like Griggs to offer such luxuries without due cause. But Kit wasn't going to look a gift horse in the mouth. She saluted and went to dismiss her squadron. She finished her paperwork by three and headed home, the chance to try out the motorcycle quickening her step. She changed into an old flight suit and hurried up to the carriage house with her precious jars of gasoline. She rolled the motorcycle outside and cleaned off some of the years of dust and grime. Using a bent metal funnel from the crate of tools, Kit carefully filled the tank then replaced the gas cap. She swung her leg over and adjusted the choke then turned on the key. She stomped down on the kick start, but nothing happened. She made a few adjustments and tried again, groaning as she used all her strength and weight on the starter. She was able to coax a little grumble from the engine, but it threatened to stall.

"Come on, sweetheart." She rotated the throttle to keep it running. "Purr for me, baby. That's it." Finally the engine began to chug uniformly. Kit revved the engine to clear the dust from the carburetor and exhaust. "Yes!" she exclaimed with a satisfied grin. She sat down on the seat, its well-worn leather cupped around her bottom like a soft glove. She fiddled with the clutch and gear shifter, testing whether they were in working order. After allowing the engine to idle for a few minutes, Kit was confident it was time for a test drive. She shifted into first and slowly released the clutch, giving the throttle a gentle twist. The motorcycle pulled forward, responding without hesitation. She raised her feet and increased the speed, heading down the driveway toward Digby Lane.

Kit sailed down the road toward the stone bridge with the

wind in her hair and a smile on her face. For the first time in a long time, she was roaring along the road without thought for the airfield, the airplanes or her pilots. She was content to ride the wind if even for a few minutes, or however long her two liters of gasoline would allow. She crossed the bridge and was tempted to turn left, away from Alderbrook and the airfield, out into the open countryside. But the motorcycle hadn't earned her complete confidence yet. She turned right and cruised into town, weaving her way along the narrow streets lined with shops and houses. She turned down the street that formed the perimeter of the airfield. She followed it in a complete circle around the airfield before heading back through town. Just as she took the bend in front of the church, she swerved sharply to avoid a pedestrian in the road. Kit struggled to maintain control and not lay the bike over. It suddenly dawned on her who the pedestrian was. She made a U-turn and pulled alongside Emily.

"What happened to your bicycle? Why are you walking?" Kit asked.

"I had a puncture in the tire. I see you got Grandfather's motorcycle running."

"Yes, and thanks for the gasoline."

"You're welcome. It was the least I could do."

"Let me give you a ride home. That's the least I could do."

"No, I don't think so," Emily said.

"Why not? It's your family's motorcycle. You deserve a ride on it." Kit brushed off the back pad then patted it.

"Thank you for the offer, but I'll walk." Emily continued for home.

"It's two miles. I can have you home in five minutes," Kit said, rolling up beside her.

"Thank you anyway," Emily said, keeping a healthy pace to her stride.

"Are you sure?"

Emily nodded, her back rigid and her arms swinging at her side as she made her way along the dirt road. Kit finally gave up and slowly pulled away, trying not to leave Emily in a cloud of dust. Just as she reached the carriage house, she felt the first drops of rain from a dark cloud that had moved across the afternoon sky. She looked down the drive for signs of Emily but saw no one.

"Why didn't she just accept the ride?" Kit said to herself. She heaved a sigh and studied the increasing rain. "What the heck?" she said and threw her leg over the seat. She started the motorcycle and roared down the drive. She crossed the bridge and headed for town, expecting to see Emily walking along the edge of the road, drenched and disgruntled. Kit got all the way to the center of town but didn't see her. She turned around and retraced her route. As she rounded a curve in the road she saw Emily standing under a large tree, trying to stay out of the rain. Kit's flight suit was drenched, and her hair was matted against her head as she rolled to a stop and smiled over at Emily.

"How about a ride now?" Kit asked, the rain running down her face.

"You are soaked," Emily said, remaining against the tree trunk.

"So are you."

"I told you, I don't need a ride."

"You don't need one or you don't want one?" Kit asked skeptically.

"Does it matter?"

"If someone else was offering a ride would you take it?"

Emily scowled bitterly.

"I thought so. You don't like me and I can accept that, Miss Mills. But rather than stand there discussing the fact I rented your grandmother's cottage without your permission, would you please swallow that ever-loving British pride and get on the back of this motorcycle before I use up the last of the gasoline idling here on the side of the road? Please?" she added with a forced smile.

Emily looked up at the increasing rain and over at Kit who

was being drowned by the downpour. Without a word, she came out from under the tree and climbed on the back of the motorcycle.

"Put your feet on the pegs and hold on," Kit said, waiting impatiently for her to get situated. Emily positioned her feet on the pegs and modestly placed her hands on Kit's waist. "Hold on tighter."

Emily slowly eased her arms around Kit but she held back, trying not to commit her whole body to the hug.

"Scoot up," Kit said, revving the engine eagerly.

"You Yanks sure are a pushy lot." Emily finally did as she was told.

"We don't fall off motorcycles either." Kit released the brake and pulled away.

They roared down the road, the motorcycle slinging a plume of muddy spray in its wake. Kit could hear Emily gasp and felt her grip tighten as she shifted through the gears, slowly gaining speed. Kit kept the bike on a steady course, but with each gradual turn she could feel Emily's bear hug increase. As they rounded the house and stopped in front of the carriage house, the rain was coming down in buckets. Emily climbed off and scurried into the safety of the garage, dripping wet and shaking from the cold. Kit turned off the engine and rolled the motorcycle inside.

"Thank you for the ride, Lieutenant," Emily said, folding her arms for warmth.

"You're welcome." Kit shook her head and ran her fingers through her wet hair.

"And by the way," Emily said, looking over at Kit. "What makes you think I don't like you? Do you still think I did those terrible things to you on purpose?"

Kit looked back at her and chuckled. "Now be honest. That first time you came to the airfield to tell me to move out of your grandmother's cottage, you weren't exactly thrilled to meet me."

"Well," Emily stammered.

"And when you barged in on me when I was taking a bath, it

wasn't because you wanted to wash my back, now was it?"

Emily blushed bright red.

"And having to ask me to sign as your reference on the job application was about the last thing in the world you wanted to do. Am I right?"

"That was a complete misunderstanding."

"You don't like me, and we can work around it."

"I do not dislike you, Lieutenant. I have apologized for the smelly pan of water incident and the runaway truck. You must admit your reaction to my misfortune was somewhat rude and boorish. But yes, I have to take the lion's share of the blame. My record doesn't inspire much confidence."

Kit laughed. "You British tickle me. Why not just say everything you touch turns to shit?"

Emily raised her eyebrows as if she didn't approve of such language.

"What? You don't say stuff like that?"

"As a literature teacher, I prefer to use a more descriptive vocabulary."

"Oh, come on. Say shit."

"I will not." Emily frowned indignantly.

"Then try damn."

"No." Emily scowled.

Kit chuckled and shook her head. "I've got a few more, but I won't suggest them."

"I can just guess." Emily studied the skies for a long moment as if considering her next statement carefully. "Will I be sent off to Manchester right away, or will I have a few days to prepare?"

"Why are you going to Manchester?"

"You know what I mean, Lieutenant. How soon can I expect the incident with the truck to cross Commander Griggs's desk?"

"What truck? Did you have a problem with a truck I should know about?" Kit asked innocently. When Emily finally looked over at her, Kit smiled shyly. "I don't need to report anything. Do you?"

Emily stared at her blankly, seemingly surprised at her forgiveness.

"I'm not the evil person you seem to think I am, Emily." Kit smiled at her, their eyes meeting for a long moment. "Now if you'll excuse me, I think I'll go change out of these wet clothes. I think it has stopped raining."

"Thank you, Lieutenant," Emily said, touching her arm.

Kit nodded then trotted down the drive toward the cottage. As she opened the door, she looked back through the woods toward the big house. She couldn't see Emily, but Kit could feel her heart pounding in her chest over the way Emily's eyes had fallen so softly on her and the way her body molded against her back on the ride home.

"Maybe she doesn't hate me," Kit said, raising her eyebrows. "Maybe she even likes me just a tad."

She stripped out of her wet clothes and toweled off, fluff drying her hair as she stood naked in front of the window. She scanned the spaces between the trees for a view of the house. The memory of the feel of Emily's breasts against her back and of her thighs curled around her hips as she straddled the motorcycle washed over Kit. It wasn't like her to fantasize about someone she knew she couldn't have, but she couldn't stop it. Emily was lovely. Even when she couldn't stand to be in the same room with Kit, there was something about the smile that curled her lips and the twinkle in her eyes that captured Kit's heart. Emily Mills may be a tea bag, but she was the cutest tea bag Kit had ever seen. Too bad she couldn't tell her that.

Chapter 13

Kit knocked on the side door to the big house early the next morning, ready to thank Lillian for allowing her to use the motorcycle and to offer Emily a ride to the airfield. To Kit's disappointment, Emily had already left. Nigel informed her she had left well over an hour before, carrying the bicycle's flat tire with hopes someone at the airfield could fix it for her.

"I wish she had told me. I could have taken it," Kit said.

"She said she had a ride on the back of Sir Edmund's toy. I can't imagine it was very comfortable, especially in the rain," he said, glowering at Kit. "Her Ladyship will undoubtedly worry every moment you are on that dreadful thing. And knowing Miss Emily is straddling the back like a sack of potatoes going to market will only make matters worse."

"Tell her I'm very careful. She can trust me not to crash land."

"By the way, Lieutenant," he said, pulling a slip of paper from his vest pocket. "Lady Marble asked me to give you this."

"What is it?" Kit asked, taking the small certificate.

"Her Ladyship's petrol ration card."

"I can't take this," she said, handing it back. "You'll need it for the car."

"Her Ladyship is giving you her second card. This one has never been used. Bellhurst is allowed two ration cards." He pointed out the faint number two in the corner of the card. "Do take care of it. They are a devil to replace."

"Thank her for me, will you?" Kit said, grinning broadly at the present. "This is wonderful. I had no idea how I was going to get gas."

"She assumed as much. Have a pleasant day, Lieutenant, and do be careful."

Kit roared up the road and entered the airfield gate, turning heads as she rode by on the Indian. She parked and locked it outside the ATA office and went inside to check the assignment sheets. As predicted, the day would be hectic. The pilots received their orders and were sent off on their first sortie just after seven o'clock. Kit was about to cross the field for her first flight when Griggs waved her back.

"You're taking a Lancaster to Ashton Down," Griggs said. "It's being finished up at the MAC unit and needs to go back straight away. I'll oversee the other deliveries until you get back."

"Do they have something for me to bring back?" Kit asked, not wanting to spend her day hitching a ride along the road.

"I believe they have a Mustang that's coming back for a complete engine replacement."

"Peachy," Kit said, knowing that meant the one that was in it had damage. "They can't swap it up there?"

"Not a Mustang. There aren't enough spare engines to go around." Griggs went back to her office.

Kit gathered her flight gear and checked in at the MAC unit. A row of airplanes in every size from antiquated biplanes to four-engine bombers and seaplanes were waiting repair. The mechanics units were responsible for the major repairs the individual airfield crews couldn't handle. Many of the crippled and damaged aircraft were littered with bullet holes and blood-stained cockpits.

"Which Lancaster goes to Ashton Downs?" Kit said to the man on the telephone. He pointed to the one at the end of the row. He snapped his fingers to get one of his mechanic's attention and pointed for him to assist Kit in getting the big bomber away. As she climbed into the left seat, she noticed a glob of dried blood and gooey brain matter stuck on the altimeter. She sat frozen, unable to take her eyes off it.

"Ready, Lieutenant?" the mechanic called up to her.

"Yeah," she said, her eyes still on the glob.

"Okay, wind her up," he said, pulling the chocks from behind the wheels.

Kit forced her attention to flying the mission. She started the engines and preformed her pre-flight check then released the brake and pulled away, slowly rolling across the field and onto the runway. She had to throttle back and wait behind three Spitfires for her turn to take off. While she waited, she allowed her eyes to return to the altimeter. She was mesmerized by the blood and tissue. She touched it with her index finger, drawing back a long string of sticky substance. Kit swallowed hard, fighting the tears that suddenly filled her eyes. She found a scrap of paper under the seat and was ready to wipe it off, but hesitated. She crumpled the paper and tossed it out the window, leaving the glob of blood where it was. If someone wanted it removed, they would have to do it. She wasn't going to be the one to take away this medal of honor.

The last Spitfire took off, and she eased forward on the throttle. The bomber began its run across the grass, effortlessly rising above the trees as she cleared the end of the airfield. There was a strong tail wind, and Kit made good time. She rolled to a stop at the end of the runway at Ashton Downs, an airfield much like Alderbrook, but one that housed a bomber squadron instead of a fighter group. A few smaller aircraft were lined up as trainers and escorts, but it was the twenty-six bombers that gave the airfield its punch. She checked in with the command center then climbed into the Mustang for her return flight.

"She's a little testy, Lieutenant," the mechanic said as he helped get her seat-belted into the cockpit. "Watch the oil pressure."

"Did you fill it?" Kit asked, checking the gauges.

"Six liters. You should be all right. Don't pull any loops." He patted the canopy and climbed down the wing.

"That's comforting." She closed the canopy and started the engine. It belched a cloud of blue smoke then chugged into service. She tightened the straps on her parachute as she rolled toward the runway. "Okay, baby. Let's go home, and make it quick." She roared down the runway and eased back on the stick. As soon as she had cleared the fence at the end of the runway, she headed southeast for Alderbrook, setting as straight and fast a course as she could. The Mustang normally was a fast and fun fighter to fly, but this one was sluggish and heavy. Kit fought with it the entire trip, trying to keep the nose up and the speed steady. The wind pushed the plane as well, making corrections to her heading necessary every few miles. The oil pressure began to drop as she neared Alderbrook. By the time she crossed the river and made her turn for an approach, the gauge showed no oil pressure at all. Kit knew it was just a matter of time before the already damaged engine began to seize up, cooking its pistons and welding the parts together. A loud bang and a jerk of the stick took Kit's breath away. It was all she could do to hold the airplane in a straight line as it lost altitude, sailing in over the end of the runway like a leaf in the wind. She had no time to make adjustments, and the choking black smoke billowing from the engine obscured the runway. The Mustang was on a course, and she hoped it was one that would set her down on grass, not trees or buildings. She braced herself and held the stick with both hands, straining to keep it against her body as the wheels came crashing to the ground, gouging a pair of ruts in the soft grass. The tail of the airplane swung around, pulling the left wing tip up at a sharp angle. It finally came to a stop, jolting Kit forward it her seat, her head striking the edge of the canopy.

All she knew was she wanted out. If the engine was going to blow up, she didn't want to be sitting in the cockpit. She scrambled to release her seat belt and threw back the canopy. Climbing out of a fighter's cockpit was usually easier if the pilot waited for one of the ground crew to assist with the straps, but she wasn't waiting for anyone. She pulled herself out and slid down the wing then ran for safety. She didn't look back until she was well away from the crippled aircraft. The mechanics surrounded the plane, spraying foam on the engine to stop the smoke and fire danger. Kit unhooked her parachute harness as she headed across the infield, glad that mission was behind her. The ready room was empty. Even Commander Griggs was out of her office. From a look at the assignment sheets, Kit assumed her girls had been sent out on their next delivery.

The door opened and Emily stepped in, carrying a box full of folders.

"Lieutenant Anderson," she said, noticing Kit studying the map.

"Hello." Kit looked up. "What have you got there?"

"These are for Commander Griggs. I brought them back from Luton." Emily's face changed from pleasant to horrified. "Lieutenant, what happened to your head?" she asked, dropping the box in a chair.

"What are you talking about?" Kit asked, touching the tingle she felt on her forehead. She drew back bloody fingers.

"Did you have an accident on the motorcycle?" Emily asked angrily. "I knew it was too dangerous to ride." She came to see Kit's wound.

"I didn't have an accident on the motorcycle. This must have happened when I lost power on the P-Fifty-one and had to land with a dead stick." Kit rubbed her forehead again.

"Don't do that. Sit down and let me have a look." Emily pulled a white hankie from her pocket and prepared to administer first aid. "That's a nasty looking gash."

"It's nothing," Kit insisted, still wiping the blood that was now trickling down her cheek.

"Sit down," Emily ordered, steering Kit toward a chair then pushing down on her shoulder. Kit had no choice. She decided it was better to give in and let Emily tend to her wound than to continue dripping blood onto the flight jacket. "Lean your head back and hold this." Emily pressed the handkerchief over the cut. "I'm going to get some water and a bandage."

"That's all right. It'll stop bleeding in a minute."

"Just hold it, Lieutenant. I'll be right back." Emily placed Kit's hand over the hankie and hurried out the back door. She was only gone a few minutes and was back before the bleeding stopped. She carefully removed the handkerchief and dipped it in a pan of water then went about dabbing at the cut.

"Ouch!" Kit flinched as Emily touched it. It hadn't hurt before. Kit had barely noticed she was injured. But now it stung and was beginning to throb. "Just press the handkerchief on it, and I'll be fine."

"You'll be fine when I tell you you'll be fine," Emily said, pushing Kit's hand away. "Now hold still. You've got it bleeding again."

"And you thought we Americans are pushy."

"Lieutenant Anderson, what happened?" Andrea exclaimed, stepping through the door.

"Nothing," Kit snapped.

"I saw your landing in the Mustang. That must have been a hairy flight." Andrea came to Kit's side to see her wound.

"You may require stitches, Lieutenant," Emily said.

"Oh, no I won't," Kit said decisively and stood up.

Emily grabbed her sleeve and pulled her back into the chair. "Oh, yes, you will."

"No, I won't. Doris had stitches on a tiny little cut on the back of her head, and she said it hurt worse than having a baby. And she ought to know. She had two of them."

"Would you rather bleed to death?" Emily scowled, still dabbing away the blood.

"You better listen to her, Lieutenant," Andrea said.

"I'd rather put a bandage on it and forget it."

"You're worse than my students. At least they sat quietly while I tended their scrapes and bruises."

"No stitches," Kit insisted.

"We'll see." Emily gently pressed her fingertips around the cut, examining the depth of the wound. "It isn't as bad as I thought. It's just a small flap of skin that has been sliced open. I believe I can close it with some tape, if you'll remain still."

"Good."

"Looks pretty nasty. Do you want me to take her to the infirmary?" Andrea asked.

"No, she'll be fine," Emily said, her face just inches from Kit's as she inspected the wound. "Close your eyes, Lieutenant." Emily pulled a small brown bottle from her pocket.

"What are you going to do with that?" Kit asked suspiciously. "And what is it?"

"It's Miss Mills Magical Fairy Potion. At least that's what I told my students."

"Looks like iodine," Andrea said.

"Iodine!" Kit glared up at Emily. "Where did you get that?"

"In the first aid box." Emily unscrewed the cap and pulled the dauber from the bottle. "Now hold still and close your eyes."

"That's going to sting," Andrea said, leaning in to watch.

"You are not helping," Emily said, frowning at her.

"Couldn't you find something else?" Kit asked.

"There wasn't anything else unless you want me to sprinkle foot powder on your face." She pressed Kit's head back and held it there. "It will only sting for a moment, and it isn't that bad. Besides, you're one of those brave Yanks. I thought you could take anything."

"Very funny."

"Hold still." Emily touched a few drops of iodine to the cut. Kit immediately jerked her head.

"Ouch, Goddamn it. That does too sting." She waved her hand over the cut, trying to fan away the sting.

"I told you," Andrea said.

"Wait," Emily said, holding Kit's hand out of the way and gently blowing across her forehead. Kit closed her eyes as Emily's tender care cooled the pain.

"Better?" Emily asked between breaths.

"Yes." Kit said, her eyes still closed.

"It wasn't that bad, now was it?" Emily said then pressed a kiss on Kit's forehead.

Kit opened her eyes and stared up at her, surprised at Emily's kiss. Emily blushed, as if she too was surprised at her action. Andrea stood staring at the two of them.

If Emily kissed all her students' cuts and scraps like that, Kit was ready to go back to school. It may have been instinctive for Emily as a teacher, but for Kit it was a gift from the gods. She was only sorry Emily had done it in front of one of her pilots. She hoped Andrea didn't find it awkward or embarrassing.

"I should apply the adhesive before your cut starts to bleed again," Emily stammered, fumbling nervously with the roll of tape. Kit took the roll and peeled off a strip. Emily pressed it across the cut, diverting her eyes from Kit's stare.

"There we are. All finished," Emily said, collecting the first aid supplies.

"Lieutenant Anderson, what happened to you?" Griggs asked as she strode through on her way to her office.

"Nothing, Commander. Just a scratch," Kit replied.

"Good. The MAC unit just telephoned. They have a pair of Hurricanes ready to go back to Ringway. And, Mills, Commander Wilkes needs a driver to take him down to Whitechurch. Check with his office to see what time to pick him up, then check out a car from the motor pool."

"Yes, ma'am," Emily replied, pulling her attention away from

Kit and her wound.

"Thank you, Miss Mills." In spite of Commander Griggs and Andrea's suspicious stare, Kit couldn't help herself. She gazed into Emily's eyes and found something tender there.

"You're welcome, Lieutenant. Anytime you need bandaging, please do not hesitate to call on me."

"Grab your gear, Paisley. We're going to Ringway," Kit said, leaving Emily with a smile as she headed out the door.

"Do be careful this time, Lieutenant," Emily said softly.

As they crossed the infield toward the runway, Kit looked back at the ATA office and saw Emily standing in the window. Emily pressed her hand against the glass. Kit's heart skipped a beat. She tapped her forehead, saluting back at her.

Chapter 14

"You have anything else for me, Commander?" Kit asked, sticking her head in Griggs's office.

"No, that's all for this evening. Have you seen Officer Peacock? She left her log book in the mess hall." Griggs held it up. "And I noticed she hasn't made entries in four days. I thought I made it clear log entries were to be made daily."

"Yes, ma'am. I'll remind her."

"Find her and remind her now." She held the log book out to Kit.

Kit wanted to admit she knew Red had already left for the day, but thought better of it.

"And Officer Loveland is still having a bit of trouble with her landings, Lieutenant."

"She did much better yesterday. She brought that plane in so soft it barely bent the grass."

Griggs looked up at her skeptically.

"But I'll have a talk with her about it," Kit added. "Did she get back from Telford?"

"No. She's spending the night and bringing back a Grumman tomorrow."

"I'll see that Officer Peacock gets her log book."

"And I want those entries made tonight. Tell her I want to see it first thing in the morning."

"Yes, ma'am." Kit saluted and disappeared out the door. "Thanks a bunch, Red." Kit fanned through the log book, groaning at the empty pages.

It was nearly dark by the time Kit made it to the rooming house where Red, Lovie and several of the other women pilots lived. She opened the front door and felt her way up the narrow staircase to the second floor. The only light came from the downstairs dining room where a single lamp dimly welcomed the residents. The women paid a stiff rent to live in the three-story brick house, with two meals a day and shared bathrooms. The landlady was a sour-humored woman who ruled the comings and goings of her renters like she was their mother. The rooms were small but clean, that Mrs. Block insisted on. Lovie lived on the third floor under the eaves. Red had the last room on the second floor, the smallest room, but the one with the most privacy since it was next to the storage closet and looked out onto the back garden. Kit walked to the end of the hall and knocked on the door. She could hear the muted sounds of giggling. She knocked again. The voices stopped.

"Who is it?" Red said.

"Kit."

There was a long pause.

"You left your log book in the mess hall," Kit added. "And Griggs found it. She wants your entries made before tomorrow morning so she can check them." There was still no reply. "I brought it over." She tapped again.

"Just a second," Red said nervously.

Kit could hear whispering. Finally, the lock was turned and

the door opened a few inches. Red peered out with a forced smile as if hiding something behind the door.

"Hi, Kit," she said, clutching a robe around her body and smoothing her ruffled hair.

Kit slid the book through the opening in the door. Her curiosity pulled her gaze inside, searching for what sinister thing Red and her friends were up to. Kit suspected a bottle of Scotch and some black market cigarettes were at the root of Red's secrecy, something the landlady wouldn't allow. Kit also assumed once Red realized it was just her, she would be invited in, or at least teased about scaring them. But Red held her post at the door, doing her best to block the opening.

"Thanks, Kit. I'll get this filled out right away."

"Griggs wants you girls to make log entries daily. You put my butt in a ringer when you don't." Kit scowled at her then smiled. "Watch it next time."

"Yeah, I will. I'm sorry."

"What's up?" Kit asked, looking over Red's shoulder. "Are you having a party Lovie is going to be sorry she missed? I heard she won't be back tonight."

"Yeah, I heard she got stranded." Red leaned on the door jamb, obviously not intending on inviting Kit to join the party.

"Why do you look like that?"

"Like what?" Red's expression was suspicious at best.

"Like you have the crown jewels hidden under your mattress."

"I don't have anything in my bed. What makes you think I have anyone in my bed?" Red seemed surprisingly defensive. "There's no one in my bed."

Kit laughed at her.

"I didn't say you did, Red. Why are you so nervous?" Kit peeked through the gap between Red's chin and the door. She couldn't see the bed, but she could see the small mirror hanging over the dresser. The reflection in the mirror caught Kit completely off guard. A woman lay across the bed, naked, uncovered and seductive among the rumbled sheets. The woman's breasts were full and round, the dark nipples as plump as raisins against her white skin. Kit couldn't see the woman's face, but her body was gorgeous. No wonder Red had her in bed, Kit thought. But that fact brought a gasp from Kit. She had no idea Red was a lesbian. She had suspected it. She had suspected it of several of the women at the airfield, but considered it none of her business, just as her own choices were no one else's business. Kit took a step back, trying to hide her surprise. Red seemed to know her secret was out by the look on Kit's face.

"Lieutenant?" she stammered.

"I better go. I'll see you in the morning." Kit turned and hurried down the hall. She was halfway down the street when she heard footsteps behind her.

"Kit?" Red called, running to catch up. "Wait, Kit." She grabbed Kit's arm. "Will you stop?"

"What?"

"I need to talk to you," Red said, buttoning the coat she had put on over her robe. Her shoes weren't tied and her hair was a mess.

"Talk to me about what?" Kit asked, continuing up the street with her hands in her jacket pockets. Red walked alongside, struggling to keep up with Kit's hurried pace.

"About what you saw in my room."

"I didn't see anything." Kit didn't mean to fib, but she didn't want to make Red uncomfortable either.

"Her name is Eve," Red said softly, as if that fact would break the ice. "She's from Luton."

Kit kept walking, her eyes on the pavement.

"She's an ambulance driver," Red said out of the blue.

They walked in silence.

"How long have you known her?" Kit finally asked.

"Six months."

They continued up the street and turned the corner.

"Kit, I have to ask," Red said, taking Kit by the arm and stopping her. "Are you going to say anything?"

"Say what?" Kit asked, looking over at her.

"You know what I mean. Are you going to say anything about Eve and me?"

"To who?"

"I don't want to lose my wings," Red said solemnly.

"Why would you loose your wings? Your private life has nothing to do with flying airplanes. If you can't do your job, then you can worry about losing your wings. Otherwise, I don't plan on taking them away from you."

"There are some people who would," Red replied, scanning the darkness. "Some people would love to have me fired over this."

"But you already knew that before you and Eve . . ." Kit said, nodding her head back toward the rooming house.

"Yes." Red lowered her eyes.

"I thought we were friends, Red. Why didn't you tell me?"

"Tell you what? Hey, Lieutenant Anderson, I'm from Australia, I love flying airplanes in your squadron, and oh, by the way, I like to bed women." Red scowled at her. "I'm sure that would have gone over well at the base."

"I didn't mean like that. But my God, Red, I thought you and Lovie and I were close. We were the three Musketeers. You could have said something."

"I couldn't take the chance." Red's eyes grew misty. "I didn't know how you'd take it."

"Didn't you trust me?"

Red shrugged and diverted her gaze. Kit reached out and touched Red's cheek.

"You can trust me, Red. We're friends. Believe me, it's okay."

"It doesn't turn your stomach?"

Kit allowed a smile to grow across her face while she waited for Red's eyes to meet hers.

"No," Kit said quietly.

"Are you sure, Lieutenant? I've heard some of the women at the airfield talk about *those kind of women*."

"Lieutenant Anderson is sure. And so is your friend Kit." She offered Red a hug, one she accepted warmly.

"I was so afraid I'd ruined our friendship and my job," Red said, a tear rolling down her cheek.

"You didn't ruin anything," Kit said, wiping the tear away.

"Lovie was right. She said you'd understand."

"Lovie knows and I didn't?" Kit said sternly then chuckled.

"Well . . ." Red started then hesitated.

"Don't tell me. Lovie is a member of your sorority too?"

Red looked up and down the street then nodded.

"She and I found out we were both interested in the same woman."

"Eve?"

"No, no. Her name was Cecilia and she was French, at least half French. The other half was pure bitch." Red shook her head and grimaced.

"Sounds bad."

"Not really. It was lucky for both of us. We grew closer and saved ourselves a lot of heartache down the road. But you can't let on I told you. Lovie was devastated for a while."

"Was that back in August? I remember she was moody, not the normal Lovie."

"Yes. So I fixed her up with a girl from Leeds. She had the most gorgeous eyes. I told Lovie nothing fixes a broken heart like a fresh pair of eyes," Red said, winking mischievously.

"Oh, really?"

"Listen to me. Carrying on about things you don't want to hear. I'm sorry, Kit."

"That's okay. I'm glad you were able to help Lovie past her heartache. Her flying was terrible that month. I just figured she had a period from hell."

"It was rough on her for a long time."

"Is she still seeing the woman with the gorgeous eyes?"

"Let's just say Lovie isn't spending the night alone." Red smiled.

"Let me guess. The girl from Leeds was transferred to Telford, right?"

Red nodded.

"No wonder Lovie volunteered for that assignment."

"You don't mind that two of the girls in your squadron are daisies?" Red said.

"Daisies?"

"That's what we call them back home in Queensland."

"I don't mind at all, so long as they do their job. You know, the squadron may have more daisies in the flowerbed than you think," Kit said and started up the street again.

"Who?" Red asked, catching up with her.

Kit just smiled and kept her eyes on the pavement.

"Come on, Kit. Let's hear it. I can keep a secret. Who is it? Viv? Patty? I know, Susan."

"You may have to go up the chain of command a bit."

"Commander Griggs?" Red asked with wide eyes.

"Too high up."

Red walked along, thinking.

"The only rank between Griggs and Susan is you," she said.

Kit raised her eyes and stared at her, waiting for a reaction. It took Red a minute, but slowly Kit's revelation sank in. She drew a deep breath and held it.

"You?" Red whispered, her eyes as large as plates.

Kit continued to watch her, pulling a slow smile.

"My God, Kit. I was right," Red exclaimed, hugging her again, this time holding her in a bear hug. "The first time I met you I said to myself, there's one of us."

"I don't suppose you have a problem with your Flight Lieutenant being a lesbian then."

"I think it's great. Wait until I tell Lovie."

Kit held Red by the shoulders and gave her a critical gaze.

"I know. I know," Red quickly said, reading Kit's warning.

"Protect the wings. Be careful who you tell. Right?"

"Something like that. You don't want to lose your wings, and neither do I.

"No one will hear it from me, Kit. If you want someone to know, you'll have to tell them. It's my solemn promise."

"Thank you, honey. I appreciate that. You just never know who might use something like this against us."

"It's none of my business, but do you mind if I ask you a question?"

Kit chuckled, hunching her shoulders to the chilling wind.

"What do you want to know? Am I am doing any gardening in the daisy bed?"

Red smiled back at her and raised her eyebrows as if to agree with the question.

"Not at the moment. I left my gardening days back in the U.S."

"That's a shame. The British flowers are very sweet," Red whispered.

"I'm sure they are, but sometimes it's better to leave the entanglements behind."

"Ah, the entanglements of love," Red said, smiling at the moon. "Is that why you're here in England, to escape those dreaded entanglements? And don't say you're here to make a difference. We all came for that reason. But there has to be something stronger to make a person give up a secure, uncluttered life back home to live in a war zone."

Kit scooted a pebble across the ground with the toe of her shoe.

"You might say I needed to get away. I just got tired of giving and giving and never getting anything in return."

"I've been there." Red sighed. "You invest yourself in someone just to find out you're in love alone."

"Something like that."

"Is your journey here to find someone new?"

"No. Sometimes it isn't the person at the end of the journey.

It's the journey itself that's important," Kit said reflectively.

"Sometimes it's both."

"Don't you have someone waiting for you?" Kit nodded back toward the rooming house.

"Yes, I guess I do," Red said then gave Kit a hug. "I'll see you tomorrow, Lieutenant." She snapped a salute then turned and ran back down the street.

"Good night," Kit said then headed for the airfield. She collected her gear and rode the motorcycle home, parking it in the carriage house and away from the nearly daily threat of rain. As she walked down the drive toward the path that lead to the cottage, she noticed a sliver of light showing through the curtains in the upstairs corner window, Emily's window. She saw Emily's face peeking between the blackout curtains. She smiled down at her shyly. Kit waved up at her, expecting Emily to disappear behind the curtains, but instead she opened the window.

"You're working late, Lieutenant."

"Aren't you worried about the blackout ordinance? Someone might turn you in for showing a light from your window," Kit said kindly.

"I'm not worried. There's a very nice ATA officer living on the grounds, and I'm sure she wouldn't turn me in. She's very understanding." Emily leaned out the window, propping her elbows on the sill.

"Seems like you should be calling her by her name when she isn't at the airfield."

"Perhaps I should." Emily smiled. "By the way, don't forget Saturday night. The women's guild is having the dance at the community center. I can personally guarantee there will be refreshments."

"Does that mean you are going to try working in a kitchen again?"

"Oh, dear," Emily gasped, covering her face with her hands as she blushed. "Don't remind me. That was so embarrassing."

"I guess I should be there to witness this return to kitchen duty." Kit was captivated by Emily's innocence and the way the moonlight sparkled on her hair.

"I'll try to do better. I really should go before someone notices the light. Good night, Kit." Emily smiled down at her then closed the window and drew the curtains.

"It's a good thing you don't know about me, Miss Mills," Kit said to herself as she unlocked the cottage door. "What would you think if you knew the Flight Lieutenant you thought was your friend was really a lesbian who fantasized about taking your gorgeous body to bed? I doubt you'd be insisting I come to your dance."

Chapter 15

Kit walked to town, crossing the stone bridge then winding the meandering streets to the brick community center. The dance was all her girls had been talking about all week. A live band, refreshments, a chance to let their hair down was all it took to turn the squadron into a frenzy of anticipatory delight. And like all the other ATA women, Kit spent a little extra time in front of the mirror, getting her uniform and hair just right. Most of the women wore their dress uniform skirts and jackets. Kit wasn't comfortable in her skirt, especially if she was going to dance. She wore her uniform trousers neatly pressed to a razor sharp crease. As she rounded the corner, she could hear the faint sound of the band in the distance. Several guards stood outside, their rifles on their shoulders as they marched around the building, protecting the gathering.

Inside, the dance floor was filled with couples. Some in uniform. Some locals. Since there were more women at the dance than men, there were also a few pairs of women happy to dance with each other rather than spend their evening as wallflowers. The band was playing something lively. The dancers were doing the jitterbug, the women being tossed and swung like rag dolls. Kit dropped some coins in the donation box then pushed her way through the crowd and found the refreshment table. Lillian was dipping cups of punch, and Emily was refilling the sandwich and cookie trays. Several women were busy making sandwiches in the kitchen and mixing batches of punch. The line was long for both the punch and the food, the fresh bread and sweets a welcome treat for many of the locals.

"Hello, Lady Marble," Kit said, taking a cup of punch from the table.

"Lieutenant, how nice to see you," she beamed. "I told Emily you'd be here. She was afraid you might avoid our little event."

"It's very nice of your ladies' group to put this on," Kit said, trying to talk above the band.

"We have been planning it for months. There's nothing like a dance to put a smile on everyone's face."

"Hello, Lieutenant," Emily said, her eyes sparkling as she held up a tray for Kit. "Would you like a sandwich? These are cucumber."

"No, but thanks."

"We have jam sandwiches too."

"No, really. Nothing right now. Maybe later."

"Did you ride the motorcycle?"

"No, I walked. Motorcycles and clean uniforms don't mix."

"I imagine not." Emily chuckled. "If you'll excuse me, I have to refill the trays. Everyone seems famished." She slipped away into the kitchen.

Kit roamed the edge of the dance floor, watching the couples and looking for anyone familiar. Tables and chairs surrounded the dance floor, most of them packed with people, laughing and visiting like old friends. Across the room Kit could see Red, Lovie and several of the girls from the squadron crowded around a table, giggling and having fun.

"Hey, Lieutenant," Lovie said, seeing her approach. The group immediately stood up and saluted, something they were supposed to do but seldom did. Kit didn't demand it unless someone was around to notice. She reciprocated, smiling as she touched her temple.

"Sit down, Kit." Red pulled up another chair. "We are discussing important matters."

"Like what?" Kit asked.

"Proper proportions," Lovie said, a bit giddy.

"Proportions for what?"

"Punch," Andrea said, also smiling strangely.

"That's right, Kit," Red added. "We are trying to establish the correct proportions of ingredients for the perfect cup of punch." Everyone giggled.

"Let me guess, one of the ingredients is something other than seltzer water or fruit juice." Kit sipped her cup.

"Our Flight Lieutenant is so smart," Lovie said, toasting Kit.

"And I bet your cup doesn't contain the perfect punch," Red said, leaning over to her.

"It doesn't taste like it has anything extra in it, no."

"Then it is our duty to make that addition," Andrea said, taking the cup from Kit's hand. "Officer Loveland." She held it out to Lovie.

"Absolutely," Lovie said, producing a silver flask from under the table. She looked around then poured a splash into the cup.

"Lieutenant Anderson, your punch." Andrea placed the cup in Kit's hand again.

Kit took a sip, sucking wind at the bitter flavor.

"Wow, that's definitely punch," she said, swallowing hard. "What is it?"

"Homemade hooch," Patty said, grinning triumphantly. "I traded for it."

"Do I want to know what you traded?"

"Don't ask," Red whispered.

156

"I hope you didn't trade for a lot of it," Kit said, swallowing the last of her punch then pushing the cup back. "You are all going to be cross-eyed before midnight at this rate."

"We only have one jar of it," Lovie said then dipped her finger into her cup and put it in her mouth.

"That's more than enough."

"Oh, damn. It's him," Andrea gasped then ducked her head and tried to hide her face.

"Who?" Lovie asked, scanning the room.

"That bloody bastard, Officer Powell," Andrea said, peeking up to see if he was still coming toward them. "The one with the stupid look on his face heading right for us."

Kit looked over shoulder at the brash young man in the RAF uniform striding confidently through the crowd. The rest of the women at the table gave him an accusatory stare.

"Hello, Andrea," he said with a cocky grin. "Would you like to dance?"

"It's Officer Paisley," Kit said, giving him a terse glance.

"Would Officer Paisley like to dance then?" he said without looking at Kit.

"Are you Officer John Powell?" Kit asked nonchalantly.

"Yeah." He kept his eyes on Andrea.

"Well, I am Flight Lieutenant Anderson. If I'm not mistaken, I outrank you. Isn't that right?"

"Well, yes, technically." He didn't show much interest in Kit or her statement.

Kit smiled at the women around the table then slowly stood up and turned to face the young man, giving him a cold stare.

"Then unless you want to spend this war digging ditches with a spoon, I suggest you show my rank the respect it is due," she said.

"Excuse me, Lieutenant," he replied and raised a salute but quickly dropped it, not waiting for Kit's reply.

Kit stepped closer and squinted at him.

"Is that the way you salute your superiors, Officer Powell?"

"No, Lieutenant," he said and raised his salute again, holding his hand sharply in place and standing erect.

The girls at the table giggled, enjoying the young man's humiliation. Kit turned and walked away from the table without returning his salute, leaving him with a curious look on his face and his hand frozen against his forehead. She crossed the room to the refreshment table. He had begun to lower his salute, not sure if she planned on returning. Kit looked back through the crowd, staring daggers at him. He raised his hand, again holding the salute and stiffening his posture. She picked up a cup of punch, took a sip then slowly made her way back to the table. She stood face to face with him and took another sip of punch as her eyes cut through him.

"If you ever drop your salute in my presence again, Powell, I'll report you for insubordination so fast you'll curse your mother for giving you birth. Is that clear?" she said in a quiet but firm voice.

"Yes, ma'am," he said, his eyes staring straight ahead.

"That's all, Powell," she said, sitting down but not yet returning his salute. Once she was settled and placed her cup on the table she looked up at him. "Carry on," she added and saluted.

Powell dropped his salute and disappeared through the crowd, an angry, embarrassed blush on his face. It wasn't like Kit to pull rank on anyone, but he deserved it. If she couldn't protect her girls, what good was her rank, anyway?

"Wow, Lieutenant," Viv exclaimed, once Powell was out of sight. "That was great."

"The little twerp had it coming," Red added, smiling over at Andrea. "Next time he bothers you, I'll knee him in his balls."

"Thank you, Lieutenant," Andrea said sheepishly. "I should have said something, shouldn't I?"

"You did just fine," Kit said. "The less said to guys like that, the better."

"Hello, everyone," Emily said, trying to smile, but there was a worried look on her face. The women at the table smiled greetings. "Lieutenant," she said, touching Kit on the shoulder. "I have a bit of a sticky situation. Could I bother you for a moment?" She cast her gaze toward the kitchen.

"Sure." Kit followed her into the kitchen.

"I'm terribly sorry to take you away from you friends." Emily had a frightened look on her face.

"What's wrong?"

"I have locked the car," Emily said apologetically then whispered. "With the tins of cookies inside."

"Where are the keys?"

Emily just looked at her, her eyes telling the sad truth.

"You locked the keys in the car?"

"They fell out of my pocket on the floor in the backseat. I can see them through the glass. What am I to do? We promised refreshments, and I can't very well announce they are gone in the first hour."

"Does your grandmother have an extra key?"

"I doubt it. She never has before. She leaves that sort of thing to Nigel or me. I used his keys this evening."

"Where's the car?"

"In the parking lot across the street."

Emily led the way, slipping out the back door and around the building. They crossed the darkened street and snaked through the parking lot to the long black car. Kit cupped her hands to the window and peered inside. Sure enough, even in the dim moonlight, she could see a pair of keys on the floorboard. She tried the doors, but they were all locked. She circled the car, scratching her head in thought.

"Shall I break a window?" Emily asked.

"No, not yet." Kit went to the back of the car and turned the handle. The trunk lid swung up.

"I wish I had put them in there instead of the backseat."

"I may be wrong, but some of these cars have fold down seats. Does this one?"

"I don't know. I've never tried to fold it down. I just ride in it."

159

Emily was wringing her hands nervously.

Kit removed her jacket and handed it to Emily then crawled into the trunk and began thumping on the back of the rear seat.

"I don't suppose you have a flashlight," Kit said from deep in the trunk.

"Yes. It's in the glove compartment."

"Then, no, you don't have one." She kept thumping. Suddenly the seat back fell forward and Kit scrambled inside. She grabbed the keys and opened the back door. "Your coach, me lady." Kit climbed out, dropping the keys into Emily's hand.

"Oh, Lieutenant. Thank you. Thank you," Emily exclaimed. She had a huge smile on her face. She threw her arms around Kit and kissed her cheek repeatedly. "I can't tell you how much I appreciate your help." Emily was bubbling with relief, her arms still around Kit's neck. Kit folded her arms around Emily, holding on as she thanked her again and again. "I didn't know what to do or who to ask. I'm so grateful."

"You're welcome."

"Another one of my silly mistakes. At least it wasn't actually in the kitchen," Emily added with a chuckle.

"I'm glad I could help." With Emily hanging around her neck and her enthusiastic body pressed firmly against her, Kit had all she could do not to kiss Emily right on the lips. But a kiss, even one, would tell Emily something she probably didn't want to know. Nevertheless, Kit wanted that kiss so badly it hurt. She wanted her lips on Emily's, tasting her and touching her. Kit hadn't expected these feelings to rush her all at once. She just wanted to be Emily's friend. She had sworn off kissing women, at least for now. She came to England to fly airplanes, not fall in love. Emily had the breeding, the looks and the education of a British aristocrat. Kit was certain somewhere in Emily's past or future waited the perfect man with her best wishes at heart. Kit had no intention of interfering with that. But Emily's nipples were doing a jitterbug against Kit's chest, and they were becoming harder and harder to ignore.

"Perhaps we should take the cookies inside," Kit said, giving Emily a friendly pat on the back and diverting her eyes.

"Yes, perhaps we should," Emily said, drawing her arms from Kit's neck. She collected the tins and headed inside, leaving Kit to replace the seat and close up the car. Just as Kit was about to cross the road and follow Emily back inside, a jeep roared around the corner and stopped in front of her.

"Lieutenant Anderson, I was sent to find you." The man driving had on greasy coveralls and a dirty cap pushed to the back of his head. "Lucky you haven't gone in the dance yet."

"But I have," Kit said, watching Emily round the corner of the building. "What do you need?"

"Commander Griggs said they need a pilot right away."

"It's after eight o'clock." She scowled, checking her watch.

He took a folded piece of paper from his pocket and handed it to Kit. She opened it and held it to the dim headlight.

"Tonight?" she exclaimed, rereading it. "I'm supposed to do a test flight tonight?"

"It's a Lancaster, and it is going out at zero six hundred. We replaced two engines and need a flight check on it tonight, Lieutenant. It won't take long."

"Yeah, sure, it won't take long," she mumbled under her breath as she gave a last look where Emily had gone. "Will I at least get runway markers?"

"I heard Captain Gilford order flares to be lit just before you take off."

"That'll give me what, fifteen minutes?"

"Maybe. Twelve for sure."

"Okay. You wait here. I'll need one of my girls for a copilot. Then you'll have to take me home to get my gear." Kit went inside and weaved her way to the table where her squadron was sitting.

"Where have you been?" Red asked, handing her a cup of punch.

"Getting an assignment," she said, shaking her head at the

161

cup. "I need a volunteer to be my copilot for a test flight."

"Ask me in the morning," Red said, downing the last of her cup. "I won't remember tonight."

"I need one now."

"Now?" Viv asked, giggling then hiccupping.

"I'll go," Lovie said, standing up and saluting with the wrong hand.

"Thanks, Lovie, but I think you're better off on the ground tonight," Kit said.

"I'll go, Lieutenant," Andrea said, standing up. "I haven't had much of their punch. I didn't care for it."

"Have you ever flown as copilot in a Lancaster, Paisley?" Kit asked sarcastically, knowing full well she hadn't.

"No, but I may be the only sober pilot at the table," she replied, looking around the table.

Kit groaned and nodded.

"Get your gear and meet me at the ready room in twenty minutes."

"Yes, ma'am." Andrea saluted crisply, a wide grin on her face. "I can't wait to fly one of the big bombers."

"It won't be much of a flight. I'm testing the engines, and that's all. Ten minutes, up and down."

"But it's still a Lancaster, Lieutenant." Andrea grinned like she had just been promoted.

Kit went home and changed into her flight suit then had the driver drop her off at the ready room. Soon after she arrived, Commander Griggs walked in, her coat buttoned to the neck.

"Sorry to roust you out, Lieutenant." Griggs said. "But the Lancaster has to be ready in the morning. It's a rush job and there was no way around it."

"So long as I have lights along the runway, I won't have any problem."

"Who did you get to sit in the right hand seat?"

"Paisley," Kit said.

"Paisley? She's a Class One. She's never flown a Lancaster."

"She's about ready to move up to Class Two. She's doing a great job."

"You need at least a Class Three as copilot."

"There aren't any available."

"Aren't they at the dance in town?"

"Um, yes, but, no." Kit raised her eyebrows. She didn't want to admit the girls were halfway to hangovers.

"Are they or aren't they?" Griggs frowned.

"Commander, let's just say we didn't expect to need pilots tonight. They are a little under the weather."

"All of them?"

"All but Paisley."

"All right, Lieutenant. If you think she can handle it, I trust your judgment."

Andrea strode in, her parachute over her shoulder and her flight jacket zipped to the collar.

"I'm ready, Lieutenant," she said with a wide grin.

"I'll have the balloons lowered," Griggs said, picking up the telephone.

"Come on, Paisley. Let's get this done." Kit headed out the door, grabbing her parachute from the chair. Andrea followed. The big bomber was parked at the end of the runway. A group of mechanics crowded around it, waiting for its test flight.

Kit could hear Andrea's little gasps of excitement the closer they got to the flight line. She knew just how she felt. Big plane, first time, night flight. The stuff of dreams for a young pilot, especially a woman who normally wouldn't be allowed inside one, let alone fly one.

"Looks kind of spooky with the light on it like that, doesn't it, Lieutenant?"

"She's a big bird all right."

"Why are airplanes referred to as she? Because they're temperamental and unpredictable?"

"That's what the men say."

"How about you?" Andrea asked, looking over at her.

"I call them ladies because they're dependable and underappreciated." Kit pulled on her flight cap and zipped her jacket.

"Sorry to drag you out tonight, Lieutenant," Willie said, wiping his greasy hands on a rag.

"I bet you are. What's the poop on this bird?"

"We replaced both right engines. I've got a list of things I want you to check," he said. "Have you got a pencil and something to write on?"

Andrea immediately began searching for paper and pencil.

"Forget about writing it down, Willie," Kit said, grabbing him by the arm. "Come on. You're going with us."

"Not me, Lieutenant," he said, pulling away. "I fix them. I don't fly them."

"I can write it down, Lieutenant." Andrea was still searching through her flight bag for a pencil.

"Nope. He's going to sit in the jump seat and watch the gauges himself. I'm not going to waste thirty minutes going over what we're supposed to do. You're going, or this test flight isn't getting done tonight, Willie," Kit said, pulling her parachute over her shoulders. "And don't argue. This Lancaster has been sitting here ready for a test flight since three o'clock this afternoon. You just forgot to get it done. Now you want me to save your sorry ass before it's due for delivery. Either get in, or I'm going home." Kit stared him down. He heaved a disgusted groan, reset his cap on his head and climbed in the cockpit.

"How many flares will be lit?" Kit asked the ground chief.

"Two, posted at the end of the runway, just beyond the threshold. Remember, the flares only give you twelve minutes. The flight command said one set of flares is all they'll allow. We don't want the whole bloody German Air Force landing with you. We'll give you ten minutes for your pre-flight, then light them up," he said and gave the signal for someone to drive to the end of the runway with the flares.

Kit and Andrea climbed in and closed the hatch. With Willie looking over her shoulder, Kit started the engines and went through the pre-flight check. After he was satisfied with the engine performance, she rolled into position and released the brakes. The airplane roared down the runway, past the flares and into the night skies. She banked away from the field, throttling up to test the engines as Willie watched and listened.

"All set?" she asked, continuing her flight pattern over the airfield.

Willie leaned in and studied the cockpit gauges one more time.

"Looks good. Set her down, Lieutenant," he said, buckling himself in his seat for the landing.

Kit lined up with the flares, trusting her instincts as she dropped from the darkness. Andrea watched intently as Kit eased the wheels on the ground. She cut the throttle and rolled to the end of the runway where a flashlight marked the parking spot. "Breathe, Andrea," Kit said, noticing her wide-eyed stare.

"That was exhilarating, Lieutenant," she exclaimed, leaning back in her seat with a grin like she had just had an orgasm.

"You did fine. Come on. Let's go," Kit said, climbing between the seats and sliding out the hatch. She wasted no time in heading back across the field.

"Where are you going?" Andrea asked, trotting to catch up.

"I'm locking my gear in the ready room then getting away from here before I'm snagged to fly something else," Kit said, taking long strides. It was late, but she hoped the dance was still going on. She couldn't get Emily off her mind. As fast as she walked, she couldn't shake Andrea either. She followed like a puppy, asking questions about Lancasters and thrilling in the test flight. She bounced along, a smile on her face as she accompanied Kit back to the community center. As Kit turned the corner, her heart sank. Lady Marble's car was gone. So were many of the vehicles in the parking lot. The faint sound of the band could still be heard, but the crowd around the door was gone, thinned out by the late hour.

"Sounds like things are still jumping," Andrea said. "I wonder if Red and Lovie are inside."

"Why don't you go ahead and see?" Kit said, hoping to lose her in the crowd.

"You're coming too aren't you, Lieutenant?" Andrea said, hooking her arm through Kit's. They stood in the doorway, watching the dancers still jitterbugging around the dance floor. Lovie and Viv were spinning and hopping to the music. The giddy grins on their faces told Kit the flask under the table was still strengthening the punch. Red was leaning against the wall, visiting with one of the RAF pilots, her hands maneuvering through the air as if she was describing flight techniques. There were several pairs of women dancing in a row, occasionally changing partners by passing one to the right, laughing and having fun.

Kit hesitated at the door, scanning the room for Emily. The refreshment table was empty and the kitchen was dark.

"Come on in, ladies," a matronly looking woman said, waving them inside. "I'm sorry the refreshments are all gone. But the band will be playing for another hour or so."

"You go ahead, Andrea," Kit said. She didn't want to dance, and she didn't want any more mystery punch. If Emily wasn't there, Kit saw no reason to stay.

"We could dance," Andrea said, smiling hopefully.

"Thanks, but I don't have the energy. Tell the girls good night for me." Kit turned to leave, but Andrea wouldn't let go of her arm.

"Are you sure, Lieutenant?"

"Quite sure." Kit pulled away and patted her on the back. "Have fun." She quickly disappeared out the door before Andrea could latch on to her again. Kit wasn't in the mood to chitchat with the girls. She had wanted to visit with Emily, but hanging around the dance wasn't something she wanted to do. "Damn test flight," she said as she started up Digby Lane for home. By the time she got to the stone bridge, she was dead tired and her feet were killing her. Another mile and she could strip out of her clothes and into a hot tub. But once in bed, try as she might to stop them, she knew thoughts of Emily would follow her into her dreams. Her enchanting eyes, her soft, pale skin and that crooked little smile, the one that brightened her face when she was amused, would be there to haunt Kit as soon as she closed her eyes.

When Kit stepped onto her porch and unlocked the cottage door she noticed a small package tied to the doorknob. It was tissue paper formed around a stack of the cookies the ladies auxiliary had served at the refreshment table. Kit hurried inside and drew the blackout curtains then snapped on the light to read the note.

Thanks again for your help tonight. I don't think I could have survived another catastrophe this week. I seem to continually make a fool of myself in front of you. Please forgive me. I saved a few of the cookies and hope you enjoy them. Sorry you didn't stay longer. Yours truly, E. M.

Kit smiled at the way Emily artistically signed her initials with elaborate swirls. She slipped the note back in the envelope, slowly drawing her fingers over it as if it held the essence of Emily.

"Please don't make me fall in love with you," she whispered then went to the window and stared out into the darkness. "We'll just be friends. Just friends."

Chapter 16

Kit opened the door to the carriage house and rolled the motorcycle out into the morning light. It was a chilly morning, but the weather ministry promised sunshine and warmer temperatures. At least that was the forecast. Kit's morning included a test flight of a Wellington bomber then returning a Lancaster to the factory near London. She hadn't been in London in weeks and hoped she could find the time for a quiet lunch and maybe a bit of shopping. She didn't need anything, but a few hours away from the airfield would be nice. She checked the gas tank on the motorcycle then turned on the key. Just as she was about to step down on the kick starter, Emily placed a hand on her arm.

"Good morning," Emily said softly. She was dressed in a tweed skirt and a form-fitting sweater. Kit loved the way the sweater hugged her body, so much so her foot fell off the starter. She quickly caught her balance, pretending she had to look at something on the side of the engine.

"Good morning. Are you going to work dressed like that?" Kit asked, looking her up and down.

"No. I'm off today."

"That explains why no ugly jumpsuit."

"They aren't very flattering, are they?" Emily said, tugging at the hem of her sweater.

"I like that outfit. You look very nice," Kit said, trying to divert her eyes from Emily's well-formed breasts, but they kept returning as if searching for the imprint of her nipples through the sweater.

"Thank you. I didn't want to keep you. I just wanted to tell you how much I appreciate your help yesterday. If you hadn't known how to get in the car, I would have had to break the window or something."

"My pleasure. And thanks for the cookies. What are you going to do with your day off?"

"I'm not sure. I thought about taking the train into London for the day. Have tea at Fortnum and Mason. Or lunch someplace. There is a little place near Victoria Station, the Chelsea. It's small, but the food is wonderful. I haven't eaten there in months and months. Perhaps I'll go there."

"So you're going all the way to London just to have lunch?"

"Sure. It's going to be a lovely day for an outing." Emily scanned the cloudless sky. "Where are you going today? Prestwick? Ringway? Dublin?"

"Actually, I am taking a bomber to a factory near Brixton. The bomb racks need replacing."

"Brixton? That's right outside London."

Kit nodded.

"Are you flying back immediately?" Emily asked.

"Not necessarily. I think I'll have a few hours to kill," Kit said, her mind already planning how she could meet Emily for lunch without sounding pushy. "When are you catching the train to London?"

"If I take the nine-twenty train, I could be in Victorian Station

169

by eleven or eleven fifteen." Emily checked her watch. "The Brixton Station is on the same line, just a few stops away. Perhaps you'd like to meet me at the Chelsea for lunch."

"Okay," Kit said immediately.

"When you come out of Victoria Station, turn right then left at the next corner. You can't miss it. It's in the middle of the next block."

"I'll look forward to it," Kit said, nervously checking her watch. She was already late, but she hated to pull herself away.

"Shall we say twelve thirty, just to be on the safe side?"

Kit nodded and depressed the kick starter.

"If something happens, if I get another assignment, how will I let you know?" Kit asked above the engine.

"You won't need to. If you don't show up, I won't wait. I'll know you had something else to do." Emily waved as Kit roared away.

Kit could just imagine the conversation between Emily and Lillian.

"Where are you off to, looking so cheerful?" Lillian would ask.

"I'm going to London for lunch," Emily would answer, rushing up the stairs.

"With anyone special?"

"Kit."

"Kit? Lieutenant Anderson? The American you hate?" Lillian would laugh at her then frown curiously at how strange it must sound, their newfound friendship after so rocky a start.

Kit waited nervously for the MAC unit to have the Wellington ready for the test flight. She circled the airfield, checking the repairs, then set the bomber down and rolled to a stop. She was out of the cockpit before the waiting ground crew could help with the door. There was no time for a leisurely joy ride around the base or pleasant conversation with the crew. She hurried over to the command office, ready to check out the Lancaster and head south for Brixton. Lovie, Red and Andrea were crossing the field on their way to deliver Hurricanes. They waved, expecting Kit to stop and chat, but she merely returned the wave and continued toward the bomber waiting at the end of the runway. She climbed in and nervously went through her pre-flight check, her fingers fumbling with the switches. She had trouble remembering the sequence to start the four engines, something she had done a hundred times before, but today she had to look at the cheat sheet taped to the side of the cockpit.

"Pull the chocks, Mike," she yelled out the window. "I'm ready. Let's go."

"Hold your horses, Lieutenant," he said. "I'm doing it. What's your hurry?"

The instant he was clear and waved his arm, she pushed the throttle forward and released the brake. Like popping the clutch in a car, the bomber lurched forward, plowing divots as it began to roll. Kit could barely wait for the airplane to reach ninety knots so she could pull back on the yoke and lift off. She retracted the undercarriage and climbed out, increasing to one hundred forty knots. She banked hard to the left, finding a course south to Brixton and lunch with Emily. But before she could straighten her wings, she saw a red flare explode over the airfield. It could be one of any number of things. Smoke from the engines on takeoff she couldn't see, route or destination change, incoming German aircraft in her flight path, change of assignment—anything. But whatever it was, it would eat up time, time she needed to get to Victoria Station by noon. She could keep her heading, arguing she didn't see the flare, but she wasn't that kind of pilot, or that kind of officer. She heaved a disgusted sigh and turned back for a landing. As she rolled to a stop she slid the window open and stuck her head out.

"What's up?" she yelled, keeping two of the engines at idle.

The mechanic waved his hand across his throat for her to kill the engines.

"Command wants you to take some parts back to Brixton," he said. "Wheel bearings and struts."

Kit closed her eyes and rested her forehead against the window disgustedly.

"How long?" she asked, almost afraid to hear the answer.

"It won't take long. Go have a cup of tea while you wait."

"I don't want a cup of tea. I want to get the hell off the ground." She slammed the window shut and climbed out. It took over an hour for five men to load a dozen crates of parts. Kit paced nervously, watching the aggravatingly slow process. She knew if she complained about their progress they would take even longer. Finally, the cargo door closed and she was cleared for takeoff. It came none too soon for her rising blood pressure. Now she would have to make up an hour somewhere along the way. By the time she banked away from the airfield and headed south, the wind was directly in her face, pushing against the airplane and adding to her frustration. When she reached the airstrip next to the factory she had to wait her turn to land. It was nearly twelve when she finally signed out of the office. She dumped her parachute and flight bag in the corner of the flight operations office and trotted toward the underground station. She raced down the stairs onto the platform and waited nervously for the next train. Checking her watch every few seconds didn't help.

"Come on, come on. Let's go," she said, pacing up and down. The other passengers waiting patiently for a ride into London stared at her curiously. She studied the schedule posted on a pole then checked her watch again.

"Does this train run on time?" she asked an elderly woman.

"Sometimes. Sometimes it doesn't."

"That's just great. I'm never going to make it in time."

"You should learn to take life more slowly, miss," the woman said. "It will do you no good to rush around, fretting over a late train. Whatever it is will wait."

"Lord, I hope so," she said, leaning out over the tracks, looking for signs of the oncoming train.

"I believe it is coming," a gray-haired man said, standing up and walking to the edge of the platform, his umbrella hung over his arm and his hat sitting squarely on his head.

Kit hadn't heard anything, but sure enough, the man was right. Within a moment she could hear the rattle of the wheels on the rails and a blast of the train whistle. She waited for the doors to open and the other passengers to step on before rushing in the car and grabbing a strap. The train left the station with a jerk and rumbled toward London central. Kit tried to will it not to stop at each and every station, but it did anyway. Finally, it pulled into Victoria Station. She bolted out of the subway and fought her way through the thick crowd to the front entrance. Right then left at the corner. That was what Emily had said. But it was already after one, and Kit felt tears welling up in her eyes. If she was late, Emily had explained she wouldn't wait. As fruitless as it seemed, Kit hurried around the corner and down the block. Like many of the shops and businesses, stacks of sandbags lined the front windows, and wooden planks covered the glass door of the cafe. The hand-painted board hanging over the door was the only sign marking the entrance to the Chelsea. She hesitated outside, wiping away the tears that clung to her eyelashes. She hated to open the door. Emily wasn't going to be there. Kit knew it. She was an hour late. It wasn't her fault, but Emily must have assumed she didn't care about meeting her and left. Nothing could be further from the truth. Kit hadn't looked forward to anything as much in years. Emily Mills may not be a lesbian, but the pure devotion Kit felt growing for her was enough to make every encounter something wonderful, even if it was nothing more than a smile and a wave across the airfield. Meeting Emily was safe. As far as Emily knew, they were just friends. And friends were what Kit preferred. No commitment. No heartache. That's what she told herself. The girlfriends she had loved and lost back home were enough to turn Kit off to serious relationships. They were past mistakes Kit had no intention of repeating. Emily would be just a casual acquaintance, one who would never know Kit's sexual desires or preferences. Kit's only problem was convincing her heart that was best for everyone.

173

Kit opened the door and stepped inside. A few dim light fixtures lit the dozen or so tables, most of them occupied with middle-aged women, uniformed soldiers or businessmen in neatly pressed suits. Kit did a quick scan of the room, squinting as her eyes became accustomed to the dim light.

"Can I help you, miss?" a woman asked, coming through the kitchen door. "We've got a lovely table in the back."

"I was supposed to meet someone," Kit said, rescanning the room as her heart sank. "I don't think she's here."

"What does she look like, love?"

"Reddish-brown hair to her shoulders. Big brown eyes. Nice figure," Kit said, letting her heart answer.

"I meant how old and how tall." The woman frowned suspiciously at her.

"Oh, she's twenty-eight and about five feet four." Kit held her hand up to the bridge of her nose to show how tall Emily was.

"Sorry, love. That describes a lot of women."

"She has a camel colored coat," Kit added, although she didn't know if Emily planned on wearing it today. The woman chuckled. Kit glanced around the room again. Several of the women were in camel colored coats.

"Have a look around, ducks. If you decide to have a bite to eat, let me know," the woman said then returned to her chores.

Kit gave a last careful look around then resigned herself to the fact Emily wasn't there. Kit couldn't blame her. How could she be expected to wait an hour for someone who may or may not show up? Kit strolled the street dejectedly, cursing herself and the cargo she had to haul to Brixton. She rounded the corner and headed back to Victoria Station. As she did, she could see someone at the end of the street running toward her. It was Emily, her hair flying and her coat open.

"Kit!" she shouted, waving at her.

Kit immediately brightened. She waved back and hurried up the street toward her.

"I'm so sorry," Emily said, hugging Kit warmly. "My train was stopped twice for a search. I thought I'd never get here."

"I was late myself." Kit was so happy to see her she could hardly breathe. "I just got here."

"I was afraid you'd leave." Emily hooked her arm through Kit's and escorted her up the sidewalk. "Have you had lunch?"

"Not yet. You?"

"No. I was waiting for you." Emily squeezed Kit's arm. "But I'm famished."

"Did you want to go to the Chelsea?" Kit asked, pointing back over her shoulder.

"Not unless you do. I have another place in mind. I thought of it on the way in on the train. Do you like fish and chips?"

"Sure," Kit said, unable to resist placing her hand over Emily's as it clung to her arm.

"Good. I have the perfect place." They hurried along the sidewalk, smiling and chatting contentedly.

Kit was sure the perfect place for fish and chips was some high-class bistro with linen tablecloths and stemmed goblets. To her surprise, Emily led the way to a food stand where freshly cooked fish and crispy potato slices were sold in paper wrapped cones.

"What'll it be, miss?" a man asked as he stood at the window, resettling his paper hat on his head. He smelled like fish. But so did the entire street.

Emily held up two fingers. He went right to work rolling a sheet of newspaper into a cone then filling it with chips and fish filets. When he was done, he folded the top down neatly and handed it to Emily then made another for Kit. Kit pulled a handful of coins from her pocket and held them out for Emily to count. She handed the money to the man then opened the top of the cone, administering a generous sprinkle from a bottle on the counter.

"What's that?" Kit asked, watching intently.

"Malt vinegar," she said, opening Kit's cone and giving hers a sprinkle as well. "If you eat fish and chips, you have to have vinegar on it."

"I do, huh?" Kit said, looking in the top of her cone at what she had to eat.

Emily pulled a chip from her package and took a bite, sighing deeply.

"It's wonderful," she cooed, taking a bite of fish.

Kit took a small taste of the fish, not sure if she liked it or not. To her surprise, it was just as Emily described it, wonderful.

"Hey, I like it," she said, taking a larger bite.

"I told you." Emily bumped her playfully. "I bet you thought I only ate roast beef and Yorkshire pudding, didn't you?"

"Well," Kit stammered, enjoying a large chunk of fish. "I wasn't expecting you to find a place like this."

"My grandmother told me about it. She eats here sometimes when she's in London."

"Lillian?" Kit asked, amazed.

Emily nodded, dropping a chip into her upturned mouth.

"Although she doesn't use vinegar. She eats her fish and chips straight. You don't understand the love affair we British have for this. It's almost as strong as you Americans' love of hot dogs. With the Germans sinking our fishing fleet as fast as we rebuild them, this might be the next thing to be rationed." With that, she took another bite of fish, closed her eyes and savored the flavor for a long moment before swallowing. Kit watched her, smiling at the way she enjoyed her food like a child with a chocolate bar.

In no time at all, they were picking the last crumbs from the bottom of the cones.

"Did you like it?" Emily asked, tossing her paper in a barrel. She pulled a handkerchief from her purse and wiped her fingers then dabbed the corners of her mouth.

"Yes, I did. I loved it." She pressed her paper in the barrel and brushed off her hands. "Am I British now that I've had fish and chips?"

"Almost." Emily smiled. "You have to learn some other things first."

"Like what?" Kit asked as they strolled down the street.

"A cup of tea is a cuppa. What I drive at the motor pool isn't a truck. It's a lorry. At least the big ones are. And if someone asks where someplace is, you say straight away up and point. Can you remember?"

"I don't know. That seems like a lot to remember," Kit mused. "I have learned some expressions though."

"Like what?" Emily said, again locking her arm through Kit's.

"The bathroom is the loo. The trunk of the car is the boot and the hood over the engine is the bonnet. And when you are talking to someone you call them love."

"Very good. You are learning a lot."

"Yes, love," Kit said, laughing at her.

"Yes, love," Emily repeated, leaning into her playfully.

They had no sooner rounded a corner than the clear blue sky and peaceful afternoon was cut by the slow roll of the air raid siren growing into a sharp scream. Before they could react, the street was a buzz of people running out of buildings toward air raid shelters and others running inside to collect family members.

"Where do we go?" Emily said as passing pedestrians brushed by them.

Kit searched the sky. Three squadrons of fighters were roaring east over the river.

"I saw a sign for a shelter on the corner. It's probably the tube station," Kit said, quickening their pace down the sidewalk. "Come on. Let's go there."

She took Emily's hand and pulled her through the crowd as residents funneled down three flights of steps to the underground station. Its long halls and tiled walls were rapidly filling with people establishing parcels of space for themselves and their families. As old hands at living out an air raid in a shelter, Londoners came prepared to stay the night or at least until the all-clear was sounded. Most had bedrolls and hampers of food. Others had small camp stoves to cook their dinner and heat water for tea or washing. Children carried their own blanket or knapsack of provisions. An old man in a tattered overcoat and weathered hat unfolded a chair and hung his umbrella over the back before sitting down. Two women still wearing their aprons were carrying what they were preparing for dinner, ready to adapt as best they could. Camp stools, crates, old suitcases, even overturned soup pots were carried into the underground for chairs. There was no panic. After months of sirens disrupting their lives at all hours of the day and night, they accepted this nuisance with steeled reserve. Their eyes showed a nervous fear for what they might return to, but there was no panic.

"Let's go down that way." Kit pointed toward the end of a line of squatters. As they weaved their way along the platform, stepping over belongings and outstretched legs, Kit and Emily noticed an obnoxious smell floating through the air like an odious fog. It was a mixture of urine, body odor, cigarette smoke, partially cooked food and moth balls. Emily held her handkerchief to her nose as she followed Kit, holding on to the tail of her jacket. Kit looked back, her eyes watering and her forehead wrinkled at the smell.

"Are you all right?" Kit asked, noticing Emily's slightly green cast.

"Frightfully strong, isn't it?" Emily said, choking back a gag.

"Yes," Kit said, clinching her jaw to keep from retching. "Maybe it will be better down at the end." It wasn't. In fact the smell seemed to follow them, hanging over their heads like a putrefied cloud.

"I don't know if I can do this," Emily said, trying to hide her face against Kit's shoulder. "If I stay here, I'm going to be sick."

"Me too," Kit said. She took Emily's hand and headed back through the crowd to the stairs up to the street. Once at the top of the steps, they both took deep breaths, coughing and gagging away the stench. "How do people stand that smell?"

"Either they have no choice, or perhaps they just get used to it."

The air raid siren had stopped wailing. The sound of anti-aircraft guns could be heard in the distance, sending round after round into the late afternoon sky over London, rattling windows. Kit and Emily huddled in a doorway, deciding what to do.

"Where shall we go?" Emily asked, clutching Kit's arm.

Kit wrapped an arm around her shoulder. Just then an explosion shook the building across the street, showering shards of glass into the street. Emily screamed and ducked as a section of wall crumbled into a pile of bricks and timbers. A cloud of dust settled around them. Kit pushed Emily back into the doorway as far as they could go, blocking her with her own body. Another louder explosion in the next block sent Emily to her knees, screaming in terror. Kit knelt at her side, holding her in her arms as blast after blast rumbled overhead. Emily buried her face in the embrace, afraid to look up.

"I'm sorry I made you leave the air raid shelter," Emily cried. "It's all my fault."

"No, it isn't. I couldn't stay down there in that cesspool either." Kit raised Emily's chin and smiled at her. "I'm right here and I'll take care of you."

"I want you to go back down there. I'll be all right," Emily said, trying to be brave.

"I'm not going anywhere without you." Kit took Emily by the hand and led her along the sidewalk, darting in and out of doorways at the slightest rumble of danger. An ambulance sped down the street, its siren screaming, followed by a fire truck. Kit pulled Emily down a narrow alley just as the whistle of a bomb ended with a rattling explosion. They scrambled down a flight of stairs that led to a basement door. The staircase was lined with sandbags, blocking the door at the bottom and making a small but cozy bomb shelter.

"I think we're safe down here," Kit said, pushing Emily into the back.

"I wish the bombs would stop," Emily cried, crouching in the corner.

"It's a daylight bombing attack, so they have specific targets. They're after the airplane factories or munitions plants. They shouldn't be targeting downtown London," Kit said, peering up through the clouds of smoke drifting across the skyline. "Have you been in an air raid before?"

Emily nodded.

"It was terrible. The bombs were falling everywhere. It was so loud, and there was fire all around us." Tears filled Emily's eyes as she huddled in the corner of their makeshift bomb shelter, a terrified look on her face Kit had never seen before. "I was so frightened. I was on the train. They made us get off, but there was no place to go. We hid under a trellis until it was over. A few of the passengers were injured from flying debris. It took two days for me to get home. The tracks were hit, and I had to wait for them to be repaired." She covered her head with her hands and began to weep. "I don't know if I can go through this again."

Kit knelt next to her and gently pulled her hands away from her face.

"Nothing is going to happen to you, Emily. Believe me, I won't let it."

"Aren't you afraid?" Emily asked, looking up into Kit's eyes.

"Yes, I little," Kit whispered. "But we're here together." She wrapped her arms around Emily and pulled her close. "We'll take care of each other." Kit kissed Emily's forehead. "Hang on to me."

Emily folded her arms around Kit, her face nestled against her chest. Each time an explosion rumbled in the distance, Emily hugged Kit a little tighter. Kit stroked Emily's hair softly, trying to soothe her. After several minutes of silence, a blast shook the building above them, showering dust into the alley. It was a small explosion, but enough to make Emily jump.

"Don't be afraid," Kit said, brushing the dust from Emily's face. "I think that was an anti-aircraft shell falling to the ground."

"I can't stay here. I have to get out of this alley and out of

London." Emily tried to pull away, but Kit held tight to her, keeping her from running up the stairs.

"You can't go out there, Emily. It isn't safe, not yet. It'll be over soon."

"I can't help it. Let me go, please. I don't want to be trapped here," Emily screamed, fighting Kit to get free.

"Emily, stop it. You can't go out there. Look. We have a wall of sandbags all around us. Iron railing over the top of us. We are safe. Look at me," Kit said, pushing Emily against the sandbags and holding her there. She took Emily's face in her hands and stared deep into her frightened eyes. "I will protect you. I want you here with me." With that, Kit pressed her lips against Emily's, kissing her full on the mouth. Emily hadn't closed her eyes. She stared wide-eyed at Kit, seemingly stunned at what had happened and too surprised to speak.

"Emily," Kit whispered, stammering for an apology.

Emily didn't draw away. Instead she slowly closed her eyes and turned her lips up to Kit expectantly. Kit kissed her again, slowly and sweetly, lingering over the taste and touch of her. Emily melted into her embrace as if they had done it a thousand times before. She may never have kissed a woman before, but Kit could tell she wasn't intimidated by the taboo.

Kit couldn't stop. She laced her fingers through Emily's hair, grabbing handfuls of the silken softness as she devoured her mouth. She pressed herself against Emily, their breasts and hips locked together as completely as their lips. With the distant rumbling all around them, they continued to explore the other's mouth with hot, passionate tongues. In the back of Kit's mind, she knew better than to start something she couldn't finish, but Emily had been an attraction, a distraction, every day since they first met. Her lips were unlike anything Kit had ever experienced, and she couldn't give them up.

"Emily," Kit gasped, holding her in her arms and closing her eyes. "We shouldn't be doing this. I didn't mean to kiss you. Please forgive me. We're just friends, and this is wrong."

"Why did you kiss me?" Emily whispered.

"I don't know. Maybe I was just scared. The bombs were exploding all around us. You were crying. I think I was trying to protect you." Kit looked down at Emily. "You have to believe me. I didn't plan to do it. It just happened. Can you forgive me?"

"You there. What are you doing?" a woman shouted from a second story window across the alley. "That's private property. I'll call the constable on you two if you don't get away from there. Mr. Haggis doesn't like people hanging round his basement, you hear me?" She glared down at them, shaking a menacing hand in their direction.

"The bombing has stopped," Kit said, taking Emily by the hand and leading her up the stairs and out of their shelter. "We're leaving," she said up at the woman. Kit was relieved the woman had interrupted them. She didn't have to face Emily's questions about why she kissed her.

"Where are we going?" Emily asked.

"If we could get to Brixton, I'm sure the factory has something ready to go back to Alderbrook. That is, if they haven't been bombed."

"What if all they have is a single seated plane, like a Spitfire?"

"If it is, then you'll sit on my lap," Kit said, wrapping an arm around her as the sound of fire engines screamed in the distance. "I'm not leaving you here in London."

"The trains and underground don't run during air raids," Emily said, seemingly glad to have Kit's arm around her guiding her down the street. "If there was any damage to the tracks, it might be a day or two before they are running again."

"Would you be up to doing a little hitching?" Kit asked.

"Hitching? What is that?"

"Hitchhiking." Kit held out her thumb to demonstrate. "If we could get across the river, I think we could catch a ride with someone going south. Are you up to it?"

Emily immediately turned them around and headed in the

other direction without losing step.

"The Thames is this way," she said, holding on to Kit's hand. They wound through the streets and crossed the river at Vauxhall Bridge then headed south on Lambeth Road.

"Look at that," Kit gasped, looking back across the river. London was aglow with orange flares.

"I hate to look at it," Emily said, looking then quickly diverting her eyes. "So many people lose their lives and their homes each time this happens."

Kit gave a last look then hurried them along.

"I want to get to Brixton before it's dark," Kit said.

They didn't see any traffic for blocks. They were both about to give up on hitching a ride when a rickety old truck came chugging around the corner. The racks in the back of the truck were covered with pots and pans, odd car parts, sections of metal fencing and anything of value, regardless of how little the worth.

"Hello, love," the woman driver said, screeching to a stop. She grinned broadly at them. Her hair was trying desperately to escape the tie that held it out of her face. She wore a man's shirt that was several sizes too large and a pair of trousers secured with a belt, also several sizes too large. Her nails were as dirty as her face. "Need a lift?"

"Are you going anywhere near Brixton?" Kit asked hopefully, stepping back at the smell the woman emitted.

"I can get you as far as Clapham," she said. "Will that help?"

"That'll be fine," Kit said.

"Get in." She motioned for them to climb in the cab next to her. "I haven't got time to stand 'round and chat." She ground the shifter through the gears, searching for first. Kit and Emily climbed in the cab. Fortunately it had open sides with no windows to trap the woman's foul smell.

"Thank you for the lift," Emily said, sitting in the middle but leaning toward Kit.

"Shouldn't you two be in a shelter someplace?" the woman said as she released the clutch. The truck lurched forward, nearly stalling. She cursed and rummaged through the gears again. "Bloody truck is going to be the death of me yet."

Emily put her hand on the woman's and helped guide the shifter into first gear.

"Sometimes double clutching helps," Emily said politely, discreetly wiping her hand on the side of her coat.

"Thanks. Where are you headed?"

Kit knew better than to confess where an airplane factory was located.

"We've got relatives in Brixton. We're worried about our aunt," Kit explained.

"Yes, she's a bit old and refuses to use her shelter," Emily added, trying to sound convincing.

"Aunt, eh?" The woman found second gear and popped the clutch, jerking them back in the seat. "I thought maybe you were on your way to the factory on Willis Road," she said, raising her eyebrows at Kit. "That's a pilot's jacket you've got on, isn't it?"

Kit just stared at her, refusing to answer.

"I guess I can take you as far as Willis Road. I wouldn't want anything to happen to your poor old auntie, not with the bombing and all." She bumped Emily's arm then winked.

The woman swerved around corners and cut through side streets until Kit and Emily had no idea where they were. The farther they traveled, the narrower and darker the streets became.

"Are you sure this is the right way to Brixton?" Kit asked, looking for anything familiar.

"You can't drive on the main roads, love. They've got them blocked to everything but emergency vehicles. There was a building collapse this morning and a fire over on Dover. The constables stopped me earlier. They wanted me truck to haul debris, but I told them to go straight to the devil. I have to make a living, don't I? I'm Sam," she said, offering her hand to Emily. "What's yours, love?"

"I'm Emily. This is Kit." Emily shook her hand carefully.

"Hello, Kit," Sam said, reaching over to shake her hand. "Me mum named me Samantha, but Sam is easier. Fits me better." She winked again. "Where are you from, Kit? You don't sound British."

"United States. Kansas."

"Kansas? Where's that? Is it near New York? I saw a flick last week. It had Barbara Stanwyck in it, and she was eating dinner in a posh restaurant in New York City. You should have seen what she was eating. Steak, French champagne, fresh strawberries, real cream in her coffee. I bet she had eggs and bacon for breakfast. And jam on her toast." Sam sighed. "I haven't had an egg in six months."

Kit didn't want to tell her the movie was probably made in California on a sound stage and the food was only props.

"Kansas is in the middle of the United States," Kit said, assuming that would be enough to satisfy her curiosity.

"Where are you from, Emily?" Sam asked, grinding through another gear.

"Alderbrook."

"Are the shortages as bad up there as here in London?"

"Meat is pretty scarce. So are eggs and milk."

"I hope this war ends soon. I'm tired of potatoes." Sam skidded around the corner and came to a stop. "There it is. Willis Road." She pointed at the long brown brick building across the street. "I hope your auntie wasn't hurt in the bombing," she said, smiling over at Kit.

"Thank you, Sam," she said, reaching over Emily and shaking her hand warmly. "Our aunt will appreciate your help." Kit climbed out and dug in her pocket for some change.

"Yes, thank you, Sam. You were very kind," Emily added, sliding out.

"I'd like to pay you for the ride," Kit said, searching through the coins in her hand.

"No, thanks, love. Me pleasure." Sam touched her forehead as if she were tipping her hat then smiled broadly. "Have a nice day." She popped the clutch and lurched forward. Kit and Emily could hear her cursing as she rolled down the street, grinding through the gears. They watched until she rounded the corner and disappeared, the sound of her shifting still audible in the distance.

"Let's go check in and see if they have anything for me," Kit said, leading the way across the street and through the gate. They showed their IDs to the guards, having to pass through two fences to get to the ATA office. Kit was cleared to return to Alderbrook with a recently repaired light bomber. It was scheduled for the airfield at Luton, but Kit convinced them once they got it to Alderbrook, a transfer could be arranged. They crossed to the flight operations office at the end of the runway on the far side of the factory. The air raid in London had put the factory into a frenzy of activity, sending as many airplanes out of the city as possible to avoid being targets on the ground. The flight commander was happy to have Kit deliver the bomber, leaving one less airplane in harm's way. The airplane was immediately fueled for their flight. There was no time for delays. In a matter of minutes, she was cleared for takeoff. Kit helped Emily get situated in the copilot's seat then hurried through her pre-flight checklist before being given the signal to start the engines.

"Here we go," Kit said, releasing the brakes. They rolled down the runway, increasing speed for liftoff. She eased back on the yoke, and the airplane gracefully rose into the sky. She retracted the undercarriage and adjusted the flaps.

"Which way are we going?" Emily asked, her eyes wide with amazement and her hands clutched around the seat belt straps.

"Southwest. We can't go north over London. I don't want to cross any German's path. They are probably heading northeast for home and almost out of fuel, but I'm not taking any chances. We'll go southwest then west and loop around to the north. It'll take longer, but we've seen all the German planes we need to see for a while." She smiled over at Emily, hoping to reassure her.

The last flickers of daylight were casting long shoulders over the runway at Alderbrook as Kit circled for her final approach.

A yellow flare told her she would have to wait for the returning combat fighters to land, many of them probably low on fuel.

"We'll be down in a few minutes," Kit said, making a wide circle over the field. She pointed at the incoming squadron of Spitfires. Emily nodded and kept her eyes out the window. Nothing had been said about the kiss since they left the alley. Kit was just as happy not to bring it up. From Emily's silent but pensive stare, Kit could tell she was wrestling with what they had done.

Finally Kit was cleared for landing. She came in low and soft, setting down and rolling to a stop just as darkness fell over the airfield. She cut the engines and leaned back in the seat, slowly turning to Emily. Their eyes met in soft yet frightened communication. Kit could see a confused look in Emily's eyes. As much as she wanted to protect Emily from what people would say and think about her, she also knew she couldn't stop what she felt for her. To apologize and promise it would never happen again seemed at odds with her heart.

"We need to talk," Emily said quietly.

"Emily, I'm so sorry," Kit whispered. "Did I scare the hell out of you?"

"Open up, Lieutenant," one of the mechanics shouted, pounding on the bottom hatch. "You've landed right enough." He pounded again.

Kit released the lock and dropped the pilot's hatch.

"We didn't expect to see you back this evening," he said, helping them as they lowered themselves out the bottom door.

"Air raid in London," Kit said, stepping aside and waiting for Emily to ease herself down. "They needed to get as many planes out as they could."

"We heard about it. The factory at Alstead took a wallop. Lost over forty planes and a warehouse full of engine parts." He shook his head in disgust then repositioned his cap on his head. The ground crew wasted no time in rolling the bomber to the hangar so it could be fitted with armaments and a radio.

"Lieutenant," Andrea called from the hangar door. Lovie and Red followed her, waving at Kit and Emily.

"Hi, girls," Kit said, greeting them with a wide grin, hoping to mask any telltale emotion between her and Emily.

"I was so scared when I heard you flew into Brixton. Did you see the bombing in London?" Lovie said, rushing up to them, looking as worried as an old mother hen.

"What was it like, a daylight bombing raid?" Andrea asked, wrinkling her forehead.

"Loud," Emily said. "And scary."

"Where did you go? Down in a tube station?" Andrea asked.

"The one we went to was disgusting," Kit said. "It smelled terrible."

"It was worse than terrible," Emily added then shuddered.

"It was so bad we didn't stay."

Andrea, Lovie and Red listened intently while Emily and Kit explained the sorry conditions in the air raid shelter and what they saw when they climbed back up to street level. Kit also noticed Red's invasive stare. It was subtle, but she couldn't keep her eyes off the two of them as if watching for some small hidden communication between Kit and Emily.

"Where did you go to ride out the bombing? You didn't just stand on the sidewalk, did you?" Lovie asked.

"In an alley," Emily said.

"We found a staircase fortified with iron bars and sandbags," Kit added. "It was small, but at least it didn't smell."

"Cramped quarters, eh?" Red said, a glint in her eye.

Kit saw it and instantly read her meaning.

"Not that cramped," she said, tossing a stern look at Red.

"We had a lift in a junk trunk," Emily said, laughing as she looked over at Kit. "It rattled and rumbled along the street so you could hardly hear yourself think."

While Emily described Sam and their odyssey through the side streets of Brixton, Red smiled coyly at Kit. Kit lowered her gaze, unable to stop the blush that covered her face. She wasn't easily embarrassed, but Red had found her Achilles heel. Red seemed to know something was going on between Kit and Emily. She may not have known exactly what, but Kit saw she was twinkling at the possibilities.

"I have to check in with flight operations," Kit interrupted. She hated to leave without talking to Emily about what she knew was on her mind, but Kit knew they wouldn't get any privacy so long as the girls were there. And Red's insinuating chuckle didn't help.

"I should go as well," Emily said. "If Grandmother heard about the bombing on the radio, she'll be worried. I best go ease her mind that I'm all right."

"Tell Lillian hello for me," Kit said, offering one last look in Emily's direction then crossing to the office.

It was after nine when Kit pulled the motorcycle up to the carriage house and rolled it inside. She looked up at Emily's bedroom window, but it was dark. For a moment she considered knocking on the side door and offering Emily another apology but thought better of it. Perhaps tomorrow, she decided. She walked down to the cottage, muttering to herself over what she had done. Her body was tired, but she knew it would be hours before she could turn off her mind and sleep. She undressed, washed and turned out the light. Once the cottage was dark, she opened the blackout curtains and peered out the window toward the big house. She couldn't see it, but she could imagine Emily snuggled in her bed. Kit slipped into bed and pulled the comforter up around her shoulders. She liked the feel of the soft duvet cover against her naked skin. But it was the thought of Emily's skin that kept her awake well past midnight.

Chapter 17

Sometime in the middle of the night, between Kit's dream about shooting down the entire German Luftwaffe in the dog-fight of the century and another where she saves Emily from a fire-breathing dragon, Kit was awakened by a repeated knock at the door. If it was one of the mechanics rousting her out of bed, she was going to strangle him. If it was Red, come to tease her about what went on in the stairwell, she was going to pull her hair out, one strand at a time. She was not in the mood to play twenty questions. Kit stumbled out of bed and pulled on her robe. She sleepily felt her way to the front door, stubbing her toe on the corner of the table.

"Ouch, damnit," she grumbled as she opened the door.

"Hello," Emily said. She held her robe closed over her chest, her knuckles white from the grip.

"Hello," Kit said with a gasp.

"Is it too late for us to have our talk?"

"No." Kit stood in the doorway, her brain still trying to wake up.

"May I come in?"

"Oh, yes. Sure, come in." Kit took her arm and pulled her through the door.

"I'm sorry to bother you. I know it's late," Emily said, stepping in hesitantly.

"That's okay. Sit down. Can I make you some tea or something?"

"You aren't required to be hospitable at three in the morning," Emily said shyly.

"What better time?"

"Is it terribly rude of me to wake you in the middle of the night?" Emily looked petrified. She searched Kit's face as if waiting for her acceptance.

"No. I'm a little groggy is all."

"I'll come back another time," Emily said, reaching for the door knob.

"No, wait," Kit said, pushing the door shut again. "Of course we can talk. This is the perfect time. What happened today made you uncomfortable, and I feel terrible about it. Now you know about me, and I hope we can still be friends in spite of it."

"All I know is when you kissed me with the bombs thundering around us, I came alive. It was as if I knew that about myself all along. I knew it but never was confronted with it before. When you touched me, it was as if I had been waiting my whole life for that one moment, that one incredible instant when you placed your lips on mine. No one ever kissed me like that before. It was soft and tender and it made me feel whole."

"Do you know what you're saying, Emily?"

"Yes." She traced her fingers down Kit's face. "I'm saying I am a lesbian."

"It isn't that easy. You can't just kiss me and decide your whole life has changed. You are just in shock. You'll wake up tomorrow and realize you were wrong. You'll wish we never kissed. You'll want some strong man to hold you in his arms and tell you what a perfect wife you'll make. Believe me, this isn't a decision you should make after one minute during an air raid."

"I want to tell you something, something very personal, very intimate," Emily said, taking Kit's hand. "I've never spent the night with anyone before. Ever." She said it almost apologetically. "I've dated, but I never . . ." She hesitated.

"You're a virgin." Kit said it tenderly.

"Yes. There was a teacher at the school where I taught. He and I dated from time to time. Nothing serious. He seemed very nice. But I was never completely comfortable with him. I never knew why until today. He suggested we spend the night at his flat, but I said no. I couldn't. He thought I was a prude."

"The way you kissed me today, you are no prude," Kit said, running her fingers through Emily's hair.

"Please don't say you are sorry for what happened."

"I'm not sorry I kissed you, but I am sorry I started something we can't finish. I'm going home in a few months. My contract is up soon. It wouldn't be fair to either of us. When I came to England, I made up my mind I wouldn't fall into another fleeting relationship. When that happens, someone always gets hurt."

"But we could be friends," Emily pleaded, looking up at Kit as if begging for agreement. "You said so. What if we keep it on that level? Friends, very special friends, for however long you are here."

Kit walked away, running her fingers through her hair as she thought. "It has to be just friends," she said, coming back to her. "We can't make anything out of this, Emily. Nothing permanent. Can we do that?" Kit asked, lost in Emily's big brown eyes.

"Even if it's just for a short time, we can have a wonderful friendship."

"No strings attached?"

"No strings attached." Emily moved closer, turning her face up to Kit's.

"You don't know what you are getting yourself into."

"Oh, yes, I do," she said then pulled Kit's mouth to hers and kissed her.

Kit slid her hands down Emily's back and cupped them over her bottom.

"I know exactly what I'm doing." Emily pressed her softness against Kit. "I know I want you."

Emily had said the magic words. She understood what they were doing, and it was okay. Nothing permanent. Just the softness one special friend shows another in the mindless tragedy of war. Kit knew they were stretching the meaning of friendship to include lover, but if it meant Emily would be in her arms, in her bed, in her heart, she wouldn't argue. Kit kissed her deeply, her tongue probing Emily's mouth urgently. She opened Emily's robe and let it drop. The thin cotton nightgown was no match for Kit's skillful hands. She pulled it over her head then opened her own robe. Emily gasped as their breasts caressed each other.

"Tell me when I have gone too far," Kit whispered as her kisses trailed down Emily's neck toward her nipples.

"I want you to go too far," Emily pleaded through closed eyes.

Kit could feel Emily's wetness on her thigh.

"Oh, sweet lord," Emily cried out as Kit's tongue found an erect nipple and sucked hard at it.

Kit's fingers flowed down over Emily's abdomen, growing teasingly closer to her valley. Gasping with anticipation, Emily dug her nails into Kit's shoulder. She raised her leg and wrapped it around Kit, welcoming her exploration. Kit traced the velvet petals of her folds. Her opening was small, but warm and welcoming. Emily drew short breaths as she clung to Kit.

"Do you want me to stop?" Kit whispered.

"No."

Kit flowed in and out of her, each time bringing on a fresh moan. It was as if Emily's body was a slave to Kit's touch, leaving her speechless to the growing ecstasy.

"I can't breathe," Emily gasped.

"Yes, you can," Kit whispered softly. "Relax and enjoy it, sweetheart."

Kit slowly increased her rhythm and the pressure as Emily's sighs and moans guided her. She pressed Emily against the wall and held her there as she plunged deeper. Emily held on to Kit, her eye's closed as if pain and pleasure were dueling for control. With a scream that seemed to start in her toes and rose up like a volcano, Kit knew Emily had reached orgasm. Kit held her lover as her body pulsed and she struggled for breath. Through Emily's soft moans, Kit could hear the sound of weeping.

"What is it?"

Emily didn't reply.

"What's wrong, Emily?" Kit repeated, brushing the tears from her cheeks. "Did I hurt you?"

"No," Emily said, then pulled on her robe and ran out the door, disappearing into the darkness.

"Emily?" Kit called from the doorway. "Come back. I didn't mean to make you cry." Kit stood on the porch, her robe open to the chilly night air. She was numbed by what had happened. Both Emily's soft surrender and her sudden escape had Kit staring helplessly into the pitch black night.

"Emily, come back," she repeated, gripped with guilt.

Chapter 18

Kit knocked on the side door just after seven, hoping Emily would accept a ride to the airfield so they could talk. But Nigel informed her Emily had already left. Kit hurried to the carriage house and started the motorcycle, hoping to catch up with her along the way to the airfield. She circled the motor pool twice then parked next to the ATA office, disappointed she hadn't found her.

"I telephoned the motor pool. A driver is on the way," Commander Griggs said from her open office door. Kit was only vaguely aware of her presence. She stood at the window, her eyes lost in space. "Lieutenant? Lieutenant Anderson?" Griggs said, but Kit was still in another world. Griggs strode across the room and stood behind her. "Lieutenant Anderson?"

"Yes, Commander," Kit said, finally coming to her senses.

"I said a driver is on the way. We're sending five pilots to the factory in Thriggle. Can you see to it, Lieutenant?"

"Yes, Commander."

"Where is your mind this morning?"

"I'm sorry. I'll take care of the pilots right away," Kit said. She went to her desk and began rummaging through the drawer for the assignment sheet. It was on top of the desk in plain sight. Griggs picked it up and thrust it in front of Kit's face then turned and strode into her office.

"Thriggle! Now there is one nasty factory," Lovie said as she stood combing her hair in the broken piece of mirror taped to the wall. "Smells like burnt rubber."

"It was a tire factory before they converted it to an airplane plant," Patty said, jockeying for a sliver of the mirror.

"No wonder it smells then." Lovie wrinkled her nose and stepped out of her way.

"What did you want a factory to smell like?" Red asked, taking a drag off Lovie's cigarette burning in the ashtray.

"I don't know." She shrugged. "Anything but burnt rubber. How about chocolate?"

"Okay, ladies, enough chitchat. We've got flights today," Kit said, finding her way back to the present. She made the assignments and gave last-minute instructions.

"Where will you be?" Lovie took the last drag on her cigarette then mashed it out. "Sipping French champagne and eating bonbons?" She giggled.

"Who is sipping champagne?" Commander Griggs said critically, coming out of her office with a bundle of papers for field command.

"Lieutenant Anderson, that's who," Lovie said gleefully, bumping Kit with her hip. "She's got a faraway, dreamy look in her eyes. She'll probably duck out as soon as we take off."

"Very funny. I'm taking a bomber to Dublin," Kit replied, ruffling Lovie's hair playfully.

"Lieutenant, keep a watch out for the weather on your way back. Might run into some fog," Griggs said, handing her a weather notice.

"The rest of you do the same," Kit announced, reading it over. "Don't take any chances. Set your planes down if you see fog. That includes you, Red. Don't try to outrun it like you did last week."

"Yes, Lieutenant." Red rolled her eyes. "All right. Who's the tattletale?"

"Never mind who told me. Just don't do it again. You were lucky last time."

Red gave Lovie a scowl and wagged a finger at her. Lovie shrugged and shook her head.

"It wasn't me," Lovie insisted.

Emily opened the door and stepped into the ready room, waiting for the end of the briefing.

"Okay, ladies, let's get to work. Fly safe out there," Kit said then looked over at Emily. "Hello," she said, unable to hide her pleasure at seeing her. They shared an awkwardly long gaze, one that broke only when Red finally cleared her throat loudly.

"Miss Mills," Kit said, diverting her eyes to the map. "You're taking five pilots to the factory just outside Thriggle. Have you been there before?"

"No, but I'm sure I can find it," Emily said, her eyes never leaving Kit. She came to the map, standing next to Kit to see the routing.

"Viv can help you. She's been there several times."

"It's easy to find, love," Viv said.

"Watch out for the bridge at Atwood," Lovie said. "I flew over it last week, and it was out." She draped an arm over Emily's shoulder. "Go by way of Thistle Downs, or you'll get stuck." She whispered into Emily's ear, "Viv can't tell left from right some-times."

"I heard that," Viv grumbled.

"But, sweetheart, you can't." Lovie grinned and pinched her cheek.

"That was just one time," Viv said. "Maybe two."

The girls collected their gear and headed across the field, still joking and teasing each other. Kit's discreet glances and yearning for a moment to visit with Emily were left at the ready room door. She knew duty came first. She was dying to know why Emily ran out of the cottage in tears, but she knew that would have to wait. More than once she had given her heart to a seemingly compassionate woman, only to find their rendezvous was nothing more than curiosity. If Emily had second thoughts, if she regretted what they had done, a few hasty words weren't what Kit wanted. She gave Emily a last look and smile then headed to the runway.

Kit was last to take off. She banked the lumbering bomber west by northwest with hopes the trip would be uneventful and she would be back in Alderbrook by dinner. She didn't want to worry about weather or cantankerous airplanes today. There was something else on her mind, and it was Emily's sweet smile. Thankfully, the trip across Wales and the Irish Sea to Dublin was a quick one, partially because the strong winds pushed her that way, and partially because she was cruising at six hundred feet with the throttle wide open to cut her flying time to the bare minimum. The crew descended on the bomber as soon as she rolled to a stop. Within fifteen minutes she was strapped into a 1929 Gypsy Moth biplane for her trip home. It was versatile and maneuverable as a low-level reconnaissance aircraft, although it wasn't as fast as the newer models. Because of the never-ending equipment shuffle, the front seat was packed with spare parts and covered with a tarp.

"Better get a wing in the air, Lieutenant," the mechanic said. "Weather on the way." He nodded back to the east, the direction she had just come. "And take care of those parts." He patted the side of the fuselage.

Kit nodded and flipped the switch, waiting for him to spin the propeller and start the engine. She held the stick between her knees as the Moth began rolling down the runway. She pulled her leather flight cap down and positioned her goggles then pushed the throttle to full.

"Take me home, baby," she said as she increased speed and nosed up into the blue skies. She circled the field and took up an easterly heading. She was halfway across the Irish Sea when she saw a gray haze forming along the horizon. That was fog, and she didn't like the looks of it. Her only question was could she make it over land before it swallowed her and the slow-moving airplane.

She pointed the nose of the airplane southeast toward Port Oer and raced the oncoming weather across the water. It wasn't the most direct route back to Alderbrook, but it was the nearest point of land on the coast of Wales. It didn't take Kit long to realize she was losing the race. The likelihood of reaching the coast and the airstrip at Hasselford twenty miles inland before the fog completely obscured the ground was in serious doubt. She knew the throttle was wide open, but she pushed it anyway. Ten minutes was all she needed. Ten minutes to be over the rocky coast and then a soft landing in a farm field. She raised her altitude to give herself a few more feet—a few more moments to find a suitable landing spot. The first thin wisps of gray fog sailed by as the Moth passed over the coast. She was flying straight into thick soup. Finding an emergency landing place was the best she could hope for.

Kit throttled back and dropped down to take a look. The maneuverable biplane gave her an extra bit of confidence, knowing five hundred feet of pasture was enough for a safe landing. As fog grew thicker, she became more worried she wouldn't find an open field. She remembered dozens of green pastures and smooth meadows the last time she over-flew western Wales, but all she could see were swampy fields and rows of trees. With no radio, she was on her own. She needed a place to set down, and now. Kit banked to the left and flew parallel to the fog bank.

"You aren't a beautiful field, but you'll have to do," she mumbled, pitching around and lining up with a narrow pasture. "I hope there are no tractors down there." She gritted her teeth and cut the engine. The front wheels skimmed the top of the trees as she floated in for a landing, bouncing over the rut-covered ground. The Moth rolled into the fog and stopped, the last turns of the propeller thrashing at the hedge row that surrounded the field. Kit leaned her head back and closed her eyes, saying a prayer of thanks for being on solid ground. She climbed out and slid down the wing then waded through the weeds to check the propeller. The thrashing sounded disastrous, but fortunately the blades looked okay. She wouldn't know for sure if there was any damage until she turned the airplane around and started the engine for takeoff.

The fog thickened, obscuring everything but what she could touch. Like most English fog banks, Kit knew it would be as thick as butterscotch pudding for a few hours then drift out to sea. If she was lucky, it would move on, leaving her enough time to get back to Alderbrook before dark. For now, she could only sit and wait. She had no idea where she was, and in the thick fog, it was unlikely anyone saw her land.

Kit sat on the wing, waiting for the fog to lift. She thought about going in search of a friendly face to help turn the Moth around, but she didn't want to get lost in the fog. It seemed like hours before she noticed the fog thinning. She hopped down and began pushing the tail around. She would need all the speed she could coax from the engine to lift the wheels over the row of trees at the far end of the field. She struggled to push the airplane around, something she had done a hundred times on smooth pavement. But a heavily loaded airplane over rough furrows was something else. She managed to move it only a few feet before the tail skid bogged down in the plowed ground. She grunted and put all her weight against it, but it was stuck. Her feet slipped out from under her, and she slid to the ground.

"Where are all the mechanics when you need them?" she shouted skyward as she sat in the dirt in disgust. She leaned back against the side of the fuselage to catch her breath. In the distance she could hear the growing sound of a motor. She scrambled to her feet and thrashed her way through the weeds and brush that bordered the field and onto the dirt road. Through the thinning fog, she could see an oncoming truck lumbering down the middle of the road toward her. She waved her arms frantically, hoping the driver would stop and lend a hand. Instead, the driver honked and roared past. The truck missed her by only inches and raised a thick cloud of dirt and dust. Bits of gravel pelted her as the vehicle sped by.

"Ouch." She waved her arms and coughed at the choking dust. "Thank you very much, you son-of-a." Kit spit and fanned the dirt away from her face. The truck was well down the road when she heard it skid to a stop. "I hope you had a flat," she said as she brushed off her clothes.

The truck reappeared from the other direction, slowing as it approached.

"Were you needing something?" a woman asked as she leaned out the window warily.

"I didn't need a dirt shower, that's for sure," Kit replied glibly.

"Sorry, but you were in the road, you know. You're lucky I didn't hit you." The woman seemed confident she shared no responsibility for the near accident. "Perhaps you should keep to the side of the road next time."

"I was in the middle of the road hoping you would stop, not run over me."

"Why would I want to do that? I don't know you. We've been warned to stay on the alert for German spies and downed pilots."

"I am not a spy."

"How do I know that?"

"I'm a pilot for our side."

"And who would that be?" asked another woman as she leaned over the driver. "You can't fool us. We know there are no women pilots in the RAF. And you don't sound British."

Before Kit could explain, she noticed the barrel of a shotgun inching its way out the driver's window.

201

"Wait a minute," she said, raising her hands over her head. "Don't shoot. I can explain. I'm an American working for the ATA."

"Who is the ATA?" the driver demanded, thrusting the barrel further out the window.

"The Air Transport Auxiliary. We deliver airplanes to the air bases. I had to make an emergency landing in that field because of the fog." Kit pointed.

"I don't see anything," the passenger said, looking in that direction.

"On the other side of the hedge row," Kit said, still holding her arms up.

"There's no aerodrome out here," the driver grumbled.

"I was on my way back from Ireland when I ran into fog. Can I put my arms down? My fingers are going numb," Kit asked, resting her hands on the top of her head.

"You wouldn't have a pistol under that jacket, would you?" the driver asked, raising the gun to her shoulder.

"No. I'll unzip and show you." Kit used two fingers to unzip her jacket and open it. "See. No pistol. Do you want to see my ID?"

"No. That could be false."

"I do have a comb in my pocket. Do you want to see that?" Kit dipped her fingers into her breast pocket and pulled out a small black comb. "See? American."

The two women whispered for a moment then climbed out of the truck, the driver still holding the shotgun on Kit. The driver was a tall woman in her fifties with short, curly gray hair. She had the weathered face of a woman who worked hard for a living, and from her tanned complexion, dirty trousers and faded jacket, Kit suspected she worked outdoors. The other woman was also in her fifties and wore a simple cotton dress and coat with two buttons missing. She had long brown hair held back on either side by barrettes. Neither woman wore makeup. The truck smelled of animal manure. They whispered again then squared their shoulders demandingly.

"Your knickers, we want to see them," the passenger said.

"What?" Kit asked suspiciously.

"That's right," the driver added, waving the gun at her. "We want to see your knickers."

"You want to see my underwear?" Kit laughed. "I don't think so."

"We heard German spies wear their own undergarments. We want to see the label on your knickers." The two women stood together, looking brave and stoic at their request. Kit had the feeling they were harmless, but the driver also had a twelve-gauge shotgun aimed at her head, and for all Kit knew, she was a crack shot. They also might be the only people she would find to help turn the airplane around.

"You want me to take my clothes off so you can see my underwear?" Kit asked through a frown.

"Yes," they said in unison.

"Okay. What the heck?" Kit took off her jacket and hung it over a nearby bush. She unzipped her flight suit and peeled it off her shoulders, letting it drop to her ankles. She raised the hem of her sweater and revealed her white underpants. "Here they are."

"Where's the label?" the driver demanded.

Kit shuffled her feet as she turned to the side then rolled down the hem to reveal a label.

"See. Made in the U.S.A." she stated, holding the label out for them to see. "I bought them at Pulman's Department Store in Kansas City." The two women leaned in to see, keeping a discreet distance.

"Those are silk," the passenger exclaimed.

"Yes, and Joe DiMaggio plays for the Yankees and the state flower of Kansas is a sunflower. Can I get dressed now?" Kit pulled her sweater down over her panties. She was cold and tired of being on display for these women's pleasure.

"Where's Kansas?" the driver asked.

"Oh, for Pete's sake." Kit pulled up her flight suit in spite of the gun barrel. "It's in the middle of the United States."

"What's the capital?" the passenger asked, still scrutinizing Kit's every move.

"Would you know the difference?" she asked as she finished getting dressed.

"Florence asked you what's the capital?" The driver slowly raised the shotgun to her shoulder and took aim.

Kit stopped her zipper halfway up and stared at the woman. "Topeka."

"I thought it was Little Rock," Florence said, frowning at the other woman.

"Little Rock is the capital of Arkansas," Kit corrected diplomatically.

"Oh, that's right." Florence smiled. "Kansas is Topeka. Volume eleven."

"What is volume eleven?"

"Florence reads the Britannica. She's on volume sixteen, letter *P*," the driver said.

"The Encyclopedia Britannica?" Kit asked in amazement. She didn't mean to sound surprised, but she wasn't sure either of these women knew how to read at all, much less that they were educated.

"There isn't much else to do on a pig farm," Florence replied. "Our radio is broken, and it's too far to go to town very often."

"How far is town?"

"About thirty minutes that way," the driver said, using the barrel of the gun to point.

"We were on our way home from market," Florence said. "Sold twelve pigs."

"That's what I smell," Kit joked, trying to be sociable so the gun-toting woman would lower her weapon.

"I told you it still smells, Edie," Florence snapped, smacking the taller woman across the arm. "Next time you'll listen to me."

"I swept it out before we left town, I did."

"You can't get that stench out with a broom. You've got to use soap and water." Florence scowled angrily. "Next time I'm going to walk home if you don't clean it better. You promised I wouldn't smell it."

"We had a dozen pigs in the back. What do you expect?"

Florence stared darts at her, her hands on her hips defiantly. Edie was well over six-feet tall and a square-shouldered woman with a twelve-gauge shotgun in her hand, but she was completely intimidated by Florence's demands and her angry glare.

"All right. I'll wash it out next time," Edie said, grumbling her displeasure.

"If she can smell it over there, I don't know why you can't smell it sitting right in front of it," Florence continued.

"All right," Edie shouted, glaring back at her. "I'll wash it."

"And quit waving that bloody shotgun around. You're going to shoot yourself in the foot. She's no German spy. You've been listening to too many tales 'round the pub." Florence grabbed the end of the barrel and tilted the gun down. It was the first time since the truck roared by that Kit felt relieved.

"If she isn't a spy, what's she doing standing in the middle of the road?" Edie said.

"She told you, love. She's a pilot of some sort or other on her way home from Ireland."

"ATA ferry pilot," Kit said. "And I honestly did make an emergency landing in the field just beyond these bushes. Do you want to have a look?"

"Yes, I would," Florence said enthusiastically. "I'd love to see a real airplane up close. All we ever see are the ones roaring overhead. I've never seen a real RAF airplane before. Edie, go put that gun back in the truck, or you aren't coming," she ordered, tossing a decisive stare her way. Edie did as she was told. "I'm Florence Milford," she said, offering her hand to Kit with a wide smile.

"I'm Kit Anderson, Lieutenant Kit Anderson." Kit shook her hand, feeling the calluses on Florence's palm.

"How do you do, Lieutenant Anderson? The one with the gun is Edie Milford."

"Hello, Edie," Kit said, offering to shake her hand as well. Edie had a firm grip, one that could have easily bruised Kit's hand had she felt inclined.

"Hello," she said.

Kit led the way through the bushes to where she had left the airplane.

"Edie, will you look at that!" Florence exclaimed as she stepped through the hedge row. "An airplane. Just like she said. A real airplane." She circled it, running her hand along the wing and across the tail.

"It's not a Spitfire," Edie said gruffly. "The RAF uses Spitfires."

"It's a nineteen twenty-nine Gypsy Moth," Kit said, pointing to the RAF insignia on the side. "We still use them for trainers and to deliver cargo."

"Have you ever flown a Spitfire, Lieutenant?" Florence asked, stroking one of the smooth propeller blades.

"Yes, many times."

"Just Spitfires?" Edie asked, looking at the engine.

"We fly lots of airplanes. Hurricanes, Lancasters, Wellingtons, Mustangs."

"I remember now. I heard about ferry pilots. Women pilots are delivering airplanes fresh from the factories to our RAF boys," Florence said.

"I remember you said the only women in Great Britain to have any silk were those pilots," Edie said.

"Silk?" Kit asked.

"Your parachute, love," Florence explained.

"Oh, right."

"We women can't get any silk to make knickers or slips," she said.

"I can't get any silk either," Kit said. "It's the military who has it all."

"How many parachutes do you pilots need? Can't you use them more than once?"

"Yes, but the paratroopers use them too. They use more than we do."

"I've heard of women coming to blows over a pilot's parachute. One poor chap landed in a street in London and didn't have a scratch, not until the women in the neighborhood ran him over to get at his parachute."

"You don't need any silk, Florence," Edie said.

"I didn't say I did, now did I? I'm just saying, a little silk is nice every now and then, isn't it, Lieutenant?" Florence looked over at Kit for agreement.

"I suppose so," Kit said. She didn't sew, so she had no idea what she would do with silk anyway.

"What kind of help did you need, Lieutenant?" Edie asked.

"I need to push the back around so I can take off once the fog lifts." Kit pushed on the side of the airplane to demonstrate, but it didn't move.

"Stand back, Florence," Edie said, taking up a place next to Kit. Kit was hoping all three of them could work together to get the tail turned. She wasn't sure one more woman pushing would make that much difference.

"There's room for her on the other side of me," Kit said.

"I'll do it." Edie braced her shoulder against the fuselage. "Florence, you tell us when we've got it lined up." She began pushing before Kit was ready. Kit quickly added her muscle, but the airplane had already begun to move, plowing the rear skid through the soft dirt. Edie's face reddened as she marched forward, swinging the airplane into line.

"Right there, love," Florence said, waving her arms. Edie stopped pushing. Kit immediately felt the weight of the plane sink into the plowed ground.

"You'll have to race your engine to get over those trees," Edie said, pointing to the far end of the field just visible through the thinning fog.

"How did you do that?" Kit asked, amazed at her super-human strength.

"Do what? You said you wanted it pushed around, didn't you?"

"Yes, but . . ."

"Strong, isn't she?" Florence said with a proud smile.

"Strong isn't the word for it."

"Edie can lift a bale of hay and chuck it over a fence."

"I don't doubt it. Your sister is one strong woman," Kit acknowledged.

"She isn't my sister."

"I'm sorry. I just assumed you were sisters."

"No. We aren't related."

"Coincidence then?" Kit suggested.

"What? That we both have the same last name?" Edie asked defensively.

"Well, yes." Kit felt she had said something wrong. "Two women named Milford would make you suspect you're related somehow."

"I'm going to tell her," Florence said to Edie.

"It's none of her business," Edie said suspiciously.

"I don't care. I'm going to tell her anyway."

"Tell me what?" Kit asked.

"My last name is actually Vorice, Florence Vorice."

"Then why Milford?"

"That's what people do, isn't it?" Florence said with a soft smile. "When they're married." She looked over at Edie lovingly.

"You and Edie?"

"That's right. Florence and I," Edie said, coming to stand beside her wife. She wrapped an arm around Florence's shoulder protectively.

"We know it isn't legal. But it is to us," Florence said, leaning against Edie.

Kit pulled a slow but proud smile that they would include her in their news.

"When did you get married?" she asked.

"October fourth, it'll be twenty-eight years," Florence replied.

"Wow, twenty-eight years. That's wonderful."

"It would have been thirty years, but she turned me down the first four times I asked," Edie said, smiling down at her. Florence blushed and giggled.

"She just wouldn't take no for an answer. She kept asking me until she wore me down." Florence brushed a stray leaf from Edie's jacket. "Way out here, no one cares. We don't bother anyone, and they don't bother us. We go about our business, raising pigs and chickens. We pay our bills, don't break the law, and they leave us alone."

"Thank you. I'm honored that you told me," Kit said.

"Then you don't mind?"

Kit smiled at Florence then hugged her warmly.

"Not in the least. If you ever come to Alderbrook, look me up. I'll show you some big airplanes."

"We don't get very far from home. The animals won't feed themselves," Edie said. "But thank you, Lieutenant."

"Thank you for helping me with the airplane. I couldn't have turned it by myself." Kit held back, not sure how Edie would accept a hug.

"Do you need us to help with anything else?"

"Actually, if you would sit in the cockpit and adjust the throttle when I spin the prop, it would be very helpful. Otherwise, I'll be chasing the plane across the field. There are no brakes, and I don't have anything to tie it down."

"Why don't you sit in the cockpit and I'll spin the prop?" Edie said.

"It's too dangerous. I can't ask you to do that. Once the engine catches, that propeller has quite a kick. It'll slice your arm off."

"I don't plan on putting me arm in the way. Besides, when would I ever get to say I started an airplane for the RAF?" A twinkle came to Edie's eye. "It looks like the fog is moving out. You better get going if you want to get back before dark."

Kit scanned the field for debris then spun the propeller to prime the starter before showing Edie what to do. Like a kid with a new toy, Edie watched and listened intently at the prospect of actually starting the Moth. Kit climbed on the wing and checked the controls. She reached in the cockpit and pulled out her parachute, ready to strap it on for her flight home. Florence was watching her every move, fascinated by the goings on. Kit hesitated a moment then jumped down from the wing. She ran over to Florence and pressed the parachute against her chest.

"An anniversary present," Kit said then kissed Florence's cheek.

"Oh, Lieutenant," Florence stammered, suddenly speechless.

"Great for knickers," she said, winking at her.

"Thank you," Florence whispered, barely able to talk. She looked over at Edie, tears filling her eyes as she hugged the parachute pack.

"Don't you need that, Lieutenant?" Edie asked with concern.

"I can get another one."

"How about this flight?"

"I'll keep it low and slow." She grinned.

"We don't want you to get hurt," Edie said, her gruff exterior giving way to her tender side.

"I'll be fine."

"You take care of yourself, Lieutenant," Florence said, stroking her precious silk parachute. "Come visit us again."

"I'd like that."

"Next time Florence will cook you some bacon and eggs, fresh from our farm," Edie said proudly. Kit went to shake Edie's hand but reached up and gave the big woman a hug instead. Edie blushed but seemed happy to accept it.

"Stand back, Florence," Kit said as she climbed in the cockpit and strapped herself in. "Okay, Edie. Contact."

Edie gave the prop a spin, sending a plume of smoke belching out the side of the engine. She spun it again. This time it caught, whipping the propeller and chugging into action. She went to stand by Florence, both of them squinting at the cloud of dust the propeller raised. Kit saluted and nudged the throttle forward, starting the Moth across the field. She bounced along the field and eased into the sky as Edie and Florence watched and waved. She rocked her wings and waved before banking to the east and the trip home.

Chapter 19

Kit knew she was late as she circled Alderbrook for her approach. Hours late. It had been a harrowing flight, and she was glad to be within sight of the airfield. If it had been one of her girls who had taken six hours more than usual to complete a mission, she would be pacing the field, grinding her teeth and thinking the worst. As she circled, awaiting the balloons to be lowered, she could see three women standing at the end of the runway, all of them waving at her. It was Lovie, Red and Emily. Her heart quickened at the thought that Emily had been waiting for her return. Kit hoped she hadn't caused worry, but knowing Emily was there, watching her turn for home, was a relief. Kit's scarf flagged out the side of the cockpit as she rolled down the runway toward the women.

"Hello," Emily said, trotting up to the plane. She looked pale and frightened but relieved to see Kit.

"Hi," Kit said, cutting the engine and pulling her flight cap from her head. She pulled herself onto the back of the seat and took a deep breath, glad to be on the ground.

"Are you all right, Lieutenant?" Emily asked cautiously.

"Yeah, I am now." She grinned down at Emily. "I ran into a little fog over the coast."

"We heard. I was worried."

"Nice landing," Red said. "See, Emily? That's how you make a landing. Not bouncing all over the place." Red bobbed her head like a bobble-head doggy in a window.

"Taking your sweet time, Lieutenant?" Lovie said.

Kit shrugged, not wanting to worry Emily needlessly.

"Was the fog heavy?" Emily asked.

"Not too bad." Kit forced a smile, but it was clear she'd had a difficult flight. She swung her legs over the side and stood on the wing, collecting her flight bag. She hopped down and unzipped her flight jacket.

"Willie said a fog bank choked down every airfield west of the Wales border. He said four bombers returning to Dublin crashed off the coast. They couldn't see to land and ran out of fuel," Emily said.

"Emily was concerned when she heard you left Dublin seven hours ago. You should have been back hours ago," Lovie said. "I told her you'd be all right. You aren't a flunky like the rest of us. If you get into a jam you can always parachute out to safety. You've done it before. I told her you were a bonafide member of the silkworm club several times over."

"Is that true, Lieutenant? Have you actually parachuted out of an airplane?" Emily asked, holding her breath.

"Yes, but there's nothing to it," Kit said, tossing a caustic glance at Lovie for worrying Emily like that. "Everyone learns to parachute out of a plane during training."

"Where's your parachute?" Red asked. "Did you leave it in the cockpit?"

"Guess I forgot it," Kit said. "Did everyone get back from Thriggle all right?"

"Yes, everybody got back. Kit, where's your chute?" Red said critically, looking in the cockpit.

"Don't worry about it."

"Aren't you supposed to wear a parachute on every mission?" Emily asked.

"Sometimes."

"What the hell is this sometimes stuff?" Red said, looking in the other seat. "Where is it?"

"I lost it, all right?" Kit replied angrily.

"Kit?" Lovie started, but Kit met her with a fierce stare as well.

"It's no big deal," she said, hoping to end the questions.

"Well, I'm glad you are on the ground and not flying around in that fog," Emily said, touching Kit's arm affectionately. "Parachute or not, you shouldn't fly when the weather is bad."

"We do it all the time," Kit said. She didn't want Emily to worry, but the thought of her concern gave Kit a warm feeling.

"We do?" Lovie asked.

"I have to check in with flight command then I need to talk with you about your PT-six transfer forms," Kit said, taking Emily by the arm. "You two complete your log entries and turn your chutes in for repacking, then you can leave," she said to Lovie and Red, ignoring their curious stares.

"What about our plans to have a drink at Brindy's?" Lovie called. "The whole squadron is coming. Remember?"

"Have a good time," Kit replied without looking back.

"You, too," Red said through a snicker.

Kit checked in then scribbled something in her log book while Emily sat quietly waiting, looking both nervous and apprehensive.

"Are you finished for the day?" Kit asked, signing her log.

"Yes, but what is wrong with my PT-six forms?" Emily asked, coming to the desk. "Do I need to redo them?"

"Nothing," she said, closing her log book and sliding it into the desk drawer.

"But you said . . ."

"They're fine." Kit smiled up at her. "How would you like to go for a ride with me?"

"A ride to where?"

"Does it matter?" Their gazes met across the desk.

"No. It doesn't matter at all," she said softly.

Kit held the door for her then led the way to the motorcycle parked behind the ready room. She stomped the starter then waited for Emily to climb on behind her.

"Hold on," she said.

"You can count on it," Emily whispered and wrapped her arms around Kit, pressing her body against her back.

Kit maneuvered between the buildings and out onto the road. She headed through town but didn't turn at the stone bridge that led to Bellhurst. Instead, she roared down the road, leaving the airfield and Alderbrook behind them. Emily held fast to Kit as they floated over hills and around the tree-lined back roads of Buckinghamshire County. For over an hour they cruised through villages and past farms in a never-ending patchwork of plowed fields, green meadows and thick forests. The road changed from packed dirt to pavement and back again. Emily seemed content to hold on and let the wind and road carry them away. Kit didn't have to make polite conversation. She didn't have to worry someone would see the way her eyes followed Emily's every move. Emily's arms were around her, and it was heaven.

Kit slowed at an intersection then roared around the corner. She pulled to a stop in front of a white two-story building in need of painting. Two bicycles, one car and a horse tied to a tree were in the narrow graveled area along the front. She turned off the engine and waited for Emily to climb off before raising the bike onto the kickstand.

"Where are we?" Emily asked, brushing her hands through her wind-whipped hair.

"Stewart's Pub and Inn," Kit said, swinging her leg over and removing her goggles. "I found it a couple months ago when I was hitching a ride home from Wadley airfield. Would you like a drink or a cup of tea? They have soup and something they call wiggle. I have no idea what it is. Some kind of meat with potatoes and gravy."

"I'd love something to drink."

Kit locked her arm through Emily's and led the way inside. The door entered directly into the pub, a narrow room that ran across the front of the building. The polished wooden bar took up much of the room, leaving a single row of small tables along the windows, each with two chairs. The bartender and four male customers turned in unison, giving a critical stare as the two women walked in and took a table. The men seemed to approve, or at least were disinterested and turned back to their glasses of ale. Kit ordered two pints, asking the bartender which he recommended. That seemed to please him, and he brought them a basket of thin crackers along with the drinks.

"Here's to Grandfather's motorcycle," Emily said, holding her glass up. She clinked their glasses then took a long drink, leaving a foam moustache on her upper lip. Kit chuckled and dabbed it off with the napkin.

"Here's to your grandmother's letting me use it." Kit clinked again and took another drink.

"I heard her tell Nigel she forgot it was even out there. She never goes in the carriage house. I think she was pleased you could get some good from it."

"Do you want to learn to drive it?"

"No. You drive it. I'll ride on the back."

"If you can ride a bicycle you can drive a motorcycle."

"No, thank you." Emily laughed. "You seem to have forgotten my past troubles with learning new skills. I think it would be better for all concerned if I left that to you."

Kit discreetly allowed one finger to touch Emily's hand across the table.

"Would you like some wiggle?"

Kit didn't mean it suggestively, but Emily instantly blushed.

"Dinner," Kit said, laughing behind her glass of ale.

"No, thank you. I'm not very hungry." She lowered her eyes while the blush subsided.

"Would I make you blush again if I said I'm hungry?" Kit whispered.

Emily diverted her gaze out the window as a second blush raced over her face.

"Should we be heading back?" Emily asked, noticing the fading sunlight. "It'll be dark soon."

"If we take long enough to finish our drink, we won't be able to get home tonight. We'll have to stay. I can't ride with the headlight on since I haven't put a damper on it yet."

"Could we have two more?" Emily called to the bartender then smiled shyly.

"I definitely like your style, Miss Mills. Now, tell me how you got to be a school teacher."

"You don't want to hear that," Emily said as the bartender placed two more glasses on the table. "It's a very dull story. I'd much rather hear about you. Are you a pilot back in the United States?"

"Yes. I'm partner in a regional airline company. We fly special cargo and VIPs from Chicago to St. Louis and Kansas City."

"Why are you here then?"

"I wanted to help. It was a hard sell, but I convinced my partners to let me have eighteen months off. Kind of a leave of absence."

"So you came to England to join the ATA."

"That's right."

"Is it difficult being a squadron leader?"

"It isn't difficult necessarily. It's just hard to send the girls off not knowing what they are flying into. Bad weather, damaged airplanes, inadequate maintenance. You name it, I worry about it."

"But it isn't all your responsibility. You aren't the only flight lieutenant or the only squadron leader in the ATA," Emily said, folding her hand over Kit's sympathetically. "All you have to do is the best you can. The rest is left to the winds." Her words were gentle and caring.

"I worry about that too," Kit joked. "Wind off the Irish Sea can be a devil on an open cockpit plane."

Emily looked out the window at the last glimpses of twilight.

"I think you got your wish. I don't think there's enough light for us to get back to town," she said, her eyes meeting Kit's.

Kit went to the bar and paid the bartender for a room, explaining their predicament, such as it was, and how they could only afford one room on their salaries. She laid on a healthy helping of regret for ignoring the oncoming darkness. Once upstairs, Kit led the way down the narrow, darkened hall to the last room on the right. The skeleton key unlocked a door hung on squeaky hinges. Inside they found a bed, somewhere between a twin and a double, and a short-legged wooden chair next to a tiny table. There was no dresser, only a series of hooks across the back of the door. The small sink in the corner dripped quietly. A chamber pot was discreetly hidden under the sink, covered with a piece of white lace tablecloth.

Kit dropped the key on the table and draped her jacket over the chair. She opened the window to allow the chilly evening breezes to flood the stuffy room. She leaned out and took a deep breath.

"It isn't Buckingham Palace, but I think it'll be all right," Kit said turning back to Emily. She was standing at the corner of the bed clutching the corner post, looking suddenly frightened and pale. "What's the matter?" she asked, coming to her. "Are you worried someone will know we are here?"

"I'm not frightened about that."

"What is it, sweetheart? What's wrong?" Kit took her face in her hands and kissed her. "I thought this is what you wanted." Kit folded her arms around her gently.

"I so wanted to be in your arms again, but now . . ." Emily said as her voice cracked.

"Oh, baby, are you going to cry?"

"I'm sorry. I can't help it," Emily said as tears began to roll down her cheeks.

"If you have changed your mind just tell me." Kit held her in her arms and rocked her as she cried. "I want you to be honest with me and yourself. If this isn't right for you, just tell me."

"Kit, I do want this. I do. With all my heart. It's just . . ." Emily started, but the tears got in the way.

"It's just what?"

Emily looked up at her desperately then pulled away and ran to the door. She fumbled with the doorknob, struggling to get it open through her tears. Kit held her hand against the door to keep it closed and pulled Emily around, pinning her against the door.

"Not tonight, Emily," Kit demanded. "Tonight you're going to tell me what's wrong? What have I done?"

"I'm ashamed," Emily managed to say between the sobs. "I'm sorry."

"Ashamed of what we did?" Kit hated to ask it, but she had to know. She had heard this apology before, usually with heart-breaking results.

"Ashamed of me." Emily slowly rolled her eyes up to meet Kit's. "I don't know what I'm supposed to do. I don't know what is expected of me."

"Oh, sweetheart," Kit whispered, taking her in her arms. "I don't expect anything of you."

Emily looked over at the bed and swallowed nervously.

"I don't want to disappoint you," she said, remaining huddled in Kit's embrace.

"You couldn't. Believe me, you could never disappoint me." She kissed Emily's tear-stained lips. Emily pressed herself into the kiss without reservation. Kit reached behind her and snapped off the light. The sapphire-hued light from the window was all that separated them from total darkness.

"Will you teach me what to do?" Emily asked softly.

"I won't need to," she said, stroking Emily's back. "You are a sensuous, caring woman. You'll know what to do."

Emily rested her head on Kit's shoulder.

"If I do something wrong, will you forgive me?" she asked.

"If you do something wrong, I'll do what any teacher would do. I'll make you do it over and over until you do it right," Kit said through a wicked little grin.

"I should pay very close attention then," Emily replied as she unbuttoned Kit's blouse. She released the last button and pulled the blouse free from Kit's trousers. She unbuckled Kit's belt and slowly lowered the zipper, making it last as long as possible. She pulled the blouse from Kit's shoulders and let it fall to the floor. Emily placed her fingertips on Kit's bra straps, tracing the outline of the lace. Emily's touch sent a shock wave surging through Kit, making her shudder and shiver. "How am I doing so far?" Emily whispered then nibbled at Kit's chin.

"Just fine. I knew this was a subject you could handle."

Kit had unbuttoned the awkward coveralls that hid Emily's delicate figure and peeled them over her shoulders. Last night Emily's naked body had been a surprise, albeit a pleasant one. But tonight, in the faint light from the window, her bra and pantied body was even more seductive. It was all Kit could do not to throw her on the bed, rip away the lace that covered her dark patch and plunge into her honey path. She unhooked Emily's bra and peeled the straps away as she painted soft kisses down her neck. Emily moaned, the kisses seeming to distract her from what she was doing.

"That feels so wonderful," she whispered, her hands clutching at the waistband of Kit's trousers.

"And this?" Kit moved to the other side and drew her tongue down Emily's neck onto her shoulder.

"Even better," she said breathlessly.

Kit's trousers fell to her feet, and she stepped out of them as she maneuvered Emily onto the bed. Emily clung to her, pulling Kit down on top of her. Kit pushed Emily's pink panties down over her hips, barely freeing them from her legs before stroking her soft belly in a determined journey down to her thick patch of hair.

Emily had struggled to pull Kit's panties down over one side of her bottom then the other, groaning and gasping as Kit moved down her body. Finally Kit's stubborn panties were freed and dropped to the floor. Emily wrapped her legs around Kit. Kit pressed herself against Emily, rhythmically moving their mounds over each other until they both glistened with a sweet sweat.

Kit's fingers danced tantalizingly close but did not enter Emily's moistness. Emily's nails dug into Kit's back. Her soft moans became demanding gasps as her body rose to Kit's teasing touch.

"Please," she gasped. "Hurry."

"Wait, sweetheart," Kit said gently, kissing her softly. "Be patient."

"I can't." Emily writhed on the bed, pulling Kit's hand tighter to her need.

"Yes, you can," she whispered. "And it will be worth the wait." Kit took one of Emily's nipples in her mouth, sucking at the tiny hardened spear. Emily covered her face with the pillow as Kit sucked and tweaked at it with her tongue. As Kit moved to the other nipple, Emily wrapped both arms around the pillow, but she couldn't muffle her gasps and shrieks.

"Wait," Emily said, her breaths coming only in short gasps. "I can't breathe."

Kit pulled the pillow away and grinned down at her.

"You don't really want me to stop now, do you?" she said coyly, rolling Emily's nipple between her fingers.

"No," she sighed, folding her arms over her head as she smiled up at Kit.

Kit wrapped her arms around Emily and rolled them over. She cupped her hands at Emily's soft bottom and pulled her against her. Emily straddled Kit's hips, massaging herself against Kit's mound. Kit could feel her own passion growing, stinging and pulsing through her core, but this was Emily's moment. She didn't dare demand what Emily wasn't yet ready to give her.

"Slide up here," Kit whispered, guiding her forward. She stroked Emily's thighs as she crawled forward. Emily placed her hands on the wall behind the bed and lowered herself to Kit's kiss, her body quivering as Kit's mouth took her in. Emily's once rigid body melted against her. Kit's tongue skirted the shores of her opening, stroking and dabbing at her tender folds.

Emily released a guttural sound and leaned her head against the wall. A trail of sweat rolled down her belly and mixed with the hot juices between her legs.

"Whatever it is you are doing, don't stop," Emily groaned. "Don't stop."

Just as Emily seemed to relax into the rhythm of Kit's exploration, she slipped her tongue inside, drawing it deep then up to the tip of her swollen nub. Emily shuddered and closed her legs around Kit's head. Slow flicks. Fast thrusts. Kit knew the hot pain and deep convulsions Emily must be experiencing. Emily moved over Kit's tongue as if she knew exactly what she wanted.

"Oh, yes. Oh God, yes," Emily cried out. She tapped her forehead against the wall with each deep probe of Kit's tongue. Her legs twitched and jerked. She pushed herself off the wall as if a tremendous volcano was about to erupt somewhere deep inside. Kit could feel Emily's climax start to grow and slowly move up her body like a tidal wave. Kit increased her pace, holding Emily's hips against her mouth as she thrust deeper, the hot nectar of Emily's flower sweet on her tongue.

Emily opened her mouth as if to scream, but nothing came out, only muffled inaudible gasps as Kit felt her flower close around her tongue, soft and strong. Emily collapsed across the bed, gulping for breath. Kit pulled her close, watching as Emily's face changed from strained ecstasy to a satisfied contentment. Emily snuggled against her.

"I've never felt anything like that," Emily whispered, drawing her leg up to expose her moist valley to Kit's thigh.

Kit cupped her hand over the last faint throbs of Emily's orgasm.

"How can I ever give you that kind of pleasure?" Emily asked tenderly.

"Just kiss me," Kit whispered, folding her arms around Emily as their lips met.

Emily slipped her knee between Kit's thighs. She was warm, moist and ready. Emily may have never touched another woman before, but it seemed instinctive as she tenderly reached for Kit's womanhood. She pressed her hand over the thick hair as if searching for the spot that would ignite Kit's passion.

"Easy, sweetheart," Kit said. "Two fingers." She guided Emily's hand to the folds that guarded her entry. "Gently at first." She showed her, holding her in her arms as Emily learned the art of a delicate touch. With tender strokes, Emily petted Kit's softness until she began to moan and move beneath her. "Yes, baby. Just like that." Kit sighed. "Just exactly like that."

Emily alternated between long tender strokes and gentle yet inquisitive ones. Kit drew her legs apart as Emily's touch lit the candle of her pleasure. Kit bit down on her lip to keep from crying out as the first tremor raced through her.

"Don't stop, baby. Don't stop."

Emily continued, alternating soft and persistent strokes into Kit's warm cavern.

"Harder, my love," Kit whispered through a sigh. "Touch me harder."

"Show me," Emily whispered, kissing the soft skin between her breasts.

Kit covered Emily's hand with her own and moved against it. Emily took up the newer and harder pace. Kit groaned and arched her back, straining against the bed. She grabbed the headboard and stiffened.

"Yes, baby. Yes," Kit urged through gritted teeth. She could feel Emily shifting on the bed and the rhythm faltering. "Don't stop." Kit hadn't felt another woman's touch in over a year, and she wanted this. She needed it. And she wasn't afraid to say so. "Harder."

"Sweetheart," Emily cooed, kissing her erect nipple. Kit heard the concerned hesitation in Emily's voice but she couldn't stop. She grabbed Emily's hand and pressed it against her, directing the pace as sweat poured down her face. Emily pulled her leg from under Kit's, but with it she pulled her hand. Kit rolled to her, anxious for more as she reached an explosive climax. She screamed, her body heaving a great shudder, her valley throbbing uncontrollably. With a loud thump, Emily rolled onto the floor, pulling Kit down on top of her. Kit couldn't stop their fall as she was still feeling the waves of her orgasm. She groaned, trying to catch herself, but it was no use. Emily still had her hand hooked inside her.

"Ouch," Emily squealed, Kit's full weight dropping on her.

"Oh, God. Are you all right?" Kit said, pulling Emily's hand free and rolling off. For a moment there was stunned silence, but the calamity of the moment was too much to ignore. They both began laughing, quietly at first, then louder and louder as they fell into each other's arms.

"What's going on in there?" a man shouted, knocking at the door. "What are you doing? This is no rugby field, it ain't."

"Sorry," Kit said, covering Emily's giggle with her hand. "I tripped over the corner of the bed. Room's awfully small, you know." Emily giggled again.

"Well, turn on the bleeding light," he replied and walked away, his footsteps disappearing down the hall.

Kit and Emily lay on the floor next to the bed, holding their breath until the footsteps were gone, then they smiled at each other.

"That's my little tea bag," Kit mused, holding on to Emily. "Dangerous even in bed."

"Can we do it again?" Emily whispered.

"Absolutely."

Chapter 20

Kit sat on the window sill hugging her knees and watching Emily sleep as the first lavender glow of light met the dawn. When Emily stirred, Kit came to her, kissing her forehead.

"Good morning," Emily said as she stretched then pulled Kit against her.

"Good morning, my love." Kit swept the hair from Emily's face.

"What time is it?"

"Early," Kit whispered. "I didn't want to wake you, but we need to start back soon."

"Kiss me awake," Emily said, locking her hands behind Kit's neck.

Kit obliged, kissing her softly then again passionately.

"I wish we could stay here all day and all night and all day again." Emily sighed dreamily. "Just you and me and our tiny bed."

"So do I, but we can't. I have to be at the airfield at seven this morning. And you have a job too."

"I want a new job," Emily teased, playing with the curls over Kit's ears. "I want to be your personal driver. I want to drive you wherever you need to go." She smiled coyly.

"I like the idea, but I'd never get anything done. We'd spend all our time in the backseat of the car."

"I know." Emily winked, pulling Kit down on top of her and locking a leg over her. Kit nuzzled her neck, making snorting noises as she rolled them back and forth on the bed. Emily giggled and wiggled beneath her. Kit allowed them a few minutes of snuggling before swatting Emily on the bottom and pulling her out of bed.

Emily gulped down a cup of coffee before climbing on the back of the motorcycle for the ride back to Alderbrook. The closer they got to Digby Lane and home, the tighter Emily clung to Kit. She rode the whole way with her head against Kit's back. Kit pulled up to the side door of the big house and let Emily off. She then hurried to the cottage to change and wash before waiting by the motorcycle for Emily to finish getting ready. As Emily rushed out and climbed back on for the trip to the airfield, they both saw the curtain in Lillian's bedroom part.

"Did she say anything?" Kit asked.

"She tried. Let's go." Emily held on as Kit roared down the drive.

If word of their nights together got out, Kit knew Emily would be subject to a whole new world of questions and suspicions. Unless they planned on weaving an elaborate web of lies and half-truths, the road they had started would have to be kept private. Kit didn't want Emily to get hurt. Kit had been through that before, and she didn't wish those kinds of stares and malicious remarks on anyone. Kit had developed the crust to protect herself from the moral bigots and hypocrites. Emily hadn't been exposed to it yet.

Kit pulled up to the motor pool.

"Thanks for the ride, Lieutenant," Emily said as if she too realized they needed to keep up a professional appearance.

"You're welcome, Miss Mills," Kit said in her best business voice. Then in a quiet voice she added. "I had a wonderful time last night."

"So did I." Emily's hand slid across Kit's shoulder as she climbed off.

"Perhaps we could have tea later in the ready room."

"Perhaps," Emily said with a soft smile. "But I'd rather enjoy a long, luscious kiss."

"That would definitely be better than tea." Kit pulled away then looked back and winked.

"Fly safe, Lieutenant."

Kit was the last pilot to enter the ready room and felt every pair of eyes follow her through the door.

"Good morning, ladies," she said cheerfully.

"You may not think so," Patty mumbled as she brushed the mud from her flight boots.

"Where were you last night?" Lovie asked quietly.

"Who wants to know?" Kit said, thumbing through the day's assignment sheets and the weather report.

"Everyone from Griggs to the field commander," Red said, nodding out the window toward the flight command office.

"What are you talking about?"

"Did you forget the monthly flight command meeting last night?" Lovie whispered.

Kit felt the color drain from her face.

"Oh, shit," she muttered, looking out the window at Commander Griggs heading toward the ready room with determined strides.

"Make up something good because she is one mad woman," Red said.

"Lieutenant Anderson," Griggs snarled, stepping inside. Her eyes were black daggers and her jaw muscles were pulsing as she slammed the door. "Where were you last night? We sent an aide to your home. We scoured the countryside in every café and pub within thirty miles. Admiral Foster was ready to have you declared AWOL." She stood toe to toe with Kit, her venom so hot, every woman in the room could feel it. "Last night's meeting was important. I told you that. The meeting was for the Admiral's staff to hear our recommendations on pilot training, squadron assignments and pilot salaries. Where in the hell were you?" Griggs didn't seem to care every pilot in the room was watching her dress Kit down for her oversight. "You better have a damn good reason." She glowered at Kit, waiting for her reply.

"I was . . ." Kit started, looking around the room at her pilots, each of them anxious to hear what she had to say. "I was out of town," she stammered.

"Out of town doing what?" Griggs demanded loudly. "I expect a full explanation and I want it right now, Lieutenant."

Kit looked over at Red and Lovie. Both lowered their eyes as if to say they knew exactly what she was doing.

"I was out of town taking a little R&R," she said, pulling herself up proudly. "I haven't taken a night off since I got here over a year ago. So last night I took one. And if you want to know why, I'll tell you. Yesterday I flew a ramshackle piece of shit airplane into a fog bank over the coast of Wales and instead of bailing out and dumping the damn thing in the drink, I put it down in a field. Two hours later, the fog lifted and I took off. I made it as far as Darnell Heath before the fog closed in again. Have you ever flown over Darnell Heath, Commander? There isn't one field long enough or flat enough to hold an airplane. I flew through two hours of fog so thick I couldn't see the propeller. I flew around in circles so many times I thought I would fly up my own ass. By the time the fog cleared and I set down on this field, I didn't have enough fuel to move the pin on the gauge. And you know why? Because some fool mechanic told me I was carrying a load of replacement parts for the MAC unit, precious Spitfire parts. So I protected them with my life. They couldn't give me a decent airplane like a De Havilland or a twin-engine transport for the precious parts. They gave me an out-of-date Gypsy Moth with so many holes in the skin you could see through to the other side. I don't mind though. That's what they pay me to do. You know what makes me mad? The Goddamn parts I was supposed to be carrying were nothing more than hubcaps and seats. Hubcaps and seats, Commander. I risked my life to protect nothing." Kit met Griggs's determined stare with one of her own. "I don't give a damn about a meeting. I'm a pilot. With all due respect, Commander, you can keep the meetings and the paperwork. If you want me to deliver airplanes, fine. But don't ask me to give up my free time to sit in a stuffy room and tell an Admiral we need more pilots with better training and more money. If they don't already know that, then my telling them wouldn't make a damn bit of difference."

A dead silence fell over the room. Griggs stood staring at Kit with narrowed eyes, her lips drawn thin. No one said a word as they watched Kit stand up to Commander Griggs's authority.

"R&R, eh?" Griggs said.

"Yes, Commander."

"Gypsy Moth." Griggs snapped a look out the window, the Moth still sitting on the flight line.

"Yes, ma'am."

"Hubcaps?" she asked.

"And seats, ma'am."

"Damn," Griggs said then strode into her office without a backward glance. She closed the door, but before it latched she opened it again. "Next month, Lieutenant, try not to find fog right before the monthly meeting," she said, giving Kit a long look.

"Yes, Commander," Kit said and saluted.

Griggs closed her door and left Kit to her work. Nothing more was said about Kit missing the meeting. Lovie, Red and the others knew better than to tease Kit about the incident with Griggs. It was very unlike Kit to snap back at the Commander like that, especially in front of such a large audience. Kit's even temper had been tested to the limit, and everyone knew she was better left alone. She gave out assignments and wasted no time in getting flights in the air. Several of the pilots were sent to a small factory near Paddington to pick up Hurricanes. Kit was left to fly test flights for the MAC unit. She made several trips across the infield. Each time she allowed her eyes to drift toward the motor pool. The building was too far away to see who was standing outside, but just a glimpse in that direction brought a smile to her face.

"Log your entries, ladies. Then you can call it a day," Kit said, passing through the ready room on her way to Griggs's office. She knocked on the door and waited for permission to enter.

"Come," Griggs said.

"All flights have been completed, and all pilots are back, Commander." Kit set a daily report on her desk. "And, Commander . . ." she started but waited until Griggs looked up from her work.

"Yes, Lieutenant."

"I want to apologize. About this morning, I was way out of line. I'm sorry." Kit stood at attention.

"Accepted," Griggs said and went back to her paperwork. "Just don't make a habit of it."

"Thank you, Commander," Kit said and saluted then turned to leave.

"Lieutenant?" Griggs said without looking up. "You still haven't turned in your contract renewal. Can I expect it within the week?"

"I don't know."

"Anything I can do to help?" Griggs asked, looking up.

"No, ma'am. It's something I have to decide for myself. But thanks for the offer." Kit closed the door. She felt the growing pressure about her renewal. She had agreed to spend eighteen months in England, working for the ATA. After that, she would go home, return to her job and the company she helped form. That was her plan. If she stayed longer, she ran the risk of losing her company and her future. But now Emily was a new factor in that equation. They had agreed their fun and games would be just temporary, but that was becoming harder and harder to remember.

For the next three days, Kit was so busy she didn't have time for anything but ATA business. She was sent to Scotland to pick up a heavy bomber then flew a seaplane to Ireland. She spent the night waiting for a return flight. The blue skies over England meant the ferry pilots were flying a nearly continuous stream of missions. Emily was busy too, shuttling pilots to the factories to pick up new aircraft, chauffeuring officers to meetings and keeping the vehicles in the motor pool clean and ready for service. Late meetings, night instructions and overnight trips meant there wasn't time for even the shortest rendezvous.

Kit was walking one of her pilots to the MAC unit to discuss a test flight when she saw Emily heading toward her. They smiled at each other as they passed on the infield. Emily's eyes followed Kit so intently she didn't seem to notice a field marker and stumbled over it.

"Good afternoon, Miss Mills," Kit said politely, taking her arm to help her up. "Are you all right?"

"Hello, Lieutenant Anderson," Emily replied. "Yes, thank you. I'm fine."

"How is your grandmother?"

"She's well. She asked how you are."

"Tell her I'm sorry I've been too busy to stop by for a visit, but soon, I hope." Kit squeezed Emily's arm, telling her the visit she was talking about was meant for the two of them, not her grandmother.

"She'll be pleased, I'm sure." Emily smiled discreetly. "She has missed you."

"I've missed her too. I'm late," Kit said, checking her watch. "Have a nice day, Miss Mills."

"You too, Lieutenant."

Late that night, after Kit closed the carriage house door on the motorcycle and walked the path to the cottage, she waited in the darkened bedroom for a knock on her door. It was just after midnight when Emily's faint tapping brought Kit rushing to greet her.

"I missed you so terribly. It has been three whole days," Emily said, throwing herself into Kit's arms. "Hold me."

"I missed you more," Kit said, kissing her wildly. She drew Emily inside and closed the door with her foot. They fumbled their way to the bed, kissing and pulling at each other's clothing with desperate gasps. What started as soft sighs soon grew to shrieks and cries even thunder couldn't hide.

"I never knew this cottage could hold such magic," Emily said breathlessly, snuggling against Kit's exhausted body.

"And just think, you wanted me to move out," Kit said, spooning her body behind Emily's.

"I had a dream about you last night. We were drifting down the river in a little boat with moonlight shining down just on us."

"Just us?"

"Yes," Emily sighed, wiggling her bottom into Kit's lap. "We went on for miles and miles, holding on to each other just like this."

"Sounds like a fabulous trip. Can we do it for real sometime?"

"I'd love that. Just you and me and the moonlight. Promise we'll take a boat ride before you go back home," she said, hugging Kit's arm around her.

"I promise, sweetheart."

"I wish I didn't have to leave you tonight," Emily whispered.

"Your grandmother will have questions, and I know exactly what she is going to think."

"I don't care." Emily closed her eyes and held tight to Kit. "I don't want to leave you."

"I care." Kit laced her fingers through Emily's hair and smiled down at her. "Tomorrow we will have tea in the ready room and maybe a ride on the motorcycle. Tonight you have to be a good girl and go up to your own bed."

"You sound like my mother when I misbehaved."

"Believe me, I wish you could stay too. But we have to be careful." Kit kissed the back of Emily's neck. "And besides, if you stay here I won't get any sleep at all. I'll have my hands all over you, and you know it." She bit her neck playfully.

"I know you are right, but can't I whine just a bit more?"

"No. If you don't stop that, I'll give in and let you stay."

"Oh, goodie," Emily said childishly and turned over to face Kit. She took one of Kit's nipples in her mouth and sucked hard on it.

"Ouch," she shrieked, clamping her hands over her breasts. "You little brat."

"Kiss me," Emily demanded. "Kiss me hard."

Kit kissed her, hard at first then passionately, pulling Emily to her. Finally Emily slipped out of bed and dressed. They stood in the doorway, kissing and holding each other, unable to end their evening together.

"I love you, Kit. I want you to know that. I know what we said. I know we may not have a future, but I still love you," Emily said, stroking Kit's face. "And I know you love me too."

"This is the hardest thing I have ever done," Kit said, holding Emily in her arms. A tear rolled out of Kit's eye and ran down her cheek.

"I want you to know I am yours, forever and ever," Emily said, her chin quivering as she looked up into Kit's eyes, then she turned and hurried up the path.

Chapter 21

Lovie exploded through the door and rushed over to where Kit was charting routes on the map.

"Hi, Lovie. What's up with you?" Kit said, jotting figures on a scrap of paper.

"Did she get back okay?" Lovie asked breathlessly.

"Who? Red?"

"No. Emily."

"Did Emily get back from where?" Kit said, looking over at her.

"Benson. She took us up there to pick up a pair of Spits."

"I haven't seen her." Kit went back to work, assuming this wasn't dire news.

"Didn't you hear?" Lovie said, grabbing Kit's arm. "We got out just in time. They were bombed this morning. We saw a hell of a dogfight just south of the river. But our boys really gave it to them. I hope Emily left right after she dropped us off and came straight back."

"Why? What did you see?" Lovie now had her complete attention.

"They hit the Hemstead Bridge and maybe the one at Norris. I could see explosions over my shoulder."

Kit went to Commander Griggs's office and knocked on the door.

"Come."

"Commander, have you heard anything about Emily Mills? Has she made it back from Benson?" Griggs was hanging up the telephone.

"No, I haven't heard. Why?"

"Lovie said they were bombed this morning, and she thought the bridges along the river were both hit. If they were, she'll be trapped on the river road."

"Yes, I heard the factory had some minor damage, but most of the bombs fell south of town."

Griggs telephoned the motor pool. Kit and Lovie could tell by her expression Emily hadn't gotten back yet.

"Let's have a look at the map," Griggs said, hanging up and following Kit into the ready room.

"This is Hemstead Bridge," Kit said, pointing to the spot.

"I know that one was hit for sure," Lovie said.

"And if this one at Norris was destroyed, this whole section along the river will be like an island. She won't be able to go anywhere." Kit traced the route with her finger as Griggs squinted at the map.

"Let me call the station master at Norris and see if he has heard." Griggs went back into her office and made the call. Kit watched as her face changed from hopeful to worried as she listened to the man's explanation.

"Yes, both bridges were hit," Griggs said, hanging up and returning to the map. "The Hemstead Bridge was more heavily damaged, but the Norris Bridge is impassible as well." She studied the map, narrowing her eyes. "He said the river is up.

It's running bank to bank. If she made it across this one, she'll be stranded. The station master said there is no other road anywhere along there. No place for her to go."

"So she could be anywhere along here," Kit said, studying the road that snaked along the river. "That's a good fifteen miles."

Kit looked at Griggs. They were both thinking the same thing. If Emily was to be plucked from the isolated stretch of road, it would have to be done by air. The destroyed bridges and high water meant ground rescue was out of the question. Kit checked her watch.

"I've got three hours of daylight. That should be enough."

"Do you want me to go with you, Kit?" Lovie asked.

"No. I won't have room. But thanks for offering," Kit said, rubbing her arm. "I'll take care of this."

"Ordinarily I would say wait until morning, but the weather forecast is calling for freezing temperatures tonight, and the river may come out of its banks. If she can't get to shelter, it'll be pretty cold," Griggs said. "Don't take the Moth. There's a Stearman biplane behind the hangar. It's yellow with red wings and twenty miles an hour faster."

"That's yours, isn't it, Commander?" Kit asked, surprised Griggs would suggest it.

"Yes. And I expect it back in one piece, Lieutenant. She just had an oil change and new plugs."

"Are you sure about this?"

"Yes, Lieutenant, I'm sure. Now get going. You're wasting valuable daylight." She followed Kit out the door. "Watch out for bomb craters. The fields may be littered with them."

"I will." Kit tossed a salute back at her then trotted across the field. Mary Griggs's 1935 Stearman was a sweet little biplane. Kit had always thought so. It had a golden yellow fuselage with crimson wings and support cables and saddle brown leather upholstery. Every detail of the cockpit had been painted and scrubbed, making it the cleanest aircraft on the base, bar none. Even the factory fresh Spitfires that came right off the assembly line weren't as clean as Commander Griggs's baby. She kept it covered with a tarp and filled with petrol at all times. It wasn't unusual for Griggs to hop in the cockpit and fly off into the afternoon sun without warning then return just after sunset, coasting in and landing as light as a feather. Griggs used her own airplane when she was summoned to London or Whitechurch for a meeting, preferring it to the more modern twin engine transports used by most of the RAF brass.

Kit whistled for one of the mechanics to follow her behind the hangar. She pulled back the tarp, climbed in the rear seat and checked the gauges.

"All set, Lieutenant," he said, motioning for her to start the engine.

Kit pushed the rudder pedals and moved the stick, testing its response as the engine warmed up. She pulled her flight cap over her ears and nestled her goggles into place. The mechanic waved her forward, helping guide her around the building and onto the runway. She saluted, released the brake and began her roll across the grass, increasing speed and rotating into the sky before she had used even half of the runway. Griggs wasn't kidding when she said the Stearman had more speed than a Tiger Moth. Kit couldn't help but smile as the spirited little plane rose above the trees and darted across the sky, its nose heading northwest. Kit had planned her search pattern, and by the time she reached the outskirts of Norris, she was just three hundred feet above the ground. She banked back and forth, rocking from side to side as she scanned the road below for signs of a green truck with a canvas covered cargo box. When she roared over the bridge at Norris, she could see the damage. It wasn't completely gone, but a blast on each end of the bridge left craters large enough to block the roadway. Kit headed for the Hemstead Bridge. A canopy of trees obscured sections of the road, making her search harder. The river ran parallel to the road, and in places the murky water was creeping out of its banks and touching the shoulder. When Kit reached the Hemstead Bridge, she stood the biplane on its wing, pivoting above the bomb-leveled debris. Both ends of the cement and stone bridge were still intact, but the center thirty feet were completely missing. Kit headed north toward Benson. Perhaps Emily hadn't made it to the bridges. But if she hadn't, she would have had plenty of time to reroute herself through Kimball, Tuttle Crossing and back to Alderbrook. Kit made a slow turn and headed back toward the river road. On this pass she would fly lower and slower, crisscrossing the road, hoping to see through the tree cover.

"Where you are, Emily?" Kit said as she scanned the road. She didn't see a truck, but she did see several bomb craters along the side of the road. She also saw the remnants of an airplane. It looked like a fighter shot down or crashed during the dogfight Lovie had seen. Tiny plumes of smoke still rose from the wreckage. She tried to see a wing insignia, but it was too damaged to make out the mark. She continued up the road, staying low to the treetops. Just as she cleared a row of tall trees and returned to her search altitude, she saw the hint of something green between the trees. It wasn't the same green as the branches, but a dingy, almost olive green. Kit quickly pulled the stick and banked around, making another pass.

There was definitely something under there. A truck? Maybe. But something. Kit wished Emily would pop her head out from under the trees and wave, indicating she was all right. Kit couldn't tell if the truck was damaged, if it was indeed Emily's truck. Kit made several passes over the spot, trying to get a better view. She finally made a wide turn and came in low, flying right next to the trees, hoping to see in from the side. It was a truck. A dirty green truck with a canvas cover, Emily's truck, according to the markings on the side. Kit banked hard to the right. She roared across the field, looking for a place to set down, a place that would offer a safe takeoff as well. With bomb craters on both sides, Kit lined up with the center of a pasture, cleared the hedge row and touched down gently. The Stearman hopped over rocks and plowed rows, but rolled to a stop near the road. Kit revved the engine and turned the airplane so it would be ready for takeoff. She released her parachute straps and climbed out, hopping the fence and trotting down the road toward the truck. It was parked in the middle of the road, and the keys were still in the ignition.

"Emily," Kit called, checking the back of the truck. "Emily." She cupped her hands to her mouth. "Emily Mills." All Kit heard was the sound of rushing water from the nearby river. "Emily, where are you? It's Kit." Again she listened.

"You don't have to shout," Emily said, standing next to a tree.

Kit spun around, the sound of her voice bringing a relieved smile. "There you are."

Emily remained against the tree, her arms crossed and her face stone cold serious. Kit was so thankful to have found her alive and safe, she didn't immediately notice Emily's pale color or frightened eyes.

"Are you all right?" Kit asked, walking toward her.

"Yes. But you might want to stay where you are," Emily said quietly.

"Why?" Kit asked, moving closer.

Before Emily could reply, a young man stepped out from behind the tree. His uniform jacket was ripped and covered in blood. He stood close to Emily, one hand hidden behind her back.

"Who is he?" Kit exclaimed.

"I am Luftwaffe," he said with a heavy German accent. "You stop." He couldn't have been more than twenty years old. He was obviously scared and confused.

"You're under arrest," Kit said quickly, hoping to intimidate him. "You are a prisoner of war." She took another step closer, but he immediately produced a pistol he was holding to Emily's back.

"*Nicht gefangener!*" he said angrily, the vein on his forehead popping out.

"He said he is not a prisoner," Emily said, stiffening as he poked her with the barrel of the pistol.

"*Nicht gefangener,*" he repeated.

"Okay, okay." Kit could see the fear on Emily's face. Kit desperately wanted to snatch her out of the jaws of danger, but the pistol in Emily's back kept her frozen. "Emily," she gasped helplessly.

Emily stared back, her face as white as a ghost.

"How did he get here?" Kit asked carefully, not wanting to upset the nervous soldier.

"His plane was shot down. It's over there in a field. He bailed out and stopped me on the road. We've been driving along the river looking for a road out. Both bridges were destroyed in the air raid."

"*Keine brucken,*" he said, frowning at Kit. He didn't seem to know what to do next as his eyes darted up and down the road.

"That's right. There are no bridges left standing on this road."

"Thanks to your terrible aim," Kit said.

Emily scowled at Kit for her remarks that might enrage him further, but he didn't seem to understand.

"I believe our little visitor has only a marginal English vocabulary," Emily said.

"*Ich spreche Englisch,*" he insisted, recognizing a word or two.

"He says he speaks English," Emily said.

"Yes, the pencil dick does indeed speak English," Kit said. She wasn't intimidated by his youthful scowl.

"Was ist pencil dick?" he asked with a frown.

"It's a slender young man, *schlank junger Mann,*" Emily quickly said, tossing a glare at Kit.

"*Ja, ich bin pencil dick,*" he said proudly, puffing his chest.

Kit stifled a snicker, coughing instead.

"What's your name?" she asked.

"Peter," he stated. "Lieutenant Peter Strauss."

Emily raised her eyebrows at Kit as if to stop any remark she might have about his name, but it was too late.

"Peter. Perfect name for a pencil dick," Kit said, swallowing a chuckle.

"Peter has an abrasion to the back of his head," Emily said, picking her words carefully. "A rather severe one."

"Are you hurt? Are you injured?" Kit asked him, trying to sound concerned.

"*Verletzt*," Emily said.

"*Nein.*" He snapped to attention. "Not injured." But his eyes betrayed him. He was pale and sweaty in spite of the chilly day.

"We want to take very good care of Peter," Kit said, casting a worried look his way. "We don't want him to sit down." She nodded at Emily as if sending her a message.

"I agree." Emily also offered him a motherly glance. "We'll take good care of him."

"Maybe we should walk that way," Kit said, pointing up the road, away from the truck and the Stearman she had left in the field. "There is a road around the bridge. It's that way." She pointed.

"*Strasse rund brucken*," Emily said. "*Vier kilometers*," she added, holding up four fingers.

"Walk," he ordered, waving the gun at them as if it was his idea. Kit and Emily walked down the middle of the road, the German following and pointing his pistol at them ominously. Kit occasionally checked to see if he was keeping up with their brisk pace. He frowned, using the pistol to wave them onward. As they marched down the road, they could hear his gasps and groans becoming louder and more frequent as he struggled to keep up with them. Kit looked over at Emily, her eyes passing silent messages to keep a fast pace.

"Two kilometers," Emily said, pointing over the rise in the road. Both women knew there was nothing two kilometers up the road. Only more road. By the time they reached the bombed out bridge at Norris, they hoped Peter's head injury would be enough to drop him in his tracks. At least that was the plan.

Peter tried to keep up, but he began to falter. His steps were uneven and his balance shaky. He struggled to keep one foot in front of the other.

"Halt," he stammered, waving the gun at them. He had a crazed look in his eyes. Sweat streamed down his face as he staggered from side to side. Kit and Emily turned around just as he raised the pistol and pointed it at Emily, the barrel shaking wildly.

"No!" Kit shrieked. She could see his finger tighten around the trigger. She shoved Emily to the ground then charged him just as a shot rang out, missing both of them. He took aim again, pointing directly at Emily's head. Kit lunged at his outstretched arm. A blast exploded from the end of the barrel just as she pushed his hand to the side. The bullet struck the ground inches from Emily. Kit tackled him, using all her weight to force him down. She grabbed his wrist and whacked it on the ground until he released the pistol. She doubled up her fist and hit him across the face.

"You son of a bitch," she snarled, hitting him again and again. There was little fight in him. His head wound left him weak and dazed. That didn't matter. Kit continued to hit him, unable to contain her rage.

"Stop, Kit," Emily said, pulling Kit off the man. "Stop. He's unconscious."

"I hate him! I hate him!" she screamed, fighting Emily to hit him again. "Why did he shoot? Why did he do that?"

"You stopped him, sweetheart," Emily said, pulling Kit away. "He can't hurt anyone now."

Kit picked up the pistol and zipped it inside her flight jacket.

"Are you all right?" Kit asked, grabbing Emily by the shoulders and looking her up and down. "Did he hurt you?"

"No, he didn't hurt me."

"Oh, my God." Kit wrapped Emily in a hug. "He tried to kill you."

Kit could feel Emily weaken in her arms and begin to cry.

"I was so scared. I couldn't get away from him. He pointed that pistol at my head and told me to drive." Emily held on tighter, a new round of sobs consuming her.

"Shh," Kit cooed. "It's all right now."

"Is he dead?" Emily glanced down at the soldier.

"No. He's just unconscious. I was so frightened. I never thought I could wish death on someone, but when he pointed that gun at you, I felt something inside snap."

"I know. I was afraid he would shoot us both."

"I didn't know you spoke German," Kit said, brushing the hair from Emily's face.

"I never had to use it before, but I speak a little German, a little French, a little Spanish. I've picked it up from books."

"Let me guess. Most kids played kickball. You read novels, right?"

"Yes."

"I'm glad you did. You were wonderful," Kit said, giving her another hug.

"How did you get here?"

"I flew in. I left the plane back that way. I was afraid he had heard it. That's why I suggested we walk this direction. I didn't want him to see the plane and try to leave in it."

"What are we going to do with him? We can't leave him here, can we?"

"No. He'll just wake up and cause trouble." Kit thought a moment. "We're going to have to take him with us, I guess."

"Did you bring a large airplane?"

"It's just a two-seater, but I'll figure something out. Can you drive the truck down here to pick him up?"

"No. I ran out of gas from all the trips up and down the road."

"Okay," Kit said, unbuckling the pilot's belt and pulling it off his pants.

"What are you going to do with that?"

"Tie him up. You stay here with him while I run back and see what I can find." Kit tied the belt around the unconscious man's hands. "Don't touch him, and stay back. If he wakes up, yell. If you have to, kick him in the you-know-what."

"Pencil dick?"

"You got it." Kit winked then headed for the truck.

Kit returned ten minutes later, dragging the canvas tarp that had covered the back of the truck. She had two hanks of rope over her shoulder.

"Is he still out?" she asked as she trotted up the road.

"Yes. He's groaning a bit, but he hasn't opened his eyes." Emily had taken up a post ten feet away, far enough so the prisoner couldn't reach her if he came to, but close enough so she could see his every move. "What are we going to do with that?"

"Drag him back to the plane." Kit stretched out the tarp beside him and rolled him onto it. She then bundled him like a baby in a receiving blanket, using one of the hanks of rope to tie him neatly and securely. She left his head exposed. "Can you pull this corner?"

"Sure," Emily said, grabbing hold.

Together they dragged their prisoner back down the road to the opening in the hedge row near the Stearman. In spite of the jostling, Peter never woke up. Kit checked his pulse and pupils after they reached the airplane.

"What now? Are we going to put him in the seat?" Emily asked, trying to figure out how they would hoist him into the cockpit.

"No. You are riding in the seat. He is riding on the wing," Kit said, pulling the bundle into place beside the airplane.

"On the wing?" Emily exclaimed. "Is that safe?"

"Safer than leaving him here to bother someone else." Kit grabbed him under the arms and heaved him onto the lower wing next to the cockpit. "He has to be as close to the fuselage as we can get him for balance. It'll be hard enough to take off across this rough field without a lead weight on the wing. I'll tie him to the struts and cover his face with the ends of the tarp. He should be okay."

"Maybe I should stay here. You could take him first then come back for me."

"No!" Kit said adamantly. "I'll drop him in the river before I'd leave you here. You're the reason I came. You are going with me, or I don't go. You climb in the front seat while I finish tying him down. We're running out of daylight." Kit motioned toward the horizon where the sun had already set. Emily swallowed hard as she gazed up at the cockpit.

"What is the trick to getting in?" Emily asked as she stood on the wing and tried to swing her leg over the side.

Kit looked up and laughed. She forgot not everyone was familiar with how to hoist themselves in one of these babies. She stepped up onto the wing next to Emily, scooped her up in her arms and set her inside.

"Like this," she said then went back to tying Peter into place.

"Thank you, I think," Emily said, settling into her seat and buckling her seat belt. She looked out the side of the cockpit then pulled the belt tighter.

Kit checked the knots and made sure Peter was secure then climbed in the backseat. She hit the switch and spun the propeller, the airplane responding instantly.

"Slide down in the seat once we get up. The wind won't seem as bad," Kit shouted above the noise of the engine as they began to roll across the field. Emily nodded. Kit could tell she was nervous. "Is this your first time in a plane like this?"

"Yes." Emily had a death grip on the sides of the cockpit.

"I think you'll like it," Kit said, pushing the throttle wide open. She didn't have enough field to increase the speed slowly. She needed every inch to get up to eighty knots. She wasn't sure how the extra weight on the wing would effect the handling, but she was about to find out. "Here we go," she said and pulled back on the stick. The little yellow biplane rose into the waning light of day, clearing the row of trees at the end of the field by only a few inches. For Kit, it was the first time since she heard Emily might be trapped along the river road that she could breathe easy.

The wheels of the Stearman touched down just as the last glimmers of light faded across the airfield. Kit rolled to a stop and signaled the ground crew for an ambulance. Emily remained in the cockpit until Peter was untied and loaded for transfer to the hospital. He had come to, screaming and shouting profanities in German. As soon as the ambulance doors slammed shut, Emily climbed out.

"Are you sure you're okay?" Kit asked, helping her down.

"Yes, I'm fine. I never thought I'd be so happy to be back at the airfield."

"I never thought I'd be so happy to have you safe on the ground." Kit wrapped an arm around her as they walked across the infield. Emily leaned into her, resting her head on Kit's shoulder.

"I can't tell you how glad I was to see you running up the road toward me. Even with that pistol in my back I just knew everything would be all right. I knew you would take care of me. Do I sound cowardly?"

"No," Kit said with a squeeze. "You were very brave. You remained calm, and that was important. Things might have been very different if you hadn't kept your composure." Kit placed a small kiss on Emily's forehead. She knew she shouldn't, but no one was watching. For Kit, having Emily safe and sound was enough to bring tears to her eyes. It was either kiss her or fall to her knees and cry like a baby.

"I suppose I should go tell Sergeant Sprague where I left his truck," Emily said with a deep sigh.

"Do you want me to go with you?"

"No. I can handle it. I imagine the paperwork will keep me busy for hours," she mused.

"Vehicle abandonment, enemy contact, combat involvement, equipment malfunction for running out of gas." Kit chuckled. "Sounds like writer's cramp to me."

"And a PT-six form for you," Emily added, grinning up at

her.

"If you need help with that one, let me know," Kit said, holding Emily against her side. "I'll be glad to offer my complete assistance."

"I love your assistance, Lieutenant," Emily said, smiling adoringly. They stopped where the path across the field forked.

"I'll give you a ride home when you're finished. I'll wait for you in the ready room."

"You don't have to wait. It could be hours. Sergeant Sprague gets a little long-winded when it comes to misplacing vehicles. One of the girls parked a car behind the supply trucks instead of in the garage, and she had to listen to a twenty minute lecture."

"That's okay. I don't mind." Kit brushed her fingers through Emily's wind-blown curls. "Take as long as you need. Send up a flare if you need me."

"I always need you," Emily whispered sweetly then headed for the motor pool.

Kit was surprised Lovie hadn't come out to meet them and expected her to be in the ready room, but it was empty. She crossed the room, but before she could knock on Griggs's office door, it opened and Griggs met her with a somber scowl.

"The boys will refill your Stearman, Commander," Kit said. "Willie said he'd replace the tarp when they are finished. It sure handled like a dream. Did you hear about the German pilot?"

"Yes, the hospital just telephoned. He'll recover and be sent to a POW center. Come in, Lieutenant." She stepped back and waited for Kit to enter then closed the door.

"Emily did a great job. She didn't panic, even when he had that Luger in her back. It was touch and go for a minute, but no one was shot. Thank goodness for that."

"Yes. That is good news," Griggs said, but it was plain something else was on her mind.

"Did you have another mission for me?" Kit asked. Often the secret missions Kit was asked to fly came behind closed doors when no one else was around. She had been called to the airfield

247

in the wee hours of the morning on several occasions to deliver surveillance photographs or fly high-ranking officers to clandestine meetings on offshore locations. Her ability to fly seaplanes and her rank made her indispensable.

"No. Sit down, Lieutenant." Her eyes were hard and focused.

"Thank you, ma'am. Is there a problem?" Kit asked, reading something worrisome on her face.

"Yes, Anderson, there is a problem, and I'm sure it won't come as a surprise to you." Griggs sat down behind her desk and leaned forward ominously.

"I beg your pardon, Commander." Kit had no idea what she was talking about.

"The problem is with Miss Emily Mills."

"Emily? I don't understand. If you are talking about her leaving the truck out there on that road, believe me, it wasn't her fault. Both bridges were bombed. She was cut off."

"I am not talking about that, Lieutenant. I am talking about you and Mills," she said sternly.

Kit took a deep breath, suddenly aware what she was talking about. But Kit didn't want to make assumptions. If Commander Griggs was talking about their relationship, their personal relationship, she would have to be more explicit than that.

"Emily and me?" she asked innocently.

"This is a very small airfield, Anderson. Everything that goes on here will be seen by someone. Did you think no one would notice?"

"Commander, I don't know what you are talking about. If you have a problem with my work, I'd like to hear it. If this has anything to do with my private life, with all due respect, Commander, it is no one's business."

"You are an officer and squadron leader with the Air Transport Auxiliary. Our duties go well beyond the airfield. Accusations like this reflect on everyone. Every officer, every woman in the ATA has a responsibility to conduct herself without reproach."

"Commander, may I ask exactly what you are accusing me of?"

"Up to now, I've considered the reports and rumors I've heard, just that, rumors. I assumed, as squadron leader and Flight Lieutenant, you were a responsible pilot and wouldn't do anything to jeopardize your position or your wings. What I saw just now, out my window, has only reinforced the truth behind those rumors. I assume you and Emily are having some sort of intimate relationship."

Kit stared angrily at Griggs but didn't say anything.

"Your wings and the right to wear them are a privilege, Lieutenant. I would hate to see you lose them over this. Don't force me to exercise my authority. This is your one and only warning, Anderson. You are to conduct yourself as an officer, a morally responsible officer. Do I make myself clear, Lieutenant?"

Kit stood at attention as Griggs finished her tirade. She kept her eyes fixed on the wall behind her desk. She refused to allow Griggs to see her resentment. Yes, Kit was a lesbian. Yes, she was in love with Emily Mills, and yes, perhaps she had used poor judgment in displaying that affection for all to see. But Kit was not going to give Griggs the satisfaction of seeing her skulk out the office with her tail between her legs. Griggs had undoubtedly seen her cross the field with her arm around Emily and probably even witnessed her kiss Emily's forehead. Kit realized it was naïve to expect Griggs would judge her on her merits as a pilot and officer, nothing else. She knew better than to expect that. The subtle rumors of them riding together on the motorcycle or perhaps being seen at Stewart's weren't enough to indict. But an innocent hug and kiss on the forehead was. Kit's reputation and achievements didn't seem to matter.

Kit snapped a salute and turned on her heels, leaving Griggs's office without a backward glance. She was too mad to sit in the ready room and wait. She crossed to the motor pool to check on Emily, hoping she was nearly finished with her paperwork.

"Is Emily Mills with Sergeant Sprague?" she asked one of the drivers.

"She was. But she left." The woman went back to sweeping the floor.

"Left? How long ago?"

The woman shrugged.

"Sprague was talking to her when I went to the loo. When I came back, they were both gone."

Kit gave the garage a quick scan but didn't see her. She decided she must have missed her and returned to the ready room. She wasn't there either. Kit rounded the building to the motorcycle with plans to circle the airfield in search of her. She was worried Sergeant Sprague had raked Emily over the coals about leaving the truck on the river road, something that wasn't her fault. As Kit was about to toss her leg over the seat, she noticed a piece of paper tucked under the shifter bar.

Kit, Sorry for standing you up like this, but Grandmother needed me to come home straight away. Nigel picked me up. Talk with you tomorrow, E.M.

Kit stuffed the note into her pocket then stomped the starter and roared toward Bellhurst, praying all the way that Lillian hadn't had another heart attack. Knowing Emily needed a ride home and she wasn't available to take her only made Kit even more furious with Commander Griggs. Kit knocked on the side door and waited nervously for someone to answer. Finally, Nigel opened the door.

"Good evening, Lieutenant Anderson," he said. Like always, Kit couldn't read Nigel. The house could be burning to the ground or he could have just been knighted by the King, but he kept the same stoic expression.

"Nigel, is she all right?" Kit asked frantically. "Did she go to the hospital?"

"Is who all right? Whom are you talking about, Lieutenant?"

"Lady Marble, of course. Is she all right? Did she have a heart attack?"

"I assure you Lady Marble has *not* had a heart attack. However, ing." He hadn't changed his expression, making Kit think maybe there really was nothing wrong.

"But I thought she was ill."

"No one is ill. Are you ill, Lieutenant?"

"No. How about Emily? Is she okay?"

"As far as I know, she is well."

"I was told she had to hurry home and you picked her up. Is she here?" Kit asked, looking past him to catch a glimpse of Emily in the hall.

"I'm afraid Miss Emily and Lady Marble are busy at the moment. Would you like to leave a message for her?" Nigel hadn't asked Kit inside, and that surprised her. He had resumed the same distant posture he displayed that first time she walked up the path to rent the cottage.

"Just tell her I'll be in the cottage. When she has a minute, I'd like to discuss her assignment for tomorrow." That was a fib, but a small one, Kit thought.

"Yes, Lieutenant. I'll tell her, but I was informed they expected to be occupied all evening. Is there anything else?"

"No. I guess not," Kit said, disappointed she couldn't see Emily. "But if she does get finished, be sure and tell her I'll be home. It doesn't matter how late. Will you tell her?"

"Yes, miss. I will tell her." He nodded.

"You're sure I couldn't see her for just a few minutes?" Kit asked, finding Nigel's explanation thin at best.

"They left specific instructions not to be interrupted. And before you ask, no, I am not privy to their meeting," he added.

"Thanks anyway, Nigel. Good evening."

"Good evening, Lieutenant." He closed the door.

She started for the path to the cottage but hesitated in the driveway and looked up at Emily's window. It was dark. Kit stood staring up at it, hoping Emily would notice her and open it. Several minutes passed, and no one came to the window.

"Is there something else, Lieutenant?" Nigel asked, opening

the front door.

"No. Good night," Kit said and begrudgingly headed for the cottage.

Chapter 22

Kit awoke early and dressed then hurried up to the house, ready to give Emily a ride to the airfield.

"Good morning, Lieutenant," Nigel said, opening the door. "I'm sorry, but Miss Emily has already left. She said something about a trip to Luton."

"This early?" Kit frowned as she checked her watch. "It's only quarter to seven."

"I believe she rode her bicycle."

"Did you give her my message? Did you tell her I needed to talk to her?"

"Yes, Lieutenant. I told her last evening." He didn't volunteer anything else.

"I better get going then," she said and hurried around to the carriage house. By the time she pulled up to the ATA office, the entire squadron was waiting inside. With only three missions to fly, the ready room remained full all day. Some of the women played cards, some wrote letters home and others just visited. Kit caught up on log entries and the monotonous paperwork left on her desk. After lunch, she slipped away from the group and headed for the motor pool. She hoped she and Emily could have a few minutes together. Kit was dying to know what happened last night to pull her away.

"Is Emily Mills back from Luton?" Kit asked, stepping into the driver's room. Someone pointed to the garage without looking up from her magazine.

"Out there somewhere," she said.

Kit roamed through the garage and out the back door, looking for Emily.

"Hi," she said, looking into the back of a truck where Emily was sweeping out clumps of mud.

"Hello." Emily continued to sweep.

"Is Lillian all right?"

"Yes, Grandmother is fine."

"I was worried when I read your note. I was afraid she had another heart attack. Is everything okay?"

"Things are fine."

"Good." She stepped aside as Emily flipped her sweepings onto the ground. "I left Nigel a message. Did you get it?" Kit offered Emily a helping hand as she climbed out of the bed of the truck, but she didn't take it.

"Yes, he told me you were home and something about discussing an assignment." Emily returned the broom to the rack then collected a clipboard and went to the cab to record the mileage and finish her trip report. Kit climbed in the passenger's seat and leaned over to Emily.

"Would you like to spend the night with me in the cottage? I'll make you a nice cuppa and we can take a hot bath together. It'll be crowded, but I'm sure we can work it out," Kit said, leaning in and speaking softly.

"I'm sorry, but I can't tonight," Emily said, continuing to write her report.

"How come?" Kit didn't mean to, but she sounded like a spoiled child.

"I just can't." Emily kept her eyes on the clipboard and away from Kit.

"Okay. Then how about tomorrow night? I'll save my hot water for you."

"Thanks, but I don't think so."

"I'll let you take a bath alone. You'd probably be more comfortable anyway. I'll just watch." Kit raised her eyebrows devilishly.

"I can't. Grandmother asked me to take her to the women's guild meeting at the community center." Emily folded down the visor and signed her initials and date on the card.

"Emily, what's wrong?"

"Nothing," she said in a very unconvincing tone then turned to climb out. "I've just got a lot to do today, but nothing is wrong."

"I think there is." Kit said, taking her arm. "Now tell me what it is. Does this have anything to do with Peter and what happened yesterday?"

Emily scanned the report she had just written, seemingly desperate to keep her eyes away from Kit.

"It does," Kit declared. "Did something happen out there on that road with that son-of-a-bitch you didn't tell me?"

"No. Nothing happened. He was too injured and frightened to know what he was doing."

"If you are still upset, I'll understand. That was a very terrifying experience. That pistol in his hand looked as big as a cannon. Maybe you should ask for a few days off. They'll approve it, I'm sure. I'll tell them what happened. No one will blame you if—"

"I can't see you anymore," Emily said quietly, not waiting for Kit to finish.

"What did you say?"

"I can't see you anymore."

"Why?" Kit gasped, her heart skipping a beat.

"I just can't. Please, Kit, just accept it."

"Look at me," she demanded. "Look at me and tell me why."

"It doesn't matter why." Emily slowly looked over at her. "I just can't do this anymore. I thought I could, but I can't. We knew it was only temporary. It's better if we stop now before someone gets hurt."

"Gets hurt?" Kit felt her heart crumbling in her chest. She knew this day would come, but she didn't expect it so soon, and certainly not like this.

"We have only known each other a few weeks. Let's end it with a smile, not a dramatic, unpleasant scene."

Kit sank in the seat and stared out the windshield.

"Don't I at least get to know why?" she finally said, looking back at Emily.

"It doesn't matter why, Kit. Believe me, it doesn't." She touched Kit's hand tenderly. "I wish you every happiness."

Emily's news hit Kit so suddenly and so hard she couldn't find words to argue or to plead for her to change her mind.

"That's it?" Kit chuckled. "Just like that, we're done? Don't I have a say in this? I thought it was a two-way relationship. You know, give and take, talk things over. You made this decision without even consulting me?" Kit looked over at her, tears filling her eyes. "I thought it would be different this time. I can't believe I am so stupid. I just keep making the same old mistakes."

"I never meant to hurt you," Emily whispered, tears rolling down her cheeks. "I blame myself. It's all my fault."

"No, it's mine." Kit leaned her head back, closed her eyes and took a deep breath. "I knew better." She turned to Emily soulfully. "I loved you, Emily. I'm sorry I got you mixed up in something you couldn't handle." Kit tried to smile, but it was no use. Her chin quivered and tears silently ran down her face. "Thank you for allowing me to rent your cottage, Miss Mills. It was quite an experience."

Kit climbed out of the truck and headed back across the field, leaving Emily sobbing in the cab. Kit took the long way back to the ready room, by way of the road that circled the field. She needed time to come to grips with what Emily had said. She needed time for the tears to stop. From the first moment she saw Emily's heart-stopping smile and innocent eyes, Kit felt they would build memories together, but she never thought they would end so bitterly. Even though they knew their time together would be short and someday they would part, deep in her heart, Kit never really believed it would happen. She was convinced they would drift on and on, locked in each other's arms forever. But now, even those daydreams had been shattered. Kit didn't know if Emily wanted someone who could offer a permanent relationship, or if she couldn't accept being a lesbian. Kit kicked herself for not asking, but at that moment all she could think about was where had she gone wrong. She continued around the field, recapturing her emotions and clearing her mind.

"Lieutenant Anderson," Commander Griggs called as she stepped out of the field office. "I was looking for you. Where have you been?"

"I was at the motor pool," Kit said, seeing no reason to lie.

"With Emily Mills? I thought I made myself clear."

"There is nothing to worry about, Commander. Not anymore. The source of gossip no longer exists." Kit clenched her fists as she said it, fighting back the pain. Griggs narrowed her eyes at Kit as if reading her heartache.

"Lieutenant Anderson, there is a Lancaster that needs a test flight. I planned on you doing it tomorrow. Would you prefer to do it today?" Griggs asked.

"If you mean do I need something to do, no, I am fine. But thank you."

"I put an order on your desk. Ringway has three Spitfires that need to come down to the MAC unit for repair. They're going to be modified and reassigned here. They'll have the bigger engine and longer range. Who can you spare in the morning?"

"Are they in good enough shape to make it back here?"

"They said so. They lost half their mechanics. Bloody German Luftwaffe targeted their hangars and the hospital."

"Loveland, Peacock and Paisley," Kit said. "That just leaves Norton. The rest of the girls are going to Martingale to pick up P-Fifty-ones."

"Send them up early. Have Norton take them up in a De Havilland. I don't want to take the whole day on just three planes."

"I'll see to it, Commander." Kit saluted then headed to the ready room. Thankfully, she had something to help take her mind off Emily.

"Lovie, Red, Andrea and Viv," she called as she stepped inside. "I've got a mission for you."

"Did I hear my name?" Lovie asked cheerfully.

"Yes, you did. You're going up to Ringway in the morning."

"Oh, goodie. I can hardly wait. Are we getting a three-day pass to see the sites?"

"No. You're going to pick up three Spits. Viv, you're flying them up in a De Havilland. The rest of you are going to Martingale to pick up Mustangs. Check the invoices. Last time they gave us the wrong planes. Someone in operations can't read." The pilots made their way to the map to check routes, headings and landmarks. "See you back here tomorrow. Fly safe, ladies."

Kit dismissed the squadron but stayed to field questions. Finally, the pilots drifted out one by one, leaving Kit and Lovie the last to leave.

"Did you want to play a little cribbage this evening, or do you and Emily have plans?" Lovie asked, pulling on her jacket.

Kit shot a look at her.

"What are you talking about?"

"Oh, come on, Kit. This is your buddy, your friend," she said, coming to sit on the edge of Kit's desk. "You don't have to pretend in front of me. Besides, I think you two make a cute couple." She pulled a cigarette from her pocket and struck a match on the bottom of her shoe.

"Well, we aren't a cute couple anymore," Kit said, sorting papers.

"Why? What happened?" Lovie slipped down into a chair and pulled herself closer. "I thought you two were getting along so well. I know it was only a couple weeks, but I could see it in your eyes, both of you."

"See what? Fear? Shock? Stupidity?" Kit tried to keep busy.

"What I saw was pure love. Emily loves you. That much I do know."

"I believe Miss Emily Mills, the teacher, would say the proper tense of that verb would be loved, not loves. Past tense." Kit gave an artificial laugh. "Whatever it is she wants, it isn't me."

"What happened between you two? If you had a tiff, surely you can kiss and make up. She's a proud Brit, and you're an ever-loving independent Yank. Surely you two can find a way to work it out." Lovie blew a smoke ring. "Don't let this war come between you and the person you love, Kit."

"The damage is already done. And I really don't want to talk about it, but thanks, Lovie." Kit went to the bulletin board to post the latest weather reports for the morning.

"You're going to give up, just like that?" Lovie asked, following her.

"I didn't give up. Emily did." Kit went back to her desk, Lovie right on her heels. "But maybe she was right. Our paths just crossed somewhere between love and war. That's all. Maybe it is better to end it now."

"Better than what? A poke in the eye with a hot stick?" Lovie mashed her cigarette out and pulled a letter from her shirt pocket. "It's never better to just give up. I thought it was. I walked away from the most wonderful person in the world, but come July, this girl won't be staying a minute longer than I have to. I'm going home." She kissed the letter and replaced it in her pocket then patted it. "It took me five thousand miles and a year to realize the woman I had back in Toronto is all I'll ever need or want."

"You aren't renewing your contract?"

"Heck no. I am running home just as fast as my little legs will take me. I got Lynette's letter three days ago. I didn't open it until last night. I was afraid she was telling me she found someone else. When I left Canada for England, she was furious with me. She thought I should have stayed so we could work out our troubles. But I was too pigheaded. I was afraid she wanted nothing else to do with me."

"Have you written her back?" Kit asked.

"Nine pages. I was up until four o'clock this morning." Lovie chuckled. "It'll cost me a fortune to send it. But it'll be worth every penny. I'd love to see her face when she reads it. I was so stupid. I almost missed out on something really wonderful."

"I'm very happy for you, honey. I can't think of a more deserving person to find happiness."

"You deserve it too, Kit. Give Emily another chance."

"Thanks, but I don't think so. I've only got a couple months left. Maybe I'll find something special myself. Kansas City is a big place." Kit took a deep breath as if trying to convince herself she was right. "Now, you go home and get some sleep. You have a mission tomorrow early."

"Yes, ma'am." Lovie smiled and saluted. "Are you going to be all right, honey? Do you need some company tonight? I'll let you win at cribbage."

"I'll be fine, Mother Loveland." Kit walked Lovie to the door. "I may take a ten-inch deep bath."

"If you need anything, anything at all, call me, okay?" Lovie hugged her and kissed her cheek.

"I will. Fly safe tomorrow."

"I will. And don't worry about Andrea. She's a good pilot." Lovie stepped out of the ready room then looked back. "I'm so sorry about you and Emily. I wish I could do something to help."

"You did. You listened. Good night, Lovie."

"Good night, Kit." She waved then headed for the rooming house.

Kit finished her work and went home. She parked the motorcycle in the carriage house and closed the door then walked the path to the cottage. She didn't stop in the driveway to look up at Emily's window. She couldn't. It hurt too much. She went to bed, looking forward to tomorrow, another day to take her mind off losing Emily.

Chapter 23

Kit sent the pilots off on their missions then made a quick flight to Luton. She spent the rest of the day helping the RAF instructor train new combat pilots in diversion tactics. Even though she had never flown a combat mission, as an experienced pilot and instructor, she knew what a Spitfire could and couldn't do and how much stress it could take. By three o'clock, she was ready to pull her hair out. The new batch of pilots arrived with little more than textbook knowledge of flying. Some of the men had no combat training at all. One young man had only twelve hours in a trainer and none in a Spitfire or Hurricane. She had to start with the basics, making for a frustrating and exhausting afternoon. She dropped her flight cap and goggles in the grass outside the hangar and sat down, stretching out her legs and leaning back on her arms.

"Lieutenant Anderson?" one of the young men said, trotting over to her. "Would you sign my log book?"

"Sure," she replied with a tired groan and pulled a pen from her pocket. She scribbled on it and handed it back. "Keep an eye on the threshold, Jimmie. Watch your speed on approach," she added.

"Yes, Lieutenant," he said then hurried away.

"Hello, Lieutenant?" Emily said, crossing the field to her.

"Hello," Kit replied with mixed emotions.

"Could you sign these PT-sixes forms? Sergeant Sprague asked me to return them for signature." She handed Kit a stack of papers. "I'm sorry if this is awkward for you. But there was no one else to bring them to."

"Sure. No problem. We have to work together, Miss Mills." Kit sat up and scanned the forms. She folded her legs, placed the papers on her lap and began signing. Emily stood nervously, waiting for her to finish. "You can sit down if you want," Kit said, patting the grass. "I promise I won't bite."

"Here they come," Willie shouted, standing in the doorway to the hangar, shading his eyes from the afternoon sun. He pointed to the three Spitfires roaring over the row of trees at the end of the runway.

"Is that Lovie, Red and Andrea?" Emily asked, shielding her eyes from the sun.

"Yep." Kit checked her watch. "A little late, but that's my girls." She smiled at their tight formation and the way the sun glistened off their wings. "Red said she would be back in time for tea. Looks like they just made it."

Emily and Kit walked to the edge of the runway and waited for the barrage balloons to be lowered so they could land.

"Your girls would do anything for you. You know that, don't you?"

"They're good kids." Kit stuffed her hands in her jacket pockets.

They watched the trio fly in formation around the field in preparation for landing. The group finally split, the first airplane lining up for approach.

"Wow, Andrea. Cut your speed, girl," Kit said, sucking air through her teeth. "Go around." She waved her arms, frantically motioning for the first airplane to circle the field and try again. The other two banked away from the runway, allowing the first to make another approach.

"How do you know that is Andrea?"

"I know Red and Lovie. They always have the rookie land first."

"That's very polite of them."

"It's more than polite. It offers less experienced pilots more room to land. Red told me she didn't want some rookie landing behind her and flying up her rear."

"I don't blame her."

"Throttle back, Andrea. All you need it sixty knots to set that thing down," Kit said, watching intently.

"What would happen if she is going too fast when she touches down? Will she overshoot the end of the runway?"

"That, and if she's going too fast, it's hard to steer once you put the wheels on the ground. Our runways are too rough for hot landings."

"How much damage do these planes have?"

"I don't know, but I bet Lovie made sure Andrea is flying the least damaged plane. She's like a mother hen. You'd think she was personally responsible for every pilot in the squadron."

"Here she comes again," Emily said.

"That's it. That's it," Kit murmured, her eyes fixed on the airplane's descent and speed. "Easy does it." She flexed her knees, unconsciously helping the wheels onto the ground. As the Spitfire touched down, Kit gave a bounce, rocking up and down on the balls of her feet. "Atta girl," she sighed.

"Who's a mother hen?" Emily joked.

Even before the airplane came to a stop, the ground crew was pursuing it down the runway, ready to move it to the hangar. The second Spitfire rounded the field, banking sharply to line up with the runway.

"Is that Lovie or Red?" Emily asked.

"Red. No one does a bank like her. She loves to stand the plane on the tip of the wing when she comes around. She can circle the field in a tighter radius than even the combat pilots. Watch. She's going to hold it until the last second before straightening out." Kit grimaced and shook her head, waiting for the airplane to level off. "Pull it over, Red. That's enough. Don't stress the wings if they're full of bullet holes." Kit's fists rustled in her pockets. "Throttle back and drop it right down the pipe."

As if the pilot could hear her instructions, the Spitfire flattened out and cruised in for a spotless landing. Kit could see some rudder damage and a row of bullet holes down the fuselage that made it handle sluggishly once it was on the ground. It swerved from side to side as it rolled to a stop.

"Must have hydraulic damage," Kit said, turning her attention to the last Spitfire. "Come on, Lovie. Crank down the undercarriage and set that baby down. Let's go have some dinner."

Kit watched closely, expecting to see two wheels unfold from the underbelly of the plane but only one came down. The other started down but hung only partially deployed.

"Crank it some more, Lovie. It's not all the way down." Kit cupped her hands to her eyes for a better view. The partially extended wheel rolled back up and started down again, but it still didn't lock into place. Lovie circled the field as she made several attempts at retracting then extending the stubborn wheel.

As the airplane flew overhead Kit could see a gaping hole in the underside of the fuselage between the doors that covered the wheels. "God, the undercarriage is all shot up. She can't get it down."

"Please, God, help her," Emily gasped. "Can she land with the wheels up?"

"Not easily. Not with all the potholes we have."

Red and Andrea had climbed out of their airplanes and ran over to where Emily and Kit were watching.

"The left wheel won't come down," Kit said, pointing skyward.

"It was all shot up, but they were supposed to fix it so she could get it down." Red's eyes traced the flight. "That's why we're late. Put some muscle in it, Lovie," she yelled. "Lean on the crank."

Slowly the wheel went back up then started down again. This time it was slow but it rolled all the way down.

"That's it, you little Canuck," Red cheered, slapping Kit on the back. "She got it down."

"Is that Loveland?" Griggs asked, joining the women at the edge of the runway.

"Yes," Kit said. "She had a problem getting the wheels down."

"I saw the damage. Looks like it took quite a bit of flack."

"I wanted to fly it, but Lovie wouldn't hear of it. She said I was too reckless," Red said, smiling over at Kit. "She said it needed her tender loving care."

"I bet she got blisters on her hand from cranking that winch up and down," Kit chuckled, relieved to see both wheels down for landing.

"She'll never let us forget that either," Red teased.

Lovie came around and lined up for her landing. She throttled back and floated in for touch down. The wheels caught the grass but didn't stay down. The Spitfire bounced up and came down again hard.

"NO!" Kit screamed. "Don't bounce the landing, Lovie."

The left landing gear couldn't stand the jolt and folded up under the bottom of the fuselage. The left wing dropped down and scraped the ground, digging a trench through the grass. The sound of five women gasping in horror couldn't drown out the terrifying sound of the left wing digging into dirt and cartwheeling the airplane wing over wing, flipping it high in the air then landing on its top. A cloud of dust rose from the crash site as the engine stopped, the propeller mangled under the cockpit.

Kit and Red started toward the crash at a dead run. Emily, Andrea and Griggs followed as fast as they could. They could see

266

Lovie hanging upside down in the cockpit, trying to unlatch the bent canopy. A group of mechanics who had seen the crash were also racing across the field toward Lovie's crumpled airplane. As the dust settled, an eerie hiss could be heard. Before Kit and Red could reach Lovie, the air was split by an explosion sending a ball of flame straight up. The airplane rose off the ground then split apart, sending metal fragments out in all directions. The concussion of the blast knocked Red and Kit backward and onto the ground. Emily, Andrea, Griggs and the mechanics stopped in their tracks and covered their heads as the shower of airplane bits settled around them. Kit scrambled to her feet and began running toward the wreckage, still on a mission to rescue Lovie from the crash.

"No, Kit, Wait!" Emily screamed, lunging for her arm.

"Let go. I've got to get Lovie out of there," she said, fighting against Emily's grip.

Red was slowly climbing to her feet, her face white as she stared at the burning wreckage. She didn't seem to be aware she had several small gashes on her face from flying debris. The fire crew sprang into action and roared toward the crash, the tanker truck always just a few yards from the runway.

"Let go," Kit repeated, trying to pull away. She could feel the sting from her wounds from the tiny bits of flying shrapnel and saw the trickle of blood on the back of her hand but she was too consumed with saving Lovie to care.

"You can't save her," Emily said, holding on to her.

Kit couldn't make sense of what Emily was telling her. She continued to lunge forward, desperately trying to reach the cockpit. Emily grabbed Kit around the waist and held her in a bear hug.

"Kit, stop. You can't help Lovie. You're going to get burned. You have to stay back."

"No. No!" Kit screamed. Her adrenaline rush gave her super-human strength. Just as she was about to pull away, Emily tackled her, forcing her to the ground.

"Lovie!" Red screamed, a stunned, glassy look in her eyes. She took a deep breath and let out a shriek of terror then fell to her knees. Andrea came to Red's side and hugged her, trying to comfort her. But it was no use. Red was inconsolable. She rocked and sobbed, Andrea holding her in her arms.

Commander Griggs stood motionless, her hands to her mouth as tears streamed down her face.

Kit's body continued to fight, unable to accept Lovie's loss. Emily held on to her as if waiting for reality to set in.

"Please let me go," Kit begged desperately. "I have to get Lovie."

"Kit," Emily said, placing her mouth close to Kit's ear. "Kit, Lovie is dead." Emily's voice cracked as she said it.

"She can't be. She can't be," Kit replied, the fight leaving her body. "I saw her. She was unlocking the canopy. I saw her." She looked back at Emily, searching for her to deny what Kit knew in her heart.

"I know you did. We all did. But she couldn't get out of time." Tears welled up in Emily's eyes. "She's gone, sweetheart. She's in no pain now."

Kit was silent for a long moment, staring blankly at the flames. Finally, the reality came crashing down on her. Tears began streaming down her face. She slumped into Emily's arms as great sobs consumed her. Emily cried with her, the two of them rocking in each other's arms.

Chapter 24

For three days, the women in Kit's squadron walked around in a daze. No one could think of Lovie without relaying a fond memory of her then falling to tears. Kit was left with the job of going through her things and shipping them back to her family, including the letter to Lynette. Red spent most of her time drowning her sorrow at Brindy's. The field commander authorized a memorial service for Lovie, but it was interrupted by a scramble order.

"Can't even have a lousy memorial service without the damn war interrupting things," Red said, her speech slurred. She stood looking at the picture of Lovie in her uniform. The simple black frame stood on the table next to a small bouquet of flowers. Kit was sitting in the front row, staring at the ground. "Don't you have an airplane to take up or something?" Red asked, leaning on the table to help her balance.

"No. They're all up."

"They can all blow up as far as I'm concerned," Red said, stumbling over to sit next to Kit. "I don't give a rat's ass." She dug a silver flask from her pocket and took a drink. "How about a snort?" she asked, handing it to Kit. "For Lovie's sake."

"No, thanks. And I think you've had enough." Kit pushed it back at her.

"The hell I have. I've just started. Come knock on my door about midnight if you want to see a good drunk." Red laughed.

"Red, this isn't going to help anything."

"Maybe not. But some of us aren't as fearless as you." She took another drink then slipped the flask back in her pocket.

"I'm not so fearless," Kit said, going to the table. She stared down at Lovie's picture. "Lovie was the brave one. Did she tell you about Lynette?"

"Yes. She couldn't wait to get home to her. She said whatever problems they had weren't worth not being together. Poor little fool. Lovie would still be alive if she had stayed in Toronto."

"I guess she had to come to England to realize just how much she loved her." Kit rubbed her fingers across Lovie's smiling face.

"If you love someone, you love them. She should have stayed." Red's voice cracked.

"But if she had stayed in Canada, we wouldn't have got to know her. We should thank God for that, Red."

"I do," she said as she succumbed to her tears. She buried her face in her hands and sobbed. Kit came to sit beside her and hugged her. "I loved that little Canuck. I'm going to miss her so bad," Red said through her sobs.

"We all loved her, and we will all miss her." Kit smoothed Red's hair and smiled at her. "And Lovie loved us too. She died doing what she always did, taking care of her friends."

"She was good at that, wasn't she?" Red said, wiping the tears from her cheeks. "Taking care of her friends. Even Emily. She liked her."

"I know. And Emily liked her too."

"Lovie tried to talk to Emily the other day when she was upset, but she couldn't catch up to her," Red said.

"When was Emily upset?" Kit asked. "The day I gave you the assignment to Ringway?"

"No. I think it was the day before that. After you rescued her from that German pilot. We had just landed and were crossing the infield. Willie said you had gone to the ready room. We saw Emily outside the ATA office."

"What are you talking about? I didn't see her outside the office."

"Yeah, she was standing outside the open window there where you park your motorcycle. She looked upset about something. She wrote a note and put it on your motorcycle then ran off. Lovie said she looked like she was crying, but she couldn't catch her. You know how Lovie was. Always ready to help her friends in a time of crisis. We assumed you would talk with her about it."

"Outside what open window?"

"Griggs's office."

"Oh, my God," Kit exclaimed, standing up and going to the window. "If she was outside the office, she heard what Griggs said to me. She heard her ultimatum."

"What are you talking about?"

Kit spun around, glaring over at Red

"That's why she did it," Kit said.

"Why she did what?" Red looked confused.

"Emily told me she didn't want to see me anymore. But the reason she broke it off is because she overheard what Griggs said to me. She heard it through the open window. She didn't want me to lose my wings. She was only trying to protect me. That little idiot." She laughed out loud.

"Told you what, Kit?"

"I'll tell you later," she said happily and kissed the top of Red's head. Kit kissed Lovie's picture too. "Thank you, Lovie, sweetheart. You were right. I know what I want, and I'm going to fight for it."

271

Kit rushed out the door and ran across the infield toward the motor pool.

"Where's Emily Mills?" she demanded breathlessly, looking past the office to the driver's waiting room. She didn't wait for a response. She hurried into the back, down the steps into the garage, searching for Emily. She checked every truck and car as she called her name.

"Are you looking for Emily Mills, Lieutenant?" a mechanic asked, rolling out from under a truck where she was changing the oil.

"Yes. Where is she?" Kit asked, looking behind the trucks in the garage.

"Didn't you hear? She transferred to Manchester. She left today."

Kit stopped in her tracks.

"Manchester?"

"Yeah. She went home to pack this morning. Someone is driving her up there at three."

Kit checked her watch. It was after three. She turned and raced across the field to the motorcycle. She stomped the starter and pulled away, slinging grass and gravel as she fish-tailed her way to the road. As she rounded the drive she noticed a car waiting in front of the big house. The driver was leaning against the fender smoking a cigarette. Kit knocked on the side door anxiously.

"Open up, Nigel," she said, pounding again. Finally the door opened slowly, Nigel smiling his passive smile.

"Good afternoon, Lieutenant Anderson. May I help you?" he said, but Kit had already pushed past him and headed down the hall for the stairs. "This is most irregular," he said. "If you will wait, I will see if Lady Marble will see you."

"I don't need to see her," Kit shouted back to him. "I'm here to see Emily."

"Lieutenant Anderson?" Lillian said, coming down the stairs. "What can I do for you?"

"Nothing, Lady Marble. I have to see Emily," Kit said looking up the staircase to where she suspected Emily was packing.

"I'm sorry, Lieutenant, but Emily is about to leave. She was just finishing her packing." Lillian stood in the middle of the bottom step, doing her best to block Kit from going upstairs. "She is going to work in Manchester."

"The hell she is," Kit said, squeezing past and vaulting up the steps two at a time.

"I beg your pardon." Lillian straightened her posture indignantly.

"I'm sorry, Lillian," Kit came back down to her and gave her a big hug. "It's just I have to talk to Emily before she leaves. It's very important." She started back up the stairs.

"Perhaps this isn't the proper time, Lieutenant."

"Oh, yes, it is. There will never be a better time for what I have to say."

"It may not surprise you, Lieutenant, but Emily has confided a great deal in me. I know all about you and her. I also know of her recent decision in regards to your relationship," Lillian said up to her.

Kit looked back at her.

"And I know why she did it," Kit said.

"Don't you think you should respect her decision?"

"No, I don't. I love her." Kit smiled then rushed up the stairs and down the hall to the corner room. She opened the door without knocking to find Emily in her slip and stockings. She looked up at Kit and screamed.

"What are you doing here?"

"I have come to see you." Kit closed the door and walked over to her. Emily grabbed her dress and held it against her chest.

"I thought we said everything we needed to say. I have to finish changing. A driver is waiting to take me to Manchester."

"You aren't going to Manchester, Miss Mills. You are staying right here in Alderbrook."

"No, I'm not. I transferred three days ago. I will be working for the flight command administration as a file clerk. They have a lovely room for me in the women's barracks, and I will have every other weekend free to visit Grandmother. I will be issued real uniforms, not those dreadful coveralls. Now, if you'll excuse me," she said, stepping into her dress and wiggling it up over her hips.

"I don't think so." Kit perched her hands on her hips. "You heard, didn't you?"

"Heard what?"

"You heard what Commander Griggs said to me in her office that afternoon when we got back with Peter, didn't you? You were standing outside her window and heard every word she said."

"No, I didn't hear anything," Emily insisted then went to her suitcase, frantically packing the rest of her clothes.

"I think you did. And what's more, I think the things you said to me were because Griggs threatened to take away my wings if we continued to see each other. Isn't that right?"

"No, I didn't say anything of the kind," she said, stuffing and closing her suitcase without looking up at Kit.

"Emily Mills, you are lying. You said those things just to protect me." Kit took Emily's arm and turned her around. "Admit it. You heard what Griggs said and you were willing to leave me just to protect my wings."

"No, that isn't it at all." Emily tried to pull away.

"Your decision had nothing to do with the way you feel about me. Admit it. Admit you still love me."

"I can't, Kit." She tried to squirm free, but Kit held on to her. "I have to go. I'll be late."

"I'm not letting go of you until you admit you still love me and want to see me."

"I will not." Emily frowned stubbornly.

"You will or else," Kit said, struggling to hold on to her.

"Or else what?" Emily tugged at Kit's fingers around her arm.

"Or I will paddle your bottom."

"You wouldn't dare." Emily glared up at her.

"Are you going to admit it?"

"No. I made my decision on my own, and you have to respect that."

"You had your chance." Kit sat down on the bed and pulled Emily across the lap.

"Let go of me, you bloody Yank," Emily said, fighting to cover her bottom with her hands.

"Not a chance." Kit began administering swats.

"Ouch!" Emily squealed.

"Are you going to admit it?" Kit asked as she struck another blow for love's sake.

"Ouch," Emily cried, kicking and fighting to get away. "You are a monster."

Kit gave her another.

"All right, all right," Emily screamed. "I admit it."

"That's better," Kit said, still holding her across her lap. "And tell me you love me."

Emily looked back at her.

"You have just beaten my bum. Why should I tell you I love you?"

"Who else was willing to stop you from running away from something wonderful?"

"Kit, I can't. I know what will happen if we stay together. You are too valuable to the ATA for me to put myself first." Emily sat up on Kit's lap and looked her in the eyes. "I couldn't stand it if you lost your wings because of me. Your last weeks here are important. I don't want to interfere with that."

"But you still love me?" Kit said encircling Emily with her arms.

"Yes, I still love you," she said softly. "I've always loved you."

"But what is this bloody Yank thing?"

"You *are* a bloody Yank. But you're my bloody Yank."

"Good, because there are going to be some changes."

"What kind of changes? We won't see each other, but we can still be friends?"

"No. I don't want you as a friend. I want you as my partner. You are all I've ever wanted, and I am staying here in England until they kick me out. If Griggs wants my wings, she can have them. I'll quit. I'll fly cargo planes, or I'll drive trucks, or I'll just live in the cottage and collect junk like Sam. But you and I are not giving up something beautiful. If they want me to fly ATA, they'll have to take me on my own terms."

"You're staying?" Emily threw her arms around Kit's neck.

"You betcha. That's a Yankee expression for I love you with all my heart, Emily Mills." She pulled Emily to her and kissed her passionately.

There was a knock at the bedroom door.

"Shall I dismiss the car, Miss Emily?" Nigel said through the door.

"Yes, Nigel. I won't be needing it," Emily replied.

"If you two would like to join her Ladyship, tea is being served in the library."

"Would you like a spot of tea, Lieutenant Anderson?" Emily asked seductively, draping her arms over Kit's shoulders.

"I would much rather have you," Kit said, laying Emily back on the bed.

"Tea is highly overrated," Emily whispered and pulled Kit down on top of her, kissing her completely.

Publications from

BELLA BOOKS, INC.

The best in contemporary lesbian fiction

P.O. Box 10543, Tallahassee, FL 32302

Phone: 800-729-4992

www.bellabooks.com

PAST REMEMBERING by Lyn Denison. What would it take to melt Peri's cool exterior? Any involvement on Asha's part would be simply asking for trouble and heartache . . . wouldn't it?   978-1-59493-103-1 $13.95

ASPEN'S EMBERS by Diane Tremain Braund. Will Aspen choose the woman she loves. . . or the forest she hopes to preserve.   978-1-59493-102-4 $14.95

THE COTTAGE by Gerri Hill. *The Cottage* is the heartbreaking story of two women who meet by chance . . . or did they? A love so destined it couldn't be denied . . . stolen moments to be cherished forever.   978-1-59493-096-6 $13.95

FANTASY: Untrue Stories of Lesbian Passion edited by Barbara Johnson and Therese Szymanski. Lie back and let Bella's bad girls take you on an erotic journey through the greatest bedtime stories never told.   978-1-59493-101-7 $15.95

SISTERS' FLIGHT by Jeanne G'Fellers. *Sisters' Flight* is the highly anticipated sequel to *No Sister of Mine* and *Sister Lost, Sister Found.*   978-1-59493-116-1 $13.95

BRAGGIN' RIGHTS by Kenna White. Taylor Fleming is a thirty-six-year-old Texas rancher who covets her independence. She finds her cowgirl independence tested by neighboring rancher Jen Holland.   978-1-59493-095-9 $13.95

BRILLIANT by Ann Roberts. Respected sociology professor, Diane Cole finds her views on love challenged by her own heart, as she fights the attraction she feels for a woman half her age.   978-1-59493-115-4 $13.95

THE EDUCATION OF ELLIE by Jackie Calhoun. When Ellie sees her childhood friend for the first time in thirty years she is tempted to resume their long lost friendship. But with the years come a lot of baggage and the two women struggle with who they are now while fighting the painful memories of their first parting. Will they be able to move past their history to start again?   978-1-59493-092-8 $13.95

DATE NIGHT CLUB by Saxon Bennett. *Date Night Club* is a dark romantic comedy about the pitfalls of dating in your thirties . . .   978-1-59493-094-2 $13.95

PLEASE FORGIVE ME by Megan Carter. Laurel Becker is on the verge of losing the two most important things in her life—her current lover, Elaine Alexander, and the Lavender Page bookstore. Will Elaine and Laurel manage to work through their misunderstandings and rebuild their life together?   978-1-59493-091-1 $13.95

WHISKEY AND OAK LEAVES by Jaime Clevenger. Meg meets June, a single woman running a horse ranch in the California Sierra foothills. The two become quick friends and it isn't long before Meg is looking for more than just a friendship. But June has no interest in developing a deeper relationship with Meg. She is, after all, not the least bit interested in women . . . or is she? Neither of these two women is prepared for what lies ahead . . .   978-1-59493-093-5 $13.95

SUMTER POINT by KG MacGregor. As Audie surrenders her heart to Beth, she begins to distance herself from the reckless habits of her youth. Just as they're ready to meet in the middle, their future is thrown into doubt by a duty Beth can't ignore. It all comes to a head on the river at Sumter Point.   978-1-59493-089-8 $13.95

THE TARGET by Gerri Hill. Sara Michaels is the daughter of a prominent senator who has been receiving death threats against his family. In an effort to protect Sara, the FBI recruits homicide detective Jaime Hutchinson to secretly provide the protection they are so certain Sara will need. Will Sara finally figure out who is behind the death threats? And will Jaime realize the truth—and be able to save Sara before it's too late?   978-1-59493-082-9 $13.95

REALITY BYTES by Jane Frances. In this sequel to *Reunion*, follow the lives of four friends in a romantic tale that spans the globe and proves that you can cross the whole of cyberspace only to find love a few suburbs away . . .   978-1-59493-079-9 $13.95

MURDER CAME SECOND by Jessica Thomas. Broadway's bad-boy genius, Paul Carlucci, has chosen *Hamlet* for his latest production and, to the delight of some and despair of others, he has selected Provincetown's amphitheatre for his opening gala. But Alex Peres realizes the wrong people are falling down, and the moaning is all too realistic. Someone must not be shooting blanks . . .   978-1-59493-081-2 $13.95

SKIN DEEP by Kenna White. Jordan Griffin has been given a new assignment: Track down and interview one-time nationally renowned broadcast journalist Reece McAllister. Much to her surprise, Jordan comes away with far more than just a story . . .
978-1-59493-78-2 $13.95

FINDERS KEEPERS by Karin Kallmaker. *Finders Keepers*, the quest for the perfect mate in the 21st century, joins Karin Kallmaker's *Just Like That* and her other incomparable novels about lesbian love, lust and laughter.   1-59493-072-4 $13.95

OUT OF THE FIRE by Beth Moore. Author Ann Covington feels at the top of the world when told her book is being made into a movie. Then in walks Casey Duncan the actress who is playing the lead in her movie. Will Casey turn Ann's world upside down?
1-59493-088-0 $13.95

STAKE THROUGH THE HEART: NEW EXPLOITS OF TWILIGHT LESBI-ANS by Karin Kallmaker, Julia Watts, Barbara Johnson and Therese Szymanski. The playful quartet that penned the acclaimed *Once Upon A Dyke* are dimming the lights for journeys into worlds of breathless seduction.   1-59493-071-6 $15.95

THE HOUSE ON SANDSTONE by KG MacGregor. Carly Griffin returns home to Leland and finds that her old high school friend Justine is awakening more than just old memories.   1-59493-076-7 $13.95

WILD NIGHTS: MOSTLY TRUE STORIES OF WOMEN LOVING WOMEN edited by Therese Szymanski. 264 pp. 23 new stories from today's hottest erotic writers are sure to give you your wildest night ever!   1-59493-069-4 $15.95

COYOTE SKY by Gerri Hill. 248 pp. Sheriff Lee Foxx is trying to cope with the real-ization that she has fallen in love for the first time. And fallen for author Kate Winters, who is technically unavailable. Will Lee fight to keep Kate in Coyote?
1-59493-065-1 $13.95

VOICES OF THE HEART by Frankie J. Jones. 264 pp. A series of events force Erin to swear off love as she tries to break away from the woman of her dreams. Will Erin ever find the key to her future happiness?   1-59493-068-6 $13.95

SHELTER FROM THE STORM by Peggy J. Herring. 296 pp. A story about family and getting reacquainted with one's past that shows that sometimes you don't appreciate what you have until you almost lose it.   1-59493-064-3 $13.95

WRITING MY LOVE by Claire McNab. 192 pp. Romance writer Vonny Smith believes she will be able to woo her editor Diana through her writing.
1-59493-063-5 $13.95

PAID IN FULL by Ann Roberts. 200 pp. Ari Adams will need to choose between the debts of the past and the promise of a happy future.   1-59493-059-7 $13.95

ROMANCING THE ZONE by Kenna White. 272 pp. Liz's world begins to crumble when a secret from her past returns to Ashton.   1-59493-060-0 $13.95

SIGN ON THE LINE by Jaime Clevenger. 204 pp. Alexis Getty, a flirtatious delivery driver is committed to finding the rightful owner of a mysterious package.
1-59493-052-X $13.95

END OF WATCH by Clare Baxter. 256 pp. LAPD Lieutenant L.A. Franco Frank follows the lone clue down the unlit steps of memory to a final, unthinkable resolution.
1-59493-064-4 $13.95

BEHIND THE PINE CURTAIN by Gerri Hill. 280 pp. Jacqueline returns home after her father's death and comes face to face with her first crush.   1-59493-057-0 $13.95

18TH & CASTRO by Karin Kallmaker. 200 pp. First-time couplings and couples who know how to mix lust and love make 18th & Castro the hottest address in the city by the bay.   1-59493-066-X $13.95

JUST THIS ONCE by KG MacGregor. 200 pp. Mindful of the obligations back home that she must honor, Wynne Connelly struggles to resist the fascination and allure that a particular woman she meets on her business trip represents. 1-59493-087-2 $13.95

ANTICIPATION by Terri Breneman. 240 pp. Two women struggle to remain professional as they work together to find a serial killer.   1-59493-055-4 $13.95

OBSESSION by Jackie Calhoun. 240 pp. Lindsey's life is turned upside down when Sarah comes into the family nursery in search of perennials.   1-59493-058-9 $13.95

BENEATH THE WILLOW by Kenna White. 240 pp. A torch that still burns brightly even after twenty-five years threatens to consume two childhood friends.
1-59493-053-8 $13.95

SISTER LOST, SISTER FOUND by Jeanne G'Fellers. 224 pp. The highly anticipated sequel to No Sister of Mine.   1-59493-056-2 $13.95

THE WEEKEND VISITOR by Jessica Thomas. 240 pp. In this latest Alex Peres mystery, Alex is asked to investigate an assault on a local woman but finds that her client may have more secrets than she lets on.   1-59493-054-6 $13.95

THE KILLING ROOM by Gerri Hill. 392 pp. How can two women forget and go their separate ways?   1-59493-050-3 $12.95

PASSIONATE KISSES by Megan Carter. 240 pp. Will two old friends run from love?
1-59493-051-1 $12.95

ALWAYS AND FOREVER by Lyn Denison. 224 pp. The girl next door turns Shannon's world upside down.   1-59493-049-X $12.95

BACK TALK by Saxon Bennett. 200 pp. Can a talk-show host find love after heartbreak?   1-59493-028-7 $12.95

THE PERFECT VALENTINE: EROTIC LESBIAN VALENTINE STORIES edited by Barbara Johnson and Therese Szymanski—from Bella After Dark. 328 pp. Stories from the hottest writers around.   1-59493-061-9 $14.95

MURDER AT RANDOM by Claire McNab. 200 pp. The Sixth Denise Cleever Thriller. Denise realizes the fate of thousands is in her hands. 1-59493-047-3 $12.95

THE TIDES OF PASSION by Diana Tremain Braund. 240 pp. Will Susan be able to hold it all together and find the one woman who touches her soul?
1-59493-048-1 $12.95

JUST LIKE THAT by Karin Kallmaker. 240 pp. Disliking each other—and everything they stand for—even before they meet, Toni and Syrah find feelings can change, just like that.   1-59493-025-2 $12.95

WHEN FIRST WE PRACTICE by Therese Szymanski. 200 pp. Brett and Allie are once again caught in the middle of murder and intrigue.   1-59493-045-7 $12.95

REUNION by Jane Frances. 240 pp. Cathy Braithwaite seems to have it all: good looks, money and a thriving accounting practice . . .   1-59493-046-5 $12.95

BELL, BOOK & DYKE: NEW EXPLOITS OF MAGICAL LESBIANS by Kallmaker, Watts, Johnson and Szymanski. 360 pp. Reluctant witches, tempting spells and skyclad beauties—delve into the mysteries of love, lust and power in this quartet of novellas.   1-59493-023-6 $14.95

ARTIST'S DREAM by Gerri Hill. 320 pp. When Cassie meets Luke Winston, she can no longer deny her attraction to women . . .   1-59493-042-2 $12.95

NO EVIDENCE by Nancy Sanra. 240 pp. Private investigator Tally McGinnis once again returns to the horror-filled world of a serial killer.   1-59493-043-04 $12.95

WHEN LOVE FINDS A HOME by Megan Carter. 280 pp. What will it take for Anna and Rona to find their way back to each other again?   1-59493-041-4 $12.95

MEMORIES TO DIE FOR by Adrian Gold. 240 pp. Rachel attempts to avoid her attraction to the charms of Anna Sigurdson . . .   1-59493-038-4 $12.95

SILENT HEART by Claire McNab. 280 pp. Exotic lesbian romance.
                                                          1-59493-044-9 $12.95

MIDNIGHT RAIN by Peggy J. Herring. 240 pp. Bridget McBee is determined to find the woman who saved her life.   1-59493-021-X $12.95

THE MISSING PAGE A Brenda Strange Mystery by Patty G. Henderson. 240 pp. Brenda investigates her client's murder . . .   1-59493-004-X $12.95

WHISPERS ON THE WIND by Frankie J. Jones. 240 pp. Dixon thinks she and her best friend, Elizabeth Colter, would make the perfect couple . . . 1-59493-037-6 $12.95

CALL OF THE DARK: EROTIC LESBIAN TALES OF THE SUPERNATURAL edited by Therese Szymanski—from Bella After Dark. 320 pp.1-59493-040-6 $14.95

A TIME TO CAST AWAY A Helen Black Mystery by Pat Welch. 240 pp. Helen stops by Alice's apartment—only to find the woman dead . . .   1-59493-036-8 $12.95

DESERT OF THE HEART by Jane Rule. 224 pp. The book that launched the most popular lesbian movie of all time is back.   1-1-59493-035-X $12.95

THE NEXT WORLD by Ursula Steck. 240 pp. Anna's friend Mido is threatened and eventually disappears . . .   1-59493-024-4 $12.95

CALL SHOTGUN by Jaime Clevenger. 240 pp. Kelly gets pulled back into the world of private investigation . . .   1-59493-016-3 $12.95

52 PICKUP by Bonnie J. Morris and E.B. Casey. 240 pp. 52 hot, romantic tales—one for every Saturday night of the year.   1-59493-026-0 $12.95

GOLD FEVER by Lyn Denison. 240 pp. Kate's first love, Ashley, returns to their home town, where Kate now lives . . .   1-1-59493-039-2 $12.95

RISKY INVESTMENT by Beth Moore. 240 pp. Lynn's best friend and roommate needs her to pretend Chris is his fiancé. But nothing is ever easy.1-59493-019-8 $12.95

HUNTER'S WAY by Gerri Hill. 240 pp. Homicide detective Tori Hunter is forced to team up with the hot-tempered Samantha Kennedy.   1-59493-018-X $12.95

CAR POOL by Karin Kallmaker. 240 pp. Soft shoulders, merging traffic and slippery when wet . . . Anthea and Shay find love in the car pool.   1-59493-013-9 $12.95

NO SISTER OF MINE by Jeanne G'Fellers. 240 pp. Telepathic women fight to coexist with a patriarchal society that wishes their eradication.   1-59493-017-1 $12.95

ON THE WINGS OF LOVE by Megan Carter. 240 pp. Stacie's reporting career is on the rocks. She has to interview bestselling author Cheryl, or else!1-59493-027-9 $12.95

WICKED GOOD TIME by Diana Tremain Braund. 224 pp. Does Christina need Miki as a protector . . . or want her as a lover?   1-59493-031-7 $12.95

THOSE WHO WAIT by Peggy J. Herring. 240 pp. Two brilliant sisters—in love with the same woman!   1-59493-032-5 $12.95

ABBY'S PASSION by Jackie Calhoun. 240 pp. Abby's bipolar sister helps turn her world upside down, so she must decide what's most important.1-59493-014-7 $12.95

PICTURE PERFECT by Jane Vollbrecht. 240 pp. Kate is reintroduced to Casey, the daughter of an old friend. Can they withstand Kate's career?   1-59493-015-5 $12.95

PAPERBACK ROMANCE by Karin Kallmaker. 240 pp. Carolyn falls for tall, dark and . . . female . . . in this classic lesbian romance.   1-59493-033-3 $12.95

DAWN OF CHANGE by Gerri Hill. 240 pp. Susan ran away to find peace in remote Kings Canyon—then she met Shawn . . .   1-59493-011-2 $12.95

DOWN THE RABBIT HOLE by Lynne Jamneck. 240 pp. Is a killer holding a grudge against FBI Agent Samantha Skellar?   1-59493-012-0 $12.95

SEASONS OF THE HEART by Jackie Calhoun. 240 pp. Overwhelmed, Sara saw only one way out—leaving . . .   1-59493-030-9 $12.95

TURNING THE TABLES by Jessica Thomas. 240 pp. The second Alex Peres Mystery. From ghosties and ghoulies and long leggity beasties . . . 1-59493-009-0 $12.95

FOR EVERY SEASON by Frankie Jones. 240 pp. Andi, who is investigating a 65-year-old murder, meets Janice, a charming district attorney . . .   1-59493-010-4 $12.95

LOVE ON THE LINE by Laura DeHart Young. 240 pp. Kay leaves a younger woman behind to go on a mission to Alaska . . . will she regret it?   1-59493-008-2 $12.95

WHEN THE CORPSE LIES A Motor City Thriller by Therese Szymanski. 328 pp. Butch bad-girl Brett Higgins is used to waking up next to beautiful women she hardly knows. Problem is, this one's dead.   1-931513-74-0 $12.95

UNDER THE SOUTHERN CROSS by Claire McNab. 200 pp. Lee, an American travel agent, goes down under and meets Australian Alex, and the sparks fly under the Southern Cross.   1-59493-029-5 $12.95

SUGAR by Karin Kallmaker. 240 pp. Three women want sugar from Sugar, who can't make up her mind.   1-59493-001-5 $12.95

FALL GUY by Claire McNab. 200 pp. 16th Detective Inspector Carol Ashton Mystery. 1-59493-000-7 $12.95

ONE SUMMER NIGHT by Gerri Hill. 232 pp. Johanna swore to never fall in love again—but then she met the charming Kelly . . .   1-59493-007-4 $12.95